CW01360302

BOOK ONE OF THE ORATA
SEEK THE THROAT
FROM WHICH WE SING

BY ALEX CF

Copyright © Alex CF 2016

www.artofalexcf.com

The Author asserts the moral right to
be identified as the author of this work

Edited by Gary Dalkin
tothelastword.com

Typset in palatino by Mark McClure
www.markmcclurestudio.com

Printed and bound in Great Britain by
ASAP Digital, Sheffield

All rights reserved. No part of the publication may be
Reproduced, stored in a retrieval system, or transmitted
In any form or by any means, electronic, mechanical
Photocopying, recording or otherwise without the prior
Permission of the author.

For Elizabeth, Tabby, Susie and Steve

The Oscelan
Norgan Kingdom
House of Bone char
Orn Megol
The Crool
Fractured sects
House of Erithacus
Bazaar
The Stinking city
Moterion
House of Tor
The Pinnacle
Kingdom of Esperer

Bestiary

Amfier – Newt
Ardid - Crane
Athlon - Horse
Aurma - Cow
Aven - Blue tit
Baldaboa - Pigeon
Bloodson - Robin
Caanus - Dog
Cini - Wolf
Corva - Crow
Collector/Corva-il - Magpie
Crechlin/Torplic - Beetle
Crepic - Crab
Creta - Mice
Danor - Black Bird
Effer - Sheep
Embree - Giant Sloth
Eprica - Gazelle
Grim - Bear
Harend - Song Thrush
Lanfol - Starfish
Malor - Pheasant
Maar - Weasel/Stoat
Morwih - Cat
Muroi - Rat
Naarna Elowin - Gull
Necros Anx - Hooded Vulture
Nighspyn - Hedgehog
Norn - Whale
Oraclas - Elephant
Oreya - Deer
Orkrek - Frog
Rauka - Sabre tooth cat/Big cat
Rersp - Woodpecker
Runta - Wild Boar/Pig
Speakers/Cheon - Parakeet
Sqvre - Squirrel
Startle - Starling
Storn - Owl
Tasq - Rhino
Tetek - Vole
Throa - Badger
Toec - Mole
Tril - Rabbit
Ungdijin - Fish
Voin - Bee
Vulpus - Fox
Wroth - Human
Yoa'a/Drove - Hare
Yowri - Lark

Language

Ora - The Sun
Naa - The Earth
Seyla - The moon

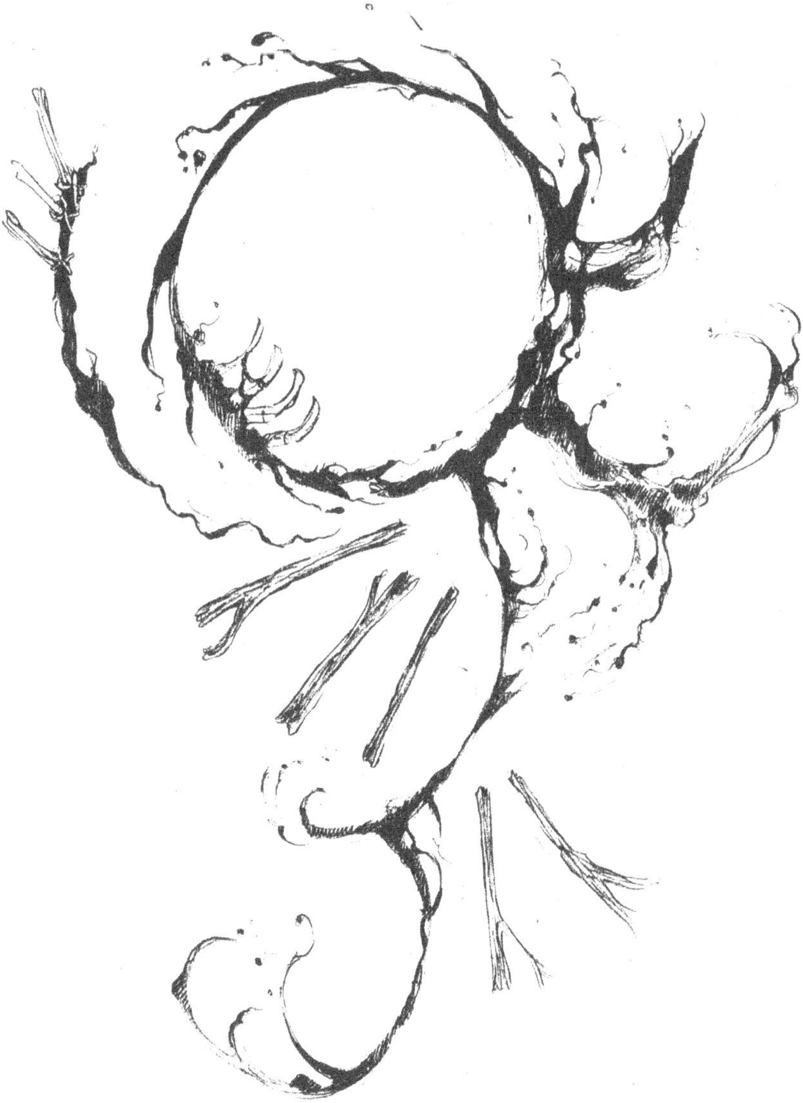

The Orata

Spoken scripture of the Vulpus
Prayer for Vorn, Vors and Alcali

Cradle me, nestle me,
In the brook of enmity
Unravel your veins
From which you shed blood

It pools in the arteries
Of the forests burgeoning
Their fertility vowed
In the blood left unsung

We promised glad tidings
In the presence of their barrow
Conceal the vertebrae
Our beloved trinity

Choir lauds the melodies
Written in matrices
Primordial symphony
In stones yet to sing

So we pray for the mantle
To offer its sanctuary
Bequeath to us the love
Of the city and its song

Prologue

Grom felt the pain like a cavity opening within. It pulled him from his slumber and fuelled his ascent; he felt the lick of bile in his gullet, the nauseating sense of foreboding nagged at him and he beat his wings in fraught succession until he flew out of the Pinnacle and into the world. He drank it in, reclaiming himself in the sting of cold, and for a moment the fervour subsided. He found a place to rest upon the roof and closed his eyes tight, feeling the furore evaporate. For many nights the same discomfort had awoken him, an ambivalent yet meaningful anxiety. He tried to make sense of it, yet it would not reveal its intention. He rested for a while upon the slate, looking out on to the land below.

The sea stirred, the fulgent foam broke across the shattered remnants of wood and concrete, the black of the ocean barely discernible against the waning light of Seyla.

It was mesmerising, he saw patterns in the reflections, the patina of light play, the staccato glint awash with implications. He considered every nightmare, every vision and only upset himself further by his lack of comprehension. The monotonous drag of dread that sang in him was all he could perceive.

The caw of the Gulls pierced his daze and he cast a weary eye in their direction. A dozen or so flew in formation, arching and wheeling, and then a dozen more. That same dull ache started to rise in him once again, and an inkling came with it. It was a warning, an omen that had barely registered before.

The legions of the Gull army spilled out over the quiet land. They wore slate armour crude and gracile, they carried with them stones clasped in their webbed talons, they held a singular perceptible focus, and it was clear to Grom.

They were coming for his kin.

For so long the rumours of rebellion within the Gull clans had circulated. Such empty threats had been wholly ignored by the Startle. The threat now flew towards his home with determination, and it kindled fear, stalling any sense of impetus in him. He had to get up, he had to alert his flock to this. It sank heavy in him, and it took every effort to tear himself away from the roof, barrelling down into the assembly roost atop the Pinnacle.

Before him the quorum perched sleepily in a loose circle, 'The Gulls! Please! They are coming!' He exclaimed. The flight chiefs awoke from their stupor and raced to the window ledge to make out the hostile flock that flanked the Pinnacle. It was quite clear what was to come.

They heeded his word and flung themselves from the banister that encircled the assembly roost, and down into the vast shaft below.

'The Gulls. They bring war!'

The word proliferated throughout the tired mass of flock, and like the rising molten ash upon a fire they soon whirled within the Pinnacle, a helical torrent of frenetic bodies.

They fanned out, flying towards the many exits cut into the wood by ancient nimble beaks, paths they had flown every morning upon waking. They would gather above in labile formations; the enunciations of the Startle. In these acts they found their strength.

Yet shapes loomed at the exits, shapes that seemed sharp and bright and merciless, beady eyes bled into their line of sight, and soon their own bodies collided with solid forms, not the night sky. The Gulls were blocking the exits, heads lashed and tore at the air, 'You cannot escape!' They jeered.

The Startle whirled; some directing themselves at the bodies that now hindered their flight; talons and beaks stabbed and wounded, caws rang out, but the Gulls would not move. Some Startle pushed themselves through, threading bills through muscles and flesh. Mouths closed on their little heads, bones cracked and blood spilled.

Grom watched in horror from above. He chided himself; had he become so arrogant? Too reliant on his gifts of foresight? His sudden inadequacy only stifled by another dread realisation; within the Pinnacle nest his mate and son resided. He quickly took flight from the Quorum, sailing out on the irascible currents once again.

The sky raged. The seismic wing beats of a hundred Gulls greeted him; the few Startle that had escaped their barracks now flew in splintered configuration; their wing blades slicing assured wounds in the necks of their thuggish aggressors; they veered and swivelled in concertina arcs; saltatorial gambols that rained down upon the Gulls. But these animals were huge and they saw this as sport. The Startle fled for their lives, and Grom was left, darting between the craws of every enemy soldier.

He spied a cavalry of Gulls who hovered near a larger hole, tearing furiously at the wood to allow them entry. He called out to them, and they stretched their sinuous necks up to greet him with barbed screeches. They set a frantic course, and he flew hard, taking one momentary glance back down to see a single Gull enter his home. His stomach turned.

Not far from the Pinnacle lay a dejected ticket office. Within, the Gull prince Esperer sat upon the dank piles of decomposing theme park promotional pamphlets and fliers that had been his father's throne. He was drunk on his irreversible decisions. At his feet lay the body of his father, Malca. Esperer cocked his head to one side to make out the still profile of his decaying face, that same face that had looked so reticently at him his whole life. The scowl was now permanent, sallow skin taut over a stubborn head. Esperer had left him there to lie in the presence of his former seat. To rot away like so many of his machinations. If his father would refuse to listen to reason then his choices were limited. Even in the face of death that obstinance had remained. Stupid flock. Why hadn't he just moved aside?

Esperer felt the shame of his act take hold, and so he waddled towards the window that gave him clear sight of the remaining squadrons who now readied themselves for flight. He buried his remorse in self-congratulation.

Beyond, the staggering effigy of the Pinnacle glowered at him, the highest point on the landscape, hugged with a shroud of water vapour. It dwarfed his domain. He felt its presence, felt its potency. It would be his.

He thought of all that had stood in his way and how easily it had all grovelled in subservience to him, how easily the neck had broken; how eager the Gull troops had been to enact his word. The Startle had held the throne for generations. Their Murmuration, the orchestration of bodies arising and undulating as one single organism, was the one constant that had vexed him beyond all. Their vain collective, a storm of deluded ideas, sparks of misshapen genius that spread like neurones firing in a mass of feathers and sharp eyes. So much potential floundering in their concept that they were not rulers but wards, Wards! His hatred for his father had a worthy successor; the Thousand Headed King.

Yet they were not kings, nor in any sense a monarchy, their sublime ballet the crux of their rule, to say, 'We are here'. They were caretakers, guides who found love in their work. They tended the needs of all, both below and in flight. They asked of the people what was needed of each of them to maintain stability and achieved a state of harmony. This was the will of the Thousand Headed King, and it had pained Esperer every waking moment. He had never understood their lack of fortitude, their idleness infuriated him. They held power with weak sensibilities, they did not value it, or harness it, or gain from it. They existed, they did not live. It was wasted on them. He was made, nay, *forced* to take it from them.

*

He turned to observe the mould-ridden corpse of his father's fiefdom one last time. He thought of the countless raided nests, the aimless feuds between the Gull clans, the failed coup of neighbouring rulers. It was all so pitiful. He exited the outbuilding as his warriors took flight, they hovered in the brawl, awaiting their call to arms. Orders were barked and the tirade ascended, their bodies caustic white, like knives. They were soon imperceptible in the gloom, and he retired to the roof and awaited word of success before he would make his entrance. He dressed himself appropriately, in armour taken from his father's body. In time, his lieutenants approached him with agreeable news and they escorted him in regal procession toward that which he had sought with lustful eyes for so long. Seyla seemed pleased, shining unhindered by the sky, the cobalt of a distant dawn venerating his ascent.

*

Within the assembly roost, the forum of the fallen rulers sat silent. Those who had been allowed to live were cowed into the corner, the brutish Gull sentries hissing and corralling them. Among the living, the flight-chief Ara, and Elistis, the appointed speaker of rule. The bodies of other flight chiefs splayed in crimson curvatures upon the floor. Esperer landed upon the balcony outside, taking a moment to revel in his element. He seemed to breathe in the sensation of it, drew the sanctimonious prize into him and smiled. He wore a crown of charcoal rock that ran across the brow of each eye socket and down about his beak, it was imposing. He cleared his throat and entered, as though crossing some venerable threshold.

'I hereby claim the Pinnacle as sovereign land under my rule. I deny your monarchy and stake claim of this roost and the land the Startle once resided over. You are no longer fit to rule, I dare say that you never were.'

Ara scoffed. 'No one will ever recognise your kingship, Esperer.'

Esperer grimaced. He moved towards the body of one of Ara's fallen comrades. He kicked at the corpse. He felt the rising lump of his last meal fester at the base of his craw, and regurgitated it, hacking it up on to the poor soul at his feet. His soldiers laughed. Ara hissed. 'You despicable ...'

'Silence!' the closest soldier stabbed at him with his beak, sending him reeling. Against the far wall sat a raised wooden platform. Esperer sidled over and sat himself upon it. He surveyed his throne room with gluttonous malice. His lieutenant, a large and imposing Gull approached, 'Lord Esperer, we have assured control of the Pinnacle. The Startle are trapped within, those who escaped we have dispatched. What are your orders?'

'Maintain control of the exits, enter where you can and kill a few families. Take control of any food stocks. Let them starve in there. In a few days they will be far more compliant.'

*

Outside, Grom hid himself beyond the sight of the sentries until they abandoned their search for him and returned to the Pinnacle. He knew this land, knew its hidden routes and sanctuaries. He ducked down towards the base of their stronghold, and at its widest point, far below the nests within, he found an entrance. Old doors hung on corroded hinges. The Startle had never made use of it and the acrid stench of urine spoke of their reason. Predators lurked here, and their presence would keep the

Gulls at bay.

Grom took advantage of this and entered. Above him lay a lattice of fallen, sodden floor boards. He sought a gap within the wood and began to scramble up, through the generations of discarded nests which honeycombed the breadth of the structure.

The muffled cries in the shaft above focused his resolve, and he dug through countless generations of shattered eggshell and knitted grass, the manifold ages of life and death like stratum layers. He fought his way amongst the timber and straw, the dust blinding him, until finally he felt the presence of bodies. He tore at the base of a new nest, and was confronted by terrified faces.

'Please,' he said, a mother and chick pulled away from him.

'It is Grom,' she said, with relief, and he continued to struggle free of the nest. He was exhausted as he birthed himself into the hollow above.

There were many dead in the Pinnacle. Their bodies lay in crumpled agony. He flitted between the corpses, fearful, desperate. The Gull guards stood motionless. They recognised him - the Shadow Starer, feared his gift, yet watched his suffering with glee. They sensed his helplessness.

His family resided close to the wall of the great tower, perched between two support beams. A Gull stood beside it. Grom could see nest material strewn, batted, clawed up and thrown asunder. Something flurried in him, something arresting, something cruel and sharp. He could see blood on the Gull, he could see that it had been wounded.

He could not bring himself to look, and so he cried out.

The Gull enjoyed this. Like a performance, he saw the intention of this Startle, he saw him sob with raw anger. He watched him veer away from the shortest path, as though he didn't wish to see this, see what the Gull had done.

The Gull felt something like remorse, soon eclipsed by wanton desire. He wanted this Startle to see what he had done. *Come closer*, he thought to himself, *come see this splendid disaster*. Grom locked eyes with the great white beast, saw that foul assuredness. The Gull stepped aside willingly, almost offering out a wing as if to say, 'Please, after you.'

The hunger of loss imbedded itself in Grom. The strangling sensation ribboned about him, pulling taut around his beak. It wanted him, in all its suffocating rapture. His son was bloody but alive, and he pulled him free. Amongst the incalculable sadness, the love of his life lay before him.

Everything became laboured, a slew of impassable unctuous blackness. Time hung off him in gobbets, forcing him to witness every bleeding facet of her. The glib bleating of the perpetrator ran from him. Like oil on water, it did not penetrate. The muffled voice of friends enclosed. They cried, they cloyed. The prophet had not foreseen. Why had he failed them? They took his son away, away from it all, and left Grom to despair.

Chapter 1

Ara stood at the edge of the Pinnacle and embraced the bullish draw of the wind. He felt it deep, fought its gnaw. A knot of dark appeared on the horizon, amongst the paroxysmal surge of funereal grey that promised more rain. It had been many turns since this land had been lost, taken by their tormentor, Esperer. Living under the Gulls, he was thankful for every small virtue, the rain brought a distinct aroma to the land and he enjoyed listening to its clatter upon the roof of the Pinnacle.

The object that grew in girth held grave tiding. Ara was almost blind, yet the blurred shape was discernible, angular. It landed beside him.

'Dominus?' Ara asked the dark figure.

'Yes,' it said.

'Will we fly?' Ara said hesitantly. The shape flexed its wings and turned to the ocean. 'You will not fly. The Sisters do not will it. This is a time in flux; we cannot interrupt the bones.'

Ara grimaced. 'What do the bones say?'

'The Shadow Starer is lost to us.'

'So you need another?'

'There is one who might be fit for the task. But we cannot force it, we do not place the bones where we wish them to lie.'

There was a calm that stripped the sea surface of sentiment. A dull turquoise blossomed beneath in the dwindling light, the odd flitting marine shadow breaking the monotony as the Startle made their final evening ballet upon the currents of air cast up by the ocean. They pirouetted silently, gracefully, in unison. From the guard towers on the balustrades, the sentry Gulls watched cautiously.

The sea was sluggish at the shore. Some boats remained, waterlogged and half-sunken, for the Wroth had begun to lose their endless grip on all things.

The stark coastline had been a popular tourist attraction, gradually receding into a quiet cove, where a theme park had been constructed. An unpredictable climate had led to rising tides and excess flooding, rendering it unusable. It had been forgotten, not even worthy of demolition. The carcasses of fairground rides slumped like prehistoric carrion against brittle crumbling tarmac. Under gaudy, paint-flecked wood the masonry jarred against the horizon. It broke the patterns of cloud with jagged edges and violent angles, unwilling to dance with its surroundings. When the wind picked up any speed it groaned with age.

A single ailing wooden tower; the Pinnacle, rose at the centre of the parklands, the remains of what had been the apex of an impressive rollercoaster. Buckled former peaks and troughs lay in its wake, as though grovelling at the Pinnacle's shabby feet. A vulgar medieval theme was now spoiled and mouldy, streams of oxidised blue green running in striation patterns across mock ramparts and battlements, stained with generations of faeces.

The Startle began to land and file in ranks upon the rooftop of the Pinnacle, pruning and chattering. They were festooned with crudely-honed yet beautiful and elaborate armour, they fastened the lightest filigreed metals to each flight feather, cutting the air with bold inefficiency. Most were ancient hand-me-downs, of legendary wing battles, owned by the old guard, those who had once flown against the Gulls in war and lost. Lost the tower and gained subservience. Of all the flocks, the Startle were one of a few whose armour was cast in ore, and for this they were known as High Wrought.

Ara stood alone below the spire that protruded from the centre of the roof. With eyes closed, he felt the pull of magnetic north, the consistent drafts communicated their paths. He was aware of every member of his flock, ducking and swerving, every mind was focused. They curlicued and revolved, iridescent green and purple and darkest brown.

He felt their warmth and sighed with contentment. Shadows danced, their silhouettes their identities, every gait unique. A young Startle stepped ungainly before him, slumping to the ground with fatigue, his armour old and unforgiving. He removed his face and head plates, pausing to catch his breath. Ara smiled and walked towards the little feathered. His name was Rune, son of Grom. His feathers like white tipped barbs, wet with rain.

Ara keened his head, 'A little nut grease on those joints will help them move with your body. It's old but its good, remember, your father flew with this armour.'

Rune nodded with resignation, jostling his armour with discomfort. The older guardskin bustled past him, tending and smoothing feathers between pristine plates of pretty metal. Rune was jealous of those who seemed so in tune with their armour. He was also restless. It was the night before First Flight. Anxiety rang through them all, but for Rune, it was particularly shrill. Tomorrow the Gull Prince Artioch would take his first flight, and they would kill him.

Above the meandering, broken edge of coastal cliff and beach, both occupied by Wroth settlements, or left to erode, the Gulls had made the sky their dominion, the sentry guards perched upon rotting groins and atop sheltered benches, always waiting. They were brutal knights, endlessly squabbling, and lacked the grace of those they presided over. Ground dwellers felt little of the grip held by Esperer, yet those who flew were privy to his will, above all the Startle.

Esperer had grown old and stoic. His formidable throne room atop the Pinnacle had once been an observation platform for visitors to the theme park. The winding staircase which had fed upwards had collapsed long ago, leaving a void in which his servant flock, the Startle resided. Flanked on all sides by a weather-battered balcony, it served as his seat of power and housed his throne of filthy down, the many blood-encrusted pelts of his fallen sons.

He had lived far longer than any Gull, stayed only by his desire to not let his kingdom fall into lesser talons. He seemed resilient against death, but with every turn his mind would wear, the whine of exhaustion deafening, the steady hiss of fate assuming the form of a pale figure who stood at the foot of his throne and smiled an assured smile, taking incremental steps towards him as the days fell away. It was fear of this certainty that, perhaps, kept him alive. Fear of death and fear of losing that which had cost him so much.

Despite the tradition of Gull monogamy, to increase his chances of producing a son and heir, Esperer had decreed the right to have many mates. These illegitimate lovers bore those sons for him. Daughters he knew nothing of and cared nothing for. A son would take his throne, a worthy lineage. Yet every son had been killed by the Startle, every one consumed by their needle beaks. He cursed himself for his lack of foresight; to steal the throne came with a price he had not predicted.

After his coup, he had offered them banishment. At first the Startle unanimously agreed to leave. But something had changed their mind and they refused his offer. They remained silent and did not question his rule, until the birth of his first son.

The Prince Altibron.

The Startle slaughtered Altibron as he flew out to bathe in the glory of his people and receive the throne from his father. The flock took him in midair and swore, for every son born, they would seek his life in recompense for those taken. And they did. The Startle would suffer greatly with each act of vengeance, but every year, Esperer would lose his heir.

The Gull Lord was steadfast. He would not give up his seat.

The fourth son had been born and had grown to an age suitable to rule. Artioch, the Gull Prince, held his petulance and pomposity like a prize. He knew nothing of the fate of his siblings, kept wholly unaware of his possible end. The act of pageant and the threat of death had come to be known as First Flight. Willingly, Esperer would hand his kingdom to his son, but each year before this could occur the unfortunate tradition would play out. It had become something of a rite of passage, embraced by the Gulls. With every son they were assured by their naive belief in their own self-worth. No Startle could kill a fourth prince surely? The death of each and every male child seemed to not unsettle this delusion. Esperer ruled, yet he relied on tradition to maintain his choking grip, every attempt to quash First Flight had failed and no son would forgo this chance to relish in his glory.

Esperer held a semblance of hope that this son would live. For death had moved a few paces forward and now blocked his vision like a graze upon his retina, and he was unable to rid himself of it.

He knew his life waned.

One more night.

*

Rune picked at his tail feathers and glanced restlessly at his kin. He listened to his brethren wax lyrically about the prince, how proud and stupid he was. Their vitriol was panicked and unsure, they spat prejudices to cloak their fears. To fight a beast so much larger, so much more virile than any Startle, was a challenge most would turn from. Some Startle had heard that Artioch would wear armour made of dried skins, light and hardy. Startle beaks could not pierce them, strapped tight across each muscle, moving gracefully with every beat of his wings. He was a strong boy, his eyes were furious and metallic. In the mornings he flexed and cawed at the females from the balcony, fought with the other boisterous Gulls and won every time.

The Startle talked of massing upon the prince. That sheer numbers would rain on him, his wings would buckle and he would fall from the sky. They called and cooed with rancour. For hours the hubbub of excitement and fear broiled, until the night stole away the heat and they sought warmth in the bowels of the Pinnacle.

Rune was last to enter, a void in the side of the tower like an open wound, chewed wide by its inhabitants, far larger than any Gull. The hole let a great gust into the interior yet was kept open, kept unhindered through fear of past atrocities reoccurring. Most of the flock roosted in the lower levels, where it was far less drafty, the ruddy colours of the unpainted wood panelling giving it a warming hue.

Generations of nesting had created a hive-like architecture; untold layers of hollows and crevices, reworked and rebuilt with each new birth. Upon the walls great painted representations of warrior gods and old mythologies, a profusion of enigmatic characters, some frightening and others heroic. Rune knew every face, every story. As he wheeled down to his perch he settled before his favourite image. Rising up was a mural, scrawled in dirt, berry juice, chalk and charcoal. The etched lattice of lines and smudges had taken many turns to complete. It depicted the Thousand Headed King liberating the Pinnacle from the Gulls.

The mural was drawn in abstract, so that any wandering Gull who dared enter their domain would not comprehend it. Yet with Startle eyes it showed the eventual death of Esperer and the reclamation of the land. Despite the significance of this scene, his favourite part was to the left, a silhouette of a single Startle, upon a rendering of the cliffs, looking up at Seyla, the light of the night, as it cast its great fluorescent gaze upon everything. It was Grom, his father.

Ara appeared beside Rune. 'I never saw it finished.' Ara looked up at the grand painting, 'My sight had waned by the time the last mark was made. I see a little of it, a blur. I remember when they started to create this, there was a great fuss, so much fear that the Gulls would punish us for such insubordination. But they never did.'

Rune smiled, 'They're not very clever, are they?'

Ara chuckled, puffing his feathers as a chill ran across him. 'Do you know the tale of their name?'

'Gull?'

'Long ago the Gull kin went by a different name. They were the Naarna Elowin, *sea stealers*. Esperer's father Malca was king. He would never think to overthrow the Startle, but he did attempt to invade another land. It is said that the ruler of that land was cunning and clever and instead of showing a sign of force, he played up to his vanities. Malca was so flattered by this wise ruler that a truce and a treaty were forged. The wise ruler offered Malca much in the way of land, told him to spread his troops across each province. He refused to call the Gull Lord by his people's name, said that Sea Stealer was far too crude and unbefitting for such a regal people. He spoke of a name far more fitting, he called them Gull. He told them the name was sharp and strong, and held a great and ancient significance.

'The name spread throughout Malca's people, beyond his own subjects, permeated the flocks that shared his roots. He was proud of this name given to him by his new friend. Yet the foreign ruler was far wiser than Malca, and as Malca ordered his soldiers to distant outposts, to hold vigil over his new claim, the wise ruler ordered his own soldiers, who far outnumbered Malca's army to seek them out.

'Within one night the entire Gull army was dead. Malca went to the wise ruler and demanded an explanation. The wise ruler said only that he knew nothing of this tragedy and would do anything in his power to help. In frustration and with no army to command, Malca fled, carrying the name given to him by the deceptor.

'It was not long after that Malca discovered that 'Gull' was derived from the sounds of a Wroth word, and in Malca's eyes this was the greatest insult, a terrible tarnish. But the Gulls are very proud, and refused to discard their new name through fear of showing weakness. So they carry this insult as their namesake!'

They laughed together and Ara placed his wing upon Rune's own, 'They came here, in the beginning, after their atrocious acts, they asserted themselves upon us, bullied us. Yet we offered them no resistance, no reason to punish us further. We did this, because we believed in the word of your father.'

'I know,' Rune lowered his head.

'Your father was very wise. You know this story has no ending yet. It is for you and your generation to write that ending. Make this', he gestured to the mural, 'come to pass.'

Rune nodded. 'Tomorrow, perhaps.'
Ara smiled.

*

Rune eventually reached his nest, climbing deep within the mass of pliant twigs and yellow grass. He closed his eyes and thought of his father and mother. He dwelt in the fragile memories that still clung to him, the moments that held a sense of them. His mother had died when he was very young, and yet he had shards of feelings, associations and smells that might conjure a vivid moment and her face, wide and filled with joy, looking down at him. His father had become more story than memory, lauded by those loyal to him.

Ara had made it very clear that Grom's absence was not Rune's fault. It was a fact he would raise often, and despite this, that absence still festered in him.

Ara had told Rune much of Grom. His father had been fastidious and intelligent beyond his means, which allowed him the tools to slowly unravel Naa. After Lauis had died, he had lost himself in his delusions. Ara had tried to peel him away from this folly, to no end, offering him the sure, earthen trappings of the flock. Instead, Grom had peered endlessly at entrails of insects, the joins of carapace and sinew, looking for rhyme and reason. But despite all that the world offered in its careful selection and its endless brutality and beauty, he eventually turned his attention to the Wroth.

For all the wanton destruction at the hands of the Wroth, they had made things, far more complex than any other species; the highest things that had purpose. He had looked inside their devices that most would strip for their armour and he had seen something greater than those parts. Before the tragedy, when he had been a dutiful father, he had shown Rune how the Wroth had mimicked nature, had found a way to bring the inanimate to life, carefully hewn ore into shapes that flicked and clicked of their own volition. Mechanisms that mirrored the intricacy of bone or chitin. Lauis's death drove him to deconstruct anything that he could find, to understand some crucial ingredient. For him the question always was 'Why'?

Eventually, amongst the debris of his own life and the strategies derived from his ceaseless search, he found some semblance of an answer. He did not share it with his loved ones, who continued to despair over him. He withdrew from the flock. Ara eventually found him in one of the many structures below their home. She saw a brightness become withered and black. Grom began to neglect Rune, eventually asking Ara to take him under his wing, that for him to be well, he would have to leave.

One morning, he was gone.

Rune was young when his father vanished, leaving him with unfinished stories and countless fantastical ideas, and although Rune refused to believe he had been abandoned, he was very much alone amongst the ceaseless din of his flock. It was this abandonment that sat like lead in his stomach every day. He felt such sadness that his father was probably dead, or lost, never to return. He felt that perhaps his father sought something greater than a son.

Something like the Wroth-made things. Something with purpose.

Rune would find himself with this particular thought often, and was only free of it when he remembered another far fonder memory. His father had once told him that inside him was something quite amazing, and for him to find it, he should follow the stars when he closed his eyes. So every night, Rune would close his eyes tight, and his mind would paint iridescent patterns, ever falling geometric shapes, a kaleidoscope of colour. He flew with them until they became faded glorious images that papered the infinite walls of sleep.

The inky depths pulled him under. Tiny effervescent shards of light lay at the furthest point from him, drawing against the pitch. He saw three lines drawn together, and they radiated a singular warmth.

*

He awoke to raised voices, bodies rushing by, the clack of armour and the flurry of feathers. With deft wing he flew to the roof; before him, his flock, chattering and shouting exuberantly. At the centre the spire of the Pinnacle, a small raised circular roof that tapered to a point, a pair of huge black feathered stood in conversation with Ara and his flight chief. They wore armour, wraith-like and gnarled.

Rune chirruped to his companions, 'What is happening?'

Many eyes darted back and forth with uncertainty, until an answer rose, 'Corva Anx! Arrived at dawn, no one knows why!'

Corva Anx, Rune was in awe.

He ducked under outstretched limbs, dodging the cutting edges of wing blades and made his way towards Ara, glancing up at the portentous ghouls, who returned an unfathomable stare. They knocked their heads in jarring motions as if studying him, flying up to the peak of the roof. He shivered in their presence.

Ara spoke quietly with his flight chief, halting their conversation as Rune approached. They turned to him with troubled faces. 'We will not fly. Artioch will live,' Ara spoke authoritatively.

Rune lost his words. Ara sighed sympathetically, 'Come, we must tell the flock.' The call was heard to join his ranks and assemble below. In befuddlement, Rune descended into the Pinnacle, returning one last glance at the Corva Anx, whose eyes remained upon him.

Above the labyrinthine nest great crossbeams extended out from the walls and on each sat a hundred silent Startle. With hesitation, Ara delivered the news.

'We cannot take the life of Artioch. The Gull Prince will live.'

The cavern erupted. Discarded feathers flew, heads swung on fibrous necks and the chorus of *Ballac* sang out the song of the Thousand Headed King. Accusations were spat at him with indignant fury. A single Startle shouted above the roar 'This is our right! My family died fighting them, we deserve his death, the death of every son!'

'The death of every son!'

'The will of those …' Ara raised his voice, 'The will of those who decide such things wish us to consider a greater purpose! Something is coming. We are but a small part in that which consumes us all! We all know the Wroth are dying. They have spread their sickness beyond their own. The Muroi and Baldaboa are poisoned with their ways.

'Too many of us feed on the waste of the Wroth, we grow fat and glib, lose ourselves. Something has fouled our waters and our allies below alike, the stench does not remain in the settlements anymore, and this quagmire grows, taking with it too many lives.

'If we take the life of Artioch, we are no better than the Gulls, no better than the Wroth we fear and hate above all. We are no longer separate from the slick of the Wroth. That is part of our world now, they may have left this place, but we are subject to them, and whether we fly under the wing of Esperer or Artioch, we must still stand against whatever malice rises. We must be the beacon for those who once looked to us for guidance!'

'The whims of the Wroth have no significance here!' a furious voice cried.

'I do not pretend to understand the complexities of those who decide such fates.' Ara replied, 'We ask only of the right path, and in this case, the right path is to listen to those who dwell on such matters.'

'How long will we rely on the rantings of the Corva Anx? They are all mad! What right have they to decide our fate, this is our land, not theirs, our lives! They stand over us like prison guards! Will they strike us down if we fly?' another retorted.

'This is no one's land.' Ara raised his eyes to the flock before him. 'Long ago, we were given a choice. Leave the Pinnacle, find a new home somewhere else. We were all but ready to leave, leave this land, leave all those who relied upon us, who saw something good in us.

'We were ready to let Esperer take this from us. But it took one feathered to make us reconsider. The Corva Anx share a shard of this gift, and we must trust in that. Some may not believe in such things, but we must at least consider that he was almost always right. We must have faith in the Corva Anx as we once had in him.'

Another Startle raised his voice, 'Grom fled this place and left his son, left us in the grip of Esperer. How can we possibly trust the actions of such a Startle?'

The frustration sat heavy, calls of resignation and sadness poured from despondent throats. They embraced one another and tempered their anger. Although fractured, the sharing will of the Startle remained, and much like their ballet, they found a semblance of peace in one another. Some cried for their families lost, others tore at the woodwork with furious claws and beaks.

The disassembled rabble left the roost and flew up to the roof to await First Flight. They would not kill, but they would make their presence known.

Rune seethed. He saw his mother's death, the many turns of his father's absence. They were all bloody wounds in the corpse of the Gull Prince.

*

The familiar caw of the Gulls broke the fatigue of dawn as they made passes of the Pinnacle. It stood like some ancient megalith; the pauper sentinel. The Startle had forgone their morning flight and remained upon the roof overlooking the balcony. For now they were silent.

Upon the balcony, Esperer watched them wearily, his attention periodically stolen by his impudent son. He was embarrassed by the prince, but accepted that he had once been that arrogant boy.

The brightness of the day banished the ghostly figure that drifted in the periphery of his sight. If he could he would stay in this morning light for the rest of his days, if only to never see that face again. A face he could never fully comprehend.

His kingdom was all he knew. All he wanted. He had not been a great king himself. He had squandered and fought and killed needlessly for so long, eaten too much food, made himself sick with greed. But he was wise with years, and all of this, all of this time spent *becoming*, and so little time *being* king. He shook his head with disappointment and returned his gaze to the roof.

The Startle were moving. They bayed for blood. Haranguing one another for a better view, stumbling and stooping at the roof edge, stretching tense, thewy necks over the precipice below and straining spittle-ridden beaks, cawing wildly as Artioch strode out onto the balcony, turning to his father's subjects and displaying the full girth of his wingspan; so fervent was his self-love. His pageantry appeared in full regalia, four huge Gulls stood either side of him, making raucous calls to the hundreds that now filled the sky.

Artioch mounted the fence that ran along the balcony edge. Upon the guard rail that enclosed the tower perched many fawning Gulls. He nodded brazenly to the females, who puffed their chests back at him. He pranced along the wooden bar, before throwing himself upon the air streams that buffeted and curled from the sea. His guards held banners of seaweed in their inelegant claws, great strips festooned with shells and flecks of metal, forming the crude sigil of the king. His shoulders strong, each flap of his wings confident and brave. Muscle undulated under brilliant white feathers, the ruddy plates of leather strapped taut against him. He made sparse wing beats, now large enough to carry him in a glide, and he harooed and guffawed as the guards danced in figure eight patterns beside him.

It pained Rune to watch this. He felt nothing but a death lust. His claws scratched at the tiles, his rage the violent whine of exposed nerves. He shook his head with feverish exasperation. Bright lights flashed and fizzed in his eyes, arching out beyond the path of Artioch. The Gull taunted him, goading him to pursue. What right had they to take this from him? This vital, tangible vengeful thing. He screeched his indignation, talons piercing, terse bites of pain, pacing, kicking, rocking, feeling nothing but the hot white sheer will, and then …

He was flying.

With his legs tucked high he was needle-like. The clouds were sharp and clear and the light banked to his left, he stayed in the glare and with little tight-flitted bursts he kept pace with the Gull entourage. Periodically dropping and swooping, he had to be low, low enough to dodge any backwards glance. He had little on his side, the morning light of Ora, and the stink of pride on the Gulls. Soon he was below them and he cast his eyes on the prince, cocooned in armour. He manoeuvred; flying up, wings taut. There it was, as the prince stretched out his neck, the proud smirk only the regal dared sport – where two armour plates once sat flush, was his exposed neck.

Esperer blinked to clear his eyes, glancing at the Startle. They were still. He had seen something, a flicker, a tiny speck had slid within his vision. For a moment he saw the ghostly form once again, it took the confusion in his mind and made itself of it, and he closed his eyes tight and opened them again, and it was gone. He dropped his head and cursed.

Rune flexed his flight feathers wide and felt the little blades shake free, a second jolt and they lay tight in their stirrups. He flew as close as he could, the space between Artioch's neck and wing was tiny; to place a killing blow would take some feat of flying.

He closed his eyes and felt the winds. He could sense inclines of low pressure from the east, the pulling strings of gravity strident raucous melodies tugging at the malleable sea below. He felt its weight on him, on each feather, and he saw for a brief moment a clear path. His wings would have to be spread to make his mark, and the gap was too tight. He cared no more for his own life than the one he wished to take. He rolled upwards, pulled in his limbs and darted down, catching a single breath of wind that knocked him clean between Artioch's out-spread wing and chest.

Thrust up, he aimed for his neck. There was an impact, a moment of surprise as Rune felt his beak pass through flesh. He felt the blossoming blood fill his nostrils and he pulled out, in a fraction of an instant he knew a single wound was not enough and despite the tumbling mass of lithe limbs and jabbing desperation around him, he held on with his claws and sank his beak over and over into the sodden bleeding hole before him until, despite the roar of plummeting winds pulling at him to let go, the horrifying gurgle of Artioch could be heard. Rune watched Artioch die, his glassy eyes roll up into his head, and he realised his own life would end very soon. He hovered mid-flight as the body fell, and then bullet like, disappeared from sight.

Before him, the abandoned amusement park was to him an assault of colours, sun damaged and rain soaked, signs strewn with indecipherable Wroth markings inviting the ghosts of what had once been. No Wroth came here, except perhaps collections of rowdy young who would leap over fences and scream and yelp like Vulpus cubs, hitting and biting and fighting. This strange bedraggled fortress, the Pinnacle and his family, his bloodlust sated, the loss enveloping him, leaving him cold and alone.

Rune felt the sticky ichor sink into his down, the metallic taste vibrant and sickly in his beak. Every move was difficult, muscles unforgiving. Rune looked back to see his pursuers encircle the body of Artioch, harrying the ground where he lay, jabbing his limp body with a vain hope at procuring signs of life. Rune hung in a morbid daze, his guilt courting hope that perhaps he had failed.

A pair of Gulls lifted the corpse between them, heavy and awkward, whilst the remaining guards turned their gallows wrath upon Rune. Soon they would catch him. With little left to give, his wings collapsed about him. He barely put up a fight, exhausted by his deeds, giving into the resignation of the short agonising snap of beak around his ankle. He was yanked from the air, tossed roughly to the awaiting maw of another guard. He was nothing more than a plaything. He remained limp, letting the searing pain of each muscular yank scold him, thrown unceremoniously between the angry Gulls, who dragged him back to the Pinnacle.

He found himself hauled upon the balcony. Stunned, his vision diminished into nimbus wreathes. He strained to see the Startle peering at him in utter silence from above. He saw Ara, dumbstruck. The Corva Anx squawked and hopped, seemingly laughing at his actions. He saw the Gulls lording over his kin with deadly aim. What had he done? Put his family in harm's way for a selfish, thoughtless act.

He was jostled forward by the guards, jabbed with every misstep. He was knocked to his side as he entered the throne room, the nauseating reek of warm rot fell upon him, draining what energy remained in his little frame. He gagged, forcing himself onto his feet, finding new pain in his digits, straining into the dark to make out the writhing white mass before him. It was Esperer. His mighty head pivoted erratically, tugging at a carcass.

As Rune's eyes grew accustomed, he made out scraps of leather armour, and a head, a face wide and boxy, hanging now from sinew and spine.

Artioch. The Gull Lord's dead son.

Esperer tore, stripped and flayed the pelt from the corpse, the spray of hot wet blood stark against the pristine bulk of his feathers. Esperer paused, glancing down at the connective tissue that remained attached to its pelt. He slashed with his beak, flinging the hide onto the throne. The carcass slid pathetically in on itself.

Without making eye contact Esperer spoke to Rune.

'I understand you. I understand vengeance. I would be nothing without vengeance. I have this throne because I sought it from the Thousand Headed King who had oppressed my people for so long. I see the same fever in you, an unquenchable fire, the bile in your belly is burning you from the inside.'

Esperer kicked the skinned body to one side, and paced awkwardly towards Rune. They were formidable flock, yet ungainly. The king cocked his head this way and that, robotically, letting each searing eye take in the little Startle. He lifted Rune's wing and teased at his flight feather armour. He tapped the blunt end and a single piercing blade slid out.

'I found no killing wound on my son's body, but a puncture mark in his throat.'

Rune bowed his head.

'You killed my son, my fourth son. He choked to death on his own blood.'

Rune shuddered, he felt the impending death blows, felt the viscous breath of the Gull Lord.

Cunning eyes studied the little feathered and a shard of recognition began to animate in Esperer. 'Who was your father, Rune?'

'Grom.'

'Your father was the Shadow Starer?' Esperer cocked his head back knowingly, a depraved smile arching across his face. 'I knew your father, forever tilting at Ora, and your mother, Lauis?

'Before I took the throne, I would see him sat atop the Pinnacle, watching Ora set and rise, watching the stars. He was a clever Startle, and I imagine, a great father, a teacher? And your mother, such a vibrance in her, such intelligent rage.'

Rune felt a punchline, he felt it before the words spilled from the Sea Stealer's oesophagus.

'It was my order that assured her death. I may have eaten her myself. Many of us developed quite a taste for Startle. Though you make such good slaves.'

Rune wanted to scream, but held his tongue.

The Gull Lord paused, seeing his words fester, framing his smugness. He waddled towards his throne, climbing the fetid steps, placing his wide girth on the platform of skins. He shifted like a mother hen over her clutch, flattening the fleshy pulp of his son's epidermis. He opened his wings wide, pretending to prune.

'I will not kill you, Rune. You have shown worth in your actions. Artioch was not ready to rule. He was weak, vain. If you could take his life so easily, then he would have been a paltry leader. But he was my son all the same, and for this you are banished from the Pinnacle, and from the lands over which I reside. You cannot fly here. You will descend to the ground and walk away forever. My guards will let you walk free, but you are to never know your kin again.'

Esperer turned away and shook his flight feathers like dismissive fingers. Rune felt the nudge of great bodies against him. He was corralled out to the balcony, his staggered footsteps not trepidation but blind confusion. As he neared the edge, the largest guard fixed a considered expression upon his face, as though calculating a diabolical plot.

Rune was thrown from the Pinnacle.

The skies were a sullen white, stormy and effulgent. His mind was stripped blank, limbs unable to rouse the thought to catch an updraft. He saw the Gull guards hesitate upon the balcony edge, and then dive after him as he fell backwards, gaining on him, defying their master's words. He had embarrassed them, shown their weakness. They were going to kill him.

He caught his breath, poised his wings, and swung upright. He spied a row of ruined refreshment stands, folding his wings close to his chest he fell fast, dropping from sight. His size relative to his pursuers gave him a little room for stealth, manoeuvring thread-like between the small structures, but what he gained in speed, he lacked in brute force. Soon he felt their presence, their heavy shadows eclipsing him. They straddled either side, lunging at him with dagger beaks. His saving grace was keeping low to the ground, tall grasses and rusted fencing brushing and grazing as he wheeled dangerously.

He glanced back as vengeful eyes focused every strike, every ensnaring jab. Soon he was overwhelmed, the body of a great Gull bared down on him, cutting the wind with sail arms.

Rune rolled over himself, his neck wrenched in agony, his body lost, eyes streaming, pulled down within feet of the ground. Mere moments stretched, the battered clouds like strips of milky flesh. He reached out to save himself, to hold tight. He flexed his armour, his piercing blades responding to the straightening of his back, the spasm of splayed flight feathers, his eyes closed, silent, ending.

His body lifted hard and fast, the frantic beating of something against his resigned senses. He engaged briefly to see his piercing blades had caught the clouds, and the clouds were now bleeding. Bleeding?

He shook himself from his stupor to see his wings were now caught in the chest of a Gull, its razor beak darting dangerously close as it rolled and banked, kicking and screaming at the little Startle. Rune felt no remorse.

He pulled one wing free, his muscles fluid and tight, he fell loose, waiting for the great beast to swing once more. Rune held his free wing steady, hanging between the animal's wing and legs. It cawed in anguish, it knew what was to come if it didn't free itself from him.

It turned abruptly, catapulting Rune out and around, a blur of black and brown and the brilliant glint of metal, slicing cleanly through and up, deep, scarlet rivulets curving past his face. The Gull screeched and Rune let go, let his blades retract, making use of the great speed he had gained, and he darted back down towards a stream, lined on both sides with brambles and thick heavy trees.

Still the Gulls came, pursuing at a distance, yet the stream was an impasse, the trees a tunnel of obstacles, easy for small feathered, fatal for his pursuers. They flew high, losing their prey in the brush. They surrendered their hunt.

'You are cursed boy. We'll find you! We'll kill you!' they cried, as they flew above the trees.

*

He flew for hours, the muffled alarm of those final words reverberating around his skull, driving him ever closer to the water. He eventually spied a perch, a rotting log breaking the surface, and he descended.

He felt dizzy and weak, realising he had weeping wounds, his down stiff with blood. With a sharp ache he pulled apart encrusted feathers and tended his cuts. The water was shallow at the bank and he hobbled down upon the muddy silt that had collected against the log and bathed himself. Nervously he watched the water run cloudy red, yet to bathe was soothing. He climbed out and shook himself as dry as possible before finding a hollow in the scrub to rest.

He carefully removed his armour, unclipping the tiny claws that firmly gripped each feather along the shaft, one single exceptionally light yet strong stay fastened close to the quill. He stretched his flight feathers, feeling the tension ebb from his flesh. He laid each piece before him, picking and scraping away detritus, polishing every blade with moss. He covered his armament with leaves and hopped out into the dwindling, murky light.

He spied a horse chestnut tree, and sought its fruit. Amongst the debris a stale nut, and with nimble beak and claw, cracked the husk to reveal the withered flesh. He broke a piece away, and flew back to his trove, squeezing at the morsel until beads of oily moisture began to collect on its surface. He applied the grease to each tip, rocking the blades until they were coated. Within moments the moisture had dried, leaving the oil as a lubricant.

He decided to sleep without his armour on, and nestled down for the night. His dreams were vivid and exhausting, the images of Artioch, his guilt at the Gull Prince's death, the blood-soaked corpse of that poor fool draped across his thoughts. He saw patterns in the blood. He saw his mother, saw the sliver of memory that held her own death.

His laboured breath woke him, heavy leaves had fallen against him as he had tossed and turned. Stifled, he pulled himself out of the nest and stood for a moment, the breeze off the water ruffling his hot damp down. He suddenly became aware that he hadn't eaten for hours. Unable to search for food in the dark, he pulled himself amongst the leaves and hoped for restful sleep.

With the morning glare breaking the leaf cover, he awoke to the sound of many voices. Having only lived amongst the Startle, his dawn chorus was a familiar, comforting chatter. Amidst this unknown land, there was a peculiar melodious order to the song. Ara had told him a little of this ritual, something shared by the winged folk only, yet of benefit to all. It was often religious, a call to prayer for the Harend and Yowri, invoking the melancholy of their prophets and deities. They would usher the devout to the lower branches, proselytising the word. But for the most part, the chorus was the passing of news. Along this stretch of river bank the communities of both arboreal and ground dwelling denizens relied on this report, for the movements of the Wroth were ever present in their minds.

That morning, the song was thick with word of the Gull Lord. The king's son was dead and the Gull kin were seeking his murderer. Rune hurriedly reattached his armour and skipped along branches and rocks until he found the Cryer of News. It was a Bloodson, dancing swiftly between branches, his armour cut from the segmented undercarriage of a Torplic. His red chest shuddered as each note was exhaled, rhythmic and tuneful.

'The king's son was killed by the Startle, against the orders of the Corva Anx!'

Rune stood below the little feathered and chirruped, to no avail.

'Bloodson, come down from there and talk to me!' he exclaimed after many calls had heeded no reply.

The feathered cocked its head, taking in the High Wrought before him. For someone so small, he held a certain confidence about him.

'You are Startle, far from home?' he said.

Rune hesitated. He was aware that the rule of the Gulls was not appreciated by any of the flocks, that in fact rebellion had flowed avidly throughout their rule. But he knew he shouldn't advertise his dissent, or indeed the blood on his talons. He stepped backwards, vainly seeking to hide his armour, and nodded.

'I … I am searching for the rebel Startle you speak of, Bloodson.' From the frown on his face, Rune could tell the Bloodson was unconvinced.

'They say a single High Wrought took out that wide-headed fool. I would like to congratulate such a fellow. If you see him, you tell him from me that he has a friend in the sons and daughters of blood. Sincerely.'

Rune lowered his head and smiled, shifting his feet in the dirt. 'Tell me, Bloodson, what is the news of the Gulls?'

The Bloodson rolled a single tune from his warbling throat. 'The word is revenge, the Gulls are scouring the land for the aggressor, the one who killed the prince. If I were him I would leave Gull-occupied land, follow the stream north. There are allies all along the way, he will have no problem finding assistance.'

They nodded to one another knowingly, and Rune took flight, up and up, until he could see the winding path of the stream, and began to follow it north east, inland, towards Wroth settlements.

He fed where he could, insects that swarmed the surface of the water, fleeting lives that seemed fulfilled by their dainty dances. He felt less anxious the further he moved from the Pinnacle, yet his loss lay heavy in him. Sadness was held back as he forged on, following the curve of the stream, becoming a river, its banks broken with copses of lush trees and ferns. Soon he was flying high on thermals alongside other lone feathered, higher and higher, glancing smiles from friendly faces turned to playful races.

The Gulls were known for their determination. It played on his mind and he decided to stay earthbound for a few days, where the troubles of the feathered were of little significance.

He walked along paths which ran beside the river, wary of Throa, Maar and Vulpus. Carnivores were drawn to water, their scents hung like wanton tongues. As much as he wished he could stray from this rather dubious path, the concourse provided a semblance of direction.

The dawn chorus became his only means to know of his pursuers. Each morning he rose to its symphony, fearful of what it might bring. Then one particular morning there was but one melodious voice amongst the trees. There was no threatening timbre to it. It soothed his waking panic, and drew him out from his roost in search of its source.

It was a Yowri, dancing upon a branch. Sewn within its wings was a collection of dried leaves. Torn carefully into each were patterns that spoke of its piety. He recognised one of these markings and it drew him towards the Yowri, his song was gloriously loud and Rune could hear conviction in his words. After a while Rune flew up to share his branch.

The Yowri completed his prayer, turning his eye upon the young Startle.

'These patterns upon the leaves, what do they mean?' Rune said.

The Yowri paced along the branch, 'They are prayers for Alauda, the Second Sister of the Flock, we sing for her guidance, and for her Sisters' embrace, feathers touching, the ever circle.'

Rune knew little of this belief, besides that which his father had taught him. Of the various religions of the feathered, the Sisters of the Flock were perhaps the most common.

For the Startle, their gods were not benevolent. Grom had once explained to Rune how their beliefs reflected the collective morale of his flock. Under the rule of Esperer, their gods were angry, violent entities, whose function to act as avatars for all their hatred and woe for the Gulls. These grim likenesses dwelt deep in all the Startle, reminding them of everything they should not be.

'Would you tell me of these Sisters?'

The Yowri acquiesced, finding a comfortable place to sit, 'The stories are old, before the flocks were formed. There were three sisters. They came into the world and each sister had a quality unlike the other. One sister was strong and brave, another wise and rational, and the final, compassionate and loving.

'Each of these singular qualities were strong, but without the others, they would surely die. Together they formed the perfect mind, and they gave Naa the confidence, patience and love that it sorely needed. But soon our ancestors grew to know of the sisters' wisdom, and wished to own it, and believed that to take of the sisters strengths would better their cause, and by taking they broke the balance shared between the sisters, and that is how the world fell. It is said the Wroth were born in the darkness that followed.

'The sisters were lost for a very long time, and when they found each other, they decided to abandon Naa and its peoples, finding solace in each other. Those who pray, do not pray for themselves but for the sisters, prayer is an apology to them for what their forebears did.'

'Do you believe the sisters are still listening?'

'I believe that they hear us, but choose not to listen, I believe their hearts are broken in to pieces, so we continue to ask for forgiveness. To mend that which we broke. Whether they listen or not it does not matter.'

The Yowri seemed so sure of this, Rune found his certainty intriguing. 'I am Startle, all I have ever known is my kin. I awoke every morning with them, I cleaned my armour with them, we flew together. Without them I am aimless.'

The Yowri smiled, 'We are born without aim, young Startle.' He shrugged, 'You must give yourself purpose, to experience, to learn. The sisters did not ask us to rest in apathy and ignorance, they taught us to make use of our lives for the better of all.'

Rune pondered for a moment, studying the patterns painted in berry innards and mud upon the Yowri's wings. He saw circles, like eyes, and a pattern he recognised from a dream.

He returned to the forest floor and continued his slow journey along the river bank, stopping to pull insects from decaying logs and drink a little water. He rested where he could. His experience of the countryside was distant green blurs; irregular masses of oblongs and squares, bizarre geometric patterns far away. Much of the land around the pinnacle was waterlogged, reclaimed by marshland or scrub. From where he stood now he saw the mark of Wroth on everything.

There were worn paths far wider than any animal he knew, bizarre order to the growth of trees and bushes. He had known only Wroth decay, abandoned and derelict monuments of what had been, and although many of the fields were now overgrown and left to the whims of nature; some still bore the trimmed mark of Aurma, massive gentle creatures, all children despite their size. Enclosed by the Wroth, unable to leave the bare grass, they seemed confused and untethered by past or present, some fragments of their mind long bred out of them, unable to piece together a sense of belonging. There were however shards of profound thought amongst their forgetting. Their incessant grazing broken by lines of inspiration caught up in the breeze and taken from them. Rune feared the time when he would encounter their former masters, and his imagination bore strange and terrifying fruit.

They were bad omens to him, angular, upright and violent. It was all he had ever been taught of the Wroth, to avoid them at all cost. Yet his avoidance meant he had no means to understand or protect himself from them.

He hurried himself, taking flight as little as possible. But it was flying that hastened his escape from the Gulls, and soon he had mastered flying close to the water.

He chased the blinking scales of tiny Ungdijin, the riotous green weeds caught in the river's motion, gaped at the dark pools beneath tree roots, where the brows of the hungry lingered. He shook at the mere thought, lifting up into the spatter of tiny flies, particles all caught in Ora's corona.

The afternoon was warm and invigorating and he flew a great distance, stopping briefly to exchange greetings with mammals of kinds he had never seen before. He found more chestnuts to oil his armour and slept for a while in the crevice of a bridge. The early evening took him away from the water, dancing amongst the seeds of dandelions as the last of the light caught their delicate fronds. He perched on a fence post and preened for a while, removing the spores which had attached themselves to him. They were not particularly good eating.

He could make out a black and white shape dashing about, examining a pile of scrap that seemed dug from the earth. It wore no armour; he could see the glint of the metal in its beak, yet besides its white wings nothing highlighted the contours of its body. For a moment he saw streaks of metallic blue and green along its tail feathers. He realised quickly that it was a Collector. They were not uncommon in his homeland. Before the Startle had been conquered by the Gulls, Collectors had been employed to bring items to the Pinnacle, some of which was used by the High Wrought for their armour. Once the Gull Lord appointed himself most fled to find less despotic employment, or were enslaved alongside the Startle.

Rune glided hesitantly from branch to branch until he settled upon a limb close to the Collector. She darted about the undergrowth with determination. There were piles of dirty metal amongst the leaf litter, ring pulls and beer cans, and twisted trinkets. He watched her tearing little slivers of foil, holding them between her feet and pulling delicately.

She would pause, repositioning her head to take in the angles of the metal, tugging, tearing and picking until the item was exactly how she wanted it. For tougher metal she employed a stone, and with deft beak and claws battered it into submission. He could make out parts which had been cast; much like the armour he wore, and she attached and adorned these with her claw-made filigrees. He continued to watch her for a few minutes before drawing attention to himself.

She shot an irate glare at him, her razor beak somehow a lot more threatening than he had expected. Her movements were erratic, he could tell she was afraid and he felt a little courtesy would go a long way. He bowed, lowering his eyes, and spoke, 'I am Rune, son of Grom. I mean you no harm.'

He raised an eye, she continued to stare. 'High Wrought, of the Pinnacle are you?' she said curtly. He nodded, and she relaxed a little. 'Your new king is dead, it is on the morning wind.'

Rune nodded again. He raised his head and stepped forward. She stepped back.

'What do you want son of Grom?'

Rune attempted to make his every movement sympathetic to her nerves, 'I was wondering what it is you are making?'

She hunched her wings and let out a hiss, backing herself against her possessions. Her eyes were enraged. She spat out words, 'You want my things? Want what is not yours?'

It dawned on him to leave her alone. He found a quiet spot, and sat down. She cocked her head, hopped and hissed again, her leer turning from anger to curiosity.

'So?' she said, and Rune, without looking her in the eye, spoke.

'Collector, I am alone, and I have been alone for many turns, and I wished for company, that is all.'

She frowned, sighed heavily and sat down beside him.

'I am sorry for frightening you,' he said calmly. They sat facing one another for a while as she studied him.

'Rune, son of Grom?'

'Yes.'

Her tone changed, she wrestled with whether he was friend or foe. She decided on the former and hopped towards her bounty. She tossed one piece up into the air and it landed before him. The object had been folded, cut and teased to form the shape of a vertebrae. Rune saw that it was quite beautiful.

'The Drove will pass close to here in a few turns, and I wish to barter with one for some work.'

She took the item back to the pile, a spine of some sort, and began to fasten the collection together. It was much larger than her, designed for a ground dweller. 'It is a harness, for armour plates.'

He marvelled at its ingenuity. 'It's very beautiful. But what are the Drove?'

Her eyes widened. 'You do not know the Drove? Well! The Drove are mercenaries. They can be bodyguards, escorts,' She paused, 'assassins even. Whatever is needed.'

'My name is Aggi,' she said.

He suggested that they find something to eat together. She appreciated the gesture and they flew towards the river. They spoke of loneliness and Rune's escape from the Gulls. She was disinterested in the life he had taken, exclaiming that taking lives was part of life itself, and whatever had driven him to commit such an act must have been worthy of its effort. He told her of his father's absence, and the dearth it had left in him.

'If your father's absence is an open sore, perhaps it needs attention.'

She whirled from river bank to river bank, catching the little wisps of veined wing and dainty bodies in her mouth, morsels of protein. Her eyes were sharp and black in the twilight and he saw something intense and sure about her.

They found a place to rest, Aggi studying Rune's own armour, remarking at its beauty. 'Do you know what this is made of? How the Muroi learned to smelt the ore?' she said as she admired the blades that sat tight in each clasp.

'I do!' she said with pride, before he could reply. 'It is what I seek, to make such things.'

'Did you ever work under Esperer?' Rune asked.

'No I did not, but some of my kin may have done. I have not flown with my flock for a long time.'

'Where are your flock?'

'Somewhere, I do not know. I left my family because I could not understand their ways and desires. I wanted a different life. So I flew away.'

'You fly alone?' Rune remarked.

She looked at him, 'I do. I am seeking understanding, to find my own path. I am a maker, a builder, and I love to make things, to fix things. I want to fix myself.'

'Fix yourself?'

'I wish to know why I do not see the world like my kin, why I do not fit in. That is my story. What of you Rune, do you believe your father still lives?'

Rune nodded. 'I have to believe there is a chance.'

'Then you have a cause. You say that your home is the Startle, that is where your family is, and you cannot return to the Pinnacle, so now you must find your father, find home out here in the world.'

Rune looked at her with frustration.

'But how do you find one feathered in a world so large?'

Aggi smiled, 'For that you will need someone who can see things that are not so clear. And it just so happens I seek that too.'

'A seer?'

'*THE* seer.' She grinned.

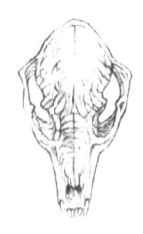

Chapter 2

Vorsa stood below the looming office block. Drizzle rain spilled out on ochre vales of sodium light, cast from lamps that crowned its roof. She sighed deeply and, disregarding their objection, dismissed her Vulpus guards. She found resolve and began to climb the exposed staircase, an endless spiral of concrete and chipped tile, the encroachment of a green film of mildew hastening its decrepitude.

As she neared its peak she could already discern the rhythmic invocations of the Corva Anx; taunting the dark sky with curses and coos. The door was ajar, her path littered with dried and dislocated limbs arranged in curious patterns, jaw fragments scratched and pockmarked with glyphic scrawl. She knew a little of their codex, yet most was hidden behind incoherent philosophy far beyond her meagre learning. She had yet to fully understand the method within their maddening spells.

The roof was clotted with a carpet of black bodies; slick feathers and severe beaks. They cawed with apprehension at her presence, bouncing hastily away from her as she walked, sweeping them aside like soot clods. Each wiry neck rotated to greet her, studying her with their dark pearl eyes. Upon the roof above the stairwell stood the Corva orthodoxy, the Corva Anx, the Bishops of Bone Char.

Like animated cadavers, they teetered and swayed. Their high priest, the ever perplexing Dominus Audagard, stood at the centre of their peculiar skullduggery, a shrine of contorted twigs and wire rising above them, bound in a broken splintered circle. Shredded black plastic sacks were draped and sewn over a collage of desiccated innards, pulled into tortured totems.

The Dominus issued commanding squawks to his bishops, and a shroud of shrivelled skins and bitumen was lifted on agile beaks and placed upon his head. It covered his eyes like a cowl. He stooped forward, shaking his wings wide, swaying and barking out prayers.

'I skry with my little eye!' the Dominus cackled, his disciples laying shards of mirrored glass on the floor before him. He couldn't see them, yet he traced decisive feathers across each fragment. His mantras grew in volume, placing further scraps of marked cloth and twig upon the ground, delicately aligning them with some strange inclination. He abruptly dug his beak into his chest and spat the bloody saliva upon the broken mirror. He keened his head this way and that, guiding the blood into a cartography. He turned his formidable head to Vorsa.

'The circles widen, moving in patterns of putrefaction, quite sublime. This is our final lesson, Vorsa. Do you feel ready to accept *him*?'

She nodded, 'I have known him my entire life, that was never a question.'

The Dominus and his kin began to utter recitations of Revenant speech. Vorsa listened; she mouthed each warbled cough, each animism; it raised in volume within, gaining clarity. Chimera skulls were brought forth and held above one another like death masks. These effigies of life. Each disciple of the Dominus took a blood-smeared mirror.

'Come join me, Vorsa Corpse Speaker.'

Vorsa bowed. She jumped effortlessly to the raised platform.

The Dominus turned his head to the Vulpus. He picked up the largest sliver of glass, and held it upright between his claws, whilst his disciples fanned around her, each placing their respective piece so that she could see herself from many angles.

'We are told to not see ourselves in shiny surfaces, to chase away our reflection. Why is that, Vorsa Corpse Speaker?'

She tried to ignore her discomfort, her eyes flinching away from the mirror. 'We tempt the Gasp, we offer ourselves as eyes for it.'

The Dominus nodded. 'We offer the Gasp our eyes, and the Gasp gains a taste for those eyes, a taste for what those eyes see. It becomes greedy, wanting. Dangerous.'

'But you already share your eyes, don't you Vorsa?'

'Yes.'

'Look in the glass Vorsa. Let him see, far from the grave where his body lies.'

She prized her eyes open wide, against every whim, every fibre of her, and looked within the glass. For a moment, all she saw was herself. Her red fur, the inflexion of the armour upon her brow. She saw the scar across her eye, something she'd quite forgotten, she felt its pain once again, noted its existence. She followed her own eyes, felt the mesmerism of each mimicked trait. Across the many shards of glass, saw each imperfection, each chink in her armour.

And then she saw him.

She had known him her whole life, had known his presence, had conversed with him in the reverie of the Gasp. But this was physical, surrounded by the tangible, he held a quality all the more unnatural. A jarring sensation struck, yielding a stab of migrainous pain. He was here, with her.

Blossoming white; the excruciating cold, the chrisom billow of ectoplasm rose limb-like from her body. Every ounce of her told her to turn away from him. Yet she held herself, promised herself. She saw his face, his empty eyes, and she gave to him her own. For a moment her reflection no longer looked back at her. It was something else, some*one* else.

It frightened her but she knew this face, knew he had been kind in life, and knew he was capable of love.

'I accept you, I accept you as my Revenant.'

The Corva were frantic with excitement as they too saw the ghostly presence manifest. Fulminations of etheric matter, gelatinous, otherworldly. And then it was gone, and her reflection returned. She slumped against the roof, exhausted. The clergy of the Dominus flung the glass from the roof. The Dominus leaned into her. 'Well done Vorsa, well done. Never have I seen such a manifestation!'

'Yes,' she managed between breaths. 'Good! Good! Now you will go to his grave, thank him! But remember your stones. He will be expecting them. Make sure you recite every word, every prayer for him, open yourself to him. He will guide you, guard you in the Gasp. ... Vorsa?

It is imperative.'

'Yes,' she said shakily. 'We leave soon, my father is frail but he will come, I worry this will be his last pilgrimage.'

'Your father will live to see the city pass to the Vulpus. But you must hurry.'

'What of the Startle?'

'With the chick's father gone, we turn to the chick himself. We hear he killed the Gull Lord's son, Artioch.'

'The child Startle killed the Gull prince?'

'Yes, quite a feat. Alone they say. He will raise many enemies. This is a precarious time Vorsa Corpse Speaker. So many divergent paths, so many broken twigs, the matrices do not lie still. When you return, you must shadow him, gain his trust.'

'Yes, Dominus.'

*

Rune squinted his eyes against the mist. The marshland sighed under a foggy torpor. In the distance he could make out an abandoned building site, massive cylindrical structures lay one on top of the other to form a pyramid, water and rotting vegetation drooled from each orifice. Far to the north east he could see a large copse of trees whose canopy shrugged the entropic haze.

Aggi was unmarred by the sluggish dawn. With spirits high she surmised their best route from above. Identifying the same trees, she urged him on.

Aggi was much larger and faster than Rune, even with the oversized armour clutched in her talons, and she whistled around him, baiting him to chase her, falling into her slipstream, feeling for the invisible tethers that Ara always spoke of. He remembered the lesson, that he must tie himself to the wind; that to feel the currents was one thing, to take hold of them was another. He felt for each infinitesimal inconsistency, finding stronger breath to carry him.

They flew for a while, over fields that steadily lost the listless fog, replaced with great swathes of corn. With each gust the golden stems rolled like choreography, and he began to see the pattern of the wind in that which it touched. More little flicks and cues, his feathers adapted to the currents, knowing when to duck and when to glide. The copse of trees was an outcrop from a much larger forest, falling over the horizon in green, glorious and dark. Aggi and Rune nodded at one another and descended to the tree line.

The trees were old, straining with age. Wrinkled and obese they sat squat and tightly packed, bound with ivy vines. Aggi busied herself by raiding the remains of nests for possible food but found nothing, Rune flitted down to the forest floor and picked under rotten wood for insects. He found a small meal of various tiny creatures, and took a few worms for Aggi, holding them in his beak. Beyond the tangle of undergrowth he could make out a clearing, and he sprung along aged limbs and mossed hillocks until he found a lookout within a holly bush.

There were others here. In the undergrowth beyond he could make out movement, mammalian faces. For a moment he was sure those eyes were full of craving, and he was ready to flee. But it was soon apparent that these were too small. Tetek, their chitin armour tiny and intricate, and Tril, amongst many others. Aggi rested on the branch beside him and tugged awkwardly at the worms in his mouth. He gave willingly, and she paused between mouthfuls to acknowledge the congregation beyond the foliage. 'It will be busy tonight, lots of business for the Drove.'

They waited in the trees the entire day, until night fell.

*

The Drove moved in steady yet tired procession from the sparse woods to the north. They had travelled without sleep for many turns to come to rest here, and begin bartering.

They were Yoa'a, all of them female. Their armour was old and High Wrought like Rune's, yet coarse and built for much more rigorous battle. They were lithe and strong under their short coats. The largest of the posse came to a standstill, purveyed her audience and closed her eyes. She stood on hind limbs, rendering her remarkably tall. She took in the dusk, deep purposeful breaths, swaying slightly with each draw, seemingly intoxicated by it.

Rune sniffed at the air and smelled the gentle sweetness of rotting vegetation and the fragrances of flowers, and the curious aroma of a cooling evening. He saw the flutter of whiskers, saw oily fur parted on her face to reveal painful scars. This Yoa'a had seen much of Naa.

The other Drove lumbered beside her, lying amongst the cool grass to rest. Some removed their armour, others slept where they fell. For a few hours the Drove lay silent as their patrons waited patiently.

Seyla's presence signalled commencement, and one by one, their huge ears rose, twitching. Aggi nudged Rune and they left their stoop to find a place amongst the crowd. Eagerly the congregation requested the ear of the Yoa'a with offers of trinkets and scrimshaw. The Drove were unhurried, each movement watched with anticipation.

'Onnar?'

Aggi gestured towards the large Drove who had caught Rune's attention. The Yoa'a turned cautious eyes towards the Collector and nodded. 'I am, what is your barter?'

Aggi offered forth the vertebrae. 'It is a new harness, lightweight, I dare say your plates will attach easily to it. I fashioned it myself.' Aggi retreated once she had placed it before the Drove.

Onnar lifted it, and felt its weight. 'This is beautiful work, very light, unlike this old brute.' Onnar shifted her shoulders, the interlocking plates upon her back clattered. 'What do you want for this?'

Aggi hesitated, 'I need vouching for. I need safe passage to the House of Tor.'

'Tor? That is a long journey. Does he expect you?'

Aggi shook her head.

Onnar smiled, 'Hence the need for my assistance!'

'That is true. I also need the same for my friend,' Aggi replied.

Onnar looked beyond Aggi at the wide-eyed Startle. 'So, the Gull Killer is still alive!' Onnar raised an eyebrow as panic ran across Rune's face. 'Don't fret little Startle, your secret is safe with me, you did us all proud.'

Rune sighed audibly and she laughed.

'I accept your barter, Collector, may I wear this now?'

Aggi agreed and Onnar threw off her armour, dislodging each aged plate and attaching them to Aggi's harness. She flung it upon her back and fastened it against her chest. In effortless leaps on lissome limbs, she sprinted about the clearing, throwing her balled paws into the air, play fighting and dancing with some invisible lover or combatant.

The Yoa'a returned panting, requesting adjustments. Aggi hopped upon her back and with nimble beak, picked and pulled at the armour until Onnar was happy. 'It is fine work Collector, fine work indeed.'

The Drove accepted other barters, which would take them to many perilous and distant places. Some animals were turned away. Curious, Rune approached a group of Muroi who sat forlorn amongst the grass. 'They did not accept your offer?' Rune asked hesitantly.

They turned and nodded. 'They cannot help us, we seek safe passage to the Stinking City, and yet they will not venture near it. We are told there is a sickness, and we worry for our families who live there.'

Rune frowned, 'What is the Stinking City?'

'It is a Wroth settlement, you can smell it on the wind sometimes. That is where the sickness lives, in the Wroth. The Wroth have made themselves ill and now that has spread beyond their people, into those who share the land with them.'

Rune offered words of comfort, but he felt them lacking. The Muroi sloped away as he rejoined Aggi and Onnar.

'The Muroi are sick,' he said as they made to leave the clearing.

Onnar grimaced, 'Yes, the Muroi, the Baldaboa, anyone who feeds on the waste of the Wroth. It is in their things, you must not eat of Wroth-made things.'

At dawn Onnar made a fond farewell to her kin, and they set off, skipping over a rickety stile, onwards amongst the gorse whose flowers were small apologies for their thorny limbs. Onnar trod carefully out into the tracts beyond, into the tawny hues of heathlands' bracken sea and the whinny of stroppy Athlon.

Rune was unaware of who they sought, but it felt good to have a goal. He and Aggi flew for a while before resting, looking up at the silhouette of feathered black against the brilliant white clouds. Eventually the wild was replaced by arable land where the signature of the Wroth was most evident. Their steady hand that sculpted and cultivated until the absence of nature was sorely felt.

The smell of the distant city was very apparent to Rune. It clung to the air, clammy and unctuous, Aggi had also become aware of it and she flew beside him. 'Can you smell it? It is them, the Wroth.'

'I've only ever seen Wroth from a distance, we were always told to keep away.'

Aggi nodded,' It is for the best, they are cruel and terrible.'

They spied Onnar in the fields below and flew down to join her.

Trails of black earth, the roads of the Wroth crept ever more frequently under her foot. Palsied grass and waning trees struggled in the shadows of larger, constructed things. Onnar made an effort to warn them of the folly of this land; that danger was not just in predators, but in traps - that the Wroth had turned the very earth against those who dared to stray upon their territory. But stray they must, for their destination lay in the bosom of this land.

It was not long before Onnar spied their goal. Piles of rusted cars heaved in an endless unmoving battle against concrete slabs that formed the perimeter of a scrapyard. Rune studied the stronghold of rusted iron cadavers beyond, imagining what use they may have served. Onnar ran along the perimeter, skittish, nervously sifting piles of leaf litter until she found her prize. It was a hole dug under the wall. Covered with vegetation, the entrance was concealed and only betrayed by the smooth ground where the great beasts who used it slid on their bellies. Onnar barked at her companions and soon all three were standing apprehensively at the entrance to the House of Tor. Neither Aggi nor Rune recognised this beast's scent, but knew to avoid it. Onnar's hackles rose with trepidation.

'Meet me on the other side,' she said in a hushed voice, as limb by careful limb she climbed down. The feathered flew overhead.

Onnar clambered under the wall, the bodies of eviscerated cars greeted her as she surfaced on the far side. There was no path to follow, no entrance to the sett. Her ward appeared above as she blinked in the low light. Eyes glowered back.

Hulking shapes shambled towards them from shadowed quarters, their armour black and threatening, mimicking the carapace of a stag torplic. Wide heads enclosed by corneous jaws, grey white streaks across their black faces and flanks, their eyes steely and unblinking. One bore a great gash across its face and various pitted scars across its chest. It keened its head quizzically as Onnar approached.

'Tordrin, my, how you have grown! Last I saw you, you were knee high and pink!'

The surliness fell from the beast's face into a wry smile as he recognised the Yoa'a before him.

'Onnar? I do not believe I was ever pink!'

'At some point in our lives my dear, we are all pink! But you are now guardskin to your father, and I am here to speak with that very daynight.'

'Tor will be glad to see you, you come at a difficult time.'

The Throa beckoned them into the sett. Down they climbed, the earth excavated by deft claws, only impeded by immovable stones or tree roots gnawed to the joint.

'The Wroth used to come here with Caanus, dig up our homes, maim and murder us. Since the previous summer they have not returned, they abandoned their pursuits in the fields and the grass they had once torn away has been left to grow wild. We hoped they had gone for good. I dare say we hoped too soon. Whilst foraging, we saw them out by the abandoned House of Ror, we believe they seek us. So we must be vigilant.'

The tunnel opened into a wide hollow. There were Wroth-made things stacked against every available space. The dull yellow grey of ageing plastic and the rusted coil of metal; water damaged yet cared for, dragged from the lap of the elements.

At the far wall, hunched over an assembly of puzzling objects, Rune saw a far larger Throa. He wore armour much like Tordrin, yet stone tools and lengths of sharpened wood hung from it. Grey whiskers hemmed his snout and he peered at a device that flickered with light as he tinkered.

'Father, you have company.'

'I do apologise!' Tor said as he turned to greet them.

Onnar bowed, and offered her paw, 'Ora bring peace, Tor old friend.'

He peered at her with solemn eyes, 'Onnar Proudfoot of the Drove!' he bellowed, 'it has been a long time, my dear.' He reached out his paw and placed it upon her and patted heartily, 'Good to see you old girl! And who do we have here? Feathered friends underground?'

Onnar introduced them. 'This is Aggi, Collector, maker.'

Tor nodded, 'A maker? Good with those claws and beak I imagine.' He grumbled as he lowered himself to all fours. Aggi stepped closer and spoke plainly, clear to all that she had rehearsed this meeting many times.

'I wish to join the Tempered Guild.'

Her eyes darted nervously, fearful of his rejection. He saw that fear and quenched it with a great clap of his paws, and laughed, 'Straight to the point!'

'I am more than happy to pass on these arts to you. No maker is complete without knowing the metals when liquid, we see the true nature, that it wishes to be so many things, like us. I am sure you'll agree, never judge a nut by its shell!'

He frowned, 'But I am afraid, I cannot make you Guild, for that you must parley with Psittacus Erithacus, he formed the Guild in the Stinking City, to learn the Wroth and their ways, to better our understanding of them.'

She considered his words, and replied hastily, 'Will you sponsor my application?'

He smiled, 'I shall consider it!' He looked to Rune, 'and this little fellow?'

'This is Rune, Son of Grom,' Onnar replied.

'Son of ... Grom?'

Tor was noticeably moved, and unfurling his large black claws he gently placed one under Rune's beak, lifting his head and turning it slightly, 'Ah yes, there he is. I can see him in you son, see that bright spark. Grom, the Shadow Starer.'

Rune swallowed hard, trying to hide the little flutter that lifted up in him. 'You knew my father?'

Tor smiled. 'Your father was the first individual I met whose interest in the Wroth eclipsed my own. He had a grasp of their ways that I could barely comprehend. It was he who inspired my work, to make use of all these disowned contraptions!'

Rune looked at the myriad of dark shapes that cluttered Tor's home. 'My father was here?'

Tor picked up the object he had been working upon. It was a rectangular shaped object, sinuous fibres extended from it, and upon these were little clear buds. He clasped a single flowerlet and twisted it. Every bud lit up like spring blossom. They stared in awe, unable to comprehend this act.

'See these lights? It is not made of Ora, or Seyla, the light is made with a puissance. The Wroth have found a way to harness the same beast that burns in fire, they have tamed it, made it bend to their will. This is the power of the Wroth – they can take a wild violent thing and make it succumb to them, and yet they cannot quell the violence in themselves.'

He turned the bud again and the lights went out, then he affixed the box to his armour. 'We collect many things from the Wroth, we find their shaped metals and wood, their complications. They hold within them a quality which fascinates me. My children have come to share in this bewilderment, how so much ingenuity can come from such a dangerous animal.'

Tor wrestled with the notion, sighing heavily, choosing to ward off such thoughts. 'We found these curious strings of luminescent flowers amongst the forgotten things above. We are yet to understand their purpose, or indeed, how they glow. Sometimes their light dies, it is my hope to one day comprehend them. But we have found many uses for them.'

'Perhaps it is magic?' Onnar smiled.

Tor pondered, 'Yes, it is possible. It would be easy to dismiss it as such, a Corvan bone hex, or other such witchery. But I believe it is far simpler. I wish to know its organs, to understand its secret.'

'Why?' Rune asked.

'Why is precisely the right word! Because there are many things in this world I am yet to understand. I wish to know so many things, to comprehend the deeper meanings of my life, and the life of my family, of your father Rune, and how all of this, all these strange and terrifying things are connected.

'You see, despite all of these Wroth creations, all of their ingenuity, they could never amount to what your father could do. It is not fortune that brings you here little feathered. Come, I wish to show you something.'

He ushered the visitors further into the sett; the smell of dry grass and the chatter of cubs at play filled his home, it intoned fond memories in Rune, he breathed in the scent of safety.

They continued on into deeper places where the walls lay thick with markings, calculations and experiments, ideas scrawled deep into crumbling clay. The deeper they went, the more fraught the earth became; it was an old place, it held something primordial, dirt untouched by the love of the life above. Here, deep below Tor's home lay a huge cavity where earth gave way to rock.

The dark cave was at once lit by the glow of Tor's collection of lights.

Amongst the eroded limestone of the water-forged grotto, stood a remarkable stone. Tear shaped and tapering to a crude point, it was prominent against the stalagmitic and stalagtitic protrusions that rose and fell around it. A series of smaller oval stones were placed at its base in a concentric circle. The earth between the obelisks was curiously marked, lines permeated the dust with jagged certainty.

'Of all the mythologies, the lore and rhymes of the Throa, the stories of this stone always remained unchanged. My father told me the tale of its provenance. It was called the Settling Stone. None knew of its original purpose, lost in the wilderness of memory, but the weight of its value to us remained the same.

'The Houses of the Throa are old. Some are even mentioned in the Vulpus Orata. We enable them to breathe with our presence, they are sewn into our very blood.

'When we are made to leave a House, through sickness or are driven out by the Wroth, it is called unsettling. The House is marked by the weight of our actions, it is hurt by ill deeds, and enriched by the good. We overwhelm a House with our sicknesses, our desires and our foibles.

'It is said that we leave a House to let it rest. It is recorded in these markings that when we left each House, with all our might we hauled the stone and took it with us, and each House had a special place for the stone, a shrine. Yet this particular stone was lost to us, buried deep within the earth.

'How it came to be lost is not known. Perhaps the walls caved in, perhaps it was hidden deliberately. To us it became another footnote, little more than a folktale. That was until your father came here Rune. He came into our home and told us where it lay. He heard it singing to him, and we dug away the soil and clay and found this place.'

The trio circled the stone, brushing nervous paws and claws upon the many crude ciphers grazing its surface.

'What does it do?' Aggi asked nervously.

Tor replied, 'Rune's father told me of something quite unique to the feathered, your ability to feel the currents, deviations and variations of the wind that course the surface of Naa. But he believed it was something even more invisible than the wind, something that lay within you, to know an unseen quality of the sky. He said he could feel it within this stone, a particular song that exhilarated him, he tuned to its euphony and felt its pull. As he learned of its subtleties, he realised that pull was directed towards a source, the source of the song. Grom believed that these stones were buried here when other animals walked Naa, our ancestors who cut and shaped them so they too could hear that same song.'

Rune joined Aggi, who peered inquisitively at the strange object. Tor continued, 'Your father was always keen on teaching me all he knew of such things, but his perception ran deeper than any consequence or idea I have ever dreamt. Let me show you.'

Tor picked up a smooth pebble, and struck the stone. A tone resounded between it and the smaller stones standing around it. Rune was at once taken by it, he saw prismatic visions, psychedelic striae unfolded in his eyes. It scared him. 'What was that?' He exclaimed.

They all placed their limbs upon the rock.

'Very rarely, there are some flock, perhaps even a ground dweller, who can actually see what we hear.'

'See?' Aggi exclaimed. 'How might one see a sound?'

'It's a very rare virtue, and in many ways, a great burden. What those exceptional souls see has a name. It is called the Umbra.'

Tor closed his eyes and listened. 'If you can see it, you are called an Umbra too, a Shadow Starer. Some will go their whole lives not knowing that which they see, it will remain a delusion, a terrifying display of dizzying lights and ideas. Some are lucky, that ability can be honed, can be focused and can be made into a quite amazing tool.'

He looked to Rune. 'Your father, he was an Umbra. He was not only able to see it, but he also began to understand it. His was the greatest gift. He could see the complexities, every intricacy in the shadow of life, every movement.'

Onnar interjected, 'But Tor, so can you?'

Tor smiled and sighed, 'If only I could do what Grom could do. I can understand this, but that does not make me a true Seer. What I know is through learning, I have gained the name of Seer because I make sense of things, I learned of life from those who understand the Wroth, who can peer inside their thoughts. But these hunks of stone are not made for such things. What the Settling Stone sees is singular, yet just as crucial. Which your father found, I may add young Rune!'

Rune glanced back at the stone.

'Your father discovered that these stones could decipher one task. To locate a single point in the world. He could see the direction, where I could not, but he found a way to let me also see.'

He pointed to the smaller stones. 'The Settling Stone plots a point in the land, and we move these smaller markers until they share its tone, to mark that direction.'

Rune was giddy. 'And can it find my father?'

Tor paused, and cast a sympathetic gaze. 'I do not claim to be clairvoyant, but I can tell you this. If your father is in the world, then he is there, at the centre of all things.'

'The centre of all things?' Rune looked at the stone. 'Can you make it sing again?' Tor smiled and knocked the pebble gently against the monolith, and the stone resonated. Rune keened in the spasmodic light of it. Onnar moved into the circle and helped Rune drag the marker stones until they too sang, designating a path.

The Settling Stone sang north.

'It resonates towards the Stinking City, much like it did for your father.'

'It cannot tell us more? Where exactly it points to?'

Tor shook his head. 'For that you must be an Umbra.'

Something caught Rune's attention. He noticed a familiar sigil upon the stone's surface. 'Tor, what is this?'

Tor blinked at the little mark. 'That my son is the symbol of Emini, Abriac and Alauda.'

'Did my father draw this?'

Tor paced forwards, 'Oh no, this is a very old symbol. It represents gods worshipped by some of the flocks. You may know these tales?'

Rune dropped to the ground. 'The three sisters who came first into the world?'

Tor nodded, 'Yes, this is how the tale goes, and your father believed that this story had some truth to it.'

Rune frowned, 'I don't understand.'

Aggi interjected, 'The stories bring much peace to many.'

'I agree, Aggi. The story is one that is repeated often in many cultures, the Sisters of the Flock are three leaders, teachers, matriarchs. Their stories are fables by which we pass on knowledge. The sisters are sometimes drawn as three trees, or a star, sometimes with their faces touching, forever connected. They are symbols of friendship, love and yes Aggi, peace. For those who worship them, often their prayers are to offer the sisters apology for what we took from them.

'Rune, your father came to me after the death of your mother. He was broken by the actions of a ruler, a Naarna Elowin, a Gull Lord who inflicted suffering upon your people. He came here looking for an answer for that pain, he needed peace too.'

'Esperer still wields that power,' Onnar added gravely.

Tor pondered, 'There is a certain kernel of truth in our legends, older than those we tell our children; they are spoken teachings, inflections and reflections of the very essences of life. We learned them in the deepest times, when our bodies were simpler, or different. We came out of the briar with new songs and we taught them to one another, healing songs, cleansing songs, we called it Ocquia. Those who ignored Ocquia became withered and black and their hearts became vacant.

'Esperer is empty. He no longer feels or even knows the fragrant currents that once fed his kin the want of creativity, and he traded it for lust, for desire. What did he get? Many dead sons and a kingdom that despises him, who flouts his rule at every turn. He would be a laughing stock if it wasn't for his stooges who act out his failure with violence. But your father Rune. Your father listened. Despite all that was done to him, he never stopped listening. He wants you to find him, I am sure.

'The Gulls are forgetting themselves; I know another animal that lost itself in its own vanity, and they have made our world sick.'

Tor let his anguish fade, 'Follow your father, Rune. The Umbra told him to go to the Stinking City, and this old thing still points in that direction. It seems the fates have bought you and your friend the tinkerer together!'

'Erithacus?' Aggi asked.

He gave her a knowing look. 'Truth hunting is tiring work! Come, we will find you something to eat and we shall rest.'

They left the cave and returned to the warm chambers above, filled with leaf litter and grass, and they each found a resting place. It was quiet and still in the sett. Rune removed his armour and let Aggi examine it and smooth out the tiny burs which had been irritating him.

'The symbol on the stone, how do you know it?'

'My father used to draw it, he said it meant a lot to him, to my mother. I sometimes dream of it.'

She held his headplate so that he could make out the various filigrees and carvings upon it. On the burnished surface, lay the mark once again. 'There is much significance, much to know. I do love a riddle!'

*

They awoke to commotion in the early hours. Tor was not alone, he spoke with urgent timbre to a number of Throa. They all carried great armour carapaces of torn wire and metal, crude and incongruous, yet with an intricacy to them. Rune discerned lightless buds, much like Tor's, coursing along each jagged edge.

Tor emitted a vibrato yelp, 'There are Wroth in the fields!'

Onnar appeared at the threshold of the den, tightening her armour as Aggi waddled awkwardly to join them. Tor exclaimed, 'I cannot ask you to run with us Onnar, it is too much.'

Onnar dismissed him, 'I won't hear of it, besides, it'll be like old times!'

They made for the surface whilst the feathered followed nervously.

Above ground a great many Throa assembled before Tordrin, the agile kin of neighbouring setts. Tordrin knocked at a discarded bucket filled with rain water, it ran between their legs and they began to dig at the soil, creating a slurry. With deft paws they collected the mud and painted each other's faces, and soon the telltale white and grey fur upon their bodies was dulled and unnoticeable. The lights upon their armour were dimmed, leaving gnarled black shapes in the dark.

Onnar watched from the entrance to the burrow, Rune flitted down beside her.

'What will they do?'

'They will protect the House of Tor, they will go out and meet whatever threatens their home.'

Onnar fell to all fours and bounded up an adjacent pile of car shells and looked out upon the field. With clear eyes she saw a streak of torch light. 'They are towards the House of Ror,' she exclaimed.

Tor acknowledged her.

'Collector!' the voice of Tordrin boomed from the group, 'the Wroth are north east, they move towards us. Will you watch them? Be our eyes in the air?'

She nodded and took flight, Rune following.

Two dozen Throa left the shelter of the abandoned junk yard, moving north to the fields. Under thickets and unkempt hedges they dug claws in the earth, the familiar draw of worn paths, places they had known as cubs.

Churned clods of earth now dry and brittle made a difficult path as they passed the great mouldered gates that marked the boundary of the deserted House of Ror. Once the home of his family, they had fled when the Wroth had lain traps and taken many lives. Strung up on wires like trophies, the broken bodies of loved ones still hung pitifully like scraps of ragged cloth, skulls bore down with permanent cries, voices unanswered by family unable to reach them, to offer a proper burial. Tor knew these faces intimately, he made a blessing as they ran beneath them.

North they bound, their stocky bodies undulating low to the ground. Aggi and Rune perceived the distant lights of Wroth vehicles, two white vans parked up on a grass verge. There were Wroth, three of them, moving across the grass, each brandishing long sticks which they held under their arms. The second white van drove off along the edge of the adjacent field. Rune could not believe his eyes. The gangly upright bodies of the Wroth were frightening.

Aggi listened to the Wroth as they spoke amongst themselves with hushed but aggressive barks. At their feet the slack-jawed lumber of obedient Caanus. They were unleashed with fractious commands, bounding off in search of the faintest scent of Throa. She made out a few sounds, yet knew nothing of their meaning. She held them beneath her tongue, able to shape the words, reciting them so as to retain each croak until she could locate her ward.

There was only a single field between the Wroth and the Throa. She landed upon Tordrin's back, clinging awkwardly. 'They have Caanus!'

Tordrin grunted, 'We expected as much.'

Onnar appeared alongside. 'I can draw off the Caanus.'

Tordrin nodded in agreement. She pulled away from the group, skirting the edge of the field. Aggi repeated the words she had overheard. Most were indecipherable, but he knew the sound for Throa.

In the dark the Throa were near invisible to the Wroth. Their bodies like cavorting grass, blue black against the dwindling Seyla light. Silently they dispersed and surrounded the Wroth. The mud kicked up by the Wroth's heavy boots resounded like the thrum of war. Against the hedgerows there was a disturbance. The Caanus howled and galumphed in search of the source. Onnar pulled herself through the dense thicket into a neighbouring field, trailing them away from their masters.

The Wroth carried threatening objects that spat pain. Deep in Tordrin's haunches lay a little of that pain, burrowed in his flesh. Panic manifested amongst his kin, they cowered against the absence of life. Tordrin looked to them with the same fear, and yet behind the commanding worry, they saw his zeal. It gripped them.

Their gait was small but assured, heavy heads aimed wide mandibles, they threw their leaden frames against the Wroth's limbs. Tearing through cloth they felt the riven skin, the appease of blood iron slick, of floundering hands in search of anchorage. The Wroth tried to reach their weapons, to cock their rifles; yet found them tangled in heavy clothing. Darkness was broken by a realisation of teeth against the clot of night.

And then lights blistered. The dizzying static of heads hard against the ground was confused further as the Throa ignited schools of lights upon their armour, making it impossible to see that which attacked them. A thousand eyes incensed the Wroth, they lashed out with feeble arms, kicking, biting that which could not be seen. Those Throa who were unfortunate to meet such lunges slumped off to breathe through broken ribs.

The Throa had brought down all three Wroth. They held throats in spasming jaws. The bitter swell of blood in Tordrin's mouth intoxicated him. He climbed upon the creature's chest, to stand over the face of that which had taken so much from him. He dulled his armour lights and the glow of his kin illuminated his fevered face. He leered at the panic-stricken eyes that lay below him. The Wroth spat at him, screamed at him.

The smell of urine and fear engulfed Tordrin's nostrils, its hairless skin, its callous eyes, the anger and hatred in that spittle-ridden mouth. He saw the facade, the acrid stench of their odour fall away, and all that was left was the hairless mammal.

Tordrin spoke, 'You have killed so many of my kin. And I take your life in recompense.' His words were meaningless to the Wroth, just strange grunts and barks, yet a vague perception transpired in its fearful eyes.

Tordrin bit down upon its neck and tore open its throat. It gargled with contempt and fear and then died. Tordrin swooned in his vitriol, in his self-doubt. His kin enacted the same upon their prey.

Rune looked down upon the Wroth. He did not feel any victory, he almost felt pity. He did not know the Wroth to know this hatred, to know the loss at their hands. But he recognised the look upon Tordrin, He could still taste Artioch's life in his mouth.

There was a loud crack and a bright burst of light from the direction of the House of Tor, he saw Aggi dart away into the black towards the source. The other van.

*

With aching breath the Throa traced their way through the dim suggestion of morning towards home. As they neared the concrete walls of the junkyard they saw the unfamiliar white van parked close; the gates to their kingdom wide open.

The beam of headlights played on a large moving figure, a Wroth, angrily digging at the earth. Close to him lay the folded body of a Throa.

Tordrin bit down and spat the words, 'Reth! He has killed her! We take him!' and without hesitation he lumbered out, blood thick on him, leaving the cover of dark, the warning yelps of his brethren only registering as another terrifying stench, followed by a hollow bark, hit his face. A huge animal emerged from behind the van, lifting the corpse of their loved one in its jaws, shaking it wildly. Caanus.

Tordrin's muscles seized, winding in each frigid limb. Teeth gritted, he sidled slowly against the vehicle, and then down, under the van. Another Caanus flanked the Wroth as it dug at the earth, squeals and barks of exasperation, baying for the Throa which lay within. Tordrin watched with terror as the roof of the sett began to collapse, and the Wroth cursed with legs buried in the soil.

Tor contemplated their options. Before him another lost home, another place unsafe for his family to reside. He knew they stood no chance in the presence of the Caanus, but he also knew the Wroth would not reach the sanctuary deep below where cubs would be hiding. So he would let this bastard dig up his home until he worked himself ragged, and leave with no quarry, and Tor would take his family far from here.

'No Throa die today,' he said gruffly, Tordrin rising from beneath the vehicle. 'We wait, and then we take our people away, the abandoned sett beyond the north stream, we will go there, it is secluded beneath great roots of a Goarth tree.'

Eventually the Wroth abandoned his digging, and with tuneless whistle he commanded the Caanus into the back of the van and drove back towards the field to find his kin.

Together they dug away the earth to free the remaining Throa, watched sorrow etch itself upon each tired face. They collected the body of Reth and dug a shallow grave, placing her amongst the few items they could rescue from the sett which held value to them. They wished her farewell and then Tor lead them beyond the gates and out along the dirt track that circled away from the field where they had drawn blood. He nodded to Tordrin to take the lead and then he returned once more to the sett.

Rune and Aggi remained in flight, not knowing what to do. They felt like helpless spectators, the roof of the sett finally giving way, the despondent old Throa sitting before the former entrance to his lost home.

Onnar lay a gentle paw on him, 'My old friend, I am sorry.'

'All our work!' he said with desperation.

'Yet you are alive, and that is something to be thankful for,' she replied.

Rune found a perch in a tree. 'The stone is lost. Perhaps there was more to learn from it. Aggi, how will we know where to look for my father?'

Aggi thought on this for a moment. 'Do you think your father always had a great stone to find his way?' She asked.

Rune frowned, 'I don't understand.'

'By all accounts, your father was a wise feathered. Can you think of what he might say at a time like this? When you felt hopeless?'

Rune considered this, 'When I was very young, when the world started to make sense to me, my father and I would climb to the top of the Pinnacle and he would look out upon the sea, and he would tell me to close my eyes, very tight, and I would ask him why we climbed so high only to shut our eyes and hide such a beautiful view. He would assure me that there is beauty beyond sight, he would tell me to listen and feel the world around me, to breathe in each current of wind, to know more than what we see, because there is much we ignore when we rely on our sight alone.'

He considered the words, and entertained the memories of his father. He felt a deep gratitude. For a moment, he closed his eyes, tracing the memories of when he first lay sight on the Settling Stone, when it had been struck; the light patterns that had made his head hurt, within them there had been something. He knew he must travel towards the Stinking City. He not only knew this, he felt it.

He opened his eyes to find Aggi smiling at him. He laughed with her, 'Do you feel better?'

'I do,' he said.

*

Tor began his slow meander towards the long deserted home of his ancestors. There would be much work to do, cleaning out the halls. It felt right to return and reclaim his birth home, and he courted fond memories as he left the destruction of his house behind.

Onnar kept a little distance and a cautious eye on the fields beyond. The distant call of the lone Wroth and his Caanus searching for his friends waxed and waned over the expanse of unkempt crops, rotting in their idleness.

They reached the peak of a small hill. Below a pair of broad trees rose beside a stream. Between their exposed roots, the wide entrance to a sett. Tor's family had already dragged the refuse of many squatters from the Throa den beneath the contorted limbs of the trees. Dust bellowed with busying bodies, as they made their home in the empty hollow.

Tor reached the wide maw of the den, drawing a deep breath and contemplating his memories, 'Many wandering spirits here, many lost souls seeking company. The Wroth came here too, took the lives of my mother and father. I was lucky to survive, these roots made it impossible to dig us out. Yet we fled, fled to another safe haven, only for the same to happen to us again. Yet we are still here. Still alive. I am still alive.'

Tordrin greeted his father with a low bleat and many faces lifted with joy to see the old Throa enter the sett.

Death lingered where it had taken lives, and for Tor this dry and compacted earth allowed him to feel each and every echo. The graffiti of many an occupant emblazoned the walls; he made out sigils of Maar and Muroi, Creta and Toec. He smiled with each delicate line placed by those of smaller stature, and the brazened gouges left by larger, less dainty claws. Beneath all of this, the hieroglyphs of his family, great twisting lines that together formed a distinctive mark, the same mark upon every Throa's face. He placed his own paw upon the mark, trying to perceive some greater meaning to all that had befallen his people. Although it offered him no solace, the great chamber, filled with the subdued smiles and hubbub of all his surviving loved ones was answer enough.

Above, Rune landed upon Onnar's back as Aggi looked for insects. He spoke quietly in her great ear, 'I have nothing to barter but … I.'

Onnar interrupted, 'I will travel with you to the Stinking City. I would only worry about you both if I were to leave, and in any case I am interested to see what will come of this adventure.'

Rune thanked her, and they waited patiently for Tor until he climbed out of the sett and called them to him.

'My people are safe, but we must mourn the passing of the life taken by the Caanus and return to the old House to rescue what we can, once the threat of the Wroth has passed. You will travel on to the city?'

Aggi hopped closer, 'Yes we shall, we shall find this Erithacus.'

'You have shown great courage today Aggi, I am sure you would make a fine member of the Tempered Guild. I will gladly vouch for you.'

He reared up on his hind legs and pulled at a thread attached to his armour, upon which hung a series of seed shells, discarded bolts and other such Wroth-made things. He loosened it and allowed one small metal nut to fall loose, refastening the thread to his armour.

'Erithacus is not a well soul. What he holds inside him, that wealth of knowledge, has cost him dearly. I once knew the way to his kingdom, but I am far too old for such a journey. But if and when you do find him, tread carefully. You will understand these words.' Give him this,' he offered the nut to her, 'and tell him that I send *the song*. He will understand.' Aggi threaded the nut upon her clawed toe.

He embraced each of them, his son standing proud at the entrance to the sett. They said their goodbyes and headed north east, away from the fields, towards the river.

*

Roak settled on the roof of a large office building that overlooked a shopping precinct. He was a large Gull, bulky and terse, he wore armour fashioned from slate, black and smooth in the morning rain, stark against his yellowing down. His percipient eyes glowering at all below. An inkling had festered in him since the death of Artioch. He had seen the shrinking spirit in Esperer at the sight of his dead son, and in this he had grasped an idea. Only royalty could claim the throne, yet it was clear that there was no time left for Esperer to father another son. Esperer would rule until his death and then the patronage would pass into unknown waters. An empty seat to be taken by any who dared.

Roak dared. Yet he wanted no fight. There were many strong candidates to begin a new reign. He needed an opportunity to prove his worth, and in Rune he found such a chance. He would bring the body of the Startle who had taken the king's son. He would show initiative that would be rewarded. Perhaps with the highest honour.

He had defied his masters word and pursued Rune after his banishment, losing sight of the Startle in the glare of the river. Despite this setback, he had returned to the water to pick up the trail. He flew swiftly, stopping only to barter for information. Most refused to do business with a Gull. In frustration, he had continued on, following the river until it reached the Stinking City. There was still no sign of Rune.

Eventually the river disappeared, and he made for the towering structures, in the vain hope of catching a glimpse of the Startle. He maintained a fruitless yet constant vigil upon the rooftop, his attention drawn by the movement below. He glanced down upon the milling Wroth. There were other Gulls here, city Gulls who held no allegiance to Esperer, who lived near parkland lakes and the great effluent-flooded river that divided the city and led to the sea. He found it difficult to understand their broken words, dismembered by colloquialism. The city was unhealthy, it left a residue in him, some olfactory melancholy. He could not imagine living in such a place.

There were Wroth here. Their usual clamour was subdued, and those that staggered around seemed completely aimless. He had studied these perverse animals and their indecipherable ways but had made little sense of them. But they stuck to patterns, swarming like insects.

There was behaviour here he had not seen before, they avoided one another with short grunts and moans and wails, there was an air of fear. The glaring lights and colours that had once shone inelegantly from their vast array of caves shone no more.

He knew they discarded things, he knew that Wroth would take the leftovers of their meals and hide them in black sacks. He had learned to tear them apart, to reach for the rich pickings within.

He saw that there were many such sacks upon the ground. The city Gulls had picked at them already. As he watched several of them reached one of the larger sacks, jabbing at it until one was brave enough to tear it open. He saw them stagger back.

Within was the body of a Wroth. One Gull leered at it, wondering if a meal could be had. Something seemed wrong. They all retreated, seeking other food.

Roak was intrigued. He spread his wings wide and flew down beside the dead Wroth. A thick residue lay about its face, its skin marbled with black veins. He cawed at the corpse, flinching as though expecting it to shoo him away. It did not. His vague awareness of a sickness which had claimed many Wroth trickled to the forefront of his mind.

Perturbed, he moved on, hopping up to a low wall that ran around a raised border, shrubs and bushes grew sickly within, scattered with scraps and detritus. He walked the length of the wall, watching the Baldaboa perform gaudy courtship rituals below him. They did not speak in Ocquia, so it was hard to decipher their clumsy fawning. He tried to catch their attention but the listless gaze he received in return held little hope of conversation. He had all but given up trying to communicate with these feathered, he assumed they were numbed by their dependence on Wroth waste, their feet mutilated and diseased, as though they cared not where they walked, into danger or otherwise, in search of food. He feared his own kin were destined for a similar fate.

A few Wroth looked warily at him. He enjoyed these moments, when the Wroth would stop and lock eyes with him, not empty glances like the Baldaboa; there was real fear that could be manipulated. Gulls stole from Wroth, Roak himself had done it a number of times. He saw this as a theft of power; he did not need to eat their food, the point was that he could if he wanted to. It was the delight in taking from them that validated the eating, that separated the Gull from the mindless Baldaboa. He reminisced about playful jabs and barbs at Wroth cubs that had incited the anger of their parents.

He studied one Wroth, not very old, who sat on a bench, leaning on its arm and making a loud, phlegmy gasp. The noise was followed by a hacking gargle, then the creature ejected something red from its throat before staggering away. Other Wroth seemed to avoid this one as he moved into the crowd. Roak cocked his head as two obese Baldaboa tottered towards the red mass on the floor. They picked at it, swallowing the foulness. Roak grimaced.

It dawned on him that perhaps this sickness was something to fear. He looked about him and saw other signs. There was more blood. Smears upon the ground and garish coloured strips in yellow and red surrounding it, glyphs that only Wroth could understand. He noticed more oblong sacks similar to that which had wrapped the Wroth corpse, and also among the shrubbery a number of Baldaboa had died, their broad rib cages split through shrivelled flesh. He had not seen such death before. He paced along the walls that encircled each border, and saw that there were more dead. Muroi, large and bloated.

Panic enveloped him and he hopped away, losing his footing, stepping into another Wroth. A flurry of limbs and feathers ensued as Roak flapped back into flailing arms, both of them now falling beneath the leaves of emaciated bushes, amongst the dead who had dragged themselves there to die.

In the moments of frenzy, Roak and the Wroth shared a very potent fear. Roak managed to gather his strength and darted from the bushes, turning back to catch the Wroth's attention. For a brief moment the Wroth, amidst his desperation to escape, saw something in Roak he had never seen in any other species, a quality to his escape far beyond pure instinct for survival. He saw something else. Upon its back, arching up along the neck and cresting atop its head - shards of slate keenly shaped and fastened, carven and considered.

The Wroth lifted his hands to clear his eyes, flinching with fear as he saw congealed innards of a corpse smeared across his hands, and soon that fear once again consumed his curiosity, and he leapt up, seeking sanctuary.

Roak fled and found a fountain, and washed himself thoroughly. He was frightened and yet the fear had brought clarity. He had flown too far, had been too hasty. He took to wing, retracing his flight back toward the river.

Evouo Vign
Corvan Bone Hex

Rend the rind!
See the wink of red enamour
Watch it glimmer, yes!
Oh putrefied malady
So sure our thaumaturgy
Gargle, spit blood
See the wink of wishes
See the lovely gore puzzle
Spoil ourselves!
Taste the niggling

Cut cut cut
Tear tear tear
Know the Magic
In our Prayer

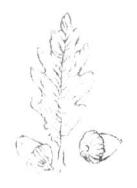

Chapter 3

Far away, beyond the periphery of the Stinking City, an atrophied chimney reverberated with a dread timbre. Below its throat the furnace had not burned for almost eighty years. The great gullet crumbled from within, soot shadows of former industry. The same soot besmeared the fineries of Victorian architecture, filigrees in brass lay beneath a black veneer.

Yet the cold furnace now held a different purpose. This was hallowed land, a place of eldritch ceremony, a litany of grey and dizzying creed. Black forms strode and flew with resoluteness, they collected their prayer words and held vigil on them.

The Vulpus clan had travelled far from the city to this place, a slow procession of ruddy coats and briary armour, reaching the frail ruin at dusk. At its entrance they howled into the chamber beyond, coaxing the black resident within. The skeletal form of an elderly feathered hobbled before them, his wing long broken and hung low at his side. His neck was twisted in such a way as to elicit a feeling of unease. His eyes were pale, body decorated with Corvan trinkets stained with coal dust. He danced before them on one good foot.

Vorsa bowed, 'Azrazion Borgal Pelt, we come to offer our thanks.'

The old Corva chittered, 'The cub is strong, the cub moans in the dirt! Come, Corpse Talker, come hither!'

The grave they sought was no longer discernible amongst the rich black loam, yet Vorsa knew precisely where her brother lay. Every winter she had returned to this place, far from home. Amidst the ziggurat of a dead science the empty vessel of industry had made good coffins for her family.

Although the trek was arduous and asked a lot of the elders, they had done so without protest, amongst them her elderly father Satresan. He paused at the resting place of his son and uttered a blessing, before allowing his daughter and her cortege to step forth and make good her promise. There lay more than the reminder of a lost loved one, for the grave also held the foundations of a long sought ideal. Each Vulpus carried a stone in their mouth, a token and a promise. One that might yet come to pass. So, very old and young alike, stood in silent veneration for their lost kin. Azrazion cleared the earth with his good wing and asked for the Vulpus to place the stones upon the grave. After this was done, Vorsa chose three; one stone was for grounding, one for the tether and the last was for her brother.

'Whilst my Corvan sons and daughters toil to enact your every wish, we lay the stones to stay perditions cough!' Azrazion squawked.

He closed his eyes and requested silence. Vorsa lay beside the grave. She stared into the cold ground and saw the dark, and the dark took shape, eclipsing her vision. She began to wade into the darkness, beyond a place she felt any sense of comfort, the currents like snake things wriggling between her limbs, beneath the cusp of life. She clawed her way beyond, until she felt the hesitant shroud of the Gasp. She passed between the planes, witnessing the vast diaspora of lightless unlife before her. There were many ghostly faces, but she only appealed for one.

The same vulpine apparition that had graced her presence on the rooftop began to reveal itself; diaphanous amidst the gloom, petal-like rills of plasma drifted in the dark, his eyes black and unforthcoming. She tilted her head to one side and smiled.

'Hello brother,' she said, 'I have a pretty stone for you, a gift for you on your day of days.'

Before her the shaking memory of the three stones, recollections of the material world. She lifted one marbled pebble in her mouth, remarking to herself how unnaturally round it was, before passing it to him. He took it from her mouth with his own, swallowing it down. He did not emote, but she could tell he was happy.

'Brother, we begin the tidings of the Meridian, and you and I are called upon to fulfil our role. To guide an Umbra to the Umbra.'

'Yes, my beloved,' he said. His words were fashioned from the rustle of leaves and creak of bow, he borrowed of ephemeral sound and coaxed it into vowels and syllables.

'We ask you to speak for the Gasp; to share with us your observations, and to act as conduit, when we ask for the city.'

The ghost kin looked behind him into the murk. An ill light threatened, it waned and ensphered; a virulent deluge of stricken bodies, the billions of former lives within the void. They moved with such veracity and yet made no sound. He whispered to them, they returned in barely audible voices, infinitesimal and gentle despite the anguish upon their faces. He turned once again to Vorsa, the pit eyes where so much life once dwelt.

'The Umbra Rune becomes brighter. He will know you, stay away from him, do not alert him to your presence. Seek the Morwih Hevridis. Let him have his way.'

'But why the Morwih? Can we trust him? He will surely harm him?'

'All Rune's paths lead to discomfort,' he said through milk white teeth. She swallowed hard, considering for a moment what had become of her quiet brother. 'If you wish the Umbra to act in your stead, you cannot save him from pain. You will let him shed a little blood for what you desire.'

"That's not fair, Petulan,' she replied. 'I do not wish him pain.'

He grinned mercilessly. 'You will have to trust me. You know I mean well, my love'.

'I know what you mean, but I cannot decipher these winding paths, how they could possibly result in anything good.'

'Good? Ah, well this is a matter of perspective. Trust me sister, I see the spectrum of colourless light, it is resplendent with the dead of good deeds!'

She sighed, 'And of the Meridian?'

'Your Corva trail the Umbra, I see their little spells prickling the walls of the Gasp. It is amusing. They have begun to deify him already. Silly Fools! Bring me an Umbra, and I will do my best.' Petulan stirred, 'But. Know this, sister. The Morwih will go to war to stop the Foul Meridian.'

'I know, and we will be prepared.'

She opened her eyes and pushed the stones away from her. She felt a little sick. She took a moment to let the nausea subside, mourn her brother, and to recite the *Nash Aka*; the will to remain alive.

A stern yet considerate Vulpus named Oromon stood beside her, steadying her by the rough of her neck. He looked at her with concern, 'You spoke with Petulan?'

'Yes. The Foul Meridian is at hand, but we must steer the Umbra.'

The crowd sighed with relief and guarded smiles were exchanged. She interjected, 'The Morwih will seek to stop us.'

Oromon scoffed, 'Wretches. The clans wish to take the streets in paw when we return. No Morwih will dare walk in their presence.'

Another Vulpus nodded, 'We are ready and willing. Nothing will interrupt this auspicious event.'

'That being said,' Vorsa added, 'Petulan asks me to use the Morwih Hevridis to track down the Startle.'

'Can we trust this Morwih?' Satresan asked. 'His offerings as spy have always been a little lacklustre.'

'Can we trust any Morwih? We open ourselves to many possibilities when dealing with such individuals. He is a traitor to his own kin, and the Morwih are traitors by blood.' Vorsa considered her words, 'Yet I believe he will complete the task, I have listened to him speak of his anger towards the Consul, he speaks with sincerity. He loved her, and he is scorned. Such hatred cannot be feigned. It is in this that I find an inkling of truth in his vow. Perhaps he wishes to double cross us, but I trust in my brother's word. He is never wrong.'

The clan agreed. They gave their blessing to Petulan's grave and began the journey back to the Stinking City.

Vorsa stood for a while, Oromon waited patiently at the entrance to the graveyard.

'Something worries you?' he said softly.

'Petulan was born with a paw already in the Gasp. He is where he feels no pain. But he was my twin, he left part of himself in me. I feel it like a cold space inside. Every time I invoke him I want to see that warmth, I want to see the part that fills me, but he is something else. He frightens me a little.'

She whispered sweet nothings then turned to join the party. As she did so, Azrazion hopped before her, peering into her with his misty eyes.

'I was once Dominus!' He spat.

Vorsa looked confused, 'You were?'

'Long ago I sought the same wretched knowledge! Look how it marks me! Be wary of Audagard, for his want is paramount!' He looked away, as though he perceived things beyond sight that scared him. She frowned, thought of the path that had led her to this place, of the Corva and their pact.

Petulan had been born albino, a dull yellow-white, with eyes that lacked any colour of life. He had been a sickly cub, and yet he lived well under the care of his sister. She had hunted for them both, had nursed him during sickness, had encouraged the little happiness that lifted him from his den and allowed him to dance amongst the dandelions. He would tire quickly, and in his exhaustive sleep he would have visions. Those visions would manifest in Vorsa too, she would share his agonies, yet they would not wait for sleep. Days would be interrupted by a deluge of shocking revelation, of futurescapes and nightmares.

It was apparent after their second birthday that much of their shared clairvoyance was of a time when Petulan no longer lived. This was not without provenance, for within the Orata, the spoken scripture of the Vulpus, the funeral of Revenant speech spoke of the sharing between a dead twin and its earthly counterpart, of being able to continue dialogue after death. This was a rare and difficult skill to acquire, taught and coveted only by the Bishops of Bone Char, the Corva Anx.

It had been many turns since Petulan's death had crept upon him, his light diminishing with each new day. The Corva Anx had become aware of Vorsa and Petulan and their bond, the children of the Vulpus king. Whilst Petulan dreamed his fever dreams, Vorsa's education began, under the tutelage of the Dominus Audagard. They met in secret places and he shared with her the Daedalian arts of invoking the dead, for one day, it was believed, a time would come when the Vulpus would need such a skill. But first Petulan would have to lose his life.

It was the Dominus who had whispered strange promises to him, guided his own wish to be bound with the earth, so that in his final days Vorsa and her family had escorted Petulan across the acres of defrosting soil that still retained winter's bite. Amongst low lying hills at the edge of a dense medieval forest they found the ruin of a coal-fired power station. Here they would lay him to rest amongst the coal dust, wrap him in incantations and invoke his Revenant.

Very few could communicate with the Gasp, the place where spirits collected. The dead had their own language, and those without the means to understand their diabolical tongue would forever be plagued by its incessant meaningless whisper.

Knowing the rhyme of the Gasp was left to the Anx, an order of pious Corva who worshipped its black influence and whose magic could decipher its dialect. Yet their appetite for its knowledge went largely unfulfilled, driving them to ever greater measures in search of answers.

It was not long before Petulan's health diminished. Their journey had come to an end before the power station as Petulan took his final breaths. He could no longer walk, and so their father, Satresan, and uncle Folcur dragged his body within the courtyard of the power station.

Much of the coal that had been stored there and which had not been stolen, lay strewn about the ground, or abandoned in carcasses of trucks, leaving layers of dust to gather upon every surface. Yet it was the coal itself that had first bought the Corva Anx, had brought the ceremony to this ruin. For the Corva Anx believed coal to be a physical aspect of the Gasp, known as the Oscelan. Millions of years of life expressed through striation seams of carbon. The Oscelan was a hallowed grave, the concentrated souls of the dead. Forests crushed into a necropolis that spanned the entirety of Naa. To all Corva, it was to be worshipped and expressed in prayer.

When The Wroth began to dig it out of the ground they considered this an act of holy war. The Oscelan was precious. They prayed to the Revenants within the carbon and pleaded with them to stay the flame, to not give of their energies. Eventually, after many generations of prayer the coal no longer burned. The power stations closed.

In the absence of the Wroth, the Corva made this consecrated ground their house of prayer. It was here that Petulan's physical nucleus would lie forever, merge with the black earth, and coalesce with the many spirits dwelling in the dark. Here he would find the other twins of necromancy, other intelligences that fed the living their trove of secrets.

It was in the courtyard flanked by the walls of the power station that Vorsa, her father and uncle had originally brought Petulan, clinging to life. Each window pane now broken, an empty socket where a collection of Corva sat silent within their cloisters, only discernible by the stark sheen of their feathers and their beady stare. In one wall rose an ornate archway. It was marred by fallen rubble, a gaping mouth, the shattered bricks its splintered teeth. A large window with a similarly resplendent arch above it. Within it had sat the Dominus Audaguard; a pupil in the cyclopean architecture.

The flock of Corva took to wing with a commanding squawk. Like collapsing books, wing beats pervaded the courtyard as they whirled beyond the arch, towards the burial grounds. The Vulpus followed, Petulan's breathing becoming ragged. They brought him to the coal shed and Satresan and Folcur dug the earth, laying their frail boy within it.

Vorsa snuggled beside him and nuzzled his face, feeling his warmth failing, his weak purring. 'I love you brother, and I will lie here until you fall asleep, and when you wake, I will be with you forever.'

His little heart soon gave up and they began to cover him. The Dominus dropped to the earth and picked out Petulan's eyes, replacing them with two lumps of coal.

They filled his mouth and packed the black earth about his body, engulfing every part of him. The Corva flock descended upon him from their pews and assembled upon the burial mound – and for a moment, they seemed to become one with it; feathers quivered and submerged with the black, losing sense of themselves. The throng routed and rucked until it broke open, a furore of feathers once again, retiring to their chancel, hidden behind ragged sheets of asbestos.

The Dominus remained and hopped towards Petulan's family. He eyed Vorsa, and beckoned her forward. He told her that Petulan would have to be found, and for that to occur, she would have to invoke the Gasp. He reminded her of her teachings, and of the simple line that should be recited from the Orata so that she could remain alive whilst summoning him. He explained that her first experience might be frightening, but she would be safe.

She held a peculiar natural talent, and it was not long before the Gasp relented and the ghost of her beloved revealed itself to her, and would become as present in death as he had been alive.

For the rest of her youth Vorsa unravelled the Orata through her brother. Learning of the Gasp, of its empyreal vagaries, and persuading the dead to give of their secrets. It was these acts that allowed her a unique perception, she found truths within the confounding phrases of the Orata and the bitter spells of the Corva, the connections of belief and the beloved dead.

It was at the height of her teachings that the Dominus bestowed her with a prestigious task. To usher in the Foul Meridian. It was in this appointment that Vorsa had seen a glint in Audagard's eye that spoke of a very specific desire.

*

Onnar made use of the gaps in the hedgerows, maintained by worried souls who dwelt in the land. She could smell a hundred lives in the earth and leaves, the families whose existence revolved around quick escape. Tied amongst the spry branches were sprigs of grass, dried berries and seed pods, left for weary travellers seeking shelter and sustenance. For most, fighting off death was a daily battle. She pondered family, the many impressions of claws and feet against the exposed mud. That a fight shared was a fight lessened. She thought of her mother, of her siblings whose impressions diluted further within her. She strained to keep their likeness present, to hold on to them.

Rune would come and join her, flying low or perching precariously on her back, providing her a little company. She was glad of it, this tiny feathered clad in armour, a fury in his head that she could read plainly in his dark eyes. She had once seen his family dance, the murmuration of the Startle, the Thousand Headed King, rollick about the sky in splendid formation, a single mind. Rune felt something like pride when she recounted this tale, to know others knew his flock, his family. They shared stories and ideas and once in a while Aggi would join them, singing songs to keep up their morale.

They entered a sparse wood, pausing to catch their breath. As they settled behind a fallen trunk they could hear the distant rattle of a Rersp, hammering the bark with its beak. The rhythm played off the trees in percussive echoes. Rune listened and thought he could decipher the meaning.

'Do you think he is calling to his loved one?' Aggi suggested.

'That I cannot answer, he may just be looking for food! You will need to ask the Speakers,' Onnar replied.

'What are the Speakers? Who do they speak for?'

Onnar pondered. 'I have never seen them, but they live in the cities, close to the Wroth. It is said they speak many languages.'

'There are those who do not speak with these words?' Rune asked.

Onnar smiled, 'The Startle have their own tongue, yes?'

Rune nodded. 'But with me, you speak Ocquia, the shared tongue. It is how we understand each other, it is imperfect, often difficult for some to make certain sounds, to mouth particular words. Some are voiceless, and use gestures to communicate. Most species speak their own words when amongst their kin. There are many fractures in our language. I do not know why. The legend goes that the Speakers know all languages.'

They soon moved on through a blossom of purple flowers, the many thousand blooms peered above their green foliage on the woodland floor. The fragrance carried with them for a while once they had left, only eclipsed by the acrid scent of the city. The horizon was lost beyond approaching hills.

From a hillock they could make out wide roads as they wove ponderously towards the city. The smell of fuel was in the vegetation, and fouled their feathers and fur. Onnar loped down towards the road, avoiding the piles of rubbish that littered the tufts of weeds that strained through unnatural black stone.

She ran the length of the side road as her ward scanned the undergrowth for morsels of food. She skirted the pavement, sniffing the air for signs of danger. Before her something lay on the road, crumpled and ragged, yet held a familiar form. Flies hung thick over it. With morbid curiosity she approached.

She veered on to the tarmac, the smear of fur and dried blood filled every footstep. The smell was appalling and she reeled back, her breath tremulous as she made sense of the scraps of armour that lay crushed and thrown aside. She saw the rich fur and the dull eyes of her kin, and she tore herself away from them, crawling up into the tall dead grass.

Rune didn't know what to do.

He made for her, but Aggi stopped him. 'Let her be.'

Eventually twitching ears rose, and with a stoic glance, she went to her kin and made a blessing, the Yoa' Ayan, a prayer to the Blithe Priestess, a plea for release. She ushered her party onwards, along the road that had brought a life to an end. She did not look back.

They travelled north east from the road and out on to a morose expanse of damp grass. There were no trees or any sense of cover, yet at equal increments, the familiar towering configurations of metal protruded up from the soil. No one knew what the Wroth had used them for and Rune circled each, following the black vines that emitted a forbidding hum.

The river again snaked back towards them after many hours. Above, the pylons sang their vibrato drone. None of them noticed the arrival of the Corva, who sat in sinister rows upon the vocal chords that sprawled from the towers, many pairs of eyes tracing the trio as they sought shelter.

Thankfully it was not raining, the cloud cover shone with a waxen yellow, tedious and moist. Onnar observed succulent grasses that fed from the water and determined that it was good to drink. She drank her fill as Rune removed his armour, joining her to quench his thirst before seeking the concrete overhang at the base of a pylon. He had become accustomed to sleeping at ground level, although Aggi reminded him it was only advisable when accompanied by a Yoa'a.

As they rested they watched the pointed forms of the Corva above them squawk and fuss over unknowable things, and Onnar told her companions the little she had learned of this curious species.

'They are intelligent, perceptive of strange things. They speak in riddles and enjoy teasing and provoking those who seek their council. Above all they worship the Gasp, the place beyond death. They seek it in all manner of ways, through magic and prayer. They crave to know what lies beyond, and will go to any length to obtain that goal.'

'Is Erithacus Corva?' Rune asked.

'I have never known anyone who has met this Erithacus. Although I have heard his name spoken with terrible omen. He is said to control the Speaker flocks and wields a potent sorcery. We shall know the truth soon enough!' Onnar said with wide eyes.

Rune studied the amassing shades of grey and blue eclipse the dusk, stars twinkled and shuddered, making their bright entrance. The Corva were silent, their gaze still upon the animals below. It made Rune nervous, and eventually intrigue got the better of him and he hopped up on to the cement base of the power line and chirruped at his audience. 'What do you want?'

A single Corva amongst the spectators cawed and bobbed his head. It tilted an eye towards Rune, as though to size him up. Then it dropped soundlessly to the ground. With ungraceful gait, it approached him.

Rune could now make out its armour, black and iridescent like its plumage, it rose to a threatening cowl that crowned its head and tapered to a violent spur, mirroring its beak. There were things sewn tight to it; clustered curios and dead scrags. They spoke of ravelled superstitions, black prayers.

The Corva peered with a knowing gape, studying each fibre of him. It lowered its head in rhythmic contortions. It got closer still, its knife-like bill tracing his contours with shrewd intent.

'Umbra!'

The entire flock squawked raucously, a throng that swept up into a typhoon of screeched inflections, a raw, enigmatic rattle.

'Umbra! Umbra!'

They fell as one, needle black, a churning contrivance of talon, they fell so close he felt their breath, he shut his eyes tight, the squall of a hundred pairs of wings buffeting, gyrating, cutting at the air.

He tucked his head low in terror. Although his eyes were closed, the protean forms amongst the black echoed that which stormed above him; a vortex of wings, cascading in spiralling arches, drawn by threads of unseeable influence that stretched beyond his peripheral vision, yet in the dark, he knew he wasn't seeing with his eyes. The turbulence subsided with a final shrill squawk.

He opened his eyes with trepidation to see the flock mere specks in the distance. Onnar sat bolt upright. She looked at Rune and saw his body quake.

'Are you alright?' she said.

He climbed down to join the pair, still shaking, 'They called me Umbra.'

Onnar watched the flock disappear. 'Ominous, I've never seen

Corva behave so strangely.'

Aggi guffawed, 'they always behave *so* strangely. And to think I am related to that flock!'

They all laughed.

*

The following day they continued on, the river becoming sluggish and broken in places, deep dark pools littered with the detritus of the Wroth, eking a path through the mud beyond. It was a sight to see, to notice how the city bled, the wafts of rot foul and unfamiliar.

Rune flew higher where he could, yet Aggi encouraged him to stay in view of Onnar. Her journey was frighteningly exposed, running along bridleways and paths that grazed the edge of the river.

Rune was still not as fast as Aggi, and allowed her to fly on, to gain a sense of direction. They assumed the water would run to its apex within the city, and beyond, to the sea. They knew little more. They rested where they could, on the roofs of cottages and under bridges, making meals of whatever they could find. One such evening they felt as though they were being watched, and looked for a particularly remote hiding place.

'How did you become Drove?' Rune said one evening as they tucked themselves under a series of large purring structures, trussed up in a cage, yellow signs with harsh black symbols that spoke of ill tidings yet offered sanctuary.

Onnar tended to her ever-increasing sores, binding her feet with saliva and moss. Rune watched her with quiet fascination, the warrior and her many salves.

'I was born into the Drove. My mother was a mercenary, she gave birth to my siblings and I on the road. I alone survived, and I had no choice but to run with them. I do not regret this.

'Drove is an honour I didn't earn. When I was young I refused to take up the mantle. I didn't feel I was strong enough, or brave enough.'

'But you are Drove now?' Rune exclaimed.

'Do you know the Sqyre?' Rune shook his head. 'They hide their food in safe places for the winter. Clever really. There was a particular dead tree they were fond of hiding their stocks in, and they dug a series of tunnels within the tree itself, and took it in turns to guard the food for each other.

'A community grew around this, and all was well until a Storn, huge white feathered, you know them? Beautiful but deadly, we call them the White Death. This male Storn who had watched the tree for weeks decided to make his home there, in the great gaping holes close to a canopy of thorny leaves. The Sqyre had to find a way to get to their food or they would all starve, and the Storn knew this. Each Sqyre who approached was easy prey. It was a feast for the White Death.

'The Sqyre came to me as I journeyed through their wood. They pleaded for my help, but I was no Drove. I had never fought a predator before. Feral Vulpus and Maar had tried to eat me once or twice, and my legs had carried me to safety. The Storn are formidable, each foot has talons, great black talons, and its beak could have pierced my flesh with no effort. It was a challenge, to defeat such a foe. The Sqyre were so frightened that eventually I agreed to help and travelled with them to the tree. It was a great grey petrified tree. It was pitted and rotten, strangled to death by the thorny leaves that wound themselves about its waist, and at its peak sat the Storn, two black orb eyes staring down at me like a spirit from the Gasp.'

Rune shuffled closer. 'What did you do?' he said excitedly, Aggi turning in her half-sleep to smile at the pair.

'Well, the Storn stretched out his huge wings, puffing itself wide, leering down at me, and the group of Sqyre was behind me, chattering with nervous terror, their bushy tails flicking this way and that in agitation. He knew my reason for being there, and like so many Storn, had a rather deluded sense of self-worth. You know, Storn have huge eyes. So big, they take up most of the space in their skull. I've seen that skull, and there isn't much room for thinking. Killing, yes. They are very adept at killing.

'So, my only choice was to parley with that arrogance, or I would be climbing up that tree and fighting with an animal that Naa had made to murder me. So I approached the tree and watched the graceful twist of that huge head follow each footstep, and I stood up on my hind legs, cleared my throat and said, "Oh great Storn, oh White Death! You are resplendent in your gown of feathers, sitting atop your throne and looking down upon us mere morsels!"

'It turned its head in a confused tilt and said, "Are you trying to flatter me morsel?" and I replied, "I would not condescend so, I merely wish to speak with you."

'The Storn crept forward so that its talons gripped the disintegrating bark of the broken hilt of the tree and gloated, "You do condescend me, assuming all Storn think too much of themselves. I am simply resting within this comfortable bow before I continue my flight north."

'I smiled, "Storn, yet here you have sat for many turns of Seyla, and with each rise of the night light, you have taken those who seek the food within this tree. You have an easy meal."

'"I do!" it said, smugly.

'"But great Storn, you are a hunter, that beak and those terrible claws are for rending and tearing and the thrill of earning a meal, yet here you are simply waiting, perhaps losing that edge, perhaps you have become too content."

'The great Storn blinked.

'"You dare to say I have become lazy atop this tree?"

'I leaned closer and with a little humour said, "Well it's hardly a challenge, is it?" And the Storn lifted itself, and flexed each razored foot and said, "Drove, you are right. In this tree I may have my breakfast brought to me, but it is not fulfilling, and Sqyre are mostly fur."

'I smiled, and curtsied. "I believe you will find much more worthwhile bounty in the fields beyond this forest."

'"Perhaps," the Storn replied, "or perhaps you offer yourself as consolation, hmm?" And then it leapt from the tree, wings exploding to engulf my vision and I was running before I knew it, and the Sqyre scattered and chittered and I kept on running.

'Soon I was out into the clearing, towards wide fields and I took only one glance back to see that menace, and I felt the throb of each wing beat batter me. I turned and moments, mere moments lay between me and that Storn, and as it descended I saw, claws first, this acute desire for blood in its fixed leer, those immense eyes, and the glare of my terrified face reflected within each, like some terrible omen. In that moment I felt I had met my match, that perhaps my arrogance had got the better of me. I had not earned the right to fight this beast. But amongst the pitfalls and successes of my life I found my mother, so strong and brave, and I felt her guiding me, each part of my body. I leapt into the air, so that his implements of torture passed beneath me, and I kicked him square in the chest.'

'You kicked him?' Rune sat perplexed.

'Have you seen these legs?' She threw out her rear legs and he saw the machinery of muscle beneath her fur. 'These legs were made for kicking!'

Rune agreed.

'The force of this brute falling upon me knocked me sideways, tearing my face on its beak. But the great beast lay splayed flat on the turned soil. I sidled up to him and sat before him.

'"Do you live?" I exclaimed.

'"Yes," it said, with muffled reticence.

'"Will you leave these woods and not bother the Sqyre? I will be staying here for a while. Its best you find a new haunt."

'"Yes," it said.

'It was that day that I accepted my role as Drove, to honour the memory of my mother.'

Rune was in awe.

'I also have a very impressive scar!' she added.

*

Rune observed the variations in the landscape below him as they continued on towards the city, the contours of green and brown turning to angular, regular forms, huge garish obstacles, sometimes faces of Wroth upon billboards, lecherous effigies that reminded him of the Gulls who would leer at the Startle from their watch towers.

He made no sense of much of what he saw, but it was fascinating nonetheless. The noxious reek of coloured patterns and smells, often terrible and choking, were once in a while new and intoxicating. He dived and withdrew and danced with Aggi as she too drank in the awful bafflements of the Wroth settlement.

Soon the city was all around them; the unwelcome malignancy of steel barricaded, as though both rejecting and imprisoning them at once. The river was reduced to not much more than a dirty trickle; Onnar skirted the dank water and scrambled over anaemic tree roots that futilely sought sustenance. Soon the banks were mere inches of rock and dirt teetering on slabs of concrete that exuded from the stream, funnelling it towards a gaping wound in the earth; a subterranean waterway.

Onnar hugged the wall and placed each step with care. From here the water now dribbled to the centre of a wide silt bed. It was flat and branches lay across it, islands of leaf litter, rock here and there. She glanced towards the other bank, a possible escape; a path worn down by those seeking water. She leapt out onto an adjacent log, it crumbled under her weight and so she kept moving, until she was close to the water.

Rune watched her awkward stagger across the mud flat, watched each wince of trepidation. Reaching one limb across to a large flat stone, she felt assured to shift her weight. In a moment, the stone turned away from her, taking with it the friction of its dry side. Her paw slid, throwing her off balance, falling forwards and hitting the surface of the slurry.

It was thick and greasy, and she was face first. She dug in her front legs to get traction but with every move she sank deeper. She pulled her head to the side, to keep her mouth and nostrils away from the slick, and with the treacherous stone against her feet, managed to push herself on to her back. Now she was sinking tail first, which gave her a little more time to find escape.

Aggi searched frantically for a trailing vine from the nearby undergrowth, spying some ivy. Tendrils had grown into the stream and drifted with the flow, and she tugged at them to bring them to Onnar's aid. They were too heavy for her, and she was too small to fly and hold the limber stem in her claws. She cawed for assistance, but no one came.

Roak was perched on a raised embankment. He had spied the companions days before, purely by chance. Staying within earshot, their proposed path had been gleaned; as he had expected, they were following the river, and he had flown on to cut them off at the opening to the subterranean stream.

He watched the two feathered whirl around the filthy Yoa'a, whose yelps and barks went unheeded. He felt that fate had played a role in this most fortuitous of events; so little effort to trace these hapless fools, then to find them withering before his very eyes.

It was pathetic. He decided to wait and watch the Drove die in the mud, or perhaps reach the point where the simpering sense of defeat would be painted upon her stricken face. The Prince's killer and the feckless Collector would perch on some nearby twig and weep, and then he would slaughter them both and take the body of the Startle back to Esperer, assuring his right to the throne.

In his gloating Roak's head had lolled back and his eyes shut as he savoured these moments, and then Aggi saw him.

'Gull!'

Roak glared. Rune cocked his head and saw the stout figure peering down upon them. He recognised him, one of the chief guards upon the Pinnacle balcony.

'What a fine mess you have found yourselves in.' His beady eyes trained on Onnar, now submerged to her waist, the whites of her eyes exposed in horror as she struggled not to move, her mouth wide, her jaw slack with fear.

The Gull gloated, 'I could probably save you, but then, what would be the point? I've followed you for days, listened to your caterwauling, your whining, your desires and successes. To watch you drown in mud would be nothing but what I deserve.'

Aggi hung from the closest branch to the Gull and hissed, 'You vile worm, you are callous and weak, like your king!'

Roak smiled at her and squawked abruptly, sending her reeling. 'My king, Esperer. You are correct he is weak, he is dying, and the stunt pulled by that little speck of dust there has drawn him ever closer to the end. A strong leader is needed to replace Esperer, yet his current successor is but a faeces-covered egg in a nest. So it turns to me to find such a … worthy ruler.'

'Let me guess,' Onnar spluttered, the mud now cradling the edge of her face.

'I am strong,' Roak nodded.

'You're just like him,' Onnar coughed out a smile, 'self-assured, violent and stupid, you will make a …' – she wretched as the smell of rot filled her lungs – '… perfect king.'

Roak was aghast, they dared speak of him in such a way? Swooping down he found a loose branch upon which to exult himself. Aggi spat caustic objections, avoiding his pernicious beak.

'You know nothing of me! I am a captain of the guard!'

He leaned ever closer so that his beak was level with Onnar's quivering ears. 'The mud will devour you.'

THUD

He felt a jolt in his back, twisting himself round to see the fleck of black swerve decisively above as he did so –

THUD

He spun full circle, his legs twisted, he reached a wing to offer balance yet instantly his flight feathers crumpled in the mud. Staggering backwards, he was no longer on his perch and his feet felt the cold mire trap him –

THUD

Aggi and Rune felt each impact hard, painful and dangerous, each turn exhausted them and on the third turn Rune fled for a branch.
'I'm too small Aggi!' he shouted and she nodded, reaching her desired height before diving towards the frightened body writhing next to Onnar, who now saw an opportunity.
The Gull's wings covered a sizeable area of the sludge before her and she pulled one limb free, feeling the bones beneath his feathers. She pushed down.
The pain was excruciating as Roak tried to twist his wing away from Onnar, yet her other forelimb was now free and she wrapped it over his chest, pulling him towards her, pushing him down as she found purchase on the stone that had failed her before. Now she was two thirds out of the mud, and Roak was almost entirely covered, unable to move. He began to sob, screaming out obscenities in fits of vehemence.
'The new king is dead, what a decidedly short reign it was!' Onnar barked as she drew ragged breaths into her lungs, wiping the foulness of the mud from her. She clung to the rock, her eyes fixed on Roak's head, the only part of him still visible.
'You see, the thing is Gull, I do not kill those who do not deserve it. I don't believe you deserve this death. I think you are party to the same delusion as Esperer, you believe ruling a scratch of land is everything.

'Yet you cannot police those who do not recognise your authority. There are bigger things, much bigger things out there. Have you not noticed the Wroth are dying? That the land is left to seed on its own accord, that their presence is not felt as much any more?

'That Startle you so desperately want to kill holds a treasure far greater than the rule of a waterlogged Wroth settlement. And what did you do? Tried to kill him. Think bigger Gull, perhaps then you will live up to the inflated sense of worth you place upon yourself.'

She spat the foul taste of mud from her mouth, snarling at him.

He lay helpless, pondering what she had said. Then he cawed, 'You mock ambition, Yoa'a? You are a mercenary, a hired murderer! You do not sit far from me.'

Onnar sighed, 'Ambition is fine, but why rule over a people who do not desire that rule? You think the Bloodsons respect you? Or the Muroi? None see the Gulls as rulers. Despots? Thieves? yes. But not kings. What If I told you there is something bigger than you and your bastard king? Would you listen?'

She was now completely free of the mud, and had climbed across a few feet to the water's edge. The sediment subsided here and she could make out stones and gravel. She began to wash herself free of the stench, glancing back at the Gull, who returned a fierce gaze. She climbed further, testing her footing on a fallen branch, it bore her weight and took her close to the river bank, and she carefully slid towards it. With each move, something wrenched in her, something frustrating, niggling. She had almost died in that mud, and that feeling of suffocation was still rife in her.

She gripped the branch and shook her head, chiding herself. It was guilt.

'Curse you Gull kin!' she said, beginning to move back on herself.

Another branch lay adjacent to her. It was half in running water and half languishing in the mud. The branch she was now upon hung close to it, and soon she was level. She balanced herself at the widest point, and with her back leg, kicked out at the fallen branch. Nothing.

Again Onnar kicked, and it gave a little. Once more and it bobbed free of the mud, its weight counterbalanced at its centre upon a rock. She felt her claws against the bark, and rolled it towards her. As she did so, the water began to collect behind it, gradually building until it flowed over and around. The water flowed towards Roak. He spluttered, exasperated, 'You'll kill me! You'll kill me!' The water washed over his wings, yet was not of a great volume, and he ducked his head down to wash his face free of dirt.

Within minutes the slurry around him was diluted and he was able to move, he swung himself forwards, and with powerful beak, tugged himself ever further from the mud.

Onnar found the safety of the riverbank. It was dry and steep and she hauled herself up into the undergrowth. A Wroth had left some soft material balled up against a tree and she lay upon it. It was not a warm day, and she shook with cold.

Rune and Aggi joined her. 'Why did you save him?' Rune scolded her.

Onnar shook her head, 'If I let him die I am no better than they are. If the roles were reversed would he have let me live? Who knows, perhaps he'll even learn something from the experience.'

Aggi pondered. 'He was following us. He may not be alone in his desire to kill Rune. We perhaps underestimated Rune's worth to others, the murderer of the Prince.'

Rune nodded, 'We hadn't seen the Gulls for so long. I assumed they'd given up!'

Aggi looked back at the whimpering Gull, who was spread across the branch. 'Do you really think he'll learn anything?'

Onnar followed her line of sight. 'I guess time will tell.'

When they felt ready to move on they climbed the levee to the road above. There was little vegetation, grey and black and the fumes of asphalt and petrol greeted their tired bodies.

They slinked along the pavement, Rune atop Onnar's shoulders and Aggi in tow, keeping an eye out for Wroth. In the distance they made out vast bleak shapes against the horizon. One of them reminded Rune of the Pinnacle. He felt the pang of home.

Continuing along the path they saw a line of shrubs and in an instant they disappeared into the undergrowth.

The mud had penetrated Roak's down, and sodden and unforgiving he made himself as flat as possible, knowing full well he was now a target for predators. His armour remained intact. Embarrassed, he coughed up his indignation, thanking Naa that no one had seen him fail quite so perfectly. He considered what had transpired, grappled with a humiliation he had not experienced since he was a fledgling.

As he had strained to see what the Drove was doing before the water flowed over his wings, he had accepted that he too would have made sure he was dead. Yet the result of her efforts had set him free.

She had saved him.

For an almost imperceptible moment he felt thankful for what she had done. He had grown up in the shadow of the Pinnacle. The galling cry of his people cacophonous, deafening. His family had been ruined after the loss of his father, what was left was torn between his siblings. His father had died at the teeth of a Vulpus, leaving, despite the tragic and arbitrary manner of his death, his mother widowed, and thus shunned. In Gull society, parents formed a lifelong partnership, not based on love or admiration but on empty tradition. It was seen as improper to ever flout this pinion, that a family divided was a family broken.

Roak had joined the infantry under the new rule of Esperer when he was very young. It was not long before his peers found out about his father. They bullied him, attacked him, and mocked him incessantly.

He kindled a very particular anger within him. In adolescence he had grown large, strong and cunning. It gave him a fighting chance and the wherewithal to become someone of great authority. His size subdued those around him, the meek boy was replaced with a shrewd and powerful adult.

Every Gull that had mocked and spoke ill of him soon feared him. The fear he wielded was inebriating. He swooned as they shook. It was in him to punish them all, to kill them all, yet that ounce of cleverness which enabled him to dominate also blessed him with foresight. Soon they fell in line, they did his bidding, and they worshipped him through their fear. He had never known true respect, always taken that which was given without thanks, or stole it if it was not readily offered. He had never tasted the ambrosia of friendship or love, had never known empathy. Never known kindness, or compassion. Just want, desire, greed and hatred. The Yoa'a, this Drove - had consented to let him live.

He tried to covet this feeling, nurture it, give it time to lay down roots. Perhaps offer him solace in knowing that not every single soul would take from him, or indeed, that to survive he must take from them. And despite this, the Yoa'a had shamed him, and for that she would be punished.

Soon he was dry enough to take short bursts of flight away from the river. His prize was long gone, and he did not know where they were headed. It would take a battalion of soldiers to seek them out, and he was alone. Once he reached a safe place to gather his thoughts he entertained the few fragments of knowledge he had gained.

The Startle Rune, he was more than the murderer of the would-be king. He was, what had she said? A treasure? Something bigger than the throne and the Pinnacle. He thought back to what he had heard in their chatter. They were looking for someone, Erithus? Eritha ... he would remember the name. These were tangible threads.

He contemplated a plan. He may not have the Startle in his talons but he now had clout, something to play with. There were events afoot that these three usurpers were tangled within. He knew he was now woven into this pattern; if not his own blood, plenty of pride had been spilt for this. He would return to the Pinnacle, offer up his knowledge as proof of his ingenuity. Then he would convince Esperer to give him the flock he needed to seek out the Startle.

He pruned his filthy feathers, pushed out his chest and took flight.

*

The Vulpus wended their way back towards the city. They took paths that were once occupied by train tracks, now reclaimed under the watch of the woodland. They loped over fences and cut new trails to aid their journey. Atop a great hill that overlooked the Stinking City, amongst the graves of many Wroth, they cast their breath with assured will.

Vorsa made her goodbyes to her father and graced Oromon's face with hers, leaping the rusted fence and down into the quiet streets below. The patter of her paws went unheard by all, she was deft at silently weaving amongst the myriad obstacles placed before her, discerning the red brick and pale concrete, the tallest apartment blocks and decrepit Victorian abodes. She knew each Wroth dwelling, and every escape from it. She saw the yellow eyes of Morwih peering out from windows, craving her liberty whilst coveting their shelter.

The city stood in silent moratorium, held in the grasp of the Wroth until such a time when its ownership passed to the Vulpus. The armistice between the Morwih Consul and the Vulpus clans allowed the Morwih to live within Wroth dwellings and the outlying lands. The Wroth enjoyed marking the boundaries of their particular plot with fences and hedgerows, which made the task of sanctioning Morwih territory a little easier. The Morwih were also free to traverse between them if no clear path was present, yet to loiter was to court danger. Vulpus held the right to kill Morwih not adhering to the laws.

Saturating light shone from a lone street lamp, it flickered periodically as distant power stations struggled to maintain service. She clung to walls, seeking the dark. In the distance she heard the familiar whine of Morwih, recognised the baritone drawl. Within moments the agile source of that howl danced along the edge of a fence and hopped down before her.

'Fighting again Hevridis?' she said.

The Morwih sighed. 'What can I say, he asked for it. I feed where I can, and if I have to liberate said meal from another party, then liberate I will!'

'Come,' she said. They paced away from the street and along a back alley where no light shone. 'Do you bring news?'

He stretched and yawned wide, she thought to herself that it seemed so rare to meet a Morwih in any state of urgency.

'I have a task for you. I wish you to locate an individual. He is Startle, High Wrought. He has not been in the city long, perhaps he has just arrived. He will no doubt have company, he was last seen with a Drove mercenary and a Collector. They were two turns walk from here.

'I want you to shadow them and determine what they seek. Please do not hurt them, there are many threats against them and it is imperative that they survive. They have much to do and their work serves our cause.'

'Can I speak with them?'

'Yes.'

'And how will I find him?'

'You're Morwih, hunt them. How often is a High Wrought, a Yoa'a and a Collector seen together? They came from the south west, follow the river that goes underground, I imagine they'll keep to the places without Wroth, the city will be terrifying to them, seek the hidden paths. ... Good?'

Hevridis nodded. 'This night I will try to meet with Consul Fraubela. The Morwih are collecting to discuss how to disrupt the Meridian. There is much talk of a treaty between the Fractured Sects.'

Vorsa sneered, 'The Familial working with the Feral? Is the wearing of armour still banned in the Consuls' presence?' She laughed, 'Your culture baffles me Hevridis.'

'I will endeavour to glean whatever I can from this. I have never seen the Consul so determined. I am likely to be ejected on sight, but I will lurk.'

'You are very good at lurking.' She drew a deep breath, turning to leave. She stopped herself and turned back. 'Hevridis? Thank you.'

He bowed and they parted ways. Hevridis had come to the Vulpus of his own volition. He had endangered himself with this act, but his sheer audacity piqued the ears of Vorsa. He had asked for her by name, and she had consented to meet with him. That night he had told a tale of excommunication, that the caste system within Morwih culture had seen it proper to strip him of his station as a Familial. He had accepted this to a degree, yet what had brought him before his enemy was far more personal. His lover, Consul of his kin, had been the Morwih who had issued the decree. His beloved, she who he had trusted and raised above all else, had thrown him to the wind. Heart broken and scornful, he had taken what he knew of her schemes to the Vulpus.

Vorsa was not naive; she knew that it was a distinct possibility that there was subterfuge at work. Yet she courted his willingness, listened to him. What she hadn't expected was to like him.

*

Panic stricken, Onnar slid under cars, skirted bollards and pavements. Aggi and Rune kept close, darting from potted tree to bus shelter to wall or doorway, avoiding corpses and dangers all the while. Now they made cautious glances at the ground below, dodging the flailing limbs of the Wroth who staggered about moaning and crying for help.

They found a quiet place to rest. Amongst terrible smelling receptacles they found shelter. They knew there were predators here, yet the pungent decay and decadence covered every scent of danger, and for Onnar this was grave news. They hid in an alcove and caught their breath. 'I have no footing here,' Onnar finally said as she calmed herself. 'I cannot read this place, we are blind. Our only choice is to seek guidance from those who live in this land.'

'I am yet to see anyone but Baldaboa, who ignore our call, I have tried to appeal to them, with no luck,' Aggi offered with resignation.

Onnar frowned. 'You won't, and with good reason. The Baldaboa will not parley with us. Come, we must keep moving.'

There was a shaded path that led between two buildings, a back alley, filled with large refuse containers. She had seen Muroi, scuttling between the soaked cardboard boxes and litter. If there were Muroi out in the open, perhaps it was safe to traverse. Onnar tightened her armour, beat her chest, breathed deeply and bound along the filthy avenue. Aggi and Rune kept low and followed, each scouting the ground for possible dangers.

They travelled north, through tunnels, along alleys, over crumbling asphalt, round puddles of stagnant sewage and nocuous doldrums of rotting garbage. Layers of it sat in decaying arrest; seeping its bacteria swamp into the earth. There was a bowl of water propped next to a post where a Caanus had once been tied. The animal was long gone. The companions all drank until little was left. They lingered, enjoying the moment of rest. Then Onnar awoke them to the danger they had exposed themselves to, and they hurried on.

From time to time glimpses of the centre of the city emerged amidst vaporous smog, contours of edifices that defied their understanding of scale. These monstrosities goaded them, through fear and curiosity. Aggi wished to see them up close, to know what they were. Their path veered towards them, so with these contrary feelings in mind, she felt certain of an eventual encounter.

Their path continued on a slight incline, walls charred with soot from street fires, occasional bodies of Wroth, dying, curled upon the ground. They tried not to stir any would-be assailants as they travelled on, continuously barraged with disgusting odours. With no one to collect them, refuse sacks split open to reveal the carcasses of animals alongside the other detritus of their world. It was not difficult to fathom that which the Wroth deigned useless or useful.

The sweet smell of grass cut the stench for a moment as Aggi spied a garden behind a gate. The gate was locked and Onnar could not climb the wall. There were other gates that lead to other gardens, all appeared to be locked. Aggi had encountered locks before and so she hung from the handle and peered into the keyhole. The mechanism was obscure, and yet she considered her options. She shook the screws in their bore holes, finding all four quite loose and old. To dismantle this was perhaps beyond her, yet the screws seemed forgiving. She sought a flat stone and turned each until gradually the lock fascia fell away. Within were many metal teeth. She proceeded to remove each piece of the assembly. Eventually the lock fell away and the gate swung wide.

It revealed a tiny refuge, the walls of which hung thick with vegetation. Onnar sat and began to eat the grass, whilst the feathered hopped about, seeking rocks to turn and worms to dig. Onnar lay back and breathed in the evocative glow of greenery. The fence hung thick with flowers, dainty, drooping yellow-pink buds. She roused herself in curiosity and loped towards them. She sniffed. 'My word!' She ran her tongue over them and smiled, 'My friends, this is a sweet treat!'

They joined her and began to taste the nectar within the delicate flowers. The sugars were invigorating and they felt elated. Rune laughed, 'I have never tasted such a thing!'

They enjoyed the respite before Onnar suggested they continue whilst there was still light. They carefully slid out of the gate and continued north. The end of their path was unavoidable. Ahead, the stampede of Wroth. Onnar cowered against the wall, petrified. She admitted defeat, realising there were no other options. Beyond this road she could discern another quiet alley.

Aggi and Rune flew low and guided Onnar through the street. She saw Wroth carrying long black objects, she knew these to be dangerous. Their faces obscured with frightening masks, they shouted muffled commands towards the Wroth before them. She stared up into boggled eyes; the wide bright teeth and stench of them. These fevered faces which could not make sense of the Yoa'a who darted apprehensively between their feet. She lurched right and left; assaulted by wayward legs and her own revulsion, barely avoiding the rancid bilge that leeched from the curb.

Onnar reached the far side. She made herself small, quieting her heart. Eventually she relaxed and regained composure. The sharp crack and scream from the street behind her spoke of death, and she hurried on.

Ahead was a pile of spoiled fruit, and a pair of Muroi chewed nervously at it. They gaped at her, perplexed by her presence. She raised her befuddled paw as a sign of friendship, and they returned the salute. She approached gently, and they ceased their feeding.

'Ora bring peace.' The closest rodent nodded to her and asked her what had brought her to the city. She explained that she was looking for a wise feathered named Erithacus.

They looked at her with caution. 'If you seek him, you will find him, or he will find you.'

They refused to say more. They offered her some food but she declined, and she explained that the sickness in the Wroth might be in their food too. The Muroi seemed unbothered, they had always eaten Wroth food as there was little else to eat in the city. Thousands of generations had lived here and it would take a lot to kill them off.

Onnar hesitated in telling them of the many Muroi who had died, and yet she stopped herself. Perhaps they were aware, perhaps they had no choice. A voice beckoned that broke her pondering and raised her hackles.

'Who do the Drove go to for guidance, Yoa'a? That is a quandary, when so many turn to you for their answers.'

The Muroi scattered. The voice was honeyed and dripped with conceit. She turned to see the lithe feline before her, its fur stark black with a tiny fleck of white on its face. It preened itself with its coarse tongue, yawning wide to display its myriad cruel teeth. It wore no armour, besides a bridle of fealty.

"Morwih cur, I guess I should have expected to see the likes of you in a place like this.'

The Morwih scowled. 'Careful Yoa'a, you may be a champion amongst dirt eaters, but this is my city, and here the plants do not grow so commonly. We flesh feeders hold court.'

'Stay back traitor!' Aggi shouted from atop a low wall, 'she has battled worse than you!'

Rune landed beside her, staring at the curious animal before him. It circled Onnar, who hunkered down, eyes bright, shoulders incisive.

'A Collector! Fine dining you bring to this neck of the woods, Yoa'a. And a Startle? A veritable plethora! And yet; why would a metal worker, a High Wrought and a mercenary come to the Stinking City?

'This is fascinating. You are in luck, because my Familiar has fed me and I am far too full to eat another bite, and I do find this ragtag team of loose ends delightful. What do you seek?'

Onnar recoiled. 'You are offering your services?'

'Do you think that all I do is murder and maim and languish in the lap of luxury? Well yes I do all of these things!' He grinned. 'But I also dabble in a little wheeling and dealing. If you wish to find someone, you needn't go any further than the Bazaar.'

Onnar had heard mention of such a place. 'You do understand that I do not, and will never trust Morwih. There is a reason you are so despised by all who walk Naa.'

The feline smiled, 'Oh I do love being so infamous. Our fealty with the Wroth aside, we care very little for the opinions of our meals, and in most cases you are nothing more than that. But for this instance, and the foreseeable future, shall we entertain a truce? I would much prefer to see this little transaction reach fruition than to simply kill and eat you all. Very unsatisfactory, what with all the armour.'

Onnar leapt atop the Morwih and pinned his barbed claws against the earth. The howl that ushered forth was venomous and reeked of death. He hissed at her. Yet her breastplate stood before his ruthless mouth and her body and the gnashing cuspids found nothing but cold metal and wood. Onnar splayed the animal flat and shepherded its gaze into hers. 'Listen betrayer. Listen hard. You hold many sharp tools in this body, many wounding implements. You are strong, you descend from the most agile and nimble of meat feeders. But you are also lazy and fat and tiresome. Your flowery utterances will not cloud my judgement. I know your kind, my own mother died at the mouth of such a cowardly creature as yourself, so killing you would be a great service to all. You wish to walk with us, show us this place, then do so, or be gone. Deal?'

'Quite so.' He spoke reticently, 'I meant no offence, simply having a laugh.'

'At our expense,' she said as she backed slowly away from him, her eyes darting to each limb as his claws retracted.

Aggi stood beside her, breathing heavily, placing a wing on the Drove. 'The Morwih wants to be helpful, let him be helpful.'

'My name is Hevridis,' the Morwih uttered between deliberately indecent licks of his fur. 'I shall take you to the market.'

*

A railway line sat upon a curvature of arches. For miles its deteriorated stoop wound towards the city centre. At various intervals along the track, old buildings were in the process of being slowly disassembled to make way for more profitable buildings. Shells and fabrications collected water, left to the spoils of disintegration in the wake of the sickness.

Seedlings rose and claimed the sun; spores of ferns whose aerial meander had ceased and blossomed in the piles of wet moss that had fallen from the roofs of slouching terraces, all of which would list until they crumbled. Miniature gardens, once incalculable in worth, had begun to grow wild, surging between the fence posts and daring to wander, clawing the wooden barriers until many would succumb to their floral desire. It was here, in an oasis of bracken, beneath the canopy of ageing iron, the unwanted denizens of the Stinking City collected and bartered meals and bought trinkets, and whispered the end of the Wroth.

From the streets that skirted this forgotten land the Bazaar was invisible. Not that it mattered, for the Wroth busied themselves with other, dire things. Hevridis studied the contours of Onnar as she strode ahead. She knew this and yet chose not to entertain his bloodlust, though she kept her great ears keened to it. The sight of rusted piles of corrugated metal and mounds of gravel appeared before them. Hevridis climbed to the top, detecting the acrid stench of his kin's markings left about the sandy shingle. He felt the desire to make his own mark, to announce himself, but the odour was quite profound. They said nothing, but his wards disgusted eyes spoke a thousand words which stayed his impulse.

The shadowed arch didn't look particularly inviting, and yet he ushered them closer. Rune shuddered, 'This would be a great place for an ambush, you know.'

Aggi nodded. 'We have wings and Onnar has, well Onnar is Onnar. We will be fine.' They hovered until the brick incline made it difficult to do so. They descended, keeping close to the Drove.

The wall of the bridge had collapsed at its centre. Water fell free from a shattered pipe and into the fracture; as they looked at one another for guidance the yellow blue flick of an Aven darted about them, before passing through the slight gap between water and wall. Moments later two city Collectors sidled close to Aggi, looking her up and down and poking at her armour. 'Excuse me?' she exclaimed as they chittered between themselves, and disappeared beyond the bricks.

'Shall we?' The Morwih offered a paw.

The water had worn the earth to form a tiny stream. It eddied across the vast space within the bridge arch, and down into the bowels below where the floor had given way. The great cavernous space was filled with life.

Hundreds danced about a grotto of colourful tapestries, the scent of oil paint and perishing canvases speaking of its former use. Flowers blossomed where the wall had caved towards the rear of the arch. A rickety staircase led to a second floor upon which hung shawls of leaves. Voin swarmed in aurous yellow and black, their caramel hives hanging in rich undulations from the banisters.

Muroi peddled their robust armour, heavy set Danor sang the praises of their harvested berries. Orkrek and Amfier sat in the mud around the water's edge and bartered rare worms and beetles. Small Storn roosted in the rafters and awaited their turn with the clever beaks of Collectors who cleaned and fixed damaged armour. The flurry of negotiations, sale and trade lifted all their spirits. 'Whatever you need you can find here,' Hevridis said. 'If you wish to rest, there is soft grass beyond the farthest wall, and warm nests above us. No one will touch you, this is a safe place, there are rules we must all abide by.'

'Whose rules?'

'Vulpus.'

'And they let a Morwih here, on Vulpus territory? That's a little hard to swallow.'

Hevridis grinned, 'I am sure *you* are a little hard to swallow. There are certain favours owed. It is true that there is a degree of friction between my kind and the cubs of Seyla. But I have history with a certain Vulpus which allows me a little leeway. I shall leave you to enjoy the

Bazaar. I have some people to see, places to be, enjoy. I shall return, perhaps with the directions you seek.'

He bounded off. Onnar frowned. 'I am unsure as to what he wants. No doubt it is nothing good, but whilst we are here, we should rest and eat. Perhaps someone can tell us where Erithacus is to be found. I will go sleep. We shall meet here when the ora rises.'

Onnar crossed the market, avoiding arguing Bloodsons and greeted a pair of Tril who shared a little food with her. The far wall had collapsed into a sheltered garden. Overgrown with tall grass, it served as a perfect resting place. Two grand Ardid stood silently above her on their stilt legs, threat enough to ward off any who dared flout the rules. Their sword-like beaks and the scraping call from their throats would terrify any assailant. She settled in the dwindling light and slept.

*

Aggi bartered her skills for food. She had begun to teach Rune how to fix armour, and he was a diligent student. His nimble little claws and bill were deft at prizing the smallest of shards. She taught him how to fold the soft metal between his legs, how to fasten one piece to another with lengths of wire. She spoke of where the best places were to locate such materials, how to shed unwanted plastic and how to know what was useful.

Their customer was a Nighspyn, its back covered entirely in barbs. It sat belly exposed, and explained how its undercarriage armour had become loose. Aggi sat and watched, letting Rune figure out what might need fixing.

'Why are the Morwih so despised?' Rune asked.

The Nighspyn ruminated, 'Most Morwih made a pact with the Wroth long ago. The Wroth think them sacred! The Morwih call the Wroth their Familiars. They are fed and want for nothing, but in return the Morwih must make offerings to show their thanks. They make blood sacrifices; they kill and take the bodies to the lairs of the Wroth.

'There are strange prayers I'm told, dark prayers that only the Morwih can speak and only the Wroth can know, incantations in their purring. It bewitches the Wroth. Sad thing is the Morwih think the Wroth are their slaves, yet I feel it is quite the opposite.

'But any who sides with the Wroth is an enemy of Ocquia, so the

Vulpus hold the Morwih as traitors. There was a battle, and bloodshed, and eventually the Vulpus conquered the Morwih, and a fragile truce was formed. But the Morwih wish for the city, they wish it to be theirs.'

'The Vulpus rule the city?'

The Nighspyn giggled, 'The Wroth rule the city! but as the saying goes, *When the city sleeps the Vulpus speaks*. The Vulpus hold quarter over the business of Ocquia, they speak for the many who live here. At night they parade the streets and declare their sovereignty. Have you not heard their sermons? The Orata? It is the prayers of the Vulpus. Every night they recite the entire chronicle. Thousands of lines of sacred riddles. Even if you do not know their language, it is quite a thing to hear.'

Aggi nodded, 'The Morwih fear the Vulpus because they know that, if the Wroth were to leave, the Vulpus will take the city back, for good.'

'But the Wroth are dying?'

'Precisely.'

Morwih rhyme

Lo and behold the city
It is but a hollow dream
Beneath the Vulpus beam
And seek the clutch eternal

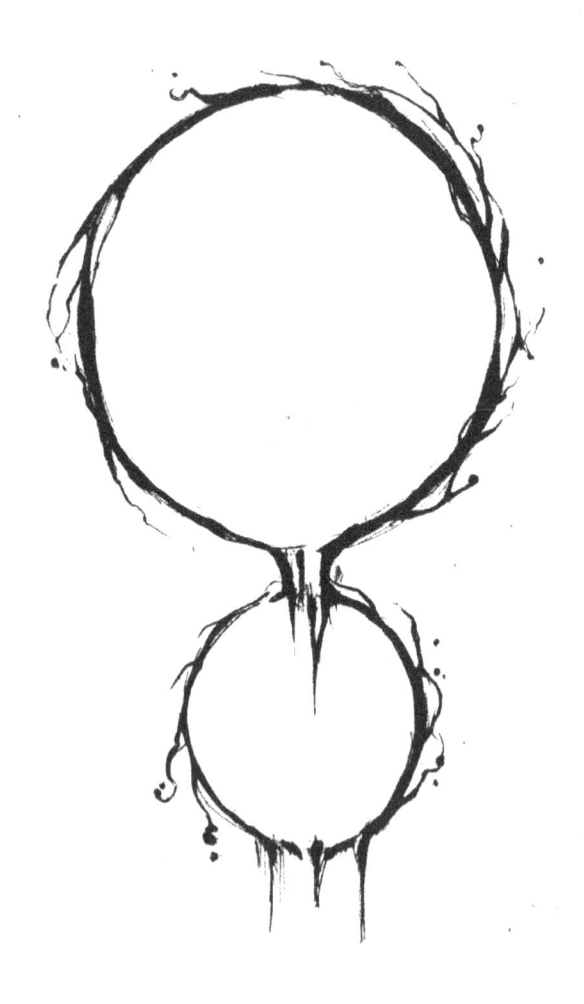

Chapter 4

Spires reached like shrivelled limbs from the cadaverous cathedral, the stain of smog upon its visage giving it a blemished menace. The central tower cast its shadow wide, as though light daren't not visit there. Upon the roof the council of Morwih sat in uncomfortable session. There was not much call for cooperation between the Sects, their agendas becoming ever more distant. The task of finding unity fell upon Fraubela, the Consul of the Fractured Sects. She sat above them, atop a raised ledge flanked by the horned effigies of gargoyles. Their snub, flattened faces mirrored her own. Such an irony was lost on her. They glared either side of her, reaching eternally for some unseen prey.

She cast a weary eye on those who had gathered there. She was a Familial, entirely accepting of her kinship with the Wroth. She wore her bridle of fealty with little resistance and performed the Ritual of Offered Blood. Accepting her familiar had brought her contentment. Like many of her familial allies, she had even accepted her Wroth name. She felt the pang of what the loss of the Wroth might bring her, it was perhaps the unknown that she found the most frightening. It had hastened her resolve.

To her left stood the Feral, for which she held a particular disdain. They had refused to remove their armour yet again, and they had never known a Wroth familiar. She accepted their loyalty to the Consul only to hasten the building of her army.

The presence of Erstwil etched himself before her. He was an Objector. Those Morwih who accepted their familiar with caution. They had other motives, which she didn't like. It was not a Morwih's place to question the Wroth. He bobbed his head in acknowledgment of her, and she shuffled forwards to return the gesture. Her bell rang. The crowd took notice and she felt the slightest cringe of embarrassment.

She had protested the presence of her bell, she could admit this challenge set by her Wroth familiar was a little hard to fathom. To hunt with such a handicap was stretching the limits of her ability. She wrestled with the notion that perhaps the Wroth considered the Morwih to be capable of miracles. Yet hunting with a contraption that could warn her prey of her presence was both a hindrance and a flamboyance she could do without.

The bell made Erstwil pity her. It was these visible shackles that had formed his own politic. It pained him to see his people chained, those Morwih imprisoned by the Wroth. He had championed their freedom, which had met with a great deal of anger from the Familials. No one dared question the Wroth. Yet he could not understand why they controlled so many aspects of their lives, whilst all of those who had accepted Ocquia went free.

Fraubela hushed her congregation and asked the heads of each chapter to come forth. They whined and yawned at one another, until finally a number of Morwih stepped forward. She was confronted by a bewildering contingent of felines of varying shapes and sizes. She asked them for their names, yet paid little attention until the velvety mewing of a particular voice reached her ears.

'Hevridis, representing the Feral Sect.'

She turned abruptly to see the impudent glare of the fallen Morwih. She hissed at him and he returned a smug smile. 'You are not welcome here Hevridis,' she spat.

'The Feral Sect does not recognise your rule Fraubela, and yet here we stand! Ready to offer our allegiance and blood to your cause. I am simply an avatar. You may refuse to accept me Familial, but you cannot refuse the Feral Sect, of which I am a member, despite my objections.'

'Your Familiar died Hevridis, you cannot claim fealty without a Familiar! And you should not wear that bridle!'

'I wear my bridle to honour the dead. Soon you will all be doing much the same. The Wroth are dying. We cannot continue to ignore the signs. How many Familial find themselves in my position?'

'The difference between you and them is that they accept they no longer have the right to wear their bridle, to grovel for leniency. There is no place for such platitudes.'

'I cannot help that my Familiar died. Soon you will find yourself much like I did. Isn't it true that the only reason we are here to hinder the ascent of the Vulpus to rulers of this city is precisely because the Wroth are dying?

'The Foul Meridian can only be performed when the Wroth relinquish control of this land. I simply wish to point out the irony, that denying me the right to my place amongst the Familial also sets a precedent, that when your Wroth familiar dies, you will also no longer be able to claim the role of Consul!'

Fraubela lifted her girth and leaned towards him so that he could smell the last meal upon her breath. 'We are not here to debate my tenure. We are here to sabotage the Vulpus scourge. How dare you come into my domain and dictate my rights! My Familiar will not die. They are healthy! They are not deterred by this sickness.

'Perhaps it is a test of resilience, separating the weak from the strong. Like this bell. I wear it as a test of my fortitude. It hinders me yes, but I still make kills, I still spill blood for my Familiar as a sign of loyalty. It is a sharing, a harmony. Something you will never again know.'

Hevridis smirked. 'I hold many secrets the likes of which might change that stubborn mind of yours!'

'I think not.'

She contemplated him for a moment and then tutted loudly, returning her attention to the Sects.

'The Vulpus have claimed this land. For generations we have lived under their paw. We are shunned by them, thought of as unclean. We have suffered indignity. We are an anchorless creed. We are born unto the Wroth, we are in their debt for our food and shelter, and it is true, the Wroth are unwell, many of you have spoken of their absence and we pray that they heal!

'But perhaps this is an opportunity to show our fortitude. If we take this city from the Vulpus, we are free to forge our own creed. Yet for this to happen we must confront them. The Foul Meridian threatens to cement their hold on us. This is one decree we cannot challenge and once it comes to pass, we are vanquished. So I ask of you to take up arms, to gather the many Morwih of this city, and to shed Vulpus blood!'

She shook with vitriol and let the idea settle in their minds. She then blessed each representative and divided the districts of the city between each Sect. They would prime the Thousands and bring them together for war.

Fraubela paused before Hevridis. 'The Feral will be scouts. The Corva Anx have been seen in the city, they are building strange things atop Wroth dwellings. Remove them.'

'And what of the Vulpus? We may outnumber them, but they are far stronger than us. How do we match their might?'

'Make use of our numbers. Many of us will be fodder. We will surge on them, we will bury them.'

The Sects dispersed quickly, finding the relief of solitude once again. The roof emptied, yet Hevridis remained.

'You loved me once Fraubela.'

'Hevridis, you may not care for our rules, but I do. The rites were decreed so that we could find comfort in our lives. I for one hold that dear. I cannot, I will not disregard that. You have no Familiar, you are no longer worthy of such a position.'

Hevridis held his head high, and darted from the roof. Fraubela lowered her eyes, considered her words and then began her journey back to the cold apartment she called home.

*

Morwih had long ago perfected the art of traversing the lengths and breadths of rooftops. They had become their unhindered domain. Not only did they allow the Morwih a clear view of the Vulpus who policed the streets during the Orata, they also allowed safe passage between the districts. Hevridis crisscrossed the many fences and walls, arches and train tracks that knitted the walkways and battlements of their lofty provinces. He sought out discarded meals of Morwih and Caanus alike, dodging the saliva-ridden maws and savage claws of many an aggressor. He even dared himself to enter the dwellings of Wroth in search of treats, not once had he been shooed away. The Wroth held the Morwih in particular high regard.

He paced along the sleepers until the canal appeared below. Spying the roof of a lockkeeper's cottage, he made use of its step and jumped down on to the towpath. There was a small brick-built island between the two locks, and he sidled over and flopped on to the ground.

Vorsa's light tread was unmistakable; his ears pricked as she appeared. He appreciated Vulpus far more than he would ever admit, they were formidable enemies. He sat up, yet held an air of aloofness, his back legs splayed in rest. Vorsa tiptoed across the lock, her eyes needling the banks for danger.

'Vorsa, my dear.' Hevridis smiled. A brief nod was her only response. 'I have taken the liberty of acquainting myself with your trio, a curious group of misfits.'

Vorsa frowned, 'It does not matter what they look like, it matters what role they play in all of this. What do they seek?'

Hevridis narrowed his eyes, 'Do not forget I have put myself in a very precarious position.'

Vorsa smiled with disdain, 'Hevridis, your choice to come to me was entirely your own, as much as I applaud you for making such a bold choice, whether the Consul has you put to death or not is on your head alone.'

'It is a drownable offence.' He shook. 'May I ask the significance of my ward?'

Vorsa pondered, 'Our prophets divined him of great importance. They have often been correct. Take it as a compliment Morwih. If you manage to keep them alive, we will reward you.'

"My dear, at this stage, I either drown at the hands of my own kin, or drown with them. It is enough for me to know that when the city falls, that I do not fall with it.'

The day disappeared over the periphery of Naa. 'Do they know where they are heading?'

Hevridis nodded, 'They seek the Grey Ghost, I cannot for the life of me guess where he resides or what they seek from him. Someone will know. I probably once ate someone who knew his roost.'

'Erithacus lives where no one dares to go. I hope they are prepared.'

The damage to Roak's wing hampered his journey. He flew as far as he could until it was unbearable and then found a perch upon a high-rise tower. He looked out over a sultry city wet with spitting rain. A drama of dark banks of grey cloud sighed and heaved over their lighter relatives, their heavy burden ready to drop unceremoniously onto all below. Out on the horizon he saw the curvature of the river, widening as it offered itself to the sea. He would find distant relatives here, ties cut, unfamiliar, wholly indifferent to the blood in their veins.

It was true Malca had burned all his friendships under the occupation. The coastal Gulls had very few allies in the city, those who might aid him could not be trusted. But he had to know what sat beyond this petty fight over a little Startle and a dead prince. In all honesty, he knew, he was in debt to Rune. He had been instrumental not only in the death of Roak's rival, but now stood to offer him that which would assure his ascension.

He took to wing once again, collecting the shards of conversation he had heard from the trio. The name they had mentioned invoked some half-memory, an inconsequential crumb thrown out by Esperer. He considered it, rolling it around within his skull.

'Erith.'

The heady stench of Ungdijin entrails was indelible. As he descended towards the docks that lined the mouth of the river it sank its oily residue into every pore. His slate armour was glaringly obvious here; most city Gulls fashioned their armour of plastic and other Wroth waste, not the cliffs that rose dark and fractious to the east and west of the Pinnacle, giving up plates of soft light rock which could be shaped and honed with their own beaks.

It was with caution he skirted the rigging and masts of the great ships that brought in the bounty. Some sat idle without their crew, no hustle of crates or cranes, or the tells that fed Gulls the knowledge of an easy meal. The estuary was littered with factions, relying on the Wroth for most of their sustenance; little more than feudal squabbles over a once bountiful land.

Rows of dilapidated factories sat fat and lifeless. He saw the flick of white against the damp roofs, Gulls lazily glid about, the angry glottal cry that was ever synonymous with home. These Gulls did not put on airs and graces like his own flock, city Gulls with their rough and discourteous temperament. He sighed deeply with trepidation as he descended.

A large warehouse festooned with Gulls lay before him. As he approached they took to wing in flanking formation and a terrible din ushered forth. He felt threatened, reducing his speed. They sideswiped him, knocking him forwards, the scowl upon each face filled with malice. He found refuge on a small tin roof and awaited his escort.

The first to land lowered his head and ejected a terrible cackling croak. It flicked its tongue and wielded its neck violently. Roak held fast. The remaining Gulls alighted, sharing their leader's disdain.

'Esperer flock,' the largest said, eyeing his armour.

'Yes,' Roak replied.

'You are far from home, boy. Why fly so far? Another coup? Land grab? I know your king is greedy.'

Roak considered his words. Gulls were vain. He knew this more than anything, knew it in himself. He could embarrass this feathered, yet it was wise to play to those vanities.

'I come seeking information, I know that your flock are wise, keep their eyes open, I come to you for assistance, where I have failed, perhaps your superiors will succeed, that is all. I am not here for anything else.'

They considered his words and then roughly escorted him down through a shattered skylight. Within was a suspended ceiling, lit dully by the light from broken tiles. It was upon this that the hundreds of gulls argued and teased one another over what little space they had, fought over females who showed them no mercy. Chaotic and filthy, it quickly dawned on him that the Pinnacle and its flock were no different.

A number of larger, well fed Gulls stood with eyes fixed on a lone trawler that chugged towards the dockside beyond the warehouse doors. Roak could imagine the whine of hunger behind those jaundiced eyes. These gulls hunted rarely, had grown too accustomed to the Wroth who discarded unwanted Ungdijin.

A stooge cleared his throat, drawing attention to himself. The Gull Master turned and noticed Roak.

'Esperer kin!' It stuck its beak up and sniffed the air, 'I could smell your stink.' His peers cawed with laughter.

Roak thought it was baffling considering the reek of faeces thick in the air.

'I come seeking a name, though I have nothing to barter but the promise of union, between my people and yours in a coming war.'

The Gull grunted. 'War? There is always war here. Nothing new, we fight without the need of your kin.'

Roak glanced at the floor and smiled.

'I do not speak of some petty feud. The Wroth are dying, you yourself must have noticed there are fewer and fewer Wroth collecting Ungdijin from the ocean. The signs are rife, the settlements are littered with the dead, Wroth and Baldaboa, even Gull die from this sickness. Without the Wroth your empire collapses quickly, no barter, no trade, and no food. Soon you will be forced to hunt and this land will be worth a great deal to the fiefdoms further inland. You will have to protect this kingdom much like Esperer protects his. Your people will turn on you.'

The Gull Master was mortified. His fierce demeanour quickly shed, he draped a facade of indifference upon himself.

'We will look after ourselves Esperer kin. But I am feeling generous. What must you know?'

'There is a wise feathered in the city. Some flock with great knowledge. He has a name I half know, Erith ...?'

'Psittacus Erithacus,' the Gull Master said gravely.

All of a sudden a hush descended.

Roak watched eyes dart towards them as though their leader had broken a promise. The assembled Gulls stared at one another as if to move would awaken some slumbering beast.

'Yes that is it! Who is he?' Roak spoke and the silence broke. The crowd began to busy themselves with anything but the conversation at hand.

'Erithacus, the Grey Ghost. He controls a terrible power. He is a dark mage. We do not speak of him. His name brings death.'

Roak comprehended the expressions of fear upon the faces of these hardened city Gulls. This was a palpable danger. What was this character that he held so much fear in his grasp? Erithacus, a wizard?

Roak cocked his head to one side.

'Where do I find him?'

*

As he flew west the soupy stench of the derelict docks soon dissipated. Warehouses and half-finished apartment blocks sank listless in the rising river; their foundations consumed by the crawling tide. It pawed at the concrete bones, needling its way deeper. Even Roak could fathom this, could see the uneasy footing of the city as it was slowly swallowed by the eroding earth. Yet he cared little. The land was always changing, and he would change with it.

Streets and signposts in their many bright colours offered him directions he would never grasp. He flew across the land the river divided. He kept the water on his left and watched the factories slip by, empty caverns that might one day make a home where the Wroth no longer lingered. Sometimes he would let his imagination drift back to the Pinnacle, the cliffs and sea that grasped his heart with their clarity.

He found this place sluggish in comparison, could hear the faint death rattle and knew that he flew over a diseased beast upon which so many now fed. Yet it was land, and land was power. He would pay it heed even if he cared nothing for it, for it would all be part of his kingdom.

The little he garnered from the city Gulls gave him a general direction. 'Fly west,' they had said, 'towards the centre of the city until you hear their cry. They will either kill you, or guide you to him.'

He didn't know who *they* were, yet this was enough. A light rain brought with it a sense of refreshment, and despite his fear, new possibilities came into focus. He not only knew the Startle Rune was still alive, and that he had a grand goal, he now knew his primary adversary, someone who held a great secret.

A weapon? Wealth? He could not guess, but he felt excitement; such a bounty to set before Esperer, such proof of his fortitude and quality that would befit a king. He manifested scenarios and laughed and chittered to himself, flying lackadaisically, courting the wind in dance. He lost himself in it.

He was soon upon the city centre, the teaming Wroth below agitated, screaming out obscenities and crying in fits of sorrow or rage as they sought to avoid each other at all cost. There were more bodies here, covered to shroud their humiliating deaths. He landed upon a phone box for a moment's rest. Here were grand Romanesque buildings, buses parked haphazardly upon the streets, piles of refuse sacks, split to reveal waste and filth. Barriers lay in piles, traffic cones scattered across streets. Horns blared, Wroth surged, holding masks over their faces.

A stout Baldaboa landed beside him. Roak stumbled and cowered from it. There was blood on its face. He cleared his throat and tried a few words in their language.

'You are sick?'

The Baldaboa gave him the cross-eyed vacant glare. For a moment a nervous laugh hovered in Roak's throat, but it wasn't mocking. He felt compassion for it.

'I'm sorry,' it said, turning away to fly, before turning back, for a moment, directing a penetrating shard of acuity into him. 'I am scared,' it said, the jolt of its neck with each step, coughing away from Roak, the dribble of bloody saliva hanging loosely from its beak.

Roak sputtered words, words he wanted to offer in kind; he didn't have anything worthy, anything salient, useful for this feathered. He only knew that it would die a horrible death, and so he lowered his eyes away from its stare.

It took to wing, and left him, dumbfounded upon the phone box. He collected himself. The fluid motion of Wroth in bizarre armour that covered their entire bodies, the muffled rumble of their voices and the shrill sirens closing in on him reached fever pitch, and he leapt from his stoop, up and up until he was too high to see any detail in the carnage below.

Further west, over crosswalks and squares and vast buildings, until he saw the green of trees, tended flowers and a distinct lack of Wroth. The park was large and flanked on one side by a remarkably straight river. He followed it on, enjoying the relative quiet of the grassy haven.

There were pools here, with water catapulted up from their centres in bizarre eruptions, and he saw Ungdijin, orange and white and yellow. He descended, hovering close to the water's edge, spying a bountiful meal. It felt too simple, and yet he cared not. Soon he was dragging the fat red creature on to the bank of the pond and knocking it back into his throat. It tasted of silt and slid down with greasy dissatisfaction. He collapsed into a sitting position and let the Undgijin die within him.

It was dusk now. Surrounding him on all sides were the black trunks of trees, their canopies leering in on him. It was not safe to be here.

There were Vulpus in the city, and Morwih. As he righted himself and shifted the heavy gluttonous feeling within, he felt something wrong. He turned to take in what lay about him, there was silence, and the black of night rolled across the city in grand ceremony. The fountain abruptly stopped flowing, which jolted him. He hopped over a few raised stones in the water and leapt upon the silent spout.

'Reee reee reee!"

The shriek was calamitous; it seemed to be all around him, and yet its host was invisible.

He did not know this sound, a virulent screech that trailed into the night. And then again, from many angles the caterwaul resounded, and he began to panic. From left and right the stark scream of the antagonist, splitting the cerulean quiet.

The sky was filled with tears of shadows darting about in ragged disarray, each slice of the stars a threat. Something hit him. It was heavy and sharp and cracked his slate armour. It rolled off him with a thud; a chunk of glass, a shattered bottle. He suddenly realised the error of his judgement.

He was too quick to dismiss the warnings of his own kin. Gulls didn't come here, and now here he was, in an open space, far from anything he knew. He looked to either side of him, he was unbalanced, unsafe. He gripped the edges of the stone ornament with his webbed feet and stooped low, throwing his beak wide, his tongue lashing, emitting his own gargling retort.

The screech came again but this time it held a condescension. They were laughing at him. 'Come forth you curs!' he bleated. They cackled, many voices discernible all around him. He pulled himself close and hissed again.

Seyla, fat and white, hung above as night took hold. The *tap tap tap* of leathery feet against tarmac heralded the approach of a single unfamiliar feathered. It walked into the light. It had an arrogant gait, as though it did not fear Vulpus or Morwih or any other predator which might be skulking in the undergrowth.

Its face was blunt, its beak curved down towards its chest, and its feathers were a curious shade of vibrant green. Its armour was similarly coloured; emerald flecks of metal and glass. It stood before him, small and stocky, with an air of mocking confidence about it.

It eyed Roak up and down, and a sound emanated from it, sharp and glottal, that made little sense to him. Again it made the sound and Roak questioned whether he was supposed to understand its meaning. It knocked its head in jarring motions and let out another cackle. The trees reverberated with laughter, amongst the foliage many eyes watched him.

'I called you Gull,' it said, with a curious wispy craw. 'It is a Wroth word, I spoke it in its original tongue.'

Roak put aside his anxieties while he tended to this fact. 'You speak Wroth?' he coughed up in astonishment. He lowered himself so that he could make out the enemies in the foliage.

'We do, we learn so much with this key. It unfolds the obscurities of their ways, we understand why they do things.'

Roak was impressed. He knew much of the Wroth, but to speak their language was an impressive feat he had never considered. 'How is this possible?'

The canopy erupted and the resplendent flock plummeted, each carrying a barbed slice of metal or glass. They wheeled above him with feverish intent, chattering and squawking their desire to maim. The green feathered turned to leave.

'Wait!' Roak screamed. The strange character stopped. The chunks of debris rained down, some striking him as he pleaded, 'Aren't you intrigued to know why I came? I seek Erithacus, you are his ... soldiers?'

The green feathered peered back at him.

'Please?' Roak imitated a grovelling cadence. 'I have travelled a long way and ignored the plea of my own kin not to venture here, to bring the great Erithacus news.'

The feathered looked unsure. 'Why do you wish to speak with Erithacus? You have no fealty here, you are an enemy.'

The bombardment ceased as the exotic flock returned to the trees. They moved as one, like a dishevelled Startle. Roak climbed down from the fountain and tended his wounds.

'I do not know Erithacus, but his name has been raised in a great prophecy yet to come. There are many parties vying for power. I made it my duty to bring this information to Erithacus and to offer him my services.'

'Erithacus craves information, we are his eyes and ears, his host. We bring him all, every scantling of information he might desire, he is the Grand Fabricator; the Tool Master.'

Roak considered these words. 'I know I have reason to fear Erithacus, and yet I stand here as proof that what I hold is worthy of my life.' His words were met with silence.

'Please,' he bleated.

The green feathered barked some orders to his kin and they took flight.

'Come. You understand that if you doublecross us we will kill you?'

'Yes.'

The park gave way to the monotonous grey once again, pockmarked by nauseating hues and jagged constructions. The flock before him flew in disarray; they fought one another in flight, clucking and clacking with no fear of being eaten. They did not hide themselves, but even made themselves known.

As they flew Roak considered this striking similarity to his own flock. Arrogant and unquestioned, the Gulls lauded themselves over their land without fear of reprimand, yet they did not walk upon the land, they did not hold the teeth and claw in their grasp, there was no healthy respect from carnivores in the shadow of the Pinnacle. Their rule was halfhearted, incomplete. Yet here was an opponent who feared no predator, where slavering mouths might fear them.

And they spoke Wroth! How could this be? The Wroth existed outside of Naa, they went about eviscerating the land, moulding it to their whims, without a thought to those who resided there. It was unique, a trait that Esperer had often spoken of; that the land should bend to his will alone. It was this imperfect interpretation of the Wroth that fascinated Roak.

But to know the Wroth *completely?* To know their majesty and also the error of their ways? This was a prize, and any wound or punishment that was to come would be worth the price. He would return to Esperer and tell him of the flock that speak Wroth tongue, and they would have to invade, enslave these bilinguals with their forked mouths. He would know this speech, and when Esperer died all this would be his. Lord Roak, Speaker of Wroth.

The flock descended towards a mass of dirtied white buildings encircled by a mesh fence topped with razor wire. All nonsensical to Roak. They flew to the largest building, a wide tilted roof. At its furthest corner a blemish, a gaping hole, which appeared to be their destination. They formed a column of bodies that plummeted into the maw and soon he too followed, his perception lost in the dark.

The flock had vanished.

He heard their chatter, yet there was no light. He could discern the drip drip of water, it was damp and cold within this place. He tried to adjust his eyes, closed them tight and saw stars; only to open to the same Cimmerian murk.

'Gull!'

The voice rose with terrifying vigour. The echo shuddered about the expanse and shook Roak's stomach.

'Your kind is not welcome here!'

Roak spread his wings in surrender. 'I come bearing news, that is all, I understand there is reason to fear you, oh mighty Psittacus Erithacus, I do not know why, but I ... apologise ... on behalf of all Gull kin ...'

'Do not placate me Naarna Elowin. I know your kind all too well. This is not the first time you have come to my city and demanded of me.'

Roak frowned. Some fragment memory was revealing itself, and yet for now, it wasn't eager to show all. He replied, 'For whatever my people did, I am sincere in my apology, yet I come here for a different purpose. I come here with word of a prophecy, of a great change, I come here to bring this news as a show of trust, and in time to build confidence in a treaty. I wish to construct an empire where a great Gull has stood, once he stands down it is my belief I will take the throne and I wish to build relations with neighbouring rulers.'

'Esperer still lives.'

Roak sighed, 'Yes. He is still king. But his son was taken by a single Startle. I believe this is an opportunity for a Gull with stature to offer his services to his people.'

'You?'

Roak nodded to the darkness. "Yes, I believe I am that Gull.'

The emerald flock chittered. An aural landscape was forming before him. He was encompassed by them.

'Gull, do you not know who I am? You are not too young to know of the great expansion of your former king's empire? Malca, the wretched fool. Do you not know this city and its army, the Speakers?'

Roak choked. The memory surfaced. In the occupation, Esperer's father Malca had sent his forces out to take the city, and had lost an entire legion to a supposed ally. Roak felt the stories click in place; the city held an army known as the Speakers, they were violent, unyielding and deadly. No Gull escaped that night of bloodshed. So many were lost.

This Green flock were the Speakers.

His heart palpitated. He must flee, but where?

'Ah, there it is! Oh Roak, son of Gepsomi, father dead and family betrayed by his own kin. I know of you and all your many foibles. There is no empire but Naa. The sooner your pathetic horde realises this, the sooner we can find the peace you feign to desire. The Umbra sees you Roak – you are a pawn, nothing but a pawn. You are ensnared in its grasp, as is Esperer, and you will never know the bounty that is offered to you until it is too late.'

Roak digested each word, each golden orb. Umbra, pawn.

Bounty?

He staggered back, what had he stumbled upon? What grand event was he now written into?

'And what of the Startle! What role did he play?'

There was silence.

'What do you know of Grom?' The voice cried back.

'Grom? No, I speak of the Startle Rune, son of Grom.'

The Speakers erupted in a chorus of chatter, their spinous caws held him in the grip of alarm. He dared not move. He felt something cold and sharp against him, great iron bars rose up to form an enclosure – a cage. Beyond him were many cages, stained with faeces. He felt some vexing malaise, it hung in the air, terrifying him.

'Rune is of no importance to you! You will not speak his name again. You will leave this city, and never return. We are watching you!'

He fled, up and up and out through the hole in the roof, catching himself on struts of decaying plasterboard and metal, he took the pain and fed from it. Soon he was high and pointing south, down, down towards the sea, to home, to his people, to Esperer.

Glaspitter the Speaker hovered before the great presence of Erithacus.

'Should we follow him?'

'No. Let him live. He has a purpose beyond his vanities.'

*

Roak flew without rest for many turns. Exhausted yet relieved, the coast appeared before him. His whole life was written into the cove from which the Pinnacle extended. The blush of Ora animated the waves that surged against the sand. He felt the invigorating relief that home still brought to him, despite the many reasons that took him far away. He even appreciated the presence of the Startle.

Gulls stood warily overlooking the turrets and battlements of the gates to the theme park. The irony was lost on those who manned these sentry towers. They saw his broad wingspan and within moments flew in convoy beside him. They held an excited fervour.

'Did you find him? Did you find Artioch's murderer?'

He descended to the balcony, and with a deep breath he entered his king's domain. The raucous laugh of courtesans greeted him. They ingratiated themselves with the tired old fool upon his pile of skins. Returning to this stale hall, Roak felt a pang of regret. There was still a sense of loyalty after all these years. Esperer swung his head to greet him, lifting himself from his lethargy.

'You defied my word Roak.'

He had quite forgotten this particular truth, that the command to follow the Startle had not been given. He contemplated the correct response.

'Sire, you must forgive a momentary lapse of judgement. My anger at that grave act took hold, I sought him purely to avenge the death of your son, the Gull who would-be king.'

Esperer narrowed his eyes, Roak could see the distrust.

He decided it was best not to embroider this lie any further. 'Forgive me, Lord Esperer.'

'Did you find him?'

'Yes. I found him and his cohorts within the Stinking City. I tracked them silently for many turns, and I learned secrets. Plans. Prophecies.'

Esperer leaned in, suddenly captivated. 'The Startle is the son of a

Shadow Starer.'

Esperer collapsed back. 'Oh Roak, please. I knew his father. I know these tales of the enigmatic Grom.'

'But Sire. The young Startle, Rune. He has taken it upon himself to seek the ear of a powerful ruler in the city. They travel to him now. I went to the Gull colonies in the city to find out the location of this mystifying character. The Gulls spoke of him with such ardour, for he appears to hold many answers. They warned me not to venture forth, and yet I did, beyond the city, in a dark place, I found this mage, this Erithacus.'

Esperer sat upright. 'Erithacus?'

'Leave!' he screamed at the courtiers who cooed and whinnied around him, and soon Esperer and Roak stood alone. The old king looked dishevelled, as though the wake of his son's death had marked him far deeper than any could have imagined. Roak traced the yellowing down and the red-ringed eyes that now stared vacantly into the middle distance.

'It has been a long time since that name was uttered in my presence. My father all but banned its use. It was the ultimate offence, to remind him of his folly. My father's failings are like stones tied to our feet. We are weighed down by his idiocy.'

Roak whispered, 'Erithacus holds a power I have not encountered before. He commands a flock as if out of fables. They have green feathers and their shrill call drowns all other feathered – and sire, they hold a quality like no other. They speak Wroth tongue.'

Esperer smiled. 'The Speakers? Ah, it is true they are a formidable enemy, but speak Wroth tongue? A parlour trick I am sure.'

'No sire, they understand the Wroth, this Erithacus taught them. They have mastered its peculiarities. They know the Wroth like no other.'

The same epiphany that had transpired in Roak now dawned on Esperer.

'A flock who can speak Wroth, now that would be quite a prize. Under my command we would learn of the Wroth dominion, know their strategies. The Wroth will surely succumb to this sickness and in their wake the world will seek new rule.'

Roak's eyes filled with stars. He had not lived long enough, had not seen war. It was perhaps overreaching for him to consider such an act, but for Esperer to command an invasion, with Roak at his right wing, he would let Esperer seize his prize, to charge into the fray. Roak would place himself within the fight, assuring that the old king went out in a blaze of glory. Roak witnessed the brilliance of his strategy, the blood would slake his desires, he would rise up from the death of Esperer. He would slay Erithacus in the name of the old king, and take his place amongst his people as the new ruler.

Esperer saw the thirst upon Roak's drooling maw, a stupor he had seen before. It had boiled in other rising stars within his infantry, some of which he had dispatched himself, to stem any dissension. Members of Roak's own family had stood in that spot, gloating of some insignificant triumph. But who was he to scold ambition? He had indulged in the bloody act himself, the same brashness which had lead him to kill his own father, Malca.

This arrogant feathered already considered himself the king in waiting, ready to walk over his corpse. It was quite a thing to see the intentions of your assassin. He savoured the knowledge for a moment, before speaking. 'And what of the Startle. What role does he play in this?'

Roak turned with scheming grin. 'Ah yes, the young murderer. I do not know the specific importance of this feathered, yet it appears he plays a part in the convergence of prophecy. He is protected by a Collector and a Yoa'a. Erithacus warned me to stay away from him. I believe this fact is pertinent.'

'Go back to the city. Seek out Rune. Take him hostage, he is now a bargaining tool. With him perhaps we can extort Erithacus. He will not give of truths if we take his throne and enslave his flock. I will ready the soldiers. I am sure they are eager for war.'

Roak bowed and took flight, below him the canny white of many hundreds of Gull, bored, restless and ready. He flew low, and let out a deliberate caw, a single word that triggered the synapses of his fellow kin. Ripples of mirrored cries lifted up, the ranks draped in stone armour, some gripping their pebble weapons. He relished this sight, his soon-to-be army. He felt the draw of rule deep in him, and it felt wonderful. All this would be his, he thought, as the word rang out against the brilliant blue sky.

War.

*

The fathoms offered serene dark, the frigid lightless places which held a world unlike any other in Naa. Here gods swam; their continental bodies graced the water with deific proportions, casting spells to perceive their paths. Here, where the rock was old and skeletons of billions hugged each other in the hyperborean dirt, a tone resounded. Cast out from the Settling Stone, pulled forth by unseen hands, it sunk beneath the waves. The great presences heard that tone and shaped their own songs in harmony. Soon it was an orchestra, a rampant cacophony below the ocean squall. Through these arrangements the swimming mountains gleaned the tone's intent, and they smiled wide and changed course, bringing their chorus with them. Their voices carried on the brine and broke the surface to be heard beneath infuriated skies. All who heard them sought their meaning.

*

'I know the whereabouts of the feathered you seek.' Hevridis said, rejoining Onnar, Aggi and Rune via the second floor of the Bazaar. He seemed confident in this fact.

Onnar approached him with a questioning gaze. 'And you gleaned this from whom?'

Hevridis smiled, 'I can see I have no chance of convincing you I mean no harm? The information comes from a reputable source. The Vulpus, to be precise.'

'Need I remind you that I am aware of how much the Vulpus despise the Morwih?' Onnar retorted.

Hevridis meandered down the staircase until he was level with Onnar. 'Did you have any luck locating him yourself?'

Onnar frowned. 'No. I garner from the little I did learn that no one seeks Erithacus. He is best avoided at all cost. He lurks in a hidden place. That's all I could gather.'

'The place I am told to take you is precisely that, a frightening place, the kind of place a character such as Erithacus would reside. It pains me to see you so distrusting,' Hevridis laughed.

Onnar thought on it. 'How far must we travel?'

'It is not as far as you would imagine.'

She rolled her eyes and gestured to her feathered friends, and together they climbed the wooden steps, following Hevridis out on to the mass of scaffolding and up to the train tracks above. They travelled west, towards the dismantled buildings. Aggi and Rune flew above, whilst Onnar and Hevridis walked precarious iron beams and jumped the dizzying gaps above great drops. The Yoa'a relied heavily on the feathered to keep an eye out for danger. Hevridis was unperturbed by the myriad of death traps. He knew these routes, knew every corridor, every traversable climb that took him away from the ground. Nevertheless, he quelled pangs of anxiety. It was rare for him to ever question his own choices, not often that he wrestled with his morality. But he had made a choice. Yet he continued on, beyond the countless office buildings, sulking high-rise housing, withering trees and vacant playgrounds. The evening came with cold and rain, nauseating spittle dragged any semblance of surety down with it into his fur. He shuddered as the discordant gloom of the cathedral spilt across the graveyard that embraced its foundations.

Rune felt his stomach turn in him as he surveyed the wretched spines of the church's architecture. It was a painful swelling, as though something he'd eaten disagreed with him, yet it held a certainty – he knew what it wasn't, it wasn't illness or even pain, it was something far less physical.

'Aggi, I am not sure this is the place.'

Aggi glanced back at him and shook her head. 'It is indeed frightening.'

Hevridis was quick to dismiss their fears, 'Come, it's up there, upon the roof, follow me.'

He leapt over the rooftops of the adjacent houses. Onnar followed warily and with difficulty, her feathered companions staying close as she struggled with her fear of falling. They weaved around chimneys and the clatter of slate tiles, until they were level with a grand stone buttress that supported the central spire. Here the roofs met and Hevridis jumped gracefully over. Onnar slid precariously on her back legs until she had purchase and dragged herself over the gap. The feathered followed, hopping close to their protector. The roof rose into the black night; the poignant silhouette of Hevridis, stoic atop the apex, his eyes like perilous orbs.

'Come,' he said, as Onnar reached the top. Beyond was a wide flat space, a lead-lined terrace that sat beside the disquieting tower.

She did not see them coming.

The Morwih pounced, pinning the Yoa'a down. Onnar bucked and screamed out against them, throwing a volley of kicks, the snap and howl as her fierce limbs hit hard ricocheting about the hallowed roof. Mouths enclosed on her; the searing ache of claws in flesh as the Morwih attempted to subdue her. She flipped herself over and pushed against the tower wall, the rattle cry of many slathering felines enclosed as they stalked low. Rune and Aggi were helpless and flew above, shouting and crying out. They hurled themselves at the Morwih, stabbing beaks into hides, fleeing the claws that replied.

Onnar shouted to her ward, 'Please, save yourselves, fly!' Her eyes were wide, her heart exploding inside her, and she felt the sure end, and the sure win, all at once. She would not be defeated by that which took her mother. She smiled at Hevridis who now pranced towards her with elegant strides.

'Utterly predictable.' She hissed at him.

'Rune,' Hevridis turned his attention to the Startle. 'you have the power to save your friend. You will all come with me, willingly, or Onnar will die.'

Rune turned to Onnar, whose throat hung in the mouth of a large armoured Morwih. She shook her head, 'No Rune! No!' She pulled herself free and backed along the wall as her enemy prowled, movements liquid, slow and calculated. She mirrored them, pulling herself back and back. They ceased their stalk; an air of mocking fell over them, and she looked on with curiosity, until she felt the cusp of the roof. They had backed her to the edge, and she now stood at the precipice. It would take little for them to push her over.

They laughed at her.

Rune stuttered. Aggi wheeled about him, 'We must help her!' She shrieked.

Onnar pleaded with them to flee, again and again, each petition to assist her quickly quashed.

'Please, you can both leave, both just go, there is nothing for us here, nothing for you. Don't let us all suffer for my misjudgement!'

'We all made this choice to follow Hevridis, it is all our fault!'

Onnar cried, 'No! It is my choice, I am your guardian, this is on my head, and I am so sorry, now go!'

Rune felt a grave pain consume him, it leered at him with disappointment, a bright kernel that scolded him for even considering leaving her. The light within him shook; its quality violent and brilliant, it took little for him to know the light was Onnar, he knew her bravery and courage and might. He knew her light was too important, too significant against the aching dark that surrounded it.

He landed upon the roof, and gestured to Aggi to do the same. Onnar sobbed, 'No Rune, please!'

The Morwih backed off from the Yoa'a as she pulled herself away from the edge.

'Come,' Hevridis ushered her towards the feathered. Onnar had no choice.

They were escorted across the roof terrace, Aggi whispering soothing words to Rune as they reached a raised incline. There were many Morwih, hungry faces that looked upon the trio with desire. Before them sat a plump grey-furred feline, her coat stood wide of her body, her face flat and ugly, eyes swollen and yellow. She studied each of them and sighed.

'Why do you bring me these creatures, Hevridis?'

'I have a story to tell, Fraubela. When my familiar died, I knew what was to come. I knew that my place amongst my people would be forfeited, that I would be sectless, I would be shunned. I knew this because I had done it myself, I had looked upon those who no longer held quarter with the Wroth and dismissed them. I knew that any affection you once had for me would be lost. And so I took it upon myself to seek other means to prove my worth to you, and to the Fractured Sects. I offered myself to the Vulpus.'

A cacophony of yowls rose, and he raised his voice. 'Let me finish!'

Fraubela shook her head, 'You continue to amaze me with your stupidity. I will not listen to your treason any longer.'

Erstwil registered his disagreement. 'Let him speak Lady Fraubela.'

She narrowed her eyes. She considered her words, so as not to lose face.

'In the interest of cooperation between the sects, you may speak Hevridis,'

Hevridis continued, 'I went to the Vulpus to offer myself as a spy. After many attempts I eventually garnered trust from their most lauded general, Vorsa.'

He held them in his grasp.

'I instilled in her that trust by offering false information, mixed with a few truths. I told them of events and certainties and many facts that would quite easily fall apart under scrutiny, and yet they did not question me. I told them a little of what they wanted to know, but what I gained in return was far greater. What you see before me is the fruit of that labour.

'This little Startle is the same Startle who killed the Gull Lord's son, the would be King of the Pinnacle, a rotting kingdom to the south. This little Startle is the linchpin in many of their plans. He is some kind of prophet. Ordained by the Corva Anx no less. This Startle holds many secrets. Many of which I imagine, he is not even aware of himself.'

The light inside Rune had now divided, it was many lights, each vying for his attention, each speaking out into the trembling mournful skies. He tried to focus on the light that seemed to be him, he sought its heat and coveted it. It was a light that felt like it might go out.

'The Corva Anx you say?' Fraubela was intrigued. 'This is quite a tale you have stumbled upon Hevridis. Yet, of what use is it to us? If we kill this Startle, it will surely enrage the Vulpus and they will seek revenge. If the Startle is unaware of his importance, then what can he tell us that we don't already know? What possible use is he to us?'

'We will barter with him. He will assure us a place in Naa beyond the Foul Meridian.'

Fraubela fumed, 'The Vulpus will all be dead! The Foul Meridian will not occur, the city will not pass into their greedy paws. We will slaughter every last one of them!'

'We have no control over these events Fraubela! You parley to the same gods as I do. You know as well as me that we cannot influence the Foul Meridian. Whatever we do, we cannot sway its outcome. If the Vulpus and the Corva Anx will it, the city will pass. The only thing we can do is hold them to ransom and demand our lives!'

Onnar's breath was laboured, she held in her a flight response. To her right ran a gully for rain to flow. It was large enough for her to fit within, and it was filling with water. She closed her eyes and laid out a map of the roof. Her great ears rose. She could hear the Morwih, their purring was distinct, each voice tremulous and low.

She separated them in her mind, dispersed herself amongst their imaginary forms, sought routes for escape. The clearest route would take her along the gulley between the Morwih, but they would surely be ready to pounce upon her. Somehow she would alert Rune and Aggi quickly, dive for the gulley and be gone with her friends before the Morwih could stop them.

'So we hold the Startle for ransom? We yield to the Vulpus yet again?'

'We do not yield, we simply exchange this feathered for land of our own. Land the Vulpus cannot walk upon. We take a district of the city and we maintain control of our walkways. If they need this Startle for the Foul Meridian to occur then they will agree to our terms. The other options? We win, take the city, remove the Vulpus and laud over the land forever. Or we die, and every last Morwih is drowned. Because they know how we murder our own.'

Fraubela drew a quick breath. 'And where do we keep him?'

Erstwil stepped forward. 'We will take him to the Crool. The Vulpus have no quarrel there. It is a Wroth place, so they will not think to visit. We can keep him there indefinitely, or dispatch him when need be.'

'So be it. You can take these others and do as you wish.'

Onnar gasped. 'Fly!' she screamed, ducking her head low and bolting for the gulley. She slid down, her feet slipping on the slimy leaf litter and algae that clung to its sides. She sought a foothold but found none; and as confused eyes darted above, down she plummeted. The Morwih wheezed and jeered at her as the water within the flue cascaded out, sliding faster as the passage tapered towards the edge of the roof. She heard Aggi's cry, wrestling free of barbarous claws and up and out, Onnar making one last turn to see if Rune had freed himself. She could not see him.

She pulled herself close and slid the final few metres before she was thrown out; high into the air. Below a wide nothing between the cathedral and the adjacent building, the tops of cars and fences and petrified thorn bushes. In a fierce moment all disappeared, and she collided with a roof. She rolled hard, fur and skin grazing, she came to a full stop and lay for a moment, bruised, battered.

'Run!' Aggi was above and Onnar roused herself enough to see the limber frames of many Morwih, now sprinting across the roof towards her, leaping across to join her. She skated on gravel, found friction and fled, across the debris of rejected sofas and mattresses, up and up and down, vaulting the menagerie of redundant things until she could run no more. She saw an opening, a dark crevice and pulled herself into it. She hid low in the shaft of an air vent, and held her breath.

The telltale jingle of a stalking Morwih betrayed it. She moved slowly left and out, skirting the edges of the various metal boxes and disused chimney stacks. She knew the sound of pads on gravel, knew there were two Morwih, one above, and one to the left. She crouched low, feeling the tension in her calf muscles build until they ached.

The Morwih rounded the corner and spied her; she leapt straight for him, the force of her body throwing him wide. He tumbled off the roof, and the hellish shriek that issued told her she was rid of him. The second Morwih hung above her and Onnar had the impression of a certain intelligence. She respected it, she saw the malign confidence, knew its death blows before they materialised. The Morwih lowered itself to her level and uttered a guttural growl. It was so unexpected, it made her laugh. The Morwih looked noticeably offended, reeling its head back. Before it could reaffirm itself, she had swung her body full circle and knocked it from the roof.

She began to run again, further and further out, scanning the sky for Aggi. Soon she was far enough away to see the entire cathedral; the yowl of many Morwih searching for her, she sat between two chimney pots and huddled down until she saw the sky brushed by Aggi's presence, the familiar flick of her turquoise tail feathers encompassed by the clutches of her white wings.

'I'm so sorry! I'm so sorry!' she cried out as Onnar called her down. Aggi was inconsolable. 'I tried! They held him down! I couldn't, I couldn't get to him!'

Onnar saw the blood now; within the black of the Collector's down deep lacerations wept. Onnar had to steady her heart, she felt everything slipping from under her. She embraced Aggi and held her until the quaking subsided. 'It's okay my dear, its okay. We will get him back.'

*

The night was long and dark. The rain never ceased, and they huddled together under a pile of wooden boards. In the morning, Onnar sought out lichens to make a healing paste. It was a long search, yet she spied a garden to feed in and places to forage for insects for Aggi. The feathered refused to eat, but allowed Onnar to tend her cuts. They were soon ready to leave the shelter, and head back towards the roof.

The Morwih would not expect them to return, and painfully, Aggi flew up to assure Onnar's safety. Upon the roof they found the stain of her blood, a feather and down from Rune's body. Aggi cried a little and Onnar left her to gather herself. She traced the scent of the Morwih to the edge of the roof, there were many paths, the winding stench of a hundred individuals. It was impossible to perceive that which had taken Rune.

'The Crool, do you know it?' Onnar turned to Aggi, who stared out on to the city and said nothing. The sky was bright yet grey, the storm front echoed in the puddles upon the rooftop. She sighed, hopping towards the Collector. 'We will find him old girl, but I will need your assistance.'

'I do not know this place, but it is in the city, so we must return to the Bazaar and seek its whereabouts.'

The bazaar heaved with trade. The rain had brought many to seek warmth and conversation. Hundreds busied themselves, laughed and skittered about the hall. There were Sqyres bartering seeds and nuts, the frantic din of the Harend announcing the morning news. Aven darted between the lethargic bodies of city Throa. Even feral Caanus sang folk songs of their weary travels to a captive audience. They wore armour made of discarded things, things they could bang and make a racket with.

Onnar and Aggi moved with the crowd until Aggi saw the Nighspyn whose armour Rune had fixed. He seemed perfectly happy with the little Startle's handiwork and they spoke for a while.

'The Crool? I can tell you it is a prison, but I do not know where it is. It is a Wroth place. I believe you will need to seek the Vulpus for directions!' He made his goodbyes and moved off, the hullabaloo of the market deafening Aggi as she sought others to ask.

A Harend upon a banister leaned down, and amongst the clamour asked what she sought. 'You seek the Crool? You know this is a Familial place? The Morwih control it.'

Aggi nodded, 'I do not know anything about it, I know that our friend has been taken there. We must find him.'

The Harend looked gravely at her. 'Is your friend feathered?'

'Yes'

'Then he will be imprisoned there. It is a place for feathered alone.'

Yowri prayer

Emini love giver,
Alauda strength bringer,
Abriac truth sayer
We exalt your names
We seek your forgiving chime

We hope for it in the wind
Listen in the bicker of rain
It is savoured in seed fall
In the amnion of braying birth

Chapter 5

Rune's vision was grazed, distorting the little light that filtered through his encrusted eyes. A multitude of shapes and patterns whirled; he felt sick. He tasted the sweet metallic glut of blood in his mouth once again, and this time it was his own. He thought long and hard, placing himself within his body, feeling each muscle scream. He was all there, he was intact.

He struggled against his atrophic limbs and turned himself over. The sore rip of blood-encrusted down broke him from any remaining fatigue, and he lay, wings splayed, upon the cold floor.

'Get up.' The words were foggy and distant and he ignored them. They returned, this time with a searing jab. He managed to part his eyes enough through the swelling to make out a feathered.

It looked down at him with tired anger. 'Get up.'

Rune stood, limping beside the great feathered.

'Armour.'

Rune cocked his head, 'I am sorry?'

'You will be. Give me your armour.'

Rune was knocked to the ground, and his armour was ripped from him. The feathered tugged at his wing blades, which would not give. When he finally got up, he untethered each piece and gave them to the green brute. It sniffed the air and glided up to a large nesting box.

Around him loomed many shadows, they swayed with a concerning lilt. Once his eyes had adjusted to the light, he saw they were far from the frightful entities he had imagined. They were decrepit, tattered, threadbare feathered, bodies covered in healed cuts, raw skin where once had been plumage, the weary gape of those who had given in. A small balding feathered darted down and with hurried wisp ushered him along.

'What are you doing out here! Come, we must get you to safety, there are many who would have your blood on their beaks.'

Rune traced the four corners of the strange place. He was enclosed. The cold concrete slabs sunk into a slurry of mud and faeces. Flat white objects stacked with rotting seed were pitched in a fouled pond. The waft of urine and decay was rife.

He looked up at a lattice of branches that had been strung from the ceiling. Each was crowded with more lowly characters, each and every one focused on him.

The small feathered pointed with tattered wing at a nesting box amongst a plethora of haphazard dwellings. He urged Rune into flight, which proved sluggish and painful. He manoeuvred with difficulty toward a small round opening.

Once inside, his companion quickly covered the entrance with bedding material. A little light still filtered through.

'How did you find yourself in such a place?' The tiny shaking feathered darted his head robotically. It made Rune nervous. He looked around him, collections of pebbles and seeds. He felt a palpable sadness in him, the little feathered's light grew dim.

Rune collapsed.

*

He slept for a number of turns, pulling himself in and out of a restless fever dream. He saw the face of his father, clear and vivid, and it filled him with remorse. He awoke each time with a sense of longing. The wounds inflicted by the Morwih were filthy, and his tiny body battled infection. He was tended by the little bald feathered who brought food and water for him, and he eventually gathered his strength.

The question was asked again, when he finally felt able to stand.

'I was captured by the Morwih, I don't know how I ended up here. I don't even know where here is!'

'I am afraid you have found yourself in a dreadful place little

Startle. This is the Crool, it is a prison. It is Familial, guarded by the Morwih. Wroth came here once. They brought beautiful feathered from places I have never heard spoken of before. Flock whose colours are like that of the brightest flowers beyond these bars. Those feathered withered and died here, or went mad. We are all that remains; the Wroth left the Crool to the Morwih. They bring feathered here to keep, they collect them for unspeakable things; blood ceremonies, they appease their familiars with our bodies.'

Rune pulled back the torn newspaper and hay from the entrance and looked out on to the internment camp. He saw the miserable spectacle of it all, old feathered huddled in any available corner, anywhere they could secret themselves away. Waterfowl listless in the stagnant pond.

There were others whose curious crests hung sick and flat. This was a place feathered came to die.

A dead place.

Rune thought long and hard. The Morwih were keeping him here until they could determine his importance. It gave him some time. Not a great deal, but enough. He turned to the little feathered. 'What is your name?'

'I am Oclio. And yours?'

'I am Rune, of the Startle. We must escape.'

*

The days ebbed as Rune learnt the rhythm of the Crool. Every few turns the Morwih would awkwardly bat a scoop towards the cage and spill seeds and grain through the bars. There was never enough.

The seed bags in a nearby outbuilding were cumbersome and impossible to move, making it difficult for the Morwih to offer the meagre pickings into the cage. Even so, they made the smallest of effort to ensure their livestock survived. To the Morwih this was only prolonging the inevitable; they had industrialised their sacrifices, catching feathered and bringing them to this diseased prison. The exotic feathered were saved for the Familial alone, Fraubela and her entourage, their innards only revealed to the most esteemed of the Morwih familiars.

It was no secret to the prisoners what their fate was to be, and only a few remained untouched, those who found sanctuary in burrows hidden under the large sheltered enclosure, or dug holes behind their nesting boxes. Yet as with every prison; there was a hierarchy. The larger flock within the Crool controlled the feeding trough, they alone could turn the fresh water tap. These feathered were rough and hardy, their leader vibrant green.

Rune caught fragments of their proselytising. They spoke with pride of their flock beyond the bars, who they would rejoin, under their great leader. That leader, Anguin, now wore Rune's armour; which was far too small for him, he looked somewhat ridiculous, and yet Rune seethed.

He stood at the entrance to the nesting box, watching the procession of hungry Feathered queue before the stocky bullies. The tap was running; water cascading across the filthy earth towards the pond. The waterfowl shuffled upon the land, their feet marked with infection. They washed themselves as best they could, the same water was drunk by the infirm feathered who had managed to descend from their nervous perches high in the cage.

'I need my armour. It is my father's. I have to get it back.'

'That old brute Anguin rules this roost. If you upset him, well then you and I are likely to starve to death here.'

Oclio sighed heavily and shuffled back to his nest. 'But if you must.'

Rune looked back and frowned. 'I am sorry,' he said.

Oclio nodded. 'I understand you are desperate to leave, but I dare say Anguin has a deal with the guards. Keeps us all in line, and he is rewarded with his continued survival. No one gets out of here, trust me! Many have tried.'

Rune dropped down to the broken paving stones that lay to the east of the pond. The water from the tap flowed into it, and it began to overflow and run out and through the cage. The smell was revolting, and Rune avoided the run off as best he could, keeping an eye on Anguin's lackeys who barked at the milling feathered who waited restlessly for their meal. The leering, ratty feathered stood in groups, bartering the little they had, scraps of grain for insects or broken chunks of cuttlefish bone. In the cold the peeling murals of forests on the wooden walls glared ironically at him, the lattice shadow of the cage cast in perfect allegory.

His feet were wet from the sandy mire that collected upon the cage floor. When the water encroached on Anguin the tap was turned off. Most would now drink from the slurry on the floor. Some grain remained dry and most managed to feed for a while, sating their hunger. Rune reached the head of the queue, his cocky presence yielding a surprised glance from Anguin.

'The little Startle lives. Thought those Morwih had done you good and proper.'

'I am a survivor,' Rune smirked.

'Give it a few more weeks and you'll soon feel differently boy!'

Anguin's cronies laughed with the preening thug, dismissing Rune entirely.

Rune sidled up to him. 'I want my armour back. It was my father's; it means a great deal to me.'

'And with that you guarantee to never get it back! You see Startle, I was once like you. I had hope. I thought to myself, I am strong, I have kin here, and it won't take long for me to get free, so we can return to our own. I was clever, made deals with the Morwih, told them I could keep things in check for them, less hassle. They assured me if I did this, I would be freed.

'That day never came, I was stupid to ever think that a good deed wouldn't go unrewarded. I soon lost any sense of hope. I gained a new perspective. Kill or be killed. So no, this armour is not yours anymore, it is mine.'

Rune felt the urge to fight Anguin for it. The formidable comrades of this feathered told him otherwise. He went to take some seed instead, scooping it up in his claws, and hopped with unwieldy gait towards his new home.

Anguin extended his wing, barring Rune's ascent. 'One clawful, don't be greedy.'

'This is for my friend, Oclio.'

'Then he should have come down himself.'

Rune emptied one clawful and with frustration continued up to the nesting box. He unfurled his claws and poured the contents before Oclio, who began to feed.

'Already eaten?'

Rune nodded. His stomach said otherwise, gurgling loudly.

'Didn't go so well?'

Rune smiled wearily. "It will take a little more persuasion to get it back.'

'You have all the time in the world my friend.'

Oclio nudged a few grains towards Rune and they fed together.

*

Onnar hung low in the shadows cast by the bridge arch. Aggi joined her, 'Any news?' Onnar asked nervously.

'Yes, I know where the prison is, what they call the Crool. It was a Wroth place, a prison for exotic feathered. It is now under Morwih control, they use it for imprisoning feathered for blood sacrifice. It is heavily guarded, and there is no easy way in or out.'

Onnar shook her head. 'We have to get him out of there, and besides the Drove I cannot think of anyone strong enough to employ in such a task. Most of my sisters are far from here. It would take me turns to track them.'

She walked out into the scrubland beyond the arch, the path they had traversed in with Hevridis. She smelt the waft of Morwih piss, and another more acrid stench, one that made its presence known above all. She recognised it. 'There is one option. It's not going to be easy.'

Aggi hopped beside her. 'Whatever it is, we have no other choice, unless we storm the place alone, and I imagine that would end in our untimely demise.'

Onnar agreed. 'We must go to Orn Megol, parley with the Vulpus. We have the benefit of information, we know a little of their enemy's plans, perhaps they will listen.'

'Orn Megol? How is that less dangerous? And pray tell, how does a Yoa'a and a Collector approach the conclave of the Vulpus clans without being stripped of our skin and bones?'

*

Aggi flew north, beyond a series of water treatment plants, terrain that stood idol, futilely awaiting those who once toiled there. The inclinations of seedlings and new shoots changed, reached roots upon sacred earth, cracked tarmac with their strong limbs, found new places to bathe in light.

Upon the ground Onnar watched her companion, her curious wing signals still opaque. Onnar smiled as Aggi jarred and jammed the sky and hollered to her, having not explained any of these intimations to her beforehand.

They travelled on, Onnar wading rivers and streams, avoiding the columns of Wroth who left the city on foot. They skirted the edges of quarantine encampments, the cries of the sick, the protective outfits, the cordons and military as incomprehensible as Aggi's sign language.

They took advantage of wide coppices of trees within parkland. Here they found shelter and exchange stories with the many creatures who lived there. They sang songs with the huge hooting flock whose migratory patterns had altered as the weather threatened, its behaviour mysterious, warm skies in the colder months, fruit maturing and spoiling too early. They spoke of their destinations beyond wide seas, lands consisting of ice, of swathes of mud, forests that seemed to swallow all with virescent beauty. They said there were more cities there, and those too showed signs of the sickness.

*

Upon the highest point of the land hung the edifice of a once proud music hall. It overlooked the city, which bowed with faint entreaty, the voices of the many thousands of guests who had once graced its opulent bowels, forever silent. Its foundations stood on old stone, the peak of the elevation chiseled flat a century or more before. Yet the underpinning had not penetrated deep into the rock, within which dwelt old eyes.

Beneath, the earth was riven with caverns, cavities controlled by subterranean occupants who held to an immemorial deed. The Vulpus did not accept those who lay claim above. They toiled in the dark, and had done so for millennia, surreptitiously holding court over the city, making decrees to refute the terrible hand of the Wroth, honed armour of glass and metal, and vowed revenge. For this particular earth had sheltered clans of differing creeds long before the use of brick and mortar. Then the sickness came, and dark prayers seemed to have been answered.

Wide green terraces tapered to the music hall atop its peak. Ora shone amidst a crisp wind, which shook the lush grass in revelling crowds, capturing the sun's rapture across each stem.

Onnar stood and watched as the clouds rolled enthusiastically, catching that same light; it blistered behind each pall, projecting an effusive radiance across the land. She could smell the rain that would follow, there was much energy here, presenting itself in broad curtains. She lifted her ears and felt the tug of the wind on her whiskers, and Aggi descended, following her line of sight towards the great dark dwelling above.

They approached with caution. They could smell the Host upon the land. Its odour held a forbidding enamour, a warning to those who might wander haplessly here.

They walked up the embankment towards the music hall, its countenance reticent against the bleached sky. Yet their goal was not the building itself, but the ground beneath, and they followed the black railing that ran beside the perimeter, long weathered, its rust bled beneath layers of paint, to the dereliction behind, hidden in its shadow.

Service ports and doors hung wide, revealing a lost bounty, the wind catching in their slack jaws. A layer of leaf litter lightening her footing, Onnar trod with care not to slide. Down they went, the road carved into the rock, leaving the bare stone exposed on the right, rising up beside them. At the base, a loading bay. It was here, beyond the wiry shrubbery, that many entrances hid.

Aggi perched upon a tree branch as Onnar searched the dead brush, she sniffed the air; the warm pungency led her, placing her own paw within the stride of another.

'Vulpus,' she said and Aggi descended, tracing the shape of the mud print.

'This is an old place,' Onnar spoke in whispers. 'This hill is riddled with tunnels, dead ends and follies. It is a maze, designed to protect that which dwells within. The entrances offer themselves to the world; all but one are false.'

Onnar eyed the undergrowth for the onlookers. Eyes peered back. She sat upright as two Vulpus guards emerged silken from the dense thicket. They fanned out, their Byzantine armour hammered into platelets that lay across graceful fur. They said nothing, yet they sized her up, exposing every facet of her. Finally, they spoke in hushed tones.

'Drove.'

Onnar bowed, 'Ora bring peace. We come to meet with the Vulpus about important matters.' One guard gestured to the other to seek guidance, the remaining Vulpus held her in its inescapable glare.

After some time the Vulpus comrade returned, and they moved off, yelping to Onnar and Aggi to follow. They cut a path that snaked amongst the haggard briar, half dug burrows that courted dead ends, until finally they approached a wide opening. Soil clung shallow to the rock, in places the grey brown sandstone exposed. The Vulpus entered without a word, and the friends followed.

There was a presence here, the stone held itself with Paleozoic wisdom, each hewn tunnel dug by water and worn smooth with the stride of ancient beasts who had made use of these natural corridors. The Wroth had not stepped here, leaving the earth to heal its many septic cuts, and like the Throa, in the polished wake of those eroded walls, the Vulpus clans had left their mark.

As they descended Aggi studied the arcane carvings that evoked the same scrawl she had seen upon the cave of the Settling Stone which had bought them to the city. Some seemed just as old, just as foreboding.

Down they went, past chasm drops unseen by careless wanderers, through hidden entrances that seemed solid walls, until finally the passages opened to a grand complex of carven rooms and vistas, the walls of which held legions of glyphic representations, bones hung from mummified skin, festooned with nuggets of coloured glass and metals, totems to unknown gods.

The Vulpus guards were silent. Between pillars a passage descended further; they ushered the pair onwards, down into the pit of Orn Megol.

Here many Vulpus plotted, pondered their veiled stratagems. They halted their clever eyes and paws to witness the unexpected guests; murmured beneath their beautiful armour.

They continued inwards, here and there light played through complexities of mirrored glass, brought down from the building above, great rooms where the Wroth once danced in curious arabesques, their reflections playing into infinity. Long shattered, they now courted the light from entrances amongst the undergrowth, and decorated the armour of the clans. As the day gave into night the light became ghostly blue. At length Onnar and Aggi reached the apex of their journey.

Giants had shaped this cave system long ago, living gods whose bodies had huddled here, hidden from the predatory Wroth. Their bones became an Ossuary, cleaned and carven with loving words, kind inscriptions, cuts to maintain a connection with what had been. They were erected high, upon the walls of the cavern, and invoked an old order, a reliquary of ancient ideas. The Vulpus lived within the watchful gaze of their deities, the first clans who had left a home for them here.

This assembly hall of the Vulpus clans was cut in a rough diamond shape; the furthest point marked by the great skulls of the Grim, and the far older Rauka; their huge canine teeth prying from the rock, half exposed from fossil tombs. Splayed out either side were legions of bones, lain in ribcage-like patterns. Amongst them tiny shrines, porticos of flowers and teeth. The floor held grooves depicting the order of the clans, and as Onnar and Aggi approached the clan leaders emerged from side passages.

Below the grin of ancient jaws sat an old Vulpus, his armour High Wrought, forming a crest of dangerous cuspates atop his head. He did not move as the pair were corralled towards him.

'My name is Satresan,' he said. 'I am the speaker of this Household. Not often is a mercenary allowed to set foot upon these lands. You hold no loyalties with the cubs of Seyla, yet these days have become unsettled. So we offer you a chance to explain yourselves.'

Onnar held herself with confidence and stepped forward. Aggi tried to feign the same stoicism, yet she felt a vivid terror.

'I mean no disrespect, but I risk my life coming here. I am employed by two feathered; the Collector, Aggi who you see before you, and another, a Startle, the same Startle who took the life of the Gull prince Artioch. He wishes to seek his father, and yet during our search it has come to my attention that this little fellow is perhaps intended for greater things.'

Satresan paused as a younger vixen requested his ear. He turned to her and they conversed. She seemed agitated, saying, 'This Startle goes by the name Rune, son of Grom?'

'Yes.'

'He is of some significance. We have charged a feral Morwih with aiding his journey. You have encountered such a creature?'

'Hevridis. You underestimated him. He sought repatriation with his kin, and so he used Rune as an offering to his leader. Rune is now held against his will in a prison, lauded over by the Morwih.'

Vorsa was visibly angered, 'If this is true this is on my head, this was my fault.'

Satresan tempered her frustration, 'We all agreed to his

involvement. We gained much from him despite his best efforts to shield the Morwih's plans. We were not completely ignorant of his intentions.'

'But I trusted him. Even a little was enough.'

Onnar interjected, 'Why did you not shadow him yourself?'

Vorsa sighed. 'Rune has a gift, much like his father, he is Umbra. I am a Corpse Speaker. Without knowing the strength of his second sight it was too risky to place me close to him. He would have seen my intentions too readily, and even if they were shrouded, he would never trust me.'

Onnar frowned, 'You have ill intentions?'

'No! Not at all. We wish to kindle Rune's abilities; in fact he is vital to our own plans. Without Rune we have no conduit. It cannot have escaped your attention that much is at stake, there is so much chaos in Naa, the Wroth are letting go of the city, and in this moment we find ourselves at a turning point.

'The Vulpus stake claim to this land, yet we must invoke the Foul Meridian, which guarantees our dominion over the Stinking City. There are so many facets, so many opportunities for error. My people and the Corva Anx know only the Gasp, the periphery of the Umbra, we cannot see the heart of it, and for us to enact certain spells, we need to speak with that heart. We need Rune. It is within him that the conduit to the Umbra dwells.'

'He will not be harmed?' Aggi joined Onnar, 'Rune is a brave and strong Startle, he is wise beyond his years.'

'No, in fact, if he seeks his father, then it is perhaps all the more necessary to your cause.' Vorsa replied.

'He is held in a prison you say? There are many prisons within the city ruled by the Wroth, prisons where our living gods are bound, declawed and dethroned. It is our role as guardian of the city to ensure they are not abandoned, that they are freed come the Foul Meridian.'

'I do not know these god prisons, yet most of the city is still unknown to me. Rune is held at a place called the Crool.' Onnar replied.

Vorsa nodded, 'I know it.' She yelped at the guards that now encircled them. 'The Morwih hold sway over the lands upon which the Crool sits. We will go to this prison and free him. It will not be easy. It is a sacred place to the Morwih. We should expect a great deal of resistance.'

*

The morning brought with it rain, and the Crool came alive. The filthy feathered descended to the ground and washed themselves. Blocked gutters above the gulag spilt clean streams of water down upon the ground, the pond began to overflow, first diluting and finally driving the putrid water out. The earth was cleansed of the covering of droppings, and for a while there was an air of tranquility. Rune watched his nemesis, Anguin, who had allowed the feathered to bathe, for even he could not ignore the stench of decay.

Oclio was unwell. He could not stop himself from scratching, leaving his skin red raw. He had plucked much of his body clean of down, which Rune found upsetting, and he could not understand why he had done this. Rune searched the prison for the lichens that Onnar had made her healing paste from, and found enough clinging to the damp woodwork to offer Oclio a little respite.

They sat together and discussed the world beyond the cage, and this seemed to lighten his friend's mood. Rune studied the marks upon the walls of the nesting box, and asked Oclio about them.

'Did you make these?' He asked as Oclio applied the paste. 'Some, yes, some were here long before me. These are old words, much of it I do not understand. The feathered hold many languages!'

Rune ran his flight feathers over the scratches, he saw reminiscences, similarities with his own people's words. 'Can you tell me what any of them mean?'

Oclio paused, struggled up onto old legs and peered at the scrawl. 'Yes, yes, some of it is legible. These markings …' he pointed at grand cuts laboured and deep, coloured with blood. 'These were lain down by the same flock that Anguin heralds from. They were brought to these lands by the Wroth. They escaped and established flocks within the city. These markings symbolise their original home. They came from a place with mountains. Long ago it seems. They make these marks to maintain their memories. Some of us only live short lives, so we must save these words for our children.'

Rune nodded, 'I recognise the Startle in these markings. Maybe not our words, but some shapes and forms.'

Oclio pondered this, 'Perhaps this is a way to entreaty Anguin, to offer him something more than a fight. He is proud, angry, but there is perhaps something deeper within him you can parley with.'

The rain died as the day continued and Ora offered the ground its warmth. Soon the puddles were all but damp patches and the prison felt refreshed.

The presence of Morwih could never be ignored, they paced the cage roof, swaggered about the path that flanked the Crool. Above Rune a black mass slinked across the wire, sinking with each heavy step. Rune hoped it would lose its footing, perhaps ensnare itself in the wire. No such luck befell the feline.

*

The day came when the slave masters delivered new blood. The heavy broken corner of the main gate was pushed open by a Morwih guard. The wooden frame had cracked at the base but was held in place by chicken wire mesh. The new inmate was clasped in the Morwih's jaws. The guard let the body slump upon the floor and whispered some unspeakable incantation, informing the prisoner of the fruitlessness of escape, before turning and leaving the way it came. Rune took to wing, dropping down to offer the tiny form a little reassurance.

As he approached the cowering body, Anguin was already upon him. Rune scowled as he circled the little feathered; it tried to stand, yet its leg was badly sprained.

'It's ok little one,' Rune said as he approached.

Anguin smiled. 'This is not your place Startle, go back to your nesting box. There is procedure here, you are not needed.'

'I wish to help,' Rune spat back. He helped the tiny Aven to its feet, allowing it to rest its weight upon him. Anguin sidled up and pushed them both to the ground. Rune sneered, 'You have spent too much time in the company of the Morwih, you even act like them!'

'How dare you!' Anguin raged, pushing Rune away from his ward. 'There is no family here, no flock to back up your little outbursts. You are all alone, that diseased old fleck Oclio is all you have!'

'Has it been so long since you knew the warmth of kin, Anguin?' Rune retorted.

'What do you mean?' Anguin paused. He backed away, seeking the brawn of the ragtag flock who made up the Crool's wardens.

Rune saw the desire for something more within that bitter old face.

'You wear my father's armour. It holds within it a history, a story of love, the love shared between my grandfather and my father, and myself. I can read each nick, each mark. It is as much me as my own feathers. It reminds me of the weight I carry. Do you not feel the nag of your own past, your own loves and wants and desires? Or is that all lost in this filthy place? Is this place worth more than the price of what you once had? You brag about your flock, but at this rate you will die here never knowing their love.'

Rune saw that Anguin was moved, yet he shrugged his emotion off and turned away.

'Do you remember the stories of your home? Where your flock once nested? In a land far from here. Do you remember your family telling you of such a place, where the air tasted different, where the world was free of all of this?'

Anguin sighed and swung his head to meet Rune's gaze. 'I remember stories, but what good are stories?'

'It's all we are, we are made up of stories, of sad times, or happy times, stories which are painful and meaningful. We cannot write stories in here. We can only remember those which were written before. You took one of my stories from me, one that is unfinished. I can only complete it by leaving this place. I must have it back.'

For a moment something resembling a concession passed before Anguin's eyes. He shook his head. He found resilience in the familiarity of the dull grey stone beneath his feet. He reminded himself of the futility of want. 'Your whimsical tales offer me nothing. No one gets out. You will die here with me.'

Rune felt his temper get the better of him, and before he could quell it he was flitting towards the great oaf, upon Anguin, confronting him.

Anguin halted his advances with little effort. Rune pushed back. Again Anguin held Rune at wing's length, yet Rune pushed back once more. He could see the stress upon the frail straps that held his armour in place upon his adversary. They strained against the broad chest, would soon break, soon be useless.

'You've lost all here Startle, you have nothing here!'

'I have my armour.'

'You have nothing!'

Rune screeched and lunged again at the great feathered, only to be knocked back. He screamed at him, 'Give me my armour!'

Anguin staggered in shock. Rune felt his strength, the swaying cursive of lights flourished and he saw echoes of possibilities, intentions and causes flicker and smoulder. Each stabbing jab he avoided, remembering every morning he had flown with his family above the Pinnacle, every turn and trick, every undulation, every foreordained divergence; there was a prism here, a refraction of paths, and he whirled above Anguin with eloquent ferocity.

He made his strike. His beak barely pierced the flesh of Anguin's neck, yet Rune held him firm. 'I ask again: give me my armour.'

Their eyes met, submerged in livid rage. They saw death in the glimmer of one another's cornea. Rune pushed his beak further into Anguin's neck. Anguin traced the oily purples and greens that perfused his down, sharp and fetid with pain. He saw beyond it all, saw the same strength he once saw in another Startle.

'Grom?'

The word hung between them and seemed to jar their vitriol. Rune felt his grip loosen and he fell back.

'Grom? Grom was ... Grom is my father.'

The great green feathered withdrew. 'You are his son? I, I did not know. I ...'

Anguin hesitated, fell back on himself and then took to wing, swooping up to his nesting box far above the yard. Rune sat perplexed upon the floor. He looked around for guidance and was greeted by the wounded Aven who seemed as confused as Rune.

'Welcome, friend.'

The Aven attempted a smile.

*

Oclio joined Rune in helping the newcomer up, guiding him away from the open, to a quiet corner where a few feathered huddled in the shafts of sunlight that challenged the cage bars. Here the Aven collected itself, shook the fear from its feathers and asked many questions.

Oclio explained the various details of the Crool whilst Rune considered his next move. Anguin had known his father, and appeared to hold Grom in high regard.

Rune slept well that night and settled on confronting the warden upon daybreak, when food and water were supplied. He readied himself, found a little courage, and both he and his new friend, along with Oclio flew down to the courtyard, where the many starving feathered waited in silent swaying queues. Anguin was nowhere to be seen.

Rune tried to find him amongst the rabble, yet the tap was held by a small stocky white feathered, one of Anguin's lackeys. Prowling Morwih spilled the seed haphazardly through the wire, and feathered nervously plucked at the morsels.

Rune hopped towards the guard, who immediately stood to attention, adopting an air of authority that sat awkwardly on its dishevelled face.

'Get back in line!' It cawed.

Rune ignored him, 'Where is Anguin?'

The feathered sneered, 'He has no time for you, get back in line or I'll do you in!'

Rune scoffed and took flight, circling the length and breadth of the prison camp. He saw no sign of the great green beast, and settled beside Anguin's nesting box. A small peg jutted beneath the entrance. Rune looked in, his eyes adjusting to the gloom. Within, a little light broke through circular windows, casting a dull orange upon the contours of a single feathered, listless, it sighed heavily, aware of Rune's presence.

'I understand,' Rune said, 'it takes very little to forget the world when you are not allowed to see it.' Cautiously, he stepped in. 'How long have you been here?'

Anguin shook his head. 'Too long. I am a fool.'

He gestured towards the far corner, where Rune's armour lay. Rune skirted the walls until he stood before it. He tugged at it, noticing infinitesimal repair work upon its joins. He attached his wing blades and breastplate and helmet, feeling each smooth surface lie flush with his body.

'You knew my father?'

Anguin turned and a half smile of nostalgia emerged in his eyes. 'Yes, he was a guest of my master. We were taught together for a time, I learned much from him, of other flock, of his gift. He spoke of you a great deal. I assumed he had lost you, and your mother?'

'Yes. My father was broken by my mother's death, and I think he went out into the world to find some kind of answer to his sadness.'

Anguin nodded, 'He learned Wroth tongue so that he might understand their ways, their sciences. My master has quite profound learning, spoke with the Wroth at length, even knew their hieroglyphs, could read their markings. He deciphered many things for your father, together they perhaps found those answers.'

Rune shuddered, 'Does my father still work with your master?'

Anguin shook his head. 'I left my flock on a scouting mission, I was caught by the Morwih whilst I rested. So pitiful. That was a long time ago. I do not know if he is still with Erithacus.'

'Erithacus! This is the wise feathered I seek!' Rune laughed, 'that makes you a Speaker, one of the Wroth-tongued?'

Rune stood bemused as Anguin chuckled, emitting a series of odd croaks. 'I just said good day to you in Wroth tongue, I am a little rusty. I have shielded my ability to speak in that woeful speech from the Morwih. I would be far too useful to them if they were to know. They would exploit me. The Speakers adhere to a strict code of conduct. If we are ever caught, we must never speak Wroth, even if threatened with death.'

Rune's eyes had adjusted to the light enough to make out more of the space before him. Piles of seed lay about and some appeared rotten. Yet beyond the squalor were walls festooned with markings, images and glyphs similar to those upon the walls of Oclio's nesting box. Though here they were vibrant, worked over and over again, some fitful and angry, some beautiful and intricate, picked and cut and chewed to reveal memories and ideologies. 'You made the marks upon Oclio's walls?'

'Yes. When I first came here, there were other wardens, violent miserable brutes. I hauled up in the furthest empty space and I hid there for days. Yet it didn't take long for me to realise I held the upper hand. I was intelligent. I made deals, found a way to mark my rivals as the perfect subjects for the Morwih's blood sacrifice.

'I wasn't proud of what I did to survive here, but survive I did. I took their place, inherited all their terrible traits. Became just as bad, if not worse. It took a little cocksure Startle to remind me of what I had become.'

Rune studied the markings. Luminescent strands swam before his eyes. Confused, he blinked to rid himself of them. He traced echoes that seemed to tether themselves to the emblems left by Anguin. 'These marks, I recognise some of them, they look a little like Startle marks.'

'That's true. There is a connection between the languages. All languages have a root, they all stem from the source. Erithacus teaches us that once there was a way to understand each and every language, that it would take very little to understand even the most alien tongue. Yet we lost this gift in our vanity, in our striving to make our voice the loudest, to make our mark. Wherever we go, we leave our mark.' Anguin turned to appreciate his works. 'It took us a very long time to form Ocquia, to understand each other again.'

He turned back to Rune, 'Long ago Erithacus found the roots of the first tongue. He called it the song, he said he could feel it in the silence between words, that between all languages there was a vibration, a resonance.

'Through the Speakers, he appealed to the heads of the many flocks and pleaded with them to listen. They were frightened by him, by his knowledge, by his words. He became infamous, he became an enigma. In his frustration he hid himself away and shaped the world around him in his own image.

'He gave the Speakers their voice, we became his limbs, and we acted out his wishes. He taught us the words of the flocks, he showed us the nuances and subtleties of the hieroglyphs of many species, asked us to seek the unifying patterns within them. We gained an almost obsessive urge to solve the puzzle, to find that which had eluded Erithacus.'

'Did you find them?'

'No. It is true that there is a quality to the scrawl of all the flocks, to many ground dwellers, an oblivious sharing of the arches and rises and stabs and breaks of the imagery and tongues of differing species. The older the markings, the more they resemble one another. Yet we lacked the wherewithal to see what Erithacus could. I sometimes wonder if perhaps his vision was true, or simply wishful thinking.'

'Yet you make these markings?' Rune frowned.

'I find solace in it. It reminds me that I still breathe, that I exist. Others will come here after I am gone and they will know a mind made these murals, that someone was here.'

'Careful,' Rune replied, 'you sound like you've given up entirely.'

Anguin smiled. 'You are wise beyond your years, little Startle. Perhaps you are right, perhaps I have given up.'

Rune spread his wings wide, 'All of this, this is not for nothing. We will escape, and you will take me to Erithacus.'

*

Oclio was noticeably perturbed as Anguin pushed himself through the tiny opening of his former dwelling. 'Either this nest has shrunk or I have grown somewhat since I arrived.'

'Grown fat.' Oclio coughed.

Anguin went to chastise him, then thought better of it. 'I deserve that. I come in peace. Your friend here wishes me to speak with you, he believes there is a way to escape this place.'

Oclio sighed, 'I'm afraid Rune has a rather awful case of optimism. I am not sure there is a way to leave alive. The only way I could fathom it is offering yourself as sacrifice.'

Rune smiled.

Chapter 6

The Starless Vulpus stood at the peak of the loading bay. Against a sky brimming with celestial forms their silhouettes were dark hollows, as though they consumed the light itself. Only their eyes determined their position.

Onnar was both perturbed and fascinated by their presence. So rarely born, the Starless had become little more than folktales. Yet here stood six, their stare fixed upon her.

She shuddered.

Her mother had told her of this peculiar pack. The legend spoke of how the Vulpus and Corva became entwined; that the Corva sought truths in the Orata, believing it to contain knowledge of the Gasp. Through their attempts to cleave those secrets from it, they became ingratiated with Vulpus society. Above all, the Corva wished to know that which lurked beyond life, that somewhere within Naa there was a tangible facet of the Gasp, something they could reach out to and touch that did not rely on vague interpretations of fallen bones and sticks. Within the Orata, they found reference to such a place, deep below the ground.

They sent the Vulpus into those caverns beneath the earth, engaged them in difficult and treacherous excavations of old Wroth mines. There the Vulpus found the Aged Grave, the Oscelan.

It was so deep that the Corva were unable to venture there themselves, and in their desperation they taught the Vulpus how to corpse speak; to commune with the dead. The first of the Vulpus Corpse Speakers had gone into the Oscelan to seek the spirits that dwelled in the coal itself. It was with these frightening souls that a trade was made, a trade that the Vulpus did not fully honour.

The ghosts had dwelt in the ground for so long that they had forgotten the sight of animated flesh, and once they glimpsed it, so rich with life, they craved it, and fell in love with it. They pleaded with the Vulpus to let them live within them, to inhabit their flesh, to know the world through living eyes. At first the young Vulpus agreed. Yet the pain of possession was unbearable, and the seal was broken. The Vulpus fled the tunnels, refusing to ever enter the earth again.

Still the incomplete task left its mark upon those Corpse Speakers; not only were they imbued with strange knowledge, they emerged from the earth with coats the colour of coal, their eyes shone under the glare of an unseen place, wreathed in the lightlessness of the Gasp. For they had made a pact with the dead, that would not go unfulfilled.

Their communion with the dead, however brief, cursed their descendants. Children born of these Vulpus did not often carry their forebears spectral gift, yet very rarely a cub would be born of the night. They became known as the *Eroua Oaza Vas;* Starless Vulpus, forever hounded by the voices of the dead, forever entwined with the Oscelan. They swore to never venture below ground again, and to never learn the language of the Gasp, for the nagging want of the Oscelan was endless.

'They say that witchery is written into their blood.' Aggi said quietly as she hopped beside Onnar. They watched Vorsa greet the Starless Vulpus, her voice hushed. She seemed to give them a command, and with that they were gone, bounding out beyond the disused playgrounds, down towards the parklands that hugged the city's edge.

Onnar called to her as she returned. 'Are they allied to your clan?'

Vorsa looked to the disappearing lope of the blackened cubs. 'The Starless live by their own creed, bound to the word of the Corva. They are the eyes of that flock, but they are Vulpus all the same, and we want for the same things.'

They were soon joined by the quiet rush of lustrous bodies, the clack of glass and metal enveloped them as the Vulpus Clans of Acrathax and Morvil, the Skulks of Vamish and Fraurora converged atop the terrace of the music hall, the vixens cackling the Orata, blessing their own stride.

Aggi grinned, 'This bodes well.'

Onnar agreed.'Yes, we will find Rune and bring him to his father, if he still lives.'

Aggi took to wing and Onnar followed the step of the Vulpus clans, descending the steep slope into the undergrowth below. She was soon running at a quick pace, beside the many cubs of Seyla, their considered lope mesmerising. She ran with flesh feeders, yet as the red river arched south, towards Morwih lands, towards the cage of the Crool, she felt safe.

Aggi looked down upon her friend, keeping a watchful eye on her, on those who would undo her if the thought arose. She felt a sense of solitude in her cause, beyond her own desires, to know of Erithacus, to further her own understanding of her place within the loose orders of the Collector flocks.

Was it simply a desire to belong? And what would she belong to? She let these ideas simmer, thinking back to her childhood. She had shunned the desire to find a mate, had found herself frustrated by the bewildering behaviour of her kin. The Collectors shared vague cultural ties to the Corva Clade, long ago perhaps those associations bore more than the teasing and name calling she received as a chick, when her own mannerisms were often compared to the bizarre enunciations of the Anx.

Aggi shook her head as the memories taunted her. Yet she had found sanctuary in the company of Rune and Onnar. She smiled as this epiphany took root and saddened her at the loss of the little Startle.

But he would be found. They were all outcasts, unwanted. Not for their faults, but for their distinctiveness. She dropped down, following the topography, the prevailing wind drawn close, animating the trees and grass with brusk tugs. Seyla loomed with tantrum glow; quarrels of cloud played peekaboo with the landscape, light shone and withdrew with excited timbre, the night exhilarated.

They pushed on, towards the city centre, the familiar carpet of stone and sheered shrubbery announcing the delineations of Wroth land. It was also by default Vulpus territory, and fluently the ragged iterations of the packs wove onwards into separate threads, their footing wide on all converging paths that led towards the Crool. Onnar stayed with Acrathax, and the Corpse Speaker Vorsa, hurtling along empty streets, under footbridges and deserted alleys, the hiss and whine of idle Morwih guards, their bodies frigid upon fences and garage roofs. The younger Vulpus pranced and rolled, seeking out these onlookers like wild currents in the stream; vital, cunning forms of teeth and red fur and metal which intoxicated Onnar.

A dense accumulation of nineteenth century terraces and gaudy supermarkets parted to reveal the dark of the walled park. Such areas within the city were sparse, yet popular haunts for all life, drawn by the lack of monotonous noise and stone, the presence of soft grass and the shade of trees, tempting to enemy and friend. Yet they were often folly to seek; with little place to hide, many found themselves dangerously exposed.

Morwih were not known to venture in such places, so it was not so strange that their occupation of the park had gone largely unnoticed by the Vulpus. The packs appeared one by one, and some had already fought. Blood streaks grazed potent faces. Vorsa conducted the rabble before her. Scouting Vulpus appeared from various entrances within the manicured bushes. They skipped towards Vorsa.

'What have you discovered?'

The leader of the pack came forth, 'The Crool is found within this curious arrangement of undergrowth. The paths are marked with tall dense thicket, which limits our ability to see the enemy. The hedgerows have staggered openings, no straight cut through, each path is guarded. There are many Morwih, the structures of glass to the north offer a dry space where they rest in shifts.

The Crool itself is a series of dwellings held together within an impenetrable lattice of metal. Yet we believe there is a way in. I advise that the clans disperse and encircle the prison, a formidable force might simply drive the Morwih away.'

Vorsa contemplated this. 'Clans, enclose the edges of these bushes, eyes wide, know the enemy lies within.'

Aggi interjected. 'Let me fly high, Seyla is bright and I may see the path clearly above these hedges, I can direct you.'

Vorsa nodded, 'That is a good plan, fly Collector!'

From above Aggi saw the concentric hedges, at the centre a neglected public aviary, to the north a large greenhouse mouldering, its panes stained with mildew. There was a gravel path that ran around the complex. Each entrance in the ringed hedges did not sit flush, there was no clear path through, and a number of Morwih stalked each space between the rows. It was a labyrinth, not unlike that of Orn Megol.

She flew back down to Vorsa, 'I see the path, I will caw once for left, twice for right and thrice for enter.'

She launched herself up beyond the damp asphalt paths that led to the maze. She could see the various clans prowling low. Vorsa entered. Aggi made her indicating caws and soon Vorsa saw the first Morwih. It moved away from her, its calm gait signifying they had gone unnoticed. She pounced high, as though seizing prey, colliding with the enemy.

Pain stricken, the Morwih rolled aside, and Vorsa swiped at its face, knocking it back against the ground. She launched her slathering jaws at its throat and dispatched it before it could issue a single yowl.

Vorsa steadied herself as her infantry overtook her, the damp rush of red fur incensed with a guided fury. She leapt on, beside her forces, to the next ring, Aggi's distant cries determining each move.

Within the forth ring stood two large Morwih. They held themselves strong and robust, their movements slow, considered. From the adjacent entrance the Vulpus cascaded like phantoms before the unprepared foe, eyes yellow-white like flames, faces low.

The Morwih pulled back against one another. The largest of the pair uttered, 'Now now, we don't want any trouble,'

*

Oclio stood beside the entrance to the cage. There were Morwih on the adjacent glass roof, disinterested in him entirely. Rune, Anguin and the little Aven sat upon a branch above him. He looked to them for motivation, they all nodded for him to begin.

'Morwih! I wish to offer myself as sacrifice!'

The feline guards ignored him. They barely moved. He looked up at Rune, who gestured to try again.

'I wish to be eaten! Take me! I am not for this life any longer!'

This time, the closest Morwih raised her head. She looked at the strange pink feathered upon the floor. Curious, she got up, stretched and slinked down to the door. By now the Morwih guard atop the cage had been drawn to the commotion.

'I wish to be eaten!' Oclio squawked, his obvious lack of enthusiasm did not register in the hungry minds of his guards.

'You wish to be eaten? Are you ill?' The larger of the two asked.

'He doesn't look very well it must be said,' The other replied. She cared little, and pushed against the door. She was now half in the cage, the broken corner of the door lying flat upon her back. Oclio was within reaching distance. He had not realised.

He even hopped closer.

Rune took to wing and landed beside Oclio. 'I wish to be eaten too! Take me first please!'

The first Morwih was perplexed, never had such an event occurred. She looked back at the larger feline, who nodded, 'Well, we shall both eat this night!'

Anguin launched himself down and landed before both feathered. 'You don't want to eat them! You want to eat me!'

Finally, this roused suspicion. 'This is a conspiracy, or our stock is sick like the Wroth. Perhaps we should just kill them!' With that the beast launched forward and latched itself onto Rune, dragging him towards her eager mouth. With a renewed sense of purpose, the Aven darted down to the hubbub.

Rune felt the claws within him, excruciating movements as the Morwih enjoyed the rubbery squeal of each barb under flesh. Rune screamed out, his eyes lulling into pins of blindness, amongst the debris of his life he saw the little Aven upon the Morwih, attempting to free him. The Morwih turned to leave, the corner of the door still propped upon its back.

Anguin was now mere inches from the cage door, still held wide upon the rump of the Morwih before him. He had little chance, little sense of a plan, but knew as soon as the Morwih moved forward the broken corner of the gate would swing shut. His fellow wardens looked on confused as he came within their line of sight, between Rune and the door. 'Anguin? What ails you?'

He heard the words, knew if he left it any longer his fragile alliance with these other feathered would fail. Even if his cronies agreed to help him, it was too late to test their loyalty. The Morwih began to move. It was now or never. He bolted towards the exit, colliding face on with the feline's hind legs, the shock sending it bolting. He felt the tear of the bare wire against his back as the broken fencing fell hard behind him.

He was outside.

He was outside!

The Morwih turned to see the perturbed Speaker. It immediately hastened towards him, claws borne; yet before it could reach him, Anguin came to his senses and took wing. He was soon above the sadistic throttle below, and he laughed to feel his weight upon his wings; he was out of shape, yet the pain was almost enjoyable as each muscle strained and surrendered to his will.

He didn't even see the Morwih above him, perched upon the roof, only the sensation of being torn from the sky. He rolled tight as the razor paws enclosed him. He pulled against them, smelled the vile stench of the Morwih's breath as jaws bit down, gnawing at him, the hot wet malaise of his own blood upon him.

But he was Speaker. He bit back. He fought hard with his own weapons, his own claws and beak found purchase, he buried his face in the crook of the Morwih's neck, and as the whirlwind of gracile blows winded and wound about him each cuspid clench and rend of flesh was met with equal ferocity. He pulled himself down, the Morwih losing him, as he clung to the edge of the roof and looked out on to the chaos below. Rune was slumped against the earth, the tiny Aven quite dead in the jaws of the Morwih, who now fed with no remorse, tearing the innocent's body apart.

'No! No no no!'

He was pulled back into the mortal embrace of the Morwih, who wished to sate his own lust.

'No!' he screamed and pulled away, his tail feathers searing as the Morwih tugged them, until his grip failed and he tumbled back towards fur and fang. His limbs shouted, his mind burned with venom, yet his eyes congealed over with insensible blood.

Black.

His life was leaving him.

Down, down down down.

Silence.

The tug was dull and meaningless, but it was followed by stillness.

'Speaker?'

The voice was sharp. Anguin felt a rough yet not unpleasant sensation about his face. Once, and then once again. It was wet, strange, but soon he could see.

The great beast before him stared with concern. It was licking his face free of blood. Before he could register his fear, the beast spoke.

'I am Rorredi of Clan Fraurora. We have come to free you.'

'Too late my friend!'

*

Onnar was not far behind Vorsa as she entered the centre of the maze, before her a maelstrom of warring shapes; the Morwih pouring forth to defend their killing floor. She arched across the gravel, skidding as she gained ground with the vixen leader, the many Morwih backed up against the entrance to the great cage.

The largest foe held a dark mass in its mouth. The mass began to fit, catching the glare of Seyla on familiar armour.

It was Rune. The bastard had Rune.

The Morwih eyed them both, a glimmer of satisfaction upon its face. It dropped Rune, holding him down.

'If you try to take him, all of this will be for nothing, I assure you,' It said. It was Familial, high in the loose echelons of the Fractured Sects.

Onnar did not recognise him from the cavalcade of leonine presences they had encountered upon the church roof. This was perhaps the governor of this encampment, who spent his days laying in the warmth of the greenhouse. Onnar relaxed and placed her paw on Vorsa, who said, 'How is this resolved Morwih?'

'You leave, the Startle lives. You stay, he dies.'

Vorsa glanced at Onnar, then back to the Morwih. 'Kill him.'

The Morwih reeled. 'You would give in so easily?'

'It is not a question of giving in. There is no barter here. Our choices were to rescue him, and if we failed, to ensure you do not benefit from his gifts. Your ultimatum is empty. If you kill him, our job is done. You lose the one thing that might sway this war, and we continue along the path to complete the Foul Meridian.'

The Morwih wrestled with these opposing ideas, that the feathered between his claws was valued by his superiors, yet he had no other leverage to guarantee his escape.

Either way he would die.

The Morwih loosened his grip. He stammered, 'I surrender.'

'They are playing you, you fool!' – The cry came from above. The slink of Hevridis was unmistakable. He loped on to the lower roof of the grain shed and smiled, but with little humour.

'They need this Startle, he is intrinsic to their plans, that's why I brought him to Fraubela. They have no desire for you to kill him, they are trying to confuse you, you dimwitted fool!'

Vorsa hissed, 'you sneaking worm Hevridis!'

Hevridis laughed, 'Oh Vorsa, I am not sure what is more enjoyable. To know I outwitted the Corpse Speaker, or that I single-handedly thwarted your plans for dominion over this city.

'Either way, the Startle will die tonight and we level this game. Both species have a great deal to lose under one another's rule. I realise now that perhaps killing Rune is the best option.'

Onnar's despair was clear as the Morwih's expression changed from confusion to steadfast determination and he lifted the limp body of Rune back into its jaws. Hevridis smiled assuredly.

'We are done here,' he said. 'Kill the …'

Anguin sprang forth, and the self-satisfied grin upon Hevridis's face was wiped clean as the Morwih was knocked off the roof. Vorsa and Onnar heard the pathetic cry as Hevridis fell awkwardly on to the gravel below.

In the panic which followed Onnar leapt to her feet and was upon the Morwih who held Rune. She kicked hard against his face and Rune fell to the earth, quickly lifted high by Vorsa in her gentle mouth, a wake of gravel shards and dust as she bound away from the maniacal deluge of teeth and limbs and fur behind her, dodging the lone fights, a shower of hot blood and irascible cries. She cut through the fracas, out of the maze, and on to the grass, her flight followed with terror by Aggi, who flew down to aid her.

Onnar bore into the Morwih ranks. Limber, they sprang forth with knifeclaws drawn, their infectious mouths clamping on her, and she whirled around, knocking them back one by one, pounding her forceful legs against ribcages and faces alike. They were many, yet soon she was joined by remorseless Vulpus soldiers, whose glass armour clashed and cut against exposed pelts.

The Morwih were pushed back, until they had no place to go other than the Crool itself. They pawed at the broken corner of the door, shoving passed one another, frantic, desperate, until they were all cowering within the cage. The Vulpus followed with murderous fever, yanking the door free, tearing the rusted chicken wire away from the broken wooden frame. They crept through the gaping hole, provoking a flurry of feathers as waterfowl and many exotic flock bolted for the ruined door, making wide births of the drooling maws. The Morwih backed against the far corner, helpless.

Outside the cage, Vorsa licked at Rune's chest, trying to stimulate breath. His head swung loosely with each lap. 'No! Vorsa cried, 'Please Rune! Please.'

Aggi was upon him too, trying to rouse his little frame, his sallow eyes empty.

*

Rune felt seething cold. It was not a winter's cold, he had known one or two of those. This was devious. It sunk within his down and skin and into the core of him. He struggled to move away from it, tried to find some existential remedy to it.

Wretched, the cold took form, great tempest drapes of smog tore up into dizzying black skies, and Rune knew a very real foreboding, a presence, disembodied feelings that at once asked everything of him, yet warned him to stay away. He could not feel his body, so could not push himself away, could not despite his best efforts make sense of himself, yet with each moment he gained more motion, his form became buoyant, unhindered, and he drifted out towards the clouds of shuddering torment that spanned the grey horizon. He felt the pull of ceaseless voices, they called to him with such sorrow, reached for him, their unseeable limbs beyond the realms of sight. Yet each voice gave him a better understanding of himself, each voice made him more manifest. His wings were barely visible yet they existed, and his will for them to be here with him only encouraged them to seek substance in the darkness.

'NO!'

The voice was a thousand wing beats, battering back the thrall of claws that reached for him. The voice was absent of form entirely, yet it swallowed the sky.

'You are not supposed to be here!'

A face formed before him, brilliant white, hewn of anaemic tumescences. Its eyes absent, black hollows, its stare terrifying. It floated in front of him, gaining clarity. A white Vulpus. It was not alive, he knew this. He could perceive the frigidity of its words, its waxen fur, liquid and transparent.

'Where am I?'

'You are in the Gasp, the Nok Langaen, the Enervation, the Lacking Sea. It has many names, all of which speak of its nature – the place where the dead exist. You lose yourself to it, to them, the many I call family. They do not mean to be cruel, yet so many who do not belong here are drawn before their time. I am Petulan. I am a Revenant. We need to take you back to Naa.'

There was something beyond the flagrant gloom that caught Rune's eye. It felt like it had no place here, impressions of golden-lighted vaults extending beyond the cloud mass: not visible, no more substantial than his own immaterial state, yet growing in volume, he could not ignore the persistence of its willingness to be seen by him.

'Wait!' he cried as the spirit-entity loomed, 'I see something here, something living! Something glorious!'

Petulan directed his eyes back towards the distance. He nodded, 'You see beyond the Gasp, you see the Umbra.'

The nucleus expanded, piercing the grey shrouds, casting a horizon that hummed and thronged in gold. 'What is it?'

'It is life. It is the spirit of Naa.'

Rune felt a longing, a grand and splendid desire to comprehend.

'My father could see the Umbra. My father? My father! Is he here, in the Gasp?'

The Vulpus smiled, a smile that held a singular kindness, and before Rune could ask the question again, it poured itself into him, a freezing torrent that corroded the inside of Rune's mind with splitting icy resolution.

He woke.

Burst forth into the damp evening. Saliva hung in gobbets against the back of his throat and he heaved to catch a single breath, savouring its ambrosia, drawing it down into his starving lungs. He blinked through tears and once again peered into the ghost-white face.

'Petulan! Please! Is my father here?'

Vorsa felt joy and confusion as the intimate name passed Rune's beak, and as the colour of her face filled Rune's vision he narrowed his eyes and he frowned, 'You are not Petulan?'

'No, I am Vorsa, his sister. Tell me little Startle, where have you been to know my brother?'

'I have been to a black place. I asked him if my father was there.'

Vorsa smiled, 'Count yourself lucky little Startle, not many return from the Gasp.'

Aggi rushed to Rune and nestled into the nape of his neck. He laughed, though his lungs were painful, 'I am well Aggi, I am well!'

Vorsa turned back towards the Crool. A number of Vulpus paced to meet her, marked with blood and cuts, awaiting further orders. 'Take Rune and Aggi somewhere safe and watch them. I will return.'

She entered the maze, following the trail of dead Morwih. The courtyard was silent. She made her way towards the place where Hevridis had fallen, yet there was no sign of him. The Crool was almost empty. The few feathered who remained sat and conversed with the Speaker. There were a number of bodies, both Morwih and Vulpus stained the ground with their blood.

She blessed those of her kin, placing grounding stones by each of them. Other Vulpus joined her in quiet ceremony, and once they had made their peace with the dead, they collected the remaining clan and departed.

Anguin stood beside Oclio, who trembled a little. 'And in the end, it was all over so quickly.'

Anguin smiled and placed a reassuring wing upon the little feathered. 'It often is my friend.'

'I am afraid Anguin, I have nowhere to go from here. This is all I have known for most of my life. Many of us are bound to this place.' Anguin cast a sympathetic eye on the tattered feathered who huddled against one another at the foot of the shattered door. To them, the open cage was as frightening as the thought of dying in the Crool.

'You will come with me, to Erithacus. There is a home there for you, for all of you. A noisy, frantic place, but many warm and friendly hearts dwell there.'

Oclio thought on this. 'The offer is very tempting. But I believe my days are numbered, and I have a world to see before they are spent. Give my best wishes to Rune.'

The little balding feathered took to wing, and several of his fellow, now liberated prisoners followed.

Vorsa approached Anguin. 'Thank you for helping save Rune. He will not be able to travel for a while. He will come with us to Orn Megol to rest, but you will return for him?'

'He is a tough little feathered. He will be fine. I imagine the Speakers still fly above the parklands north of here. Every evening I will wait for you there.'

*

Hevridis found himself alone once again. He was wounded, having landed awkwardly upon the gravel, the pain overwhelmed by his shame. He had let hubris get the better of him. He tore across the park despite his injury, up and over the wall which enclosed it. He cared little for chance encounters with Vulpus, he imagined in light of their victory they would forfeit the night's patrol. Soon he was in open streets, dodging the glow of the few remaining street lamps, clinging to the shadows until he spied his goal.

His house sat at the end of a terrace. Due to the exposed end wall it had always suffered with damp, yet had offered a singular warmth. He slinked along the fence, up on to the conservatory roof and through the open bathroom window. The rain had flooded the carpets, and the scent of stale water was rife. He wended his way down towards the front room.

His favourite spot had been beside the fireplace, curled up after his evening meal, enjoying the company of his familiar, sometimes even allowing it to touch him. But the room had lost its heart. It was dank and wet, the hearth untouched for months. There was an acrid stench that hung in the air. In the armchair sat the corpse of his Wroth familiar, still tucked under a thick blanket, the skeletal head lulled back, mouth wide.

Before the Wroth was a pile of blood offerings. The bodies of feathered and Muroi festered. He had always scoffed at those who performed these contrived rituals, yet even he had stooped to such arcane practices in hope of bringing back his familiar. For a long time he told himself he did it simply to maintain his status within the Fractured Sects, but now, with the emaciated figure before him, he realised it was much more than that. He had loved his familiar. He shook his head, and left the room.

He went to the kitchen and spied food. Leaping upon the countertop he batted the box of stale kibble to the floor. He fed leisurely, until he could stand the moist grit no longer. He made his final goodbyes, and left through the bathroom window.

There was one last place to say farewell to before he left the city for good. He had taken this path every night for a very long time, up beyond his home, across treacherous streets now completely silent, on fences and embankments, along the raised railway until he reached the modern apartments, featureless steel and glass cutting inorganic lines against the burnished sky.

A short ledge jutted out between the red brick of the arches and the grey fascia of his destination. He sidled along the various porticos and ledges until he found a particular balcony. He stepped upon it, carefully, hoping not to draw attention. The sliding door to the apartment was wide, and there were no lights inside. Sheepishly, he entered, pacing towards the sofa. There were no Wroth here, yet he detected a familiar odour, sneaking out from behind the chair leading on into the bedroom. Here he found a large bed, and upon it, the decaying bodies of two Wroth, male and female.

Fraubela lay asleep at their feet.

At first he felt anger, although it was quickly encompassed by sympathy. She looked so peaceful. He was not so callous as to chastise her. He felt remorse, and turned to leave.

'Hevridis.'

He lowered his head. 'I will go,' he said in return, but she was already beside him, and they exchanged the briefest moment of warmth. 'How long have they been dead?'

She sighed, 'A long time, perhaps longer than your own familiar. I could not bring myself to admit it. I am too proud.'

Hevridis smiled, 'We were always very similar in that regard my dear.'

They stepped out to the balcony. 'And what of the Startle?'

Hevridis frowned, 'The Vulpus came to the Crool. I imagine the Drove and the Collector alerted them.'

Fraubela scowled. 'I will call the Sects together once we know the location of the Foul Meridian. It will not be long now, we must keep all ears to the ground, have every Morwih worth its whiskers eavesdrop on the Vulpus. There are many more of us than them, despite our losses. We still have a chance.'

Hevridis nodded, 'In light of this revelation, may I return to your side?'

She said nothing, and he had his answer.

*

The warm earth was caught in a gentle breeze that raised Rune up as they left the lands of the Crool. No longer did the unsavoury odours of that dreadful place assault his senses, and he was very glad about it. He could fly for short distances, but for the most part he walked slowly with Onnar, or rested on her back, as they crossed the streets and eventually felt the soft mud and grass of the outlying scrubland and parks that swept down from the great music hall.

Vorsa walked beside them and they talked of the Morwih and the Crool.

'We must know what the Morwih plan. Have you any idea?'

Onnar nodded, 'We heard very little, but it is safe to say they will have the entirety of the Fractured Sects on their side.'

Vorsa agreed, 'There are many Morwih in the city, and they will all fall in line under their consul, Fraubela.'

Vorsa looked to Rune as he lulled up and down upon the arch of Onnar's armour.

'Not many have entered the Gasp and come back from it, it took me years to harness the strength to attempt such a feat, and even now, each time I visit my brother it feels as though I take one step further in that I will not get back.'

Rune said, 'There were things there, dead things that wanted me to stay, but your brother would not have it so. I saw something there, something beautiful beyond the dark. There was a light, great arms of light. Your brother said it was the Umbra.'

Vorsa smiled, 'That is something I cannot see, that is what separates a Corpse Speaker from a Shadow Starer. You can see beyond the Gasp.'

'My father made sense of all of this, it just frightens me.'

They reach the low path that enclosed the first step up to the hall. They wound behind it, down into the gully and beyond, into the earth of Orn Megol.

The Vulpus clans came home in fitful groups, some played and jostled with one another. Others were silent, war wounded. Vorsa escorted Rune, Aggi and Onnar to a quiet, unoccupied den where there was warm bedding. It was not long before they had curled up beside one another.

The many Vulpus collected in the great hall before Satresan and said their goodbyes to the dead. Their names were spoken by all until they became one with the Orata, and were thus remembered forever. Once this act was complete the congregation broke away, many leaving Orn Megol to return to their own dens, others finding shelter in the great city of the clans, where, unable to wait for the nocturnal embrace, they slept. Rune listened to the painful bark of the vixens as they stood upon the surface and sung the Orata. Even deep below the earth their voices were audible, a sorrowful yelp. He wished to know what they were saying. Soon they were all sound asleep, against the old earth.

*

Dominus Audagard flew high amongst the embolus clouds, gaining an eclipsing view of his work. The architect grinned at his ingenuity. Below the withered black halos rose atop the office block where he had taught Vorsa her final lesson. He trailed his eyes left and right and sure enough, upon the vacant roofs of adjacent offices and high-rise flats, electricity pylons and chimneys, many similar wreaths crept debauched and wiry into the sky. They spread wide of the city centre in perfect circumference, each structure laboured upon by his loyal flock, who continued zealously to add twisted twigs and Wroth scrap.

The binding spell enclosed the city. He cawed to his bishops, who hurled themselves up, and together they flew along the curvature of the black knot, spewing feverish cabala against the wind, coaxing their devotees to join them above the dreadful structures which groaned against the grey sky. The Dominus examined each altar, his devious eyes darting with precision; nothing would be out of place. He reached one shadowy sceptre and landed upon it. The blackened perimeter stretched out either side, curving to a distant meeting point; he could see the centre of the city even in the low light, the Moterion and its great iron stronghold, built to confine the oldest gods. He held this city in contempt; the Wroth and their ugly hands had riddled the earth. He would undo it all.

Pleased the work was almost complete, the Corva Anx made for the Moterion, dallying amongst derelict houses and overgrown gardens to seek materials; tearing strips from refuse sacks, ripping the antennas from cars and loose wires from electricity terminals. They tore tarpaulin and chewed on carrion, lifting their bounty up into the heavens. They descended within the garrison of the Moterion, a collection of squat cages amongst flower beds and food kiosks. At the centre of its grounds, at the foot of a concrete cliff, stood the Starless Vulpus. The Dominus landed before them, bowing low.

'The circle is enclosed!' He hissed.

Nox contorted his neck, plagued by something unseen. 'Their whisper grows with volume Dominus, at first their ghoulish chatter was but a slight annoyance, but their ears are turned to you and their mouths are animated. Dominus, do they speak of exorcism?'

'We toil for such an end; the city will be cleansed!'

'How much longer must we carry this burden?'

The Dominus frowned, 'Oh my lovely Starless, not much longer, soon all will be well, I assure you!'

He hid his deceit with outstretched wings, whipping up his choir into a frenzy. The Corva Anx carried their stolen wears atop the cliff and began to build the final altar. The Dominus stood silently as they ducked and weaved about one another, fusing the abundance of rough, contorted fragments into a tortuous final crescent.

A swollen moon emerged from the lowering sky, implications bloated in its waxing presence; Audagard crooked his neck and peered into the glossy iris. He wished to see the Gasp, but it was forever vague. His eyes blurred with tears and within the pearlescent formations that shuddered at the edges of his vision he saw the spheres move in conjunction, he saw meaning in each hair of light that stretched from Seyla's bulge. Yet one hair was out of place. He groaned. He recognised its shudder, the Shadow Starer. Of course, he thought. The little flotsam in his eye that burned with irritation, unable to find its source, unable to bend him to his will. Instead he must bend everything around him, in a constant insufferable theatre.

He snatched sticks meant for the shrine and scattered them before him. He made note of each position as they rolled against one another, each stick an actor in his tormented performance. Morwih, Throa, Vulpus, Gull. Even himself. Each shrieked at him, a calamity of disparate voices, all vying for his ear. The sticks came to rest about him. Three lay still whilst one teetered hither and thither atop the others, unable to find bearing. He read its meaning.

'Sisters, please!' He cursed.

The stick rolled towards him. He stepped back, and it finally rested against a length of silver birch. He narrowed his eyes. A path that required his assistance. The white stick spoke of its name to him.

'Bless you Sisters!'

He rallied his most loyal Corva and careened up, his aim for Orn Megol.

*

Rune woke sharply. Something tugged at him, a shadow danced momentarily before his eyes, and he saw that Onnar and Aggi had gone. He panicked, hopping into the corridor. Nervously he stepped out into the dark, allowing his eyes to adjust to the weak light cast down each burrow by the collections of mirrored glass. The night still held sway, and he lowered his head and listened where his eyes could not perceive. There was silence, he strained to make out the rumble of sleeping Vulpus, yet he heard nothing.

Where could they have gone? he thought, his pace quickening as he flitted awkwardly along the corridors, trying to retrace his footsteps. Something rushed past him. It caught him like a stirring of warm air or soft fur, and it was familiar, dream-like. He felt dizzy, time appeared to lag, and he considered that he might not actually be awake.

The burrow expanded into the great hall of Orn Megol, each movement sent reverberations into the black, reflecting an impression of immense size. The ceiling was distant, and he felt the desire to seek its dimensions, to fly up and trace each tapering wall. Yet again, the sluggish air stifled each movement. With effort he walked to the centre of the great void.

He froze with terror.

Huge faces stared back at him. Before him a wall of grinning skulls, their smooth grain catching the faint light, presenting the mocking leer of each great eye socket and menacing mouth. Teeth smirked with terrible girth, and he staggered back, back away from the simulacrum. At the centre, a massive blunt face; incisors glowered in yellow rage, its surface pitted with hieroglyphs, each professing some arcane desire or notion, its teeth combing the dark place with deadly certainty.

And then it spoke.

'Look at this little feathered! He is brave, or very stupid.'

Rune swallowed. 'I am not stupid.'

The huge skull reeled, suddenly free, the massive skeleton hung in the air, each bone an apparition of the fossil that protruded from the earthern wall. It moved on jets of plasmic light. It was a Revenant, a skeleton ghost.

'Now isn't this a turn up for the Orata! You see me little feathered?'

Rune nodded. 'Yes, yes I do!'

'So many questions,' it grinned. 'Did you escape the clutches of a Vulpus?'

'I am a friend of the Vulpus Vorsa, she has let me rest here before I continue my search for my father.'

'Dear Vorsa! This is fascinating, I have not conversed with the living in many, many turns. How are you able to see and speak with me?'

'I don't know, but I have been to the Gasp, perhaps that is how.'

With rich curiosity the spirit pulled close to Rune, 'You have been to the Gasp?'

'Yes, but Petulan would not let me stay.'

'Vorsa's brother? I have not seen him in an age. I believed him dead. He was always a sick pup. Perhaps I was right. I have watched Vorsa grow from a seedling to a strong tree. She is Corpse Speaker, you know?'

'Yes, she talks with her brother even in death. Can she see you?'

The great beast frowned. 'I believe she can perceive us, but she is unable to speak with us. You see, we are cursed with silence, which is why I was so shocked when you spoke to me! We are heard by no one, and we cannot leave this place, bound to our earthly bones. I am told it is because we have unfinished business, but for the death of me do I know what exactly it is we need to do! We have been here so very long, I may have forgotten!'

He smiled a terrible smile, 'My name is Bronordean.'

Rune reached out a wing and felt the chill of each ethereal limb of the beast. It looked back at him with its empty sockets.

'Tell me of the world little feathered, for the Vulpus cannot see or hear us, and we cannot hear them. So we are left to interpret, we are but mere observers, watching the rituals we performed once ourselves, watching the pups grow up, watching life ebb and flow. We are spectators of a world we have no place in, it is a little ... vexing.'

Rune looked back into the darkness, at the sterile stone and earth. 'The Vulpus are at war with the Morwih. This very night I was freed from a Morwih prison, where many suffered at their paw. The Vulpus helped us escape.'

'The Morwih! Ha!' he bellowed, 'Carcari, your kin are up to no good!'

Suddenly the wall quaked, fluorescent blues and whites effervesced against the brittle rock; spectral osteology rose as though borne of the wall itself, until another Revenant revealed itself, its head, from which two huge tusk-like teeth stabbed forth, lurching wildly.

'What is all this!' It grumbled with granite timbre.

'The Morwih have attacked the Vulpus!' Bronordean replied.

The huge feline spirit waved a dismissive limb, 'The Morwih do not organise like the Vulpus, we are far too busy for such things.' It shook its head and then noticed Rune.

'What's this? Dinner? But such a tiny thing, not even worth the effort to chew!'

Bronordean laughed loudly, 'Oh Carcari, and how does one swallow with no throat, or digest with no stomach? You are all stone bones brother, and you have not eaten in an exceedingly long time!'

'One can dream,' Carcari replied. The huge feline stretched himself flat in the midair, cavorting in fissures of cold gossamer. He stared down at Rune. 'Why are the Morwih at war with the Vulpus?'

'The Wroth are dying. The Vulpus wish to claim the city, they have a ritual, the Foul Meridian. If they perform it the city is theirs. The Morwih also wish to rule the city, and want to stop the Vulpus from performing their ritual. But all is lost, because they thought I was able to perform it like my father, but I never learned it, I was too young when he left. So I am useless to them.'

'The Foul Meridian?' Bronordean said. 'They listened to our words? This is marvellous! Carcari! It was not all in vain! They listened to our words!'

Rune frowned, 'I do not understand?'

Bronordean breathed deeply through immaterial lungs. 'This is our legacy, perhaps the only thing besides our bones that proves we once existed. This cave has been home to countless generations, of Vulpus, and before them, Cini, and before the Cini, my family lived within these caves. The great Grim made this a home, and yet even we were not the first clans to find shelter deep within the earth. Long before us, the Rauka made this their domain, in the shadow of the fallen city, and they made it a place safe from the clutches of the Wroth.'

Carcari shifted, an air of frustration fell over him, 'We had lost our words, lost our sensibilities. Unable to communicate with the other clades, we were alone in the dirt. We lived in shame, for we had driven the city away from us. It was our fault, that the city fell and we were banished, we lost everything. We deserved it, I know this now.'

Bronordean comforted his fellow Revenant, 'We each hold a piece of this shame my friend, remember this.'

He turned once again to Rune. 'When the city fell, we could no longer share a language. This divide might have given rise to our own wars and violences, much like the Vulpus and the Morwih, and yet despite our inability to speak to one another, we were united in our fear of the Wroth. They quickly took the land and hunted many of us to extinction. I died here in this hall with my children beside me, starved to death. My cubs went on to the Gasp, and yet I remained here. I have found other Revenants haunting these caves and we all held the same desire, to pass on our stories and fables, and most of all, the song. I believe this is why we were left behind.'

Bronordean smiled, 'We may have lost the words, but we knew the feeling within the words. We called it the Song, it was the voice of the city, and each sound had form, and we made marks in the mud to find that form, and those feelings were not just emotions. They had a shape, and it was for us to find, and although we had no way to know the words themselves, we mouthed each shape and we gave each sound significance, and they became new words. We clawed these words into the rock and mud, and we shared them with all who would listen.

'But we feared the words would be lost again, and so, when we were the last to know the words and the Song, we scrawled on these walls a request, that whoever should find this cave, that they learn all the knowledge that we had amassed, and for those words to be spoken out loud, and shared so that every generation would know the Song, and would find a way to know our words.'

'The Orata?'

'Yes little feathered, the Orata is our interpretation of the Song. It is all we are, and it is imperative that it is never forgotten. This cave might collapse and our legacy be lost forever. But as long as the Orata is known and spoken out loud, then our Song is not dead.'

Rune hopped towards the wall of the cave and examined the old markings of the ancient clans. Many held similarities with those on the walls of Anguin's nesting box, on the walls of the Throa set, and in his own home, far away in the Pinnacle. Amongst the clutter of markings he could make out a host of symbols which he recognised. 'This is the mark of the Sisters of the Flock?'

Bronordean drifted before the marks and examined them, 'Ah, this symbolises three very special gods. Vors, Vorn and Alcali. In fact, Vorsa's name is taken from the first. It is quite an honour to carry this name.'

Rune pointed to the symbol upon his own armour. 'This represents Alauda, Emini and Abraic, gods of the feathered. It is quite similar, isn't it?'

Bronordean brushed the symbol with a vaporous paw. 'Our gods created the world, and once they had completed it, they made us, and we were frightened, born to a strange land without the means to fend for ourselves.

'They offered us their milk for we could not feed ourselves. We drank every drop and we became strong as they withered, but soon the milk was dry and we asked for more. So they offered us their blood, and we drank all of their blood, until they were nothing but bones, and they hid themselves away because they feared us. We had become stronger than our own gods, but without them we had no nourishment, and we were forced to seek our own path.'

Rune nodded, 'The story of the Sisters of the Flock is very similar. Those who worship them pray for forgiveness. Perhaps your song is sung not just by the Vulpus, but by the feathered too?'

'Of course! This is the resonance of the Song. It permeates everything, it is a sharing of ideas and beliefs, yet it is hidden, it is obscured by traditions grown of our distance from one another. The Song bound us, fur and feather, scale and hide.'

Rune contemplated, 'I have met many on my journey who share in your desire, to know the song you speak of. There is a feathered, a magician called Erithacus that knows of it, and has tried to bring the flocks together under it. I do not know much of him, but I intend to meet him. He knew my father you see, and I hope that he can help me find him. There is another, the kin known as Throa. They have a stone, a great stone which when struck makes a sound. This sound guided me here.'

'Wait?' Bronordean interrupted, 'The Singing Stones? They still exist?'

'The Throa call them Settling Stones. They hide them deep in the earth.'

Bronordean grinned again, 'If I am not mistaken, these Settling Stones you speak of are indeed the Singing Stones of our ancestry. To think they still exist, Carcari! The Singing Stones will take you to the city!'

Rune nodded, 'They did. I have been. It is filled with dying Wroth.'

The Revenants swayed in dismay, 'No! You are mistaken! The city would not allow the Wroth within it, the Wroth broke the city and its song!'

The spectral beasts began to shudder, jettisoning globes of preternatural matter in frantic waves, losing the stark forms they had assumed.

'No! The city sings! Seek the throat from which it sings!'

*

He awoke to an empty room. The great vault of Orn Megol, flooded with a dull morning light. He was freezing, and entirely alone. Before him the skulls of Bronordean and Carcari, unmoved, undisturbed for millennia. He felt embarrassment, and quickly left, returning to the den in which he hoped to find the warm bodies of Onnar and Aggi. They lay curled beside one another. He rested for a while, and despite the bizarre occurrences of the night he felt quite refreshed.

Vorsa came to the trio, bringing with her a very large leaf folded in two, containing various worms and insects. Once they had finished eating, Vorsa said, 'My father Satresan wishes to meet with you.'

They were brought forth into the great hall. Rune eyed the skulls once again, which remained unmoving. They were flanked by the hundreds of Vulpus who stood silently, each resplendent in their armour.

Below the ashen visage of Bronordean stood Satresan. He was pale, like his son Petulan, his fur taking on a curious blue tint in the subdued light, like a living spectre. His armour snaked from his jaw in asperous curves of silver metal, meeting in a crown atop his head. It was decorated with gold and blue foils.

Vorsa gently pushed Rune towards her father. The shadows that haunched beyond the White King broke away, announcing themselves with a shrill caw. The gnarled presence of the Dominus bent fawningly towards the little Startle.

Satresan spoke, 'Dear Rune, you have been through so much, it might seem as though Naa were against you.'

Rune shrugged and gazed at his feet. 'I only wish to find my father.'

'And yet, you must ask yourself why so many wish you harm?'

'I believe they see my father in me, and my father was a great feathered.'

'Rune, you carry that same burden too. Long ago, a seal was forged between the Vulpus clans and the Corva Anx. The Anx came to us with their predictions and spoke of a way of leading the Vulpus to retake the city from the Wroth. They told us that some are born with a unique ability, the ability to see an aspect of the world hidden from almost all of life. With this ability, one can speak with the will of Naa and invoke the Foul Meridian, a spell that summons forth the Umbra and relinquishes the city from the Wroth, who have poisoned everything they have touched.

'Your father was born Umbra, and it was through him that we wished to seek that end. But when we went to find him, we learned that he had left this land.

'With your father gone, we had no way to perform the ritual. But Grom had a son, you, and the Corva believe you might also be Umbra. So we ask you here, before all who wish only good upon you, if you will ask of the Umbra for us?'

Rune hesitated. 'I am not Umbra.'

There was a great exhalation. The Dominus shook his head under the weighty hood of his cowl. He hopped before Rune, cautiously straining towards him, as though obstructed by some invisible force.

'I see it in you, Umbra,' he squawked. 'My kin can smell it on you, you reek of the Gasp. I can see the vortices like spirals of entrails, and they speak clearly of you, prince killer. My Corva already deify you, they spit after your name in service to your cause –
Find your father! Find your father! – words which have become synonymous with the holy scripture of the Anx. You are the son of Grom, who saw geometry in the innards of your mother, he was Umbra, you are Umbra.'

'Don't scare him Dominus Audagard! He is but a child!' Vorsa beseeched.

The black feathered hissed, 'Know your place, corpse chatterer!'

Vorsa snarled back, 'You are no better than I! You only see the Gasp – this child has seen the Umbra! He knows beyond the Lacking Sea!'

The other Corva shrieked, 'He has seen the Umbra! He is Umbra!'

Rune shook his head. 'I have seen it, yet I do not understand it! It is as confusing to me as the words you speak, Corva Anx. I do not know the Umbra. My father never taught me these lessons. Perhaps he learned of its meaning too late to pass the understanding on to me, or perhaps I was too young. I want to help you, but unless there is a teacher to show me how, then it will remain coloured lights and visions that do little more than scare me and make me sick.'

The Dominus coughed indignantly. This chick was stubborn, a defeatist! And yet it was in this disparity he saw a wending path. The sticks had fallen correctly.

'So be it!' he spat. 'Find another Umbra!'

*

Vorsa found Rune alone that night in the great hall, staring up at the skulls. She waited a while, trying not to disturb him, until he noticed her and beckoned her in.

'They are the old denizens of Orn Megol,' she said as she followed his line of sight to the huge bone totems above.

'Bronordean and Carcari.' He pointed with his wing at the louring craniums.

'You know them?'

'Yes, I dreamt that I spoke with them about this place, and the city. They told me of the Orata, how they forged it because they feared that their language would be lost a second time. That their families were killed by the Wroth, and that their gods are similar to the gods of the flocks. Then I woke up here,' he laughed, 'and I may have imagined it all!'

'I see them sometimes, vague visions. I could never understand them, mouthing soundless words in the dark. But I do not see them now,' she replied thoughtfully.

'I think they were supposed to speak with me, that is why you no longer see them. I think I set them free.'

'How?'

'Because I could hear them, perhaps. They needed to tell their story.'

Vorsa sighed, 'So did they tell you anything useful?'

'Maybe. I know that they were aware of the Settling Stones that the Throa worship, the same Stone that brought me here. They were upset when I told them that the city was filled with Wroth. They said that this wasn't possible. That I should find something important. Find the throat from which it sings? I don't know. What will the Vulpus do now, without me?'

'I know that the Meridian will take time to organise. The Orata tells us everything that we must do before the Meridian is invoked. We have chosen a place to perform the ritual. But we need a Shadow Starer, someone who can direct our voice to the Umbra. That was the task we wished you to fulfil.

'My father will send many Vulpus out into the world to seek another Umbra. We will attempt the Foul Meridian without one if need be. I must consult Petulan. I believe he might be strong enough to guide our voice.'

'Through the Gasp? Is that possible?'

Vorsa swallowed, 'I can open a channel and hope it remains, it might not be good for me though. Too long in the Gasp, you can lose yourself to it.'

'Will you die?'

Vorsa said nothing.

Rune returned to Onnar and Aggi whilst Vorsa sought her father.

His quarters thronged with the sepulchral caw of Corva as they jabbed and stabbed the air with their frustrations. Amidst them Satresan sat stolid and unmoved. Finally, he spoke. 'I cannot force the boy to act on our behalf. If he does not have the faculties to see the Umbra then we certainly cannot force him to do so.'

Vorsa awaited a chance to speak. The Dominus acknowledged her presence and admonished her for her previous outburst.

'You do not question us!'

'We risk everything if we do not complete this task! You taught me yourself, to hone my voice with Petulan, and I have done so. I am the strongest Corpse Speaker, stronger than any of you; I do not question your desires, simply your actions. You do not see us as thinking, feeling animals. You see us as tools, mechanisms to act out your necromancy. We are not so, Audagard. Rune is not ready, we cannot become cruel in our want.' She took a deep breath, and allowed the anger to evaporate.

'We are all tools, Vorsa! Do not think too high of yourself! Amongst the deafening cry of the Gasp we are all puppets, fetishes of life! The value of that life is only known in death. We only see our potential after the fact. I see the shadow of my pattern and I know it has worth. You too! Your role in this is messenger. The boy Rune, he is the message! We cannot shirk the nature of things simply because it doesn't suit us!'

'But I am strong enough, I can reach the Umbra. I know I can!'

'That may be so Corpse Speaker, but I have not given up on the boy.'

'No?' Vorsa questioned. 'You seemed willing to dismiss him?'

'Rune is young, little more than a fledgling. He has not borne the fruit of adulthood yet. He has his heart set on finding his father, dead or alive. That is his path, and I feel we should allow him to complete that journey. I see his path twitching in Seyla's eye. She is not done with him yet.'

Satresan said, 'We cannot force his will. All decisions must be made freely. To that end, I agree. Let him seek his father. But to be safe I will command a garrison to seek another Umbra. I have already lost one child, I cannot lose another.'

'But ... Father?'

'No Vorsa, I cannot.'

The Dominus agreed. 'Grom was Umbra, and Rune seeks Grom. I believe by the time we have prepared the Foul Meridian Rune will have our answer.'

*

As they left through the thicket that hemmed Orn Megol the Vulpus eyed their strange ensemble with a vague disdain. Rune felt chagrined, and with difficulty he buried the feeling down. Aggi attempted to lighten his mood by speaking of the sights she had seen since they had been apart. He enjoyed listening to her speak, how her words had softened, how she seemed closer to him. He did not question it, yet felt a warmth of friendship.

They were soon far from the hillock of the old music hall, heading north east towards the river once again. A frantic cry above alerted them to the jagged shadow of the Corva Anx as they scrawled a path back to the city, the quick pace of Vorsa not far behind.

Chapter 7

Roak's return to the city was laborious. Every fibre of his being seemed to wish him to stay with the sea, to catch Ungdijin and wheel about the Pinnacle. He dreamt of it, craved the salt breeze upon his down, to lay amongst the wiry sea grass that sprung from the folding sand. It was a curious state, to desire something that appeared against his better judgement, and even Roak found his argument untenable. He let it lapse into the backwaters of his thoughts and looked out on the encroaching maudlin city, all grey rectangles, the stench of a million dead. Ora and Seyla had danced but a few turns since he had taken his news to Esperer, and yet in such a small time the sickness had choked the life from the Wroth.

He settled on the ledge of a large broken window of a high-rise office complex. These dwellings served no purpose. He looked below at the festering body of a Wroth who had thrown himself from the building. Roak furrowed his brow. He felt sorry for the creature, for all these creatures. He feared death just as much as they did. He looked back at the desolate office, rows of cubicles in white plastic and steel trim, the nylon aroma of steam-cleaned carpet.

Never had he ventured within a Wroth dwelling, always an angry hand waved in his direction, a screaming Wroth to remind him of his place. He thought on this for a moment, on the absence of the Wroth. What would it mean? What would change? He knew his kind would mourn the loss of their waste, their debris, easy pickings for lazy Gulls. He had never shared the utter hatred that many feathered and ground dwellers felt for the Wroth.

He waddled into the office and hopped upon a desk, picking up a stapler and coloured pens and knocking them about, cawing with excitement at the destruction he wrought. He defecated upon a pile of files, pushing them from the table with a deft heave. He half-heartedly flapped to another desk, examining the remains of some stale yet sweet meal that protruded from a silver wrapper. He considered the scent. It was odd, delicious, unknowable. He did not trust it, and moved on.

He heard a moan and saw a Wroth in one of the chairs. It frightened him, and he lost his footing, collapsing awkwardly against a computer monitor. He steadied himself and peered at the animal. It was dying, barely able to move. Black vomit plastered its face. It was a strange sickly pale colour, and sweated profusely. Roak turned his head away and dismissed the vile creature, leaping to the floor. He found the space sterile and uninviting, and again the swell of desire to be anywhere but here, anywhere that offered the grit and grain which the Wroth removed with such zeal.

He flew out towards the centre of the city. Joining the medley of other feathered in flight. Curiously patterned flock wished him well as they cambered against the air currents.

'I seek news!' he shouted.

'Seek the Bazaar!' they crowed back.

With a little effort he found the location of the market, a myriad of species in the derelict bridge arch. He entered, garnering a little attention for his large white girth. There were feathered of every kind, and many flock he knew little about. The great stilt bodies of Ardid craned down. They had noticed him, and considered him cautiously. He followed their line of sight until he lost himself amongst the jostling barterers.

He found refuge, a place to haul up and listen. This was something he had often done amongst his own kin. As a child, before he had risen in the ranks, he had averted many fights by learning the tells and idiosyncrasies of those who threatened him. He would know their weaknesses before they did, in the gait of their walk, in the way they held themselves. It was a clever trick; one he had relied upon often. He had grown arrogant in his cunning, and it hadn't gone unnoticed. Yet here, infiltrating this world he cared nothing for, it was easy to spread his wings and absorb the mannerisms of the crowd.

...

'They'll perform it soon, I dare say!'

'Are you sure?'

'Why ever not? It is their desire. It has been foretold after all. The Vulpus wait for no one.'

'I guess you're right, but to live under Vulpus rule, will it really be any different? They already control the night!'

Vulpus! Roak baulked at the word. He leaned in to the assortment of feathered who sat beside him. They moved away from his sharp beak.

'Careful with that weapon, Elowin!' a Bloodson spluttered.

He pulled back, and feigned an apology, 'I beg your pardon, please. I couldn't help but overhear what you were speaking of. I am new to the city, from the coast, and I wish to know, what is this news of the Vulpus?'

The Bloodson accepted the apology. 'The Wroth will relinquish the city to the Vulpus. They have a spell see, a spell to take the city, but the Morwih will vie for the same rule.'

Roak frowned, 'The Morwih, they wish to rule the city?'

The Bloodson nodded. 'The war between the Vulpus and Morwih is ancient. My father told me of their battles when I was a fledgling. They have carved the city up in their bid to own it. We avoid them at all costs, but we watch them prowl the roofs and spy upon the Vulpus.'

'I see,' said Roak, 'and spells?'

'Witchery, Corva magic. The Vulpus have colluded with the Bishops of Bone Char to invoke a ritual.'

Roak smirked. 'How does this ritual guarantee the city is theirs? The Morwih have no interest in the meddling of the Anx! How on Naa do the Vulpus think they can do this?'

A scruffy feathered, of a flock which Roak could not identify, stooped forward from the shadows. It seemed emaciated, its down oily and matted. It peered up at him through pinprick eyes.

'They will see the Foul Meridian. They have an Umbra. I shared a prison with him, he freed us from the Crool,' it coughed, and an Aven offered support.

Roak spluttered. 'What is an Umbra?'

They sat in silence, none could say. 'So this Umbra is magic?'

The Bloodson shook his head. 'It must be, but I do not believe they have an Umbra. They were searching for one just this morning. Vulpus guards were here, asking strange questions.'

'So they don't have an Umbra?'

The ailing feathered raised his little voice, 'They did! They had an Umbra, his name was Rune.'

Here was a precarious choice; to side with the Morwih in a war that wasn't his. Yet the serendipity was pleasing. Revenge for his father's death was not something he had sought, not against such a foe as the Vulpus.

Roak flew low. He traced the path of the Morwih, who would pretend to laze in the warm sun, yet held a synchronicity that was easy to decipher. Information was passed through tail movements, it was clever; distance was little obstacle, the clear swish of that limb could be seen from building to building, and he tailored his path to observe the signals. Soon he made sense of it, there was a network, spanning the breadth of the city, and each join was a Morwih – a Feral, a Familial or an Objector, a feline cartography that pulled taut at the centre of the city.

He took a chance and landed beside a large tan and white Morwih who stood blinking aloofly into the distance. She did not move as he landed, but he saw the infinitesimal flex of her claws, and he chose to practice caution.

'Ora bring peace.'

She said nothing.

'If I were to offer my kin's services in the war against the Vulpus, who must I speak with?'

The Morwih smiled. 'A feathered asks to help the Morwih; all is not right with Naa.'

'It is in our mutual interest,' he retorted.

She lifted a paw and licked the fur, which seemed to serve no purpose besides a desire to look disinterested. It frustrated him, he wished to push her off the roof.

She looked up at him, 'Oh, you are still here.'

He held his tongue.

'You seek Fraubela, our Consul. We meet at that dark place over there,' she pointed at the cathedral. 'She is sometimes there, sometimes not.' Contemptuously, she added, 'Ora bring peace.'

He found a stoop to rest on atop the cathedral. From this vantage he could make out much of the city and understood why the Consul had chosen this place to meet. He observed the various Morwih at sentry posts on adjacent buildings, watched each with interest.

They were far less stupid than he had assumed, there was a clear objective in their behaviour. He enjoyed their theatrics, their blasé act. It was utterly transparent, and yet he wondered how such traits must have developed. They were an entirely unnatural concoction; he had heard the stories that the Morwih were created by the Wroth, that they had no language of their own, no place. They had to cut a niche for themselves. He admired this. It reminded him of his own path to power.

He sat for a turn, and no Morwih placed a paw upon the roof. Then, as he prepared to leave, the Consul appeared, a silver matt of hair. She sat for a moment, surveying her domain. A larger, stocky Morwih followed. Both were Familial. He could tell by the collars around their necks.

She had detected Roak before she lay her eyes upon him. He knew this and studied her; she walked away but her ears were pricked back, her whiskers grazing the air with cognisance.

Roak was pulled down hard from the raised ledge, his head pinned to the roof. The hind legs of the second feline scrambled at his armour, attempting to get purchase. Roak spun, kicking out frantically, yet rotating only made it worse, his throat was in the Morwih's mouth. The Consul sidled up beside him and leaned into his stifled field of vision.

'My guard told me you sought me, and here I find you. Hevridis will kill you shortly, but I must say I am intrigued. What does a Gull want with the Morwih?'

His vision blurred. He saw a hundred possible answers, a hundred ways to offer himself to her, but they only stuck in his throat when he recalled his last offer of parley. He decided to be honest.

'I wish to take the throne of the Pinnacle, it is a kingdom by the sea and once the current king, Esperer, departs, it is my belief I will take his place, and I wish to build relations with neighbouring rulers. I am aware of the coming war with the Vulpus. My father was killed by such a fiend, so I have something of a personal grievance with the cubs of Seyla. I hold an army, a great army of airborne infantry. We wish to forge a treaty with the Morwih sects, and offer our forces to fight for your cause.' He stuttered, 'We feel it is best to back the winning side.'

Fraubela was moved. An uncontrollable laugh erupted from her. Hevridis looked bemused. 'This is quite something; don't you agree Hevridis?'

Hevridis composed himself and let go of the Gull's neck. He stepped back and spat the down from his mouth. 'Fraubela, I think you should accept his offer.'

'Why?'

'The Gulls reduced the Startle to little more than slaves. They stole the land from under them. They are ruthless, uncompromising, and Wroth-headed.'

'And this makes them worthy allies?'

'It makes them enemies of Rune, and he says himself he is an enemy of the Vulpus. The Vulpus will seek to free the Startle from under Esperer, or any would-be king if they win. The enemy of my enemy ... and so on.'

Fraubela had never killed a Gull as large as this. She wondered if it was even possible, wondered how much the Gull wanted to kill her. She found her smile again. 'We accept your offer.'

'I ask for one thing in return. Under your rule, I wish to reclaim our title as Naarna Elowin.'

It mattered nothing to her. 'Agreed,' she said dismissively.

*

'Anguin said to wait here.' Aggi shifted her weight from leg to leg, trying to warm herself. As night drew they made for a broad-leaved shrub, it sprawled ungainly and provided enough shelter even for Onnar. It was a cold and clinical park, each edge keenly cut. The grass had once been well kempt, yet without the gardeners it was quickly becoming unruly. They saw illness here, confused Baldaboa hobbled on missing digits, their chests swollen, breath ragged, their eyes leering with fear.

They found water, a pale film coated a large pond. Onnar ran the parameter of the pool and found no corpses in the water. They waited until other feathered drank from it and felt assurance in their kin's apparent health. Yet still Onnar feared it, and found a puddle for them to drink from in the shade of a tree. It appeared clean and untouched.

They could make out flock floating upon the pond, large graceful and white, their necks exceptionally long. The city waned beyond the park, the steady decay of lights that once lit the twilight hours signalling a new character to the night. No longer would they have to avoid the alerting snare of streetlamps, they would know only the gaze of Seyla.

The cry of the Speaker flock was unmistakable. As the low wail reached them, Rune could make out their rough and tumble above him as ever-breaking shadows. They settled within the trees. Onnar and Aggi were not far behind when Rune's name was called. Anguin glid down to the grass and they greeted one another.

'Rune, you look tired.'

'I am, and you look ...'

Anguin interrupted, 'I look free! And I have you to thank for that.'

Rune smiled as another Speaker appeared before them. He was larger than Anguin, festooned with bottle caps and shards of green metal. 'This is Glaspitter, my good friend.'

The great feathered looked at Rune with an air of surprise. 'So you are the Startle who freed Anguin from the Crool. That is a feat not even we dared to attempt. We are grateful to you for assuring his escape.'

Rune nodded. 'I have my friends to thank for his safe return to you.' He introduced the Drove and the Collector.

Glaspitter acknowledged them both and then turned again to Rune.

'I understand you seek the ear of our master?'

Aggi interjected, 'We do, for many reasons!'

Onnar added, 'we are hoping this Erithacus can help us find Rune's father.' She gestured to the little feathered. 'We understand your master knew him, may even know his whereabouts.'

'Anguin has spoken a little of this. Your father was well regarded amongst our flock, so it will be a pleasure to guide you to Erithacus.'

The guardskin of Erithacus took to wing, though Anguin remained. 'Onnar, are you able to keep up with us?'

'I am used to running after these two, although please take your time!'

*

They reached the outskirts of a compound the next evening. It stood beneath a canopy of great pine trees, a damp uninviting place, made ever more inhospitable by the presence of a sprawling wire fence. Beyond this, a university building and its vivisection laboratories. Rune did not comprehend any of this, yet felt it had been an important place to the Wroth, though none seemed to dwell there anymore. Onnar squeezed through a gap in the fence. They were surrounded by stark white buildings marked by neglect. Black mould rose on sleek surfaces, attempting to reclaim them for the earth.

Aggi shuddered, 'I do not like it here.'

Onnar drew close to her, 'Come on old girl, we have seen worse!'

Aggi grimaced.

Anguin tried to reassure them, 'Erithacus did not choose this place, it chose him. He is bound to it.'

They approached the largest structure, its cold exterior unwelcoming. Anguin paused before they entered.

'The Speakers came to revere Erithacus, and for good reason. He is brilliant, and yet he has suffered intolerable pain for that brilliance. My time away from him has given me a little perspective. We must forgive those who may act with malice, but who are marked by the aggression of others. He may be upset by your presence, so please, be patient.'

The words reminded Rune of something Tor had said of Erithacus, he felt the same could be said of Anguin himself, made cruel by his imprisonment by the Morwih.

They stepped within the building through a shattered pane. They were in a corridor where glass doors separated adjoining rooms. Transparent veils hung from the ceilings, concealing stainless steel work benches and festering medical detritus. All of the doors were either open or the glass was shattered, and Onnar took care not to cut her paws. It felt as though the Wroth had put down their tools and left without warning. The place smelled strange, odours unknown to all, the stench of spilt disinfectant and mingled decay.

The corridor opened to a larger room, cold and damp, and to the steady cadence of falling water. In the far corner was a huge gaping hole where the ceiling had given way. Foliage teased at the edges and pale seedlings mourned in this dim place, straining to reach the light above.

The room was filled with rows and rows of raised cabinets, and each cabinet held a cage, foul orifices that leered at the dark. The party moved between the aisles. Rune began to feel the heavy tug of something which resided there. He peered within the enclosures. The cages were empty, yet each held some terrible residue that danced before his eyes. Aggi steadied him as he swooned in the vile presence.

'There is pain here.'

Anguin sighed, 'Yes, great pain.'

There were books scattered on the floor, volumes like many leaves pressed together, painted with Wroth speech, rotting in the water that collected below the hole in the roof. Violent metal things, broken glass; a single white feather that floated at the centre of the puddle.

They moved beyond the room, into a corridor that resounded with the chatter of the Speaker flock. It brought warmth to this place. Rune hurried along the passage, seeking the source, until at once it opened into a great auditorium.

They emerged above the stalls of a lecture hall. Above the Speaker flocks sat in silent rows, watching all below. Collapsed tables and desk spaces crowded the floor. Computer monitors lay upturned amongst a sea of strewn paper. Piles of perishing books languished about the room, and at centre stage shelving units collapsed against the seminar desk in an accidental arch; their black twisted armature appearing like some spidery altar. Their cargo of ageing scientific almanacs and compendiums spilled out in a haphazard pyramid. Here, atop piles of scientific literature, a reliquary stood. Its contents like that of a living holy artefact.

It was a cage, a large rusting portable cage.

Something dwelled within.

Rune approached hesitantly. With each step the Speakers squawked anxiously; a stranger so close to their father. Books piled to form precarious steps. He did not fly, but walked awkwardly, carefully towards the peak. He peered back at his friends, who encouraged him on.

As he reached the summit he stopped, trying to make out the form within the cage. It was too dark to discern anything in detail, yet it was clear the figure was facing away from him. It held its head low, as though in shame. Rune called upon his courage, and spoke.

'I am Rune, son of Grom. I have travelled a long way to find you. I have many questions. I am told you are very wise, and that you knew my father. Please, could you tell me if he lives?'

Erithacus stooped, turning with grave import, glowering between the bars of his cage. He studied Rune; his eyes were wild and vigorous, and they held within them something Rune had only seen in his father.

The Speaker was huge, and in his form Rune saw something reminiscent of Anguin, the blunt head and curving short beak. His down was grey, and a streak of ruddy red ran through his tail feathers. His face was stark white. The down around the ridges of his cheek was balding and ragged. There were scars too, disfiguring fissures, some so large that Rune found it difficult to look without feeling their depth upon him. Despite this, there was a youthful eccentricity to the Speaker's movements, bound to the cage he seemed to covet. Erithacus turned once again to the corner of his cage.

Rune skirted the greying books that piled beneath the cage, the door to which hung wide, squeaking against the draft that periodically drew breath. He moved closer.

'No!' Erithacus squawked.

Rune felt so many emotions in the voice, most of all he felt fear, not in himself, but from Erithacus. He took a few paces back and waited. Erithacus twitched, bobbing his head in irregular movements. He pulled at the raw skin on his wings, tearing filaments of down away. The gesture reminded Rune of Oclio. He could sense the discomfort that Erithacus felt being watched, so he turned away.

'Grom had lofty ideas.' The great feathered spoke with an orotund croak. 'He would wax lyrical about his second sight, this rumination in causality.'

Rune looked confused. Erithacus paused, considering his words.

'Every choice you make changes the face of time. Your father said he could see those paths before they occurred, said he could see every movement.'

'And ... could he?'

Erithacus pondered for a moment. 'It's possible. I believe he was capable of seeing the resonance of Naa and its many occupants, perhaps some aberration of our ability to sense the magnetic field. Which way to go?

'I for one am fascinated by the concept of choice. I would not be able to speak Wroth, I would not be able to comprehend much of what I hold dear, if it wasn't for the Wroth and their vile practices. Yes, my species is bright, tool using, multitasking. But to know what I know took learning. Did you know they inserted metal probes into my skull?'

Rune looked bemused.

'Despite the complete idiocy of the project, they believe it worked, that my comprehension of mathematics and their sciences was the result of their barbarity.'

Rune cocked his head in confusion.

'I can think bigger,' Erithacus retorted with a condescending air.

The Speakers cackled above in raucous, indecipherable words. Erithacus quieted them with a sharp squawk. His irises were wide and white, his pupils piercing black. With prehensile claws he clutched the bars of his cage.

'Your father is gone.'

Rune held his repose despite his sadness. He looked back at his friends, who sat patiently in silence. 'Where did he go?'

'He went out into the world in search of his answers, I have no way of knowing if he found them. All that I know is that he never returned. You can either see this as success, that he found what he was looking for, or that his search was folly and he is likely dead.'

Rune lowered his head. He felt despair. This seemed to irritate Erithacus, who returned to the corner of his cage.

'My father was Umbra. He could see the Umbra, he was special, he had second sight. Surely he would survive. Surely he would find his answers!'

Erithacus shot a piercing look. 'You are Umbra and you do not find your answers here!'

'I am not Umbra!'

'Oh but you are! You are just too stupid to see it! Your father was patient, he held in him that singular desire, the same desire I have, to know all. Perhaps the answer is not to seek your father, but to seek that which your father sought, to take up his mantle.'

'I do not know what my father sought, he left when I was very young. I thought it was to find why my mother died.'

'Yes! Amongst every other question he could tease from that unfortunate day – all the grief? It triggered an insatiable lust, a catalyst!' Erithacus became animated; shifting from one foot to another, the cage rattled. 'He came to me still covered in her blood. Still marked by her viscera.'

Onnar cried out, 'Do not taunt him, do not say such things!'

The Speaker's shrill retort rang out about the room. Erithacus glowered, 'I say what I wish, the boy must learn!'

Silence returned.

'Was it a pleasant journey? What have you learned of the world since leaving that tower of yours?'

Rune sighed.

'I have learned of the world. Learned how to kill a would-be king, I have seen the slow death of the Wroth, and I have met many who seek something from me.'

'What do they seek?'

'They seek my father, and without him they are left with me.'

'Can you hear it? The song?'

'What song?'

'Your father could hear it, it became louder with each turn of Seyla, and it called to him across oceans. Deafening, maddening, ceaseless. It was blinding him with its light when he slept. He was hounded by it, by the cry of it.'

'I have heard a song, in the Settling Stone, I know its voice. But I can no longer hear it. The Stone brought me to the city, to here. I thought it would bring me to my father. I thought he would be here.'

'You are young and stupid, your words are all whimsy and weakness. The song does not come from here, it sings from a different source, beyond this city. This is not the mouth, this is not the source.'

Rune considered this. Tentatively, he said, 'Seek the throat from which it sings.'

'Seek the throat from which WE sing. Seek the source,' Erithacus replied. 'Where did you hear this?'

'It doesn't matter, I cannot go back. The Settling Stone is buried beneath the earth and it is lost.'

'You must seek the source, you have overcome many obstacles, and this is but one more. Go to the Stone, find your answer. Don't be weak with whimsy, Rune son of Grom.'

There was commotion. A great black figure appeared at an open door beside the seminar desk. It lumbered on old legs up the steps of books.

When it spoke, it spoke with great sadness, 'My friends, we must look for answers elsewhere.'

Tears flooded the old Throa's eyes, the arcing jags of his armour framing his tired face. 'I am sorry Rune,' Tor said, 'we cannot go back to my House.'

Corva Omency

What a tangled web we weave
Of black masses behind walls of folly
Fashioned and partitioned and felled
The cutlass barbs declawed
And mock parliaments dismissed.
Their tread still lay sore
In the fragile earthenware fires
of all young minds
Gathered straw and sticks and stone
Amongst the cartilage of bones
Of forefathers cadavers
Strewn amongst the tidings
Of the Wroth and their travesties.

What is laid before?
Oil stained and bruised
The green pelt ragged raw
What is done and gone before
Sullied lost and moribund.

Trees have lost their eyes
Masters cocksure and idle
Buckshot sentences,
Vulpus craws now blessed silence
Taciturn, arrogant
Whilst we speak of fortune
Of prosper
We while away
At dark principles.

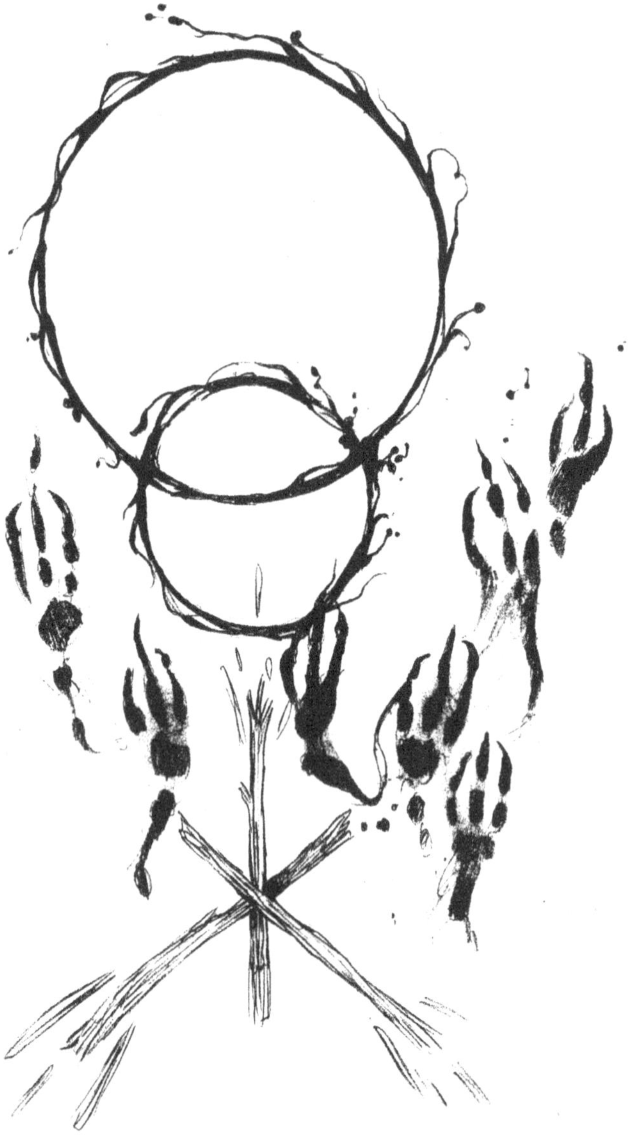

Chapter 8: Tor

For a time, the hallowed atrium of the old sett rang with the cheer of new life. Despite the loss of their former home, the unexpected change had enlivened the Throa; had given them new impetus. In the face of adversity, the empty canvas of their ancestral sett had rekindled in some an interest in arcane practices. Younger kin asked Tor of the many rituals and ceremonies of the Throa, the neglected festivals of plenty and the coming of winter.

The sett was soon filled with the same melodious laughter and clammer that had resided in Tor's old house. He did not dwell on his loses, on all the knowledge he had accumulated from those Wroth-made things. Despite dragging a few meagre scraps of his collection free of the earth, he knew he would find new contrivances to mull over, to take apart and attempt to understand. He wandered the passageways, jostled by the cubs who tumbled over one another, who pulled at his ears and nose, and despite his grumpy demeanour, they knew he enjoyed their company.

At first the sickness went unnoticed. It was insidious, spreading without symptoms. Tordrin returned from food collecting and had complained of pains in his chest. Yet they were not enough to slow him, and he returned to his work the next night, bringing in ample food for his family. Tor had only worried when he saw Tordrin coughing at the entrance to the House, clutching his chest. He asked him what ailed him, yet his son was dismissive, and had carried on with his work.

Tordrin's mate, Alberi, became sick without warning. Suddenly unable to leave her chamber, her children who were still nursing, also became unwell. The first death came in the night, Tor's grandchild, Orga.

The Throa wept for their loss, but it was not long before sickness was rife. Tordrin was strong, and shirked off the need to rest, whilst Tor, seemingly unaffected by the illness, sought out as many medicinal plants as possible. He stripped green bark and lichens; crushed berries and seeds and fed their elixir to his family. For a time this stayed the sickness, and the venomous entity that prowled the corridors of his home took no more life. Still, each night he would lie awake, awaiting the cry of his children.

He found himself thinking of the Sisters of the Flock. He imagined them, those winged paragon. He courted odd thoughts, asking them for guidance in fever moments. He scolded himself, for the Throa did not deify.

The morning came and the sickness lurked in the harrowing coughs and whimpers. He went to his son, whose face was stained with blood. Tor had seen this elsewhere, in the Wroth. Their sickness had come to his house. But how? Was it simply to be near the Wroth that one could inherit their plague? He struggled to temper his own frustrations, his ignorance was cumbersome. Those who remained well charged him with finding a cure.

In the meantime, their old remedies would ease the pain, but it would take a greater mind to cure this sickness, and Tor knew only one that might offer a salve. He readied himself that day, collected what he could of his trinkets and tools, lashed them to his armour, and left his dying home to seek the great Psittacus Erithacus.

He was an old Throa. His legs no longer served him as they had in his youth, and his fear of not reaching his destination, let alone returning, became a palpable motivation.

He found the river that would take him north to the city, a place he had not been for many years, not since his last journey to the old feathered. He studied the minutiae of change; the rise of grey stone and metal, the abundance of refuse that clogged the river, stemming its flow to a mere trickle through the stagnant mud. He would have avoided the roads, yet they too were empty, and not many would attack an old daynight like him.

The Wroth had disappeared, leaving their inanimate devices

behind, an endless trail of cars that stood silent upon the tarmac, doors wide, some crushed into one another. There were dead here too, many Wroth within their metal coffins, empty eyes and yellow flesh. He avoided them, tried not to breathe in their presence.

He hid when the packs of Caanus appeared, feral beasts without their Familiars, unable to comprehend the treatise of the city. The Vulpus would soon parley with them, or kill them. Either way, more blood would be spilled to bring the city to order. It was perhaps a lost cause.

When he was younger Tor had wished the Vulpus to leave the city, to return to the land unoccupied by Wroth settlements, to break the obsession with undoing ancient wrongs. Yet the Vulpus were stubborn and would not listen to the musings of a Throa. He had quelled his resentment by telling himself he would probably be right in the end.

The silence was not what he had expected. Traveling in the day was never advisable, yet here he was, along the main thoroughfare, observing the trappings of the Wroth, peering through windows, taking shining metal objects, discarding them when their purpose remained opaque. He dug in the earth of raised plant pots and sought worms, he drank water from a fountain that still ran. He made good progress, sleeping only a little, retracing old steps.

*

It was Erithacus who had taught him so much of the world, of crafts unknowable to those around him: he had been very young when he learned the myth of Psittacus Erithacus: of the many legends of the city, the Grey Ghost was perhaps the most infamous. Some had said that he was indeed a spirit, the Revenant of an ancient king. Others said he was not a feathered at all, but a carven effigy of some Wroth god; a statue to which the Muroi gave offerings. Yet it was the Muroi who brought with them the tempered arts to the lands beyond the city. The clever Muroi, Tor thought, who had come to the House of Ror and offered their wears, their armoury skills.

It was the Muroi whose practices enticed Tor. Even at a young age he had held their made things and examined the beauty of those crudely hewn objects, the sand and mud of the moulds they had been cast in, leaving the grainy imprint upon each surface. He had asked them to teach the Throa this skill, but they had refused. They told him to seek out the keeper of the Tempered Arts, the Arch Mage Erithacus, who dwelt in the Stinking City, who collected the brightest minds and their collective knowledge. It was Erithacus alone who could teach Tor to become part of the Tempered Guild.

So it was that when he reached an age where his father deemed him able to travel far distances he had left hastily. The same path that he now trod had changed little, despite the dizzying monoliths which had sprung from the earth. Detours were few. Tor reminisced each frightening encounter, each tooth-filled maw or cackling vixen. The cry of many flock, the patience he took to learn the language of the Baldaboa, gain their trust, know their plight. He had treated many wounded feet, and so learned much of the city through their shy and shielded existence; it was the Baldaboa who had guided him to the outskirts of the former Wroth dwelling where Erithacus conducted his Speaker flock.

In his youth the Wroth had long forgotten that torturous domain. It had once been a place of learning, yet that knowledge had been gleaned from great suffering. He learned from the Muroi that one night, some caring Wroth came and freed the many creatures that were held in the cages, taking them away through the hole they had cut in the roof. But they had left Erithacus by mistake, his cage covered with a night cloth, unseen in the dark. He had learned to keep quiet in the presence of the Wroth, and had never suspected that some Wroth meant well; some Wroth wished to end suffering. And so he sat, silent in the dark. He never knew why, but the Wroth never returned to claim their work.

It was the Muroi who had sought places the Wroth were not, who had made a home within the razor wire fences, had found the dying Erithacus at the base of his cage, his ragged breath, his starvation and thirst. They had brought him food and water, the means to survive. Yet he would not leave his cage. Every attempt had bought a terrible, desperate fear.

Once the old feathered had recovered the Muroi learned to understand his behavior. They were patient and resilient. They forgave his violent outbursts and listened attentively to his incomprehensible utterances. They fed him every day, dragging old containers filled with rain water up to his cage to refresh him. They gained his trust. It was not without reward, for once Erithacus was able he began to talk of all he knew. The Muroi saw his ingenuity and shared their own knowledge with him. They regarded him as their greatest teacher, and it was there, amongst the ruins of an abhorrent creed, that the Tempered Guild was formed.

The Speaker flocks were aliens in the land. They were once known as Cheon, brought to these cold climes by the Wroth. Imbedded in their own living memory were the stories of how they too had known cages, had escaped their bondage and eked out an existence, becoming strong. They were clever, there was cunning in their bickering turbulent ways, and when word of their colourful plumage and strange accents reached Erithacus he requested their presence.

They came with curiosity, despite their mistrust. They crowded into his domain, a typhoon of thorny squawks, driving the Muroi into the walls with their din. They harangued his cage with beady eyes, until suddenly, he spoke.

He spoke in a tongue only a few within their ranks could comprehend, the vestigial inflections of a dead language. He quelled them with the palatal consonants and vowels of their native tongue, and those capable of understanding him quieted the rabble. In those obscure shrieks Erithacus explained all that had been done to him, and all that he wished of the world. As the words became a melee of ideas that both offered a home and articles of faith, the ragtag flock gained the same fatherly admiration that the Muroi had come to cherish. He taught them the sanctity of language, his deeply held love of words, that to speak to one another conveyed so many truths. Then, above their wildest expectations of his burning intelligence, he did something seemingly impossible.

He spoke Wroth.

They would soon learn how to interpret, how to mimic their sounds with their own throats, and greater achievement still, to understand their meaning. This tool of language began to establish Erithacus's goal; to bind the air with his law. He birthed the Speakers, gave them a very real task. They would gather for him every inkling he desired, and with this his knowledge and power grew.

Tor had first reached Erithacus not long after he had tricked the Gull Lord Malca, who had sought to rule the city skies. The law of the sky and the land differed greatly. Not often did the rule of the Vulpus affect the flocks. Yet the Vulpus curiously avoided any communication with Erithacus. The defeat of Malca had left Erithacus in good spirits, which boded well for the young Throa.

He took on Tor as an apprentice.

*

Tor found himself in unfamiliar territory. Where once had been swathes of disused land, now stood rows of vast warehouses that flanked the northern end of the city. He wound his way through the abundance of dangers, great stacks of timber creaking and groaning under their own weight, the complication of pallets and their loads. He carefully manoeuvred between menacing machines, seeking out a path with his nose, the faintest scents that spoke of distant memories. He kept an ear to the sky, ever listening for that telltale cry. Eventually he acquiesced to his exhaustion and found somewhere to shelter for the day.

The evening brought the sign he sought, as an entire squadron of Speakers flew above him. He smiled to hear that terrible shriek once again. He climbed from beneath the piles of newspaper which had provided a den for his rest, shook the lethargy from himself and loped between the huge shipping containers that flanked his path, until finally he emerged before the great impenetrable fence. It took him a while to find an entry point; the wire was marked with blood spilt by previous attempts to gain access. Once within, he stood on his hind legs and awaited the guardians of the Arch Mage. They came with gusto, encircling him, demanding reason for his presence.

'I come with the Song,' he had said.

*

'Tor! Why are you here?' Rune said, worried.

Tor shook his head with confusion and embarrassment and backed away as they approached. He calmed himself, easing his tired bones into a sitting position.

'Forgive me, I have travelled for many turns and I am very tired. I heard your voices and they roused me as I rested after my journey. I am so glad to see you all, but my reason for being here is grave. For a while all was well, we were happy. But it was not long before my son Tordrin fell ill, and soon many of my kin were stricken with this foulness, the sickness of the Wroth. I did my best to treat them, but this consumption is beyond me, I cannot cure it. So I came here, seeking the guidance of Erithacus.'

Erithacus shifted in his cage. 'Tor told me of his encounter with the Wroth, and the life his son took. I believe the sickness is in the blood and spittle. I imagine through grooming and touch this sickness spread to his family. This is how it is spread within the Wroth. Through touch.'

'What is the sickness? Can it be stopped?'

Erithacus looked at Rune with something like irritation. He sighed, 'There are living things in Naa that are so small you cannot see them, they live in us, some are harmless, even helpful, and others are not. Some wish to spread and kill. This is one of the worst ones. I have no means to defeat it here. But perhaps something can be done. The study of plants and their healing abilities; perhaps amongst the flora we might find a cure.'

Onnar interjected, 'My mother taught me many cure-alls, I know a number of plants I can harvest and bring here.'

Tor smiled, 'This would be useful. I have very little time.'

It was suddenly apparent to them all that Tor was not at all well.

'How long have you been sick?' Onnar said.

Tor grimaced, 'I imagine for a while now, I have felt my body give of itself to some sickness. Perhaps my will to seek a cure has staved off the worst of it. But now, I have become tired in my search for answers, and it has caught up with me. It is best you keep a good distance. I do not want any of you to get sick.'

Erithacus spoke abruptly. 'Yet he offers us a test subject. Which is fitting considering where we are right now. This place once spoke of cures and yet seemed only capable of producing misery. We can perhaps offer a greater care than any were shown here.'

'What was this place?' Rune said as he looked about the dank room.

'My boy – It was the stuff of nightmares.'

*

Tor escorted them beyond to the library, which was filled with many more books. There was a pile of hay and torn paper where Tor had been resting, and he stumbled towards it, collapsing in a heap. Rune studied the books, 'You can understand these markings?'

Tor smiled. 'A little. Erithacus can not only read, but he knows the meaning of some of the great ideas of the Wroth. They taught him to speak, you know, taught him their symbols. They taught him the act of counting, abstractions and ideas.

'With all this he translated the Wroth tongue into Ocquia, so the many flocks and ground dwellers could understand it. There are even words that are derived from Wroth, words we use without knowing their source. Erithacus wished to comprehend the Wroth for all of us, so that we would better understand their intentions, good or bad.

'You must listen to him Rune. He may not have all the answers we seek, but he will help guide you to them. He has a way of bringing out the best in us.'

Onnar appeared, 'Tor, I will leave soon to collect plants for remedies. May I bring you anything specific?'

She began tightening her armour as Tor struggled to remember the little he knew of medicine. 'There are the autal leaves and carbry seeds. I know these will help my chest. The rest I leave to you, I am sure your knowledge of such things far surpasses mine! Thank you Onnar.'

She nodded, and headed back to the auditorium. There she said, 'Erithacus, I leave to seek plant remedies for Tor, do you have any knowledge of such things?'

Erithacus ruminated, 'The plant you call farnikan …'

Onnar frowned, 'That is poison, it will do nothing but make him sick!'

Erithacus smiled, 'Ah yes, perhaps in its raw form, but if we can produce heat, remove that poison, I believe there is a quality that will alleviate Tor's swollen chest.'

Onnar shook her head uncertainly, 'I will trust you know what is best for him, and I will bring back what farnikan I can find.'

Erithacus chirped and Anguin glided down before him. 'Anguin, please join Onnar Drove in her search. I believe a pair of eyes in the sky will be useful.'

Aggi appeared before Erithacus, 'I believe you came here with your own plight, Collector?'

Aggi lowered her head, 'I had hoped that …'

'Speak up,' he barked.

She lifted the tiny metal nut that Tor had given her. It seemed insignificant in the light of Tor's presence. 'I come with the Song, I wish to know the Tempered Arts, and to join the Guild.'

*

Tor was fast asleep as Rune and Aggi stood patiently before Erithacus. A collection of books lay spread in front of him, all of which were unfathomable to them. Erithacus peered greedily at the pages, teasing some incomprehensible meaning. Periodically he squawked for the pages to be turned.

'You both seek an art. I believe you might already know these arts better than you think.'

Aggi cocked her head to one side. 'I do not know how one bends the will of ore.'

Erithacus's eyes widened. 'Tell me, Collector, look at Rune's armour. Can you tell me how each piece joins, how the metal found these shapes, how the hieroglyphs were carved within the metal?'

'Yes, I can tell you, but I cannot do it. I do not know how to tame the molten ore.'

'Nor did the Muroi, nor did I. If I were not here to tell you how it is done, how would you do it?'

She pondered for a moment. She knew a very strong heat could melt metal. She knew that the ore was found in the earth, that the Wroth had dug it up and only some ores could be melted, the softest metals. She knew the Muroi sought places where the Wroth burned things, shaped their moulds of sand and earth. She explained all of this to Erithacus.

'I suspected as much. You see Aggi, Collector, you already hold a great deal of knowledge in you. The Muroi were inquisitive, they burrowed within the muscle of Wroth dwellings. They watched them toil away. But the Wroth did not like the Muroi in the walls, they did not like them near them when they slept. So they trapped them, and killed them. The Muroi became despised by the Wroth. Loved ones were lost, often tempted by scraps of food, only for those scraps to be lures that would only gift them with an untimely death.

'So the Muroi became clever, they learned to undo Wroth things, unmake their world. They would chew through the sinew that brought them their light, they would steal their food and wreak havoc in their homes. Each death held recompense, and it was deserved. The Muroi, despite their size, learned to infiltrate the Wroth's lives, until they were always around them, always watching them.

'They gained a potent knowledge of the Wroth; through their endless passageways, imbedded in the skeleton of every Wroth den, every Wroth settlement, watching through the slightest holes and cracks, studying, learning. Often the younger Muroi would be tempted by the traps, yet enough survived to assure their silent dominion over the Wroth. The strangest quality of this story is that the Wroth were largely unaware that they had been conquered.

'With this knowledge it is true that the Muroi went into Naa, found the places the Wroth used metals. They studied them, and much of what they learned was far beyond their means, for the Muroi were simply too small to use the great machines with which the Wroth shaped their metal.

'So they employed legions of Collectors and sent them into Naa on endless searches, sought out the lightest, most pliant metals, the softest metals that the Wroth valued the least. They found ovens – metal boxes in which the Wroth cooked food, hot enough to melt those softer metals. They harnessed this power, made an art of it. They honed beautiful things of it, the Highest Wrought, and gifted them to Naa.

'They did all of this alone. Now that the Wroth are leaving, the ovens and hot places are cold. I imagine this very moment there are Muroi attempting to make fire, to rekindle the heat so that they can continue their art.'

'So I cannot learn the Tempered Arts without these hot places?'

'The Tempered Arts are not just about tempering metal, they are about knowing ourselves. Like the metal, our strength lies within, not simply as a shiny surface. We are so often told that our eccentricities hold no value, that we must seek more useful skills.

'Tell me Collector, you sought this art, why did you wish to know how to cast armour?'

'I have always been curious; my curiosity would get me in trouble sometimes. Often I found it hard to understand the desires and traditions of my family.

'I was told my questions were pointless, I was often mocked when I did not understand the games and jokes of my flock. For so many turns I was charged with finding objects for the Muroi. I became curious of our work, I wanted to know why I was given such a task.

'The Collectors see no value in the things they collect. We simply have sharp eyes, we are clever, know where to look. But why? To put food in our bellies? Is that all I am good for?

'So I followed both Muroi and Collector and found the source, a place where the Muroi sorted through the scraps of metal, discarding a great deal of it, in search of something particular. They would use this metal in their art, the High Wrought armour forged for the Startle and the Vulpus, the armour that Rune wears. My family collected the metal for that armour.

'That night, when the Muroi had gone and the Collectors were roosting, I went to those discarded things, and I saw a purpose in them. I found I could shape that tough and unwieldy metal into shapes, my beak, my claws – they were my tools. I could shape the metal to my will. I could construct hardy armour, just as beautiful and tough as the cast armour. I did not see competition, I knew ambition.'

Erithacus asked, 'And what did you do with these skills?'

'I left my flock. I travelled south, back to the forests. I found myself alone, and I preferred it that way. I found that the Wroth discarded metal things everywhere, and I found uses for them. The soft, tearable metal could be flattened, compacted, sewn tight against other harder metals.

'I found stones to shape the metal, to cut it. I bartered my wears for food and knowledge. I kept to myself until one day, when I was trading, I came upon a Casting, a Corva with no flock. She too made things, beautiful things of thin metals and wood and seed shells. She told me of Tor, and the Guild of the Tempered Arts. She told me to seek him out, if I wished to know how the Muroi made their armour.

'At first I resisted the urge. I thought that my armour was good enough. But eventually the knowledge alone was too tempting, and so I made the finest armour I could, so that I could barter with the Drove for a guide to the House of Tor. This is how I met Rune, and Onnar.'

'In your time amongst your friends have you felt the old draw, the same desire to be alone. Do you feel discomfort around them?'

Aggi looked to Rune, who smiled. 'No, I love my friends, they are my family.' Aggi beamed.

'Then you are already part of the Guild of Tempered Arts. To smelt the ores that the Muroi covet is but a skill to be learned. The Tempered Arts are within, to accept yourself, for who you are, not for what others wish you to be. It seems that you are made to know the workings of things. I will set you tasks to perform.'

Erithacus paused, gathering his thoughts. 'That leads me to you Rune. Without the Settling Stone I cannot guide you further. The path anointed by that Stone gave you the first marker, a point on the map. Your father and Tor worked for many turns to find the path, to encourage the Stones to sing their definitive song. Yet it was more than this, it was the presence of the Umbra that enabled them to articulate their importance. Tell me Rune, do you feel a pull to things you cannot see? Perhaps, you can understand more than what is before your eyes?'

Rune recollected the multitude of coloured lines that plagued his dreams and waking vision, the mesmerism like a prism that broke into dizzying fractals.

'I see strange things, bright shapes, like staring at Ora for too long. I sense things that were once there or might possibly be in the future. I can't explain it, I feel like Naa snags on me, like it wishes me to know it better. It's difficult to explain.'

A peculiar expression appeared on Erithacus' face. 'This is the Umbra. Without a point of reference I imagine it is a nauseating affair, to be unable to steady these images. Without a teacher, these frenzied delusions will remain confusing. It would take another Umbra to allow you that ability. But I wonder if perhaps it can also be self-taught.'

'Self-taught?'

'What if we were to make a Singing Stone?'

Erithacus turned to Aggi. 'Those claws and beak are deft and precise. You have shaped metal to a fine art. Could your skills be applied to another material?'

Aggi looked at her feet, so small and fragile. 'I cannot cut stone.'

'But you can guide the tool that can.'

*

Within the grounds of the university campus was a building site. Piles of sand and shingle sat beside the behemoth machines that once toiled the land, festering plasterboard peaked out from under tarpaulin. The rain had made a mire, half-finished foundations sank in dark runoff, the collecting sky pouring its scorn on this fabrication, asking for it to sink beneath the earth.

Amidst a multitude of raindrops thousands of Muroi emerged from hidden places, they fled flood-like from beneath, searching, smelling, chewing and testing the myriad options. They searched for a particular thing, of a particular size, their delicate fingers tracing the silt and water, sensing the contours of every obstacle, until finally, beyond the new foundations they came to a pointless artifice of the Wroth; nestled in a bed of pebbles and paving stones. A great ornamental rock.

The Muroi halted, their many eyes tracing each irregular arch of the stone. They encircled it, feeling one another's concerns and queries through the infinitesimal motions of their whiskers.

Is it large enough?

Does it suit our needs?

There was consensus, too large to move; and so on they ran, beyond the slurry land, beyond the concrete expanses, the manicured trees, the tide of razor wire and security fencing. Beyond the soil besmeared by the Wroth, to the untouched wilderness that clung to the fringes of the city, the bastions of the untamed. They searched each nook, under every fallen tree. They burrowed to seek that which might dwell below. Until finally, upon the dark loam, in the shadow of a desecrated church, they happened upon a graveyard.

Dark memorials encumbered by moss and lichen, the names of the dead faded beneath the forest's green teeth, the tongue of leaf mulch licking the crumbling stone with centuries of decay. The Muroi danced in the shadows of these graves until they reached the apex. A shrine, a crucifix of sandstone.

There they saw potential.

The final word was given, not by one, but by all. The Muroi keened their ears to the earth, and began to stamp. A thousand Muroi tapping their inclinations against the hard ground. Legions of Muroi in the forests wide were alerted by the message, they listened and translated its implication, rushing urgently to the surface.

Amongst the bracken, deep within the woods far beyond the boundaries of the city, the Muroi found their goal.

Sleeping giants curled against one another for warmth, roused from their slumber. 'Come,' they whispered, 'you are needed.'

They heaved their tired bodies from the earth, their cloven hooves, their snort and whiney, the flash of tusk and sharp eye. These were the Runta, who now thrived in the absence of Wroth.

The swine made quick work of their journey, greeting the congregation before the tomb's obelisk. They considered it, and formed a plan. The Muroi ascended the trees, gnawing lengths of the ivy that hung in locks. They lay them straight and bound them, running their length, twisting each nimble creeper with another, pulling them taut into a strong cable, which was lain flat below the pillar.

The largest Runta grunted for all to move clear. Then it reared back and ran at the column, felling it with a single blow. The stone tumbled forward, the crossbar falling where the ivy lay. The Muroi lashed the ivy cable about its neck, each Runta taking the makeshift rope within its mouth. Three aside, they began to pull, and the monument lifted, until it was high enough to place the crucifix arms across the lead Runta's backs. They roared for motion – 'Onwards!' they grunted – and began to drag it, back across the unsullied copse, towards the House of Erithacus.

Chapter 9

Roak was in remarkable territory, to side with one's natural enemy, but the Morwih would hold no sway over his reign. He would have the freedom he so desired. That being said, he feared what Esperer might think of such a reckless move; how he would present this alliance to the battalions under the rule of the king. He thought of the sea once again.

He found himself above the purulent docks. This was not his sea. No Wroth vessels called here now. Some drifted in the murky water, lonesome, starving for attention. He descended, expecting a degree of reception, but not one Gull came to greet him. He found the warehouse where once he'd attempted to learn the whereabouts of Erithacus. He entered the wide steel doors and approached the hanging ceiling. Many Gulls were here, weak and malnourished. Some had stooped to hunting once again, they argued and fought for petty scraps. Hunger had got the better of any sense of courtesy.

He made for the same stoic Gull who'd once held rank over this sprawl of untidy feathered. He paid no heed to the feeble caws his presence prompted.

'What do you want?' the Gull said. He pecked at a rancid Ungdijin carcass, his henchgull shaking with hunger, eying it with envy.

'Your name.'

'I am Tawk, ruler of all you see before you!'

'You realise this is pathetic.' Roak scanned the great unfed.

'How dare you!'

'I dare! But I am not here to fight. I am here to feed you and give you something more than this.'

'Your stupid war?' The thug spat the words with a lilt of capitulation. He no longer had the strength or inclination to turn down any alternative to this slow death.

'Gather your flock. We fly to the city. I know lakes and rivers full of Ungdijin. Easy pickings. We will fatten you all, and have armour made, make you strong again. We have new allies.'

'Allies?'

Roak smiled, 'The Fractured Sects. We fight with the Morwih.'

*

Soon the old Throa was unable to leave his bedding. Medicine was brought to Tor, and he managed to drink a little water. Food would not stay down, and he shivered between distressing cries and coughs. Aggi perched above him, dripping water from moss to wet his brow.

The commotion caused by his visitors and a need to heal his sick friend had given Erithacus a purpose and vitality, and banished the damaging habits he had courted for so long. From his cage he directed the Muroi and Speakers to erect a structure from the hundreds of books, whilst other Speakers collected sticks and twine. Meanwhile they awaited the return of their brethren, with hope that they had success in acquiring that which Erithacus requested.

Aggi was asked to find a number of tools for her own use, tools that might aid her new task. She knew she required the toughest stones for cutting, yet beyond that did not know what it was she might be called upon to do. She took to wing, searching the river banks and parklands for flints. She soon spied the perfect implements and returned with excitement, completing her first assignment as a member of the Tempered Guild.

The Grey Ghost honed Rune's concentration. His fear for Tor's life had become something of a hindrance to the task at hand, clouding Rune's attention. Yet Erithacus kept his focus, taught him to breathe; to consider with less urgency and more contemplation.

The feathered would sit within his cage and describe how he pictured Grom's abilities, how he made sense of clairvoyance within his particular view of Naa. Rune found the conversation one sided, unable to add anything to the stream of thought that spilled from his tutor. Despite this, his imagination constructed vibrant visions that held facets of Erithacus's meaning. It was enough to hear the words, for Rune to gain a measure of understanding.

Erithacus found this fascinating. 'Some unseeable force conveys these thoughts through the very air, a signal. You are a receiver, how and why is unknown. I would need to cut you apart to see the blood and bone, to see the anatomy of that brain of yours.'

He peered at Rune with examining eyes. Rune recoiled.

'The ear perhaps, perhaps the eyes. There is some gelatinous mass or lens or cartilaginous mechanism in that brain of yours. I found no evidence of it in your father, but I can only imagine that the Wroth would take a blade and find the niggling architecture like that!'

He snapped his claws against the cage. A book fell beside him. Rune cowered. Erithacus gave him a wry smile.

'Rune, I am not going to hurt you, don't you worry!'

Erithacus called to the Speakers and a number landed beside Rune. His tutor spoke to them in Wroth tongue. Rune tried to make sense of it, but he could feel no residue of connection with his own words, neither Startle nor Ocquia. Not yet at least, and so he awaited quietly.

The Speakers took flight through the hole in the roof.

'Your father said he could see the movements of all feathered without witnessing them. He saw it as a latticework before his eyes, the whole of Naa. I want you to close your eyes and try to locate the Speakers that just left. Seek them.'

Rune closed his eyes tight.

Nothing.

Frustrated, he strained against the black, seeking the traces that often collected before his eyes near sleep. He opened his eyes wide, 'I see nothing!'

Erithacus sighed, 'Boy, think of it like an organ, part of you. You need to give it strength, time to manifest. Now, close your eyes, and think of the Speakers. Think of watching them leave, flying out into the night.'

Rune closed his eyes again. At once blotches and swells of light whorled before him. He squeezed his eyes tighter and followed each coloured strand. The blotches dispersed, wider than his peripheral vision.

He could make out a black horizon with no discernible difference between the highest and lowest point. He felt his eyes straining in his head. The black began to ripple, and he could sense the undulating mass. It swelled until it snuffed out every light.

Black.

Rune opened his eyes. 'There was something for a moment, but I couldn't hold it.'

Erithacus sighed. 'Time boy, time is all it takes until holding the image is but the first task.'

*

Aggi returned to find Rune waiting silently beside Erithacus's cage. There were glowing lights in the dark, they flickered in her presence and she approached them. The glow accented the edge of the Grey Ghost's face within the gloom of his cage, and this scared her a little. She asked hesitantly, 'What are these?' She gestured at the lights.

'They call them candles. They hold this fire in a constant tiny flame. The white stick is called wax, and it is a fuel. Much like the food we eat to continue moving, the flame requires fuel to keep burning. The wax melts into a liquid, this hardens when not heated, which causes these beads to form.'

Erithacus pointed at the long strands of wax that collected around the candles. 'This wax acts much like a metal exposed to fire. The Wroth learned to control fire a very long time ago, something no other species has ever achieved. It is partly why they were so successful, why there are … why there *were* so many of them.'

'Can we melt ore over these flames?' Her attention was caught by the brilliant tear of light that hovered before her. She could feel its heat.

'Some metals would melt under such a flame, we can perhaps ask the Muroi to show you. Do you have the tools I asked you to collect?'

She turned to point her wing towards several large shards of sedimentary rock, broken to form sharp cutting edges. He nodded, 'Good. These are perfect for the task ahead.'

*

Onnar and Anguin found themselves in the hills to the north, far beyond the comfort of known lands. Here the incline offered Onnar a view of the entire expanse of the Stinking City. Anguin perched upon a raised sign which displayed a map of the skyline. He traced the embossed letters with his claws.

'This place was enjoyed by the Wroth,' he said as she cleaned herself. 'The words tell me that each of these great stones,' he gestured at the buildings, 'each have names.'

'They named their dwellings?' She was surprised. 'Much like we do. I did not know they were so sentimental!'

Anguin laughed, 'The more I learn of them, the more complicated I find it to place my hatred.'

'Explain?'

'They wielded their strength with all the maturity of a child. Yet they made amazing things. They learned so much of Naa – Erithacus said they managed to leave Naa, to voyage to worlds beyond this one.'

'You mean they died and went to the Gasp?'

'Maybe, through an endless place to other worlds. I don't understand what he meant, but he holds ideas far beyond mine. The Wroth came back with such stories.'

'Rune came back from the Gasp. Perhaps Rune holds the same abilities. Rune is also a child.'

"True. I think Rune is perhaps lumbered with too many responsibilities. He is too young to hold such weight.'

Onnar agreed. 'To a degree, and yet, he holds them with a rare strength.' She gestured towards the woods. 'Perhaps we will find the plants we need there?'

They skirted the edges, seeking the odd herb or plant that might hold a cure. Onnar slipped what they found under her armour and they continued on, deep within the trees. The ferns became dense upon the floor, making it harder for Onnar to manoeuvre. Anguin could see nothing but the carpet of green and red brown, but he called to her, guiding her as best he could.

They reached a clearing and stopped to rest. As they lapped at a small puddle, Onnar's ears pricked. 'Someone is coming,' she said, moving with considered stride until she was hidden from view.

Anguin took to wing, drawing up into the trees. He saw the movement for himself, three separate forms loomed upon the clearing.

They carried themselves with a familiar lope; they were not hunting, nor stalking, their movements were not cautious.

They were Drove.

Onnar could smell them before they appeared. She let her fear disperse before freeing herself of the foliage. The three great Yoa'a revealed themselves with shared relief. A huge, grizzled older Drove and two much younger kin stood before her.

'Onnar proudfoot. As I live and breathe!'

'Tarmisil, praise the Blithe Priestess, it has been a long time!'

They met with glad tidings and Onnar was introduced to the younger Drove, 'This is Brashni and Yorkalig, from beyond the Scars River no less! I met them on my travels south.'

'What brings you to these lands?'

'Word of work, a war. The Collector flocks were being called by the Corva. We have seen a great deal of movement in the sky, and so we asked why. Strange times. The Morwih are going to war with the Vulpus.'

'Yes indeed, I am tasked myself within this war. Who will you fight for?'

Tarmisil smiled, 'Depends on the barter don't it!' She tugged at Onnar's armour, 'This is fine work, wouldn't mind some myself. Hope we don't meet on the field of battle.' She winked, 'You travel where?'

'We are seeking medicinal plants, a friend of ours is very sick.'

'We?'

Anguin descended beside Onnar, bowing to the great Drove. 'I am Anguin, of the Speaker flocks and the House of Erithacus.'

Tarmisil was taken aback, 'A Speaker? Well look at you, bright green and everything!'

Anguin gave her a look of bemusement. 'You are a rare sight yourself Yoa'a, especially by city borne.'

She laughed, 'There is only one of me, green feathers!'

They laughed together, and soon they moved through the wood and discussed the world. Anguin spoke of Erithacus, of the plight of Rune and Aggi, and of his time in the Crool. Onnar expanded Tarmisil's knowledge of the war, explaining that the city itself was at stake. Soon they came to talk of Tor and his sickness.

'You have stayed away from him? You don't carry the sickness?' Brashni asked with nervous candour.

'We have been careful. He is alone, resting. We bring him water, and hope he will soon eat again, but when we left it had been a few turns since he took a single bite. We have been asked to seek farnikan to quench the sickness.'

'The poison root? Last I used that I killed a Maar by dribbling its juices on a fallen Tril. Dead in hours. Unless you're hoping to give this Throa a quick death what could that plant possibly be used for?'

Onnar nodded, 'Yes, what you say is true, but I am told there is a way to make the poison disappear. This is what we seek. With this we might be able to help Tor, and others. We hope.'

'Fascinating, well farnikan likes dry soil. You will find it around rock, or perhaps in open space, but not here in the woods. Too damp. It is the root you seek, but be careful Onnar. I do not wish to hear you died digging for roots for an old daynight.'

'I would do the same for you, old girl,' Onnar retorted.

'Aye that you would. Well. We will see you in the throes of war, perhaps.'

'Hopefully beside one another, not against.' They both laughed.

They said their goodbyes and Anguin flew up to find a path out of the wood. They were soon back on the slopes of the hill, where the exposed yellowing grass and muddied paths greeted them. There was no sight of the plant, so they continued upwards, towards the peak.

Beside a bench stood a bin brimming with Wroth waste. At its base, by the mouldy remains of a hamburger in its greasy wrapper, they spied a rotting head of leaves. About to continue by, Onnar hesitated. For a moment she was not sure. Then she knew – farnikan. But the plant was dying. Onnar dug down, until she found its shrivelled root.

'It's the best we can do,' she shrugged. 'I have other plants, perhaps if this is no good, we might use them.'

Anguin nodded in agreement, and they began their journey back towards the city.

*

The stone was a burden yet the Runta pulled with tireless might. Through hedgerows they tore, seeking the path of least resistance, carving a deep gouge in the mud. The Muroi ran along with them, swarming over every obstacle with liquid obstinance.

They reached the fence of the compound at dusk the next turn. Dragging it to the gap in wire mesh, the grinding screech of stone against metal alerted the Speakers to the presence of the formidable animals and their load. They squealed and roared as the Speakers guided them beyond the empty laboratories; hooves against broken glass, the hollow draw of a gravestone upon carpet and linoleum.

Erithacus greeted the Runta with applause, clashing the base of the cage with his claws, swinging himself to and fro. 'Come forth! Come forth! Bring that great thing down here!'

Soon the stone lay before the mass of books that the Muroi had gathered. Erithacus peered at the huge stone cross.

'Perfect!' he exclaimed.

The Runta heaved it into a standing position. Immediately those around them pushed masses of books against its base. It leaned dangerously, until finally it was stable. The soft sandstone was shaped in a wide cylinder; old and weathered yet held its form. Aggi and Rune were engulfed by its presence, the black stanchion.

Aggi ran her wing over it. 'What is it for?'

Erithacus hopped to the front of his cage and strained to see through the bars. 'My dear, this is our Singing Stone.'

Rune turned abruptly to him, 'This is not a Singing Stone!'

'Ah, my boy, but it *will* be.'

*

'The gods are starving.'

Vorsa stood at the gates to the Moterion. Before her the Starless Vulpus and their leader, Nox. He said, 'Without the Wroth to feed them, many will die. The food remaining is almost exhausted. We can hunt for those who need flesh, and bring leaves and fruit for those who do not, but there are so many gods here, we will need a legion to sate their hunger. We must free them within a few turns of Seyla so that they might hunt and feed. Many will die without the Wroth.'

Vorsa accepted this and asked for entry within the Moterion so that she might speak with the Corva.

She passed through the gaps in the wrought iron gate. The prison was hallowed for many reasons. It was Starless territory, designated to them long before she was born. Any born Starless would immediately venerate this place, tasked by the Corva Anx with whispering the truth of Naa to the empty minds of the gods imprisoned within.

There was much Wroth debris, and a shrill din as many of the gods groaned and bleated in their cages. As her dark escort continued on, past kempt grass verges, refreshment stands and colourful signposts, Vorsa made out the phosphor of eyes watching her.

A voice snarled from a dark cage, 'Who is this?'

Vorsa did not recognise what she saw, yet it leered at her. Volatile with rage, it ran at the bars. She jumped back from the peculiarly striped beast, only to watch one Starless pace silently before the cage, and whisper in its great ear. Soon it was lulled into solace and they continued on.

Nox said, 'You will have to excuse them. They have spent a lifetime in these cages, they fear change, they even miss the constant attention of the Wroth who came to stare at them and taunt them. It is like a sickness, not knowing what you are, how you found yourself enclosed in this place. We spend our whole lives telling them of Naa, constructing the poetry of everything, giving them the hope of freedom. We must fulfil that promise.'

'We shall,' she said nervously.

Before them the rising false mountain; slabs of rock modelled to look like a gnarled cliff face, its peak festooned with Corva. The Dominus had returned to his perch, front and centre. His shifty eye needled her as she neared.

'What will it take to free these gods?'

The Dominus considered her words. 'What say the Orata, Corpse Speaker?'

She pondered. The Orata spoke of those who must be freed; it was opaque, open for interpretation. Mention of the god prison was woven into later verses.

'The Foul Meridian calls for their release, it does not speak of how?'

'They will be freed once we acquire the Umbra. For what is a Meridian without the Umbra?'

"Will the cages simply open when we have an Umbra?' she quipped.

'Do not condescend me, Vorsa.'

'I do not understand your riddles Dominus! We cannot rely on prophecy alone! I will gladly stand in for Rune if he is unable to perform the ritual. My brother is strong within the Gasp, he feels the presence of the Umbra. I will act as conduit for him.'

'You speak of heresy, Corpse Speaker! We cannot force the Umbra to give of itself!'

Vorsa scowled, 'And you cannot force Rune to act as conduit either! Your stubbornness will not win this war Audagard!'

'Let the bones lie Vorsa, let the sticks speak their intention.'

She rolled her eyes and turned to the Starless Vulpus. 'What do you need?'

'We must gather those able to bring food for the gods, and we need to break the cages that hold them. I believe there are some with nimble beaks who might have the skill to break the bonds. We know it is possible, yet such skills are rare.'

'I will send word to Erithacus. He might provide guidance in this task. For now, I will employ Collector flocks to find food for the gods. Continue preparing for the Foul Meridian, assure your wards that soon they will be free.'

The Starless Vulpus guided her back to the gates and split off into the night. Vorsa took a moment to consider her next move.

Without Hevridis she no longer had an eye on the Morwih. The Vulpus clans were busy searching the streets beyond the Moterion for spies and she greeted them as she journeyed to the city centre. She sought the office block that once served as her place of learning amongst the Corva, climbing its innards until she stood atop its roof. A number of Corva still remained, guarding the monuments of their shrouded prayer.

She could smell Morwih here, perhaps they had come seeking to disrupt the Meridian. She greeted the Corva warily, and strode to the edge of the roof.

The spectacle of dawn approached. It sank blood-like into the lay of the land. To her left and right she noticed the Corvan monoliths upon other rooftops, the intent of which was unknown to her. She traced the points in the city that gave the Morwih advantage; she would make sure each was guarded. As her eyes trailed east she saw the cathedral. Hevridis had mentioned the place often as a makeshift meeting point for the

Fractured Sects.

It was covered in Gulls. Hundreds of them.

She bound to the highest point of the roof and strained to make out movement. Some were armoured. She could see the plastic gleam of scraps hewn into breast and neck plates. And then she saw what she feared; prowling furtively beside them was a Morwih. Soon more were visible, perched upon the roof terrace. The Consul was building her army.

It took Vorsa little time to wend her way to the Bazaar. Her entrance was met with agitation; a high ranking Vulpus brought fear to prey animals. She hadn't eaten in days, she was ragged and tired. She collected herself and cleared her throat. 'I need messengers, as many as can be mustered.'

A nervous queue formed before her, and she gave each a task, to bring every able body to the Moterion, to fight and to bring food to feed the hungry gods. Word had gone far on Corva wing, which heralded many flocks entering the city. But not many claimed fealty with either the Morwih or Vulpus, they fought for whoever offered more. The Gulls she had seen were city flock, she knew this from their armour, yet there was loose loyalty between Gull kin - would Esperer fight with the Morwih? She seethed. Were the cruel and unscrupulous destined to fight alongside one another?

Once she had sent out the messengers she made her way towards the cathedral. She searched the alleys and causeways, sniffed acrid fence posts and loathsome remains of the Wroth, bodies dragged and discarded. She realised she had not even noticed their absence for a while, and the few that still remained eyed her with a palpable distress. Onwards, she reached the canal, the stench of floating corpses assaulting her as she ran beside it, and then suddenly a familiar scent, faint yet recent, drew her up to the railway track and onwards. Soon she had his trail. Only he could give her the information she desired.

The streets that circled the cathedral were thick with Morwih. Vorsa studied them from afar, as they moved around in the wreckage of a fire engine. She followed a pair, who were exchanging small talk with grating whine.

She knew a little Morwih tongue: 'It is tempting, they are so big, I would feed for days on just one! How many of us have lost our familiars, how many of us will starve for her cause?'

'It is not wise to tempt her wrath, and besides, those Gulls are huge, and loyal. They will kill you before you had a chance.'

Vorsa smiled. Defection in the ranks? Perhaps seeking the ear of an unfussy eater was a bad move on the Gulls' behalf.

She left them to squabble and ran to the right of the building. His scent hung in the air and she found him hunting Muroi in the churchyard. She watched him for a while. He was large for a Morwih, not fat, but very stocky. She considered how to approach him. He was proud, foolish.

'The Wroth bury their dead here,' she said with an air of disquiet.

He was surprised; his hackles rose and he backed away hissing. 'You are in dangerous territory here Vulpus!'

She laughed, 'Hevridis, have you finally been accepted back by your loved one?'

He sighed, 'You can condescend to me all you want, I accomplished what I set out to do, so the fate of that feathered means little to me.'

'That feathered will assure the city for us. Like it or not, you failed.'

'Vorsa, I care little for this war. I care about two things, myself and Fraubela. I care nothing for the fate of this vile place. What Fraubela desires, I support. It matters little to me.'

'She wishes to murder my people, to rule with her teeth and claws.'

'The Morwih are too loose a people to rule, we would be less authoritarian than you.'

'You would leave this land bloodied! The flocks would leave, the Muroi would leave, and it would be nothing but an empty city festering in the stead of the Wroth.'

'Ah, but the Vulpus would also leave, and she would reclaim the land which you laud over. You see, I will agree. We can be petty, aloof, uncaring. We are interested in matters of self. It is how we are born. Perhaps she is happy to let this city die, just as long as you die with it.'

Vorsa jumped at him, slathering jaws wide. Her mouth closed on his neck with precision. She held him down and spat fur.

'I want to kill you, but I know I cannot. I want to make you bleed for what you did, but you were a pawn in this just as much as I. This is not a game; we are not play fighting.' She grazed her teeth against his neck, feeling the lulling sate of blood. She shook him hard. 'Unless you leave the city, you will die along with many of us. Even me. So think carefully. I know in that thick skull of yours is the intuition to know when the game is up.'

She flung him to the ground. His neck bled. He pulled himself back, away from her.

'You're mad!' He spat, 'Why did you do that?'

'To make a point. Did it hurt? Do you feel humiliated again?'

He lowered his head. 'I understand, but it is far too late for such admissions.'

She nodded, 'If you understand, explain to me how you justify this war?'

'I cannot justify it. We forget what war means Vorsa, how much pain it will inflict. That this war will make fools of us all. In the moment we cannot see past ourselves. Regardless of who wins, so much blood will be shed. Perhaps, as you say, even ours. And for what?'

'And for what,' she spat. 'Exactly.'

Hevridis stood tall. 'So what do you want?'

Vorsa eyed him, she saw the fragment of regret, or perhaps dissension. Perhaps it had always been there, the rationality she had hoped for in him when he was nothing more than a spy.

'I want you to sway Fraubela. I want you to ask her to forget this senseless war.'

He shook his tail, 'She would never agree! She craves it above everything!'

'Even you?'

He said nothing, instead leaping atop the porch over the entrance to the cathedral. He looked back at Vorsa, her fixed stare upon him. He knew its purpose.

As Vorsa turned away she considered her words, and the taint of blood in her mouth. She could no longer quell her hunger, so she apologised to Naa for what she must take, and began to stalk the graveyard for food.

*

Onnar returned to the auditorium with Anguin in tow. Stems and shoots tucked under her armour. They took the plants to Erithacus, who greeted them with little warmth.

'You have the farnikan?' He squawked.

She offered up the root.

'This is all you could find? It is perhaps the wrong season. Regardless, we have little time. Tor will die soon.'

He called upon the Muroi, who he asked for a metal container. The rodents brought back an old tin can, filled with water. The Muroi went away and returned once more with a strange object, a large rectangular box. A candle was brought to the cage. The Muroi pulled open the box to reveal a series of long wooden sticks, each tipped with a bulbous red. They pulled one of the sticks free, then held the box firm and dragged the stick along its side. Sparks flew and a flame erupted; surprised, their audience reeled. The rodents deftly held the match and offered the flame to the candle, which after a moment or two lit.

Erithacus asked Anguin to place the farnikan root inside the can, and with his beak he held the lid like a handle over the flame. They stood in silence, whilst the can began to scorch black and sizzle.

'Stand away, do not inhale the steam!'

After a while, the Muroi approached with a bottle cap. Erithacus gently tipped some of the boiled residue of the root into the cap. He took a stick from a collection of tools in his cage and stirred, flicking fragments of root from the broth. He then lifted the stick into his mouth and tasted it.

'Vile, but not deadly. Take this to Tor, make sure he drinks all of it. I believe this will alleviate the swelling in his chest, allowing him to breathe.'

The Muroi carried the cap; they kept it level, acting as a single entity, jostling it above their heads until they reached the foot of Tor's sleeping place.

His breathing was ragged, and it took a while to rouse him.

'Come Tor, please drink this, it will help,' they whispered.

The old daynight sipped at the foul smelling water until it was all gone. Onnar mashed various herbs between stones, creating a potent aromatic odour. She placed the herbs about his den and left him to rest.

Erithacus instructed, 'Give him more of this every now and then, make sure he drinks all of it down.'

Later that night the auditorium fell silent under Erithacus's order. The Speaker flocks hung in fidgeting quiet, all enthralled by the column of stone before their master's cage. The Runta waited with similar fascination. Erithacus examined it from behind his bars, his head pivoting erratically to take in its contours. He finally appeared to come to a conclusion, and summoned Rune, Onnar and Aggi.

'Strike the stone.'

Onnar looked to Aggi, who nodded towards the collection of tools. She lifted one in her paws and hit it against the column. There was an almost inaudible thud. Onnar looked to the others for guidance. There was no resonance, no timbre.

'This does not sing like the Settling Stone,' Rune said as he hopped around it.

'No, and it won't. This stone is sandstone, it is soft, yet it matters not. We do not need it to sing, we need it to merely whisper its intention. Rune, I wish you to sit before the stone, please.'

Rune took himself to the place where Erithacus gestured. He sat, pulled his wings close and looked up at the pillar.

'Close your eyes. Picture the stone in your mind, I want you to see the stone's intention, not its surface, not the grain of the rock, or its height or indeed weight, but I want you to feel its presence. Focus Rune, as I have taught you.'

Rune nodded.

'Onnar, hit the stone again,' Erithacus squawked.

Through the piles of books that surrounded the monolith Rune felt the knock beneath him. He saw his memory of the stone, he could feel the closeness of Aggi, and he could hear Onnar's breath. He could hear the wind outside the building, the restlessness of the Speakers who looked down on them all with curiosity.

He saw the stone. 'Onnar, again please.'

She lifted the large flint, swinging her torso wide, and struck the stone with every ounce of her strength.

The stone barely registered the impact, yet Rune saw the consequence. For an imperceptible moment a vague flurry of lines expanded, the surface of his memory registered the collision with radiant strands. Most seemed to decay before they even found value, yet one single line had ambition, and skittered off beyond his perception.

'I saw something ...'

'What did you see?'

"I saw light, lines of light.'

Erithacus shook in his cage, he called upon the Muroi and the Runta to construct piles of books beside the stone. Onnar joined in to help fulfill Erithacus' request, and soon towers of literature equalled the stone's height.

'Aggi, Onnar, climb!'

Onnar stared with confusion at the irate old ghost. 'You want me to climb?'

'Yes! And take the striking stone with you!'

The Yoa'a began to mount the precarious pile, until she reached its peak, astride a tower of scientific journals and the pillar itself. Aggi flew up and sat beside her, unsure of her role.

Erithacus spoke excitedly. 'Rune will guide Aggi's tool. Once the blade is in place Onnar will strike with the stone.'

Aggi gulped. 'I will find it hard to hold without Onnar hitting me when she strikes the stone.'

'You will hold it by its side. Onnar will be precise with her strike. She will not have to hit hard, if my theory is correct.'

Aggi winced. Rune closed his eyes, and Onnar struck the stone. Again the faint striations formed; he saw the silhouette of his friends in the arc of sparking streaks, he saw the remnant line that seemed to join with the ambient light. This time the line cut clean through the stone. He took to wing, eyes shut, tugging at the adjacent edge of the tool until its blade sat across the dwindling line.

'Strike,' he said. Onnar lifted the stone and struck.

The stone made no sound, and yet one arm of the crucifix fell with a loud thud. The trio turned in disbelief to Erithacus. He bore an air of satisfaction.

Rune hopped down to the ground and assumed his resting position.

'Again!' Erithacus commanded.

Onnar struck the stone, and without willing it, the lines emerged upon Rune's mind, and each time he flew up and guided Aggi to place the tool upon the intersection. Each careful hit produced a perfect cut, and again the rock fell away with precision. The stone was now a column.

Again and again, they cut the stone, until all were exhausted. They climbed down from the listing perch to observe their work. The stone had begun to take shape; it tapered, a rough diamond wishing to make itself known.

Rune hopped towards Erithacus. 'What am I seeing?'

'You are seeing the stone's voice. It is an old voice; it seeks a tongue to annunciate. Perhaps you see the stone's request, and you encourage it to focus, to sing in tune. You see its weakest points. Each strike creates resonances that pass through its imperfections. You see its willingness to shed old skin, it becomes the object of your desire.'

'A Singing Stone.'

They each found a place to rest amongst the leaf litter of lost pages, nestled down seeking warmth. Then Rune thought of Tor, and roused himself to visit the old Throa. Anguin sat close, listening to the gentle rumble of his breathing. As Rune approached, he noticed that Tor no longer shook as he slept.

'Is he ...?'

Anguin smiled with hope, 'He is improving, the swelling in his chest has subsided, as Erithacus predicted. I hope, with a little more time, he will be through the worst of it.'

Rune felt relief, and as he made to leave, he saw the luminance that enveloped Tor swell; he saw the dimness subside. He did not understand what he saw or felt, but some inkling told him that Tor would survive.

*

Stark black and white; the rowdy Collector flock, Corva-il, sat atop the iron fortress gates of the Moterion in pairs. The Collectors' eyes were sharp and precise and honed their skill in seeking rare items, though they cared little for them beyond their trade worth. The Wroth incorrectly thought they coveted shiny objects, yet the truth was far more mundane.

The Starless Vulpus approached from the black, not even the fortitude of the Corva-il could face them without flinching.

Nox barked up at the Collectors.

'You heed the call of the Corva Anx?'

'Yes we do. We are Corva-il. We work for food and a warm place to roost.'

Nox nodded, 'We have both, first we shall see if it's possible for you to complete this particular task. Come.'

Nox joined his kin and the Corva-il followed, bouncing upon the path behind him.

The Starless approached a large cage, its entrance bolted shut. Nox reared up and laid a paw upon the lock. 'This Wroth thing, it makes this door immovable. We have seen the Wroth use a tool to open this, and yet we are unable to procure that tool. You Collectors are good with such things, perhaps you can unlock this.'

The Corva-il, Atri, took to wing and landed upon the large bolt mechanism. She peered down at the various interlocking pieces. She tapped it with her beak, shifting this way and that, examining every facet. She looked to her colleagues, who could offer no help. At last she resigned herself and hopped to the floor. She approached her kin. She sighed. A smaller Collector beside her cocked her head, 'It is not without irony, Atri.'

'Quiet. She was a difficult one. Yet we cannot complete this task without her. The Vulpus will win this war, and we lose face if we turn down this work. We must seek her out.'

'How do we convince her to work for us?'

'I have no idea.'

Atri turned to Nox. 'It is possible for us to undo these locks, yet we will need one other to help us in this task. She left our flock long ago, yet she may indeed be in the city.'

Nox sighed, 'In the meantime you can gather food for the gods. Send out word for your missing flock. We shall seek this Collector through our own means. What is her name?'

'Her name is Aggi.'

Nox frowned, 'I believe I know this feathered.'

*

Citywide, the Fractured Sects of the Morwih found themselves driven to serve under Fraubela. The slow retreat of the Wroth and the almost certain demise of that once cherished union between the Familials and their masters was hastening change in Morwih law. They were now an orphaned species. Their blood sacrifices served nothing. The Familials realised the folly of their cause and defected to the Feral Sect, asking for tutorship in hunting for survival, not just in blood ritual. The Morwih were becoming wild.

Fraubela had forgone her nightly return to the place she called home. To stretch the lie any longer seemed pointless when all the Wroth were dead. Through fear of losing the little authority she still clung to, she did not raise the issue before the Fractured Sects. The balance was precarious; to maintain allegiance with the Gull flock, to hold the gaze of the Morwih on such feeble a tenet that perhaps a better world existed if she were to rule.

From her stoop upon the roof she watched the steady succession of felines flood in from the city's suburbs. Many wore armour; in light of the approaching zenith of war she had relaxed her distaste for such an uncouth practice. She herself would stay well away from the confrontation of tooth and claw, would watch the tumult of bodies and blood from afar, until that sea of violence had calmed and she could pick the city's bones clean.

The blanket of Gulls was a sight to behold. She felt a little pride that the Morwih had battened down their carnivorous urges. Yet despite this, she knew the union was a temporary one. Once the Morwih had taken control of the city the Gulls would attempt to establish greater presence, which she knew would only lead to aggression. The Morwih would rule alone, or not at all.

Shedding the presence of the Vulpus clans and their nuanced rule might expose her incapacity to govern; to look upon the plentiful cultures and see nothing but prey might be folly. Until now her delegating did not extend beyond the rooftops upon which her people freely moved. She had little to work with. But a whole city? The Vulpus lessened the impact of the bloodlust of the Morwih upon the many animals who dwelled there. She knew this. She knew the Morwih cared nothing for the doctrines of Ocquia. Such scrawl was a pathetic attempt to preserve the concept of peace between the many flocks and clans.

Her thoughts were blunt. She saw Morwih dominion as final, that once she took seat the other species would be merely subjects to be commanded, or indeed, eaten. Including the Gull army.

Despite her feelings, she found a little place in her black heart for Roak, whose delusions of grandeur echoed her own aspirations. He wielded authority with precision. The rowdy city Gulls were unruly. He had plucked them from iniquity and taken them to the canals, let them feed on the Ungdijin. He had taken them to the Muroi who made homes in the Wroth waste piles, had armour constructed in exchange for flimsy promises of leniency under Morwih rule.

He had armed and fed thousands. He had given a starving people a purpose beyond their own dwindling mortality. This was impressive. He was a fine trophy.

Roak had however grown weary of her lulling eyes upon him. He was not blind to Fraubela and any possible betrayal she had set in motion. His time as captain of Esperer's guard had given him the tools to command battalions. It had also taught him to be cautious of the gaze of those who might be threatened by ambition.

Under his tutelage the city Gulls were beginning to not only respect him, they enjoyed the prospect of a future. They had strengthened their resolve, sourced stones for projectiles, practiced bombing runs. They had set course over the city and learned the algebra of the winds, they knew their flight paths, perceived every avenue and street upon which the foe might tread, and yet, they had not seen the enemy.

For many turns of Ora and Seyla a multitude of flocks and ground dwellers had entered the city. The dawn choruses were rife with news that the city lay bare; that the Wroth had left or died in their numbers and that new rule was imminent. These new denizens had taken sides, and for Roak it was not surprising to hear that most had allied with the Vulpus. Yet the Morwih still outnumbered them, and from his vantage, the sea of nimble grimalkin ready and waiting for Fraubela's word was a sizeable force.

The mafioso of the city Gulls stood in subservience to him. Tawk was eager, proud, glad that the authority no longer resided on his wings. Roak liked this, it was pleasurable to not have to second guess his word. Roak read his feathers like a gutted Ungdijin.

'You know the whereabouts of my homelands?' Roak said.

'More or less. I can smell the salt breeze, I have excellent eyesight.'

'Good. I wish you to fly to Esperer, alert him of the coming war. Tell him we have sided against the Vulpus; whose winged troops will no doubt be that of Erithacus. Tell him we seek his squadrons and his consent.'

Tawk nodded. 'And Roak, I ...'

Roak felt a thank you begin to form on his lieutenant's tongue, and curtailed it.

'Tell Esperer we will need his forces as quickly as possible. They should leave as soon as possible after you arrive.'

'Yes sir.'

The formidable feathered took to wing, and was beyond the glare of Ora within moments.

Roak approached the Consul. She pretended to have not noticed him.

'I send word to Esperer. With luck his troops will fly with us. He commands a vast legion. It will secure our control of the skies. The rest I leave to you, Fraubela.'

She acknowledged him with the slightest dip of her head. 'The Corva have been seen congregating over the Moterion. Do you know it?'

'No.'

'It is the fabled god prison. The Vulpus believe the Wroth imprisoned their ancient gods there, stole their memories and made them dumb and weak. They say it was a sign of the Wroth's supremacy over all other cultures.'

Roak stood mystified, 'What do these gods look like?'

'No Morwih knows. Though we can hear the great beasts in the night. A very strange contingent of Vulpus called the Starless control the land the Moterion resides upon. They say their fur was burnt black by the dead. This somehow makes them special,' she said dismissively.

'Regardless, the Moterion is the most sacred of grounds for the Vulpus clans and I believe it is the precise spot where the Foul Meridian will occur. Somewhere within that place dwells an altar or shrine of some sort where they will perform this invocation. We must obtain its whereabouts and be ready to take it.'

'I will seek the information you need.'

She smiled a thin smile and they parted ways as Hevridis approached.

'What did he want?'

'He seeks the Moterion. I believe that is where they will perform the Foul Meridian.'

Hevridis hissed. 'We play a dangerous game Fraubela. We put our paws into waters we do not understand.'

'Are you having second thoughts, Hevridis? Do you doubt my leadership?'

'I worry that perhaps the Foul Meridian is magic we do not have the slightest idea about. We fear it, we wish it to not occur, but we know that once it is performed that our cause is lost. Why is that? Do we know what it is that passes? Words spoken, rituals and words. Why do we put so much faith in Vulpus superstition?'

Fraubela nodded. 'I do not believe anything will occur. I believe that the Vulpus will be accepted as rulers of the city, that they will be anointed by every species. They will throw up their limbs and say, "It is done, the city is rightfully theirs." I do not believe in their gods, or the cursing Corva Anx, but I do believe in the power of suggestion. Just as well – it is that same power that will guarantee us rule when we stop their superstitious nonsense. The Morwih and our allies will storm the Moterion, and put an end to this farce for good.'

Chapter 10

Vorsa returned to Orn Megol to speak with the clan chiefs. She was met at the peak of the slope by Nox.

'How go the preparations?'

'We have gathered a sizeable force to feed the gods. They are much larger than any of us, yet with constant attention we will guarantee they will not starve before we can open their cages.'

'The cages are still closed?'

Nox, shook his head. 'None could undo the mechanism that holds the cages locked. They seek the Corva-il named Aggi. We are here to ask for your help in finding her. She is no longer with the clans. It is difficult to seek a single feathered amongst so many.'

'I know exactly where she is!' Vorsa said defiantly. 'I must go to her. We are running out of time.'

Orn Megol heaved with the bodies of the clans. The anxious regiments cluttered the halls. It was warm below, the old caves murmuring with commotion. Many now slept here, nesting material strewn under the feet of her comrades. Their dangerous armour lay beside them while some repaired tassets and gauntlets hewn of wood and coarse metal. She recognised distant relatives and friends alike amongst strangers from lands she had never visited.

In haste, Vorsa reached the great hall, which was amidst debate; her father at the centre. The clans divided along the scribed lines in the rock floor. The presence of countless feet had worn depressions either side. She saw Oromon, captain of the guard, strong before his soldiers. He gestured to her. Satresan quieted the ranks. He cleared his throat and yelped the Orata Tergorn; the homily of the lost words.

> Lost, lost is the cry
> The brittle shells
> Did crumble and lie
> We searched in the earth
> The corium cut
> And sought our poor mouths
> Pulled free of teeth
>
> They'd eat out our tongues
> To silence our mourning
> And with blood river run
> We find them fawning
>
> Coterie of caanus
> Lost all sense of troth
> Run with the liquor
> Of night's fluent clasp
>
> Live in the days
> Glad foretoken
> Of the land's dulcet silence
> A well hidden voice

The words held his voice in them; bore old wisdom.

'For hundreds of generations we have seen it right to heed the words of the Orata. We have kept the nag of defeat at bay, and with every litter of pups we have assured these teachings, to pass on this vital cause.

'The Orata tells us of the Foul Meridian in its opening verses. We know those words so well for they are the first we learn; the city will return to us, if we will it. We teach our children every line and recite them every turn of Seyla, each prescribed their verses, each turn a different line, and together we feel the weight of these truths.

'We meet here because the premonitions of the Orata ring true. The Wroth are dead or dying and in their wake the city stands empty. The Orata was constructed when our forebears strode the land upon which the city digs its claws. It is ours by right, and so we claim the city, claim sovereignty and act as guardians.

'It is a strange and tortured place; it is made of rock and metal, yet its endless spaces offer shelter to the myriad species with which we share it. We will not rule with our mouths, but with our minds. We will be wards, not warriors. Not endanger, but protect.

'The Orata speaks of how we should conduct ourselves, and until this time, this is how we have behaved. Policing the Morwih has become our burden. Keeping them from acting out their every whim, our priority.

'So we now face the outcome of such a charge. The Morwih wish to rule. It is not without precedent. Squabbles and violent uprisings have plagued an uneasy truce. So it comes to a head; as the Wroth depart, we must assure our position.

'We have called upon clans from the outlying lands. We have hired mercenaries and entreated thousands to our cause. Many have sided with us, have sought our ear. Yet we do not know the extent of our enemy's plans.

'We know they plot and pull rank, we have seen the presence of many Morwih in the city. This eve I call upon you all to begin the shoring of our defences.

'The Foul Meridian will take place within the Moterion. The Corva Anx have already begun preparations, and on that night we shall finally free the gods that have lain under the cruelty of the Wroth. Their presence amidst the city shall forever be felt, as we mend the weave of Naa.

'Your commanders have their orders. Each clan shall join with others throughout the city. The Moterion shall be guarded every turn of Ora and Seyla. We have little time. If the Morwih hinder us, we may never see this come to pass.

'In the name of Vorn, Vors and Alcali, I implore you all.'

The Vulpus troops signaled their approval with low yaps and barks.

Vorsa stepped within the inner circle, the soldiers eyes turned to her. 'Father, I have been to the city, I have witnessed the Morwih army.'

'What did you see?'

'They have formed a treaty with the Gulls. A huge flock is armoured and ready to fly. If they turn the head of Esperer, or the northern kingdoms of Naarna Elowin, we stand very little chance. We must perform the Foul Meridian as soon as possible.'

'We cannot perform the ritual without the Umbra.'

'I will go to him now, though my task is twofold; we seek the Collector, Aggi, to free the gods themselves. And Father, I am not sure if Rune is ready. I will perform the Foul Meridian. Petulan is strong, far stronger than any Revenant twin within the Gasp. Let me try, please?'

'Daughter, the danger to your life is too great. To lose you both, it is too much.'

'I can do this, you must have faith in me.'

'Enough,' Satresan barked. He dismissed her and addressed his captains, 'Take the regiments of Orn Megol to the Moterion. The Starless will instruct you once you are there. They know the lands deep within the city better than I. Protect the ceremony.'

He turned once more to Vorsa, his face softening as he saw the determination and anger in her, 'Go to the Umbra, Vorsa, bring him to us.'

Satresan turned away and followed the ranks of soldiers departing the great hall. Oromon remained.

'He loves you.'

'I know his intentions are good, it does not stop me from believing I am capable of surviving such an ordeal. The child Rune – he is so small, so fragile, yet my father seems to ignore the truth that invoking the Foul Meridian will just as likely kill him as me.'

'But Rune is not his daughter.'

*

For Erithacus, the world was an illusion; an uncomfortable memory. Outside the cage had always been suffering, and therefore his incarceration was quite just. It grew in him; the ache to spread his wings and fly, to know the eloquent sky with his Speaker flock. It was a notion he had entertained on many occasions.

Yet his place for now, was here. He pondered what would have been if he had not stayed, if he had not felt the unknown current of the

Umbra, had not closed his eyes tightly and imagined that which Grom had seen, and amidst the dark, had encouraged the formula of Naa to speak to him.

It did not just speak, it sang. He could not see the Gasp, much less the Umbra, yet he heard it all around him, and it was a beautiful symphony of arpeggios, flourishes that teased every molecule to convulse in joy.

The stone before him sung many splintered songs. It was incomplete and its notes were dissonant. He roused the Muroi to wake Rune and his friends so that they might complete the work.

'Strike!'

Rune commanded Onnar's deft paws as Aggi winced beneath each impact, the jolt grazing her beak and claws each time. Yet with each knock the stone found ever more perfection; no longer the blackened pillar, but a pale yellow teardrop. With each cut Rune saw the vivid lines, each cut focused their connection with the aura that lay at the fringes of his vision. Soon each strike would produce an ever brighter chord, and it strengthened his own resolve.

Erithacus felt it too, the melodies garnered a hopeful inflection. They neared the completion of the stone.

Over and over again the stone was struck, Rune rushing to guide the blade upon its gravel surface, the grain forgiving against the sharp edge. He trembled with excitement, which Onnar now courted. She felt its chorus and eagerly struck the stone with ever more refined precision. Aggi learned to stem the pain of each impact by predicting the strike and loosening her neck to compensate. Soon they perfected their craft, and the Muroi and Speakers watched as the trio made the final cut.

Rune looked upon the stone with familiarity. It was almost identical to the Settling Stone. He pressed his face against it, his eyes closed, he listened. The silence engulfed, and he placed his wings wide upon it. The lines of light were connected, they waved and meandered out into the margins, and they were permanent.

He knocked his wingblades into their stirrups and grazed the surface with the lightest mark. The sigil of his father and mother lay faintly upon the stone, and he asked Aggi to make a more significant glyph. She nodded, and began to chip away at the soft rock until the mark of the Sisters of the Flock was forever enshrined.

'Tis a Settling Stone, for sure!'

A low rumble emanated from behind Rune and he turned to see a frail, yet mobile Tor at the threshold. Anguin stood beside him, beaming.

They all embraced the great Throa. Tor felt the same draw he had once felt with Grom when they had dug the ancient Settling Stone from the earth. He looked upon Rune and saw the little feathered's father sitting there, the same enthusiasm, the same bravery.

'So Rune, son of Grom, do we wish to know the path?'

Rune pondered. 'It may lead me to my father, and for whatever dangers it may offer, it is worth it for this alone.'

They walked within the shadow cast by the stone and Tor looked to Onnar. 'May I?'

She smiled as he stood on hind limbs. She handed him the large flint.

To Rune, Erithacus said, 'I want you to take a deep breath. Focus on the lights you see within, do not think of anything but this, cleanse yourself of every single meaningless thought and think only of your father.'

He turned to Tor.

'Begin.'

Tor held his shaking forelimbs high, and brought the flint down upon the surface of the stone. The hollow quake was audible to all; it ricocheted, the shrine above Erithacus shook, loosening pages that fell like confetti. They all felt the timbre within, and their bodies responded gleefully; cells shook with delirium to hear the Song. They all looked to Rune, who sat in complete silence, enraptured.

He held his eyes shut, he could feel the tension in his eyelids, and he screwed them ever tighter as formations of light revolved and exploded and atrophied before him. He saw his cause, saw schisms of ideas, broken and reformed, silhouettes of memories faceted and harmonious fracture and fall away; and within all of this, golden lines, meridians and lay lines that intersected and fused, paths and conduits of energies; consistencies which seemed to permeate those opaline formations he chased every night before sleep.

He saw the pattern, and opened his eyes. The pattern remained, and yet beyond this, nothing but black. It hovered, cascading across the surface of his mind, casting its own aurora, and with timed blinks it seemed to react to his own perception.

The lines were thrown out beyond the periphery of his vision, they appeared to traverse the very surface of Naa. They were not marred by obstacles or boundaries, yet cut through them, unhindered.

He could see the magnetic striations of Naa itself, a confluence of inverted vacancies, lines, marks and scratches that converged and meandered across his eyes.

He could see shapes move in formation, dizzying smudges that rose and fell at the outermost reaches of his sight; smaller contingencies danced too close, so that to focus made him feel nauseous. He saw the movements of the remaining Wroth, of the flocks, of the herds and packs and swarms, the nations of Naa.

He turned his attention upon the Stone; his vision strands of golden light that connected each particle; every nucleus of every atom, he knew nothing of their significance but could see them intimately.

He looked upon Tor, who struck the Stone in succession; he could see the virus flurrying through veins, dying, retreating, seeking a futile mutiny of cells; he could see every single battle within his body, and how hard the old Throa fought to win.

He could see Tor victorious, yet there was a dark shadow he could not penetrate beyond the sickness itself. It felt like death had made itself known.

He looked upon Aggi, saw the vitality and intelligence of her, saw her sadness, but also saw her inclinations blossom and expand and encompass her doubt. He saw Onnar's strength and vibrance, saw her mother's death like vicious lacerations, saw the mark on her like fire.

He turned to Erithacus.

Lights danced fulgurant, striding blistering entanglements. Rune could discern the very brilliance of him, all the endless pain inflicted upon the Arch Mage expanding like broken memories, the consequence of the Wroth painted in each scar. He saw all of this, and he felt the deepest most profound sadness he had ever known.

His father was not clairvoyant, could not see the future, but could see every nuance, every turn, and every decision.

And so could Rune.

The light built; frothed with intention, so bright he could not look at it, yet his eyes were already open, he could not turn away. It tugged at his anatomy, braced him against the wall of reality and choked the life from him, it was shrill, aggressive in its brilliance, and soon it overwhelmed him.

He collapsed.

He felt deep time. He saw coronal light of long dead suns reach the welcome bosom of Naa. He saw the emphatic gaze of a younger Ora, an infant world. It spoke of an age lost in errant temporal folds.

He saw nations of species, nomadic like tides. They ebbed and flowed across the landscapes of Naa, some occupying the same causeways and arid grass lands with unspoken treaties. Gestures of kind were communicated through gentle howls and barks, the swaying of heads and limbs. Language was woven with many sinuous threads of the Umbra, and if one did not know the entire weave, a single strand to comprehension might be followed.

The land, sea and sky were free, unbridled by walls and borders. As the families of differing species trod hereditary patterns century upon century in the soil, there came unending tributaries of opportunities, as incremental changes within the patterns of their bodies adapted, mended and improved the certainties of survival.

Swept by currents both aquatic and airborne, languages and words and sounds travelled upon flurried winds, corridors of grey and dark marine, shuttled thoughts and feelings throughout great nations. The Umbra was entwined with the world, vibrant hues of red and ochre, green and blue, and held an endless myriad of jubilant cries, of earthen liturgy, the ceremonies bathed in rite and ruddy clay.

But where once fertile soil lay, soon became brittle and cold. The forests were now bitter places, unforgiving. Warmth was sought in migration. Where once to travel was choice, had now become inescapable.

To find any semblance of food took every ounce of energy, to push against the snow, burying frost bitten faces in search of scant calories. But something else nagged within, a primordial melody that drew creatures from their cold slumber, to march towards a single point somewhere in the warmer south. They tried to find meaning within the Umbra's strident plexus of light, in the discarded bones of their last prey, or the calligraphy of falling seeds. But they found nothing but the song, and the song dragged them onwards.

Herds of woolly Oraclas travelled alongside the broad footed Tasq, Aurma galloped like dark rivers from the frigid plains, bringing with them their hot voices, their horns bound in great crescents, ablaze with crests of autumn leaf, the older generations displaying crude markings in grey and white mud upon their flanks, signs of importance. Hoof and hide, head and horn were resplendent with armours hewn from bark and flint, bound with dried grasses and supple sapling. They travelled from the north, east and west, bringing with them the songs of their particular plot of earth.

Carnivores began the time of fasting, joining the armada of great bodies which ached its way through ancient forests and ceaseless barrens. They shared their experiences of the Song, finding solace in this act. Theirs was an array of emotions and memories invoked by these ancestral notes, yet none could perceive its meaning.

At their journey's end they found a vast arid plain, above which the sky clotted to a curdle of spiralling cloud, casting a grave malaise. A cold glow cowered beyond distant peaks as the vortex churned. A single shaft of light played upon the ground, cast down from the centre of the storm, breaking and reforming endlessly. It was here that the nations of Naa lay down their tired bodies.

Tremulous shrouds of dust and water vapour fell, brought forth by the mountains that flanked the expanse. The snow upon their summits radiated cold, condensing the warm air of the plains, binding, seething and converging to form a circular maelstrom; its eye, unseeing, cataract white and blind.

The storm, an unthinking vacancy, whipped up the anxieties of the creatures, licking each hide with rough wind tongues, lapping up their sweat and fear, dragging them within a tempestuous carousel, embellishing itself with something like consciousness. With each blast of lightning the heavens cowed the dirty hordes, they huddled in the safety of one another.

Fearing the dark, they assembled around the little light that fell upon the ground.

Those with the loudest voices let out cries of assurance against the nebulous night, commands and prayers and words of calm to their own peoples, only to tremble under the gaze of the maelstrom and fall silent, lowering their eyes to the ground.

The storm quaked with magnetic vibrato, spasming bowels of water and electricity rising and falling within. Growing in volume, the roar became constant; a stuttering convulsion, a stammered voice, and finally, amongst the heaving bedlam, a single thundering bellow which roused the very mountains to sing.

Within the rock strata veins of metal tuned to a note, a resonance low and sonorous. The tone awoke fauna and flora, the grain of branches creaking with delight, blades of grass suddenly keening in search of the source; bacteria within the soil shaking with fervour, dancing in clods of clay, jostling excitedly against one another. The sound carried such a vigour, rising to a delirium within those without senses to comprehend it, the plants, the trees, mould and algae joined the choir, letting out imperceptible cries. The rhythm cascaded to a point, deep below the earth, the same focus of the storm above.

Suddenly water changed course in subterranean channels, rising up and out, taking unnatural forms against its will, binding with ribbons of soil, becoming slurry. Discarded ancient bones knitted with slender root, stone and grass and shit and decay, bound and bound in harmonious mortar. Strutting veins of coal erupted from the sedate dust, eddying in helix patterns, massive colonnades, load-bearing walls of dirt and detritus whirling with formless grace.

The crowds who stood before were dwarfed, who heard its voice and sought its shadow. They cried terrible cries and moaned terrible moans as the assembly of muck and rock and water honed itself from Naa.

Like greedy hands, roots coiled to form digits, delving beneath the soil, tearing great gobbets of earth, raising them aloft. Forests were its towers and hills were its battlements. It hemmed its countenance into existence, a great structure, and soon an entrance, gaping and wholly uninviting.

It was the First City.

Its form was like that of a colossal hive, barely breaking the surface of the earth. It felt entirely alien, yet its substance was all the creatures of Naa had ever known. Most had never witnessed this place, all were far too young. But the Oraclas held within their ranks some old enough to have visited once before. Their weakening minds could only allow tears of oblivious joy to surface, their hearts enraptured, kindling some quiet flame deep within. They struggled forward, held up by the strong trunks of their grandsons and daughters.

A little light fell at the entrance to the maw of the structure, which breathed a warm comforting breath upon the elderly as they approached. A sweet decaying smell of forest floors coaxed nostrils, and soon the elders stood upon the unfurled tongue; a matt of mosses and lichen.

The great opening dilated ever wider. It roiled with waves of osteology; the bones of generations forming part of the superstructure, harrying in delicate kaleidoscopic patterns; rivers of dry femur, ulna and radius clattering out in two streams, beginning to manifest like scaffolding. Something ever more inconceivable assembled before them. At first confusing masses of oscillating white and grey, the chitinous clash of porcelain and yellow, spiralling splinters and shards thrown up in purposeful arcs, sewing furiously into a gigantic structure, a bone conundrum.

A skeleton.

Hundreds of feet tall, its great nasal cavities and the spears before its morbid grin gave it the semblance of its Oraclas kin. It spoke without speaking, offering words of peace and sanctuary. Soon all felt this, soon realised its purpose. The elderly came here to die, to pass on their bodies to this place, so that they could live on, unbridled by the pain in their joints and minds. The aged Oraclas were lifted up, skin and muscle let go of bone, yet no pain was felt. Their smiles were unwavering, their peace static as their essence bound with the aged cartilage of their ancestors already within the structure.

The great Mastodon, its head a thousand skulls, its tusks fossil trees marbled by a hundred thousand years, strode out on to the plain. Its ribcage an ossified forest, its legs chiseled cliff faces. Flocks of skeletal feathered eddied on its lungless breath, flitting between its china-white ribs.

Each limb so massive whole herds were displaced, it positioned gently each giant stride. It raised its head and a tremendous drone played out from its phantom trunk. The same tone that had sung from the mountains themselves.

The trumpet blast seemed to grow and the structure that towered above trembled with the same resonance. Its voice was like stone against stone.

'I am Lendel,' it said. 'I am of the First City. The city is of you and you are of it, the sum of your needs. It is a forum, a place with no prejudice. The city returns to take of your ill and infirm, of those who crave death. It feels the cold that threatens your families, but it feels another cold, the ill winds of antipathy, a far greater threat.

'You stand in the crux of all thought; the fulcrum from which every word and inspiration is forged and has come to rest. It is here that we find resolve. Use this opportunity.'

Sparks of recognition flickered within chromosomes, ancestral rhythms that had lain dormant came into focus. The fear fell away as the cathedral body of Lendel turned full circle, ushering his congregation within the city's walls.

The herds followed with trepidation, with stolen glances of one another's fear. They felt as though they were within the belly of a beast.

Soon Lendel came to a standstill, and hollow sockets seemed to ponder for a moment, allowing a hush to descend over his audience. The ancient housekeeper bowed his head, *make peace* it said, almost an afterthought, before it collapsed, concertina-like into the fabric of the city.

In the dark the walls were a movement of countless faded faces, endless identities, their grinning skulls undulating, realigning, augmenting restlessly, recognising their descendants before them. The dead were excited; fussing and bustling over one another, orthopaedic architecture that longed to know their living families. Those who were close enough to make out the skeletal utterances in the dark saw nothing but empty eyes and teeth, and they moved far away in fear.

The air was warm and calming, and soon any remaining unease drifted away like vapour. Some began to chatter, until the great Embree paced forward, standing on hind limbs, his face so peaceful. He quieted the rabble with his long and gentle claws, his deep eyes holding the gaze of all.

'The city sings for us, but it wishes for us to speak. We come here now to air our grievances, to discuss terms, to forge new treaties. I see new species amongst these ranks, faces we must know and with them find resolution. The cold is killing us, we must seek an answer.'

The murmur of agreement was only broken by the assured cry of a huge Oreya stag. His horns rose like massive bleeding hands, clawing angrily. He was stained with the blood of his mate, it was thick on his face and flanks.

He wept with every word.

'The cold is killing us, yes. But the cold is unprejudiced. It does not make eyes at our flesh. There are some here who kill with malice. My love is dead at the hands of such thieves.'

A pride of sabre-toothed Rauka snarled and batted clawed paws against the hard ground, seeking a voice. Their leader, Carcarin spoke up.

'We do not kill with prejudice! We kill for food, we hunt you for survival. My son was gored by such a stag as you, Eschea, a fair trade for those we take for sustenance. We cannot graze, our bodies are unfit for such a life.'

The Stag shook his head, 'No, Carcarin. I do not speak of your ways. The lame and unthinking are your quarry. We stand in good stead for what Naa has made of us. Yet there are those from the far south who come north and hunt incessantly. They stand upright, they hunt with made things, weapons.'

Within the bleating, cooing thousands, forms moved forward. Sometimes they fell to all fours, others used sticks to stand tall, their bodies unfamiliar to those around them. They entered the circle of light and stood at the feet of Embree. Their eyes were cold and shifting.

'We are the Wroth. The cold is killing us too and we must feed. Naa made our hands this way,' the creature grabbed at its staff with an assured grip, 'so that we can throw and kill with ease. We are here now because generations before us had the fortitude to live. We only kill for food, so that our people can survive. The Umbra shows us our quarry, would it not hide such bounty if it were wrong to kill?'

The stag ran forward, stamping his hooves, violent angular throws of his neck expelling hot clouds of breath that hung in furious echoes about his head. His eyes were black and incensed. 'The Umbra is not a tool of death! You take that which was not made for you! You take because you can, not because you need. You cut and cut and you have no remorse! You do not know the ways of those who feed as you now do. You kill mothers milking calves and let the young die. You follow no paths. You carve new paths through lands unknown by your people. You care nothing for the ways of others!'

The creature stood assuredly below the gaze of Eschea. It spoke with callousness, 'You stand so tall Stag, you have got so used to standing tall. Your mate fed our family. Her flesh satisfied my children. They will grow strong, capable of many things. Your paths are worn out, are lost in the snow. This world is cleansed. It is wiped clean by the ice. We must now make new routes to follow.'

Embree lumbered before Eschea. He placed a careful paw upon the Oreya, who hissed with uncertain rage. His anger was quickly extinguished by apology. Embree spoke, 'Your ways are unknown to us. You must understand, we have spent generations finding this peace, it is our duty to uphold it.'

'They came north because they wiped their land clean of life!' Eschea cried.

The Wroth cooed and laughed. 'He spreads fear! Is that what we travelled here for, to listen to rumours and suspicions? Our people will not take any more than those who hunt here, we are no more vicious and have no greater designs than those of the Cini, or the Rauka. We must survive, our families grow. We have no need beyond this.'

Carcarin interrupted, 'I do not know your kind, but know this, we may follow the paths, stalk the infirm and careless, but we follow courtesy. We cannot ask for more. You must see this, you must see us, see our families, and you must always know to never ask for more.'

There were voices of agreement, horns and crested headdresses bowed and swayed with encouragement. Feathered found perches on great bodies to witness the commotion.

The Wroth were corralled, surrounded by species now assured in anger. Their leader spoke up. 'We came like all others to this place, we came here when we felt the need arise, felt the keen voice of this place in us. The city sang to us too, does that not prove we are welcome here?'

Embree nodded, 'The city sang for us to come together, to find answers for what has now become a grave situation. The land is dying in the cold, we will wither if we do not find refuge together.

'Many of us left families behind with hope of us returning with answers. The forest and caves and tall grass offer no shelter now. Our salvation is in each other. If you take mothers as the Stag Eschea has reported then children starve. If there is no remorse in you then you have no place among us.'

The Wroth's gaze fell to its feet. Something like comprehension seemed to pass in glassy resolution in its eyes, then quickly this was enveloped by something else, something far stronger. Desire.

It shook its head and turned to its brethren for reassurance. 'You think this,' it threw out its arms, encompassing the great mass before it, the city and its denizens, 'you think this decides the fate of my people? You think this is the apex of our place among you? We wallow in our compromises and empty gratitudes, gestures of kind to cover our resentment. Possibly, just possibly, we are capable of more.'

'There is no more.' Carcarin circled, stalking, every muscle lithe and terse against his urge to tear out the creature's jugular. He smelt its arrogance, and it was far more pungent than fear. 'This city is us, it is the culmination of what we are. We do not ask for more, or we lose all that our families have parleyed for, for generations.'

The Wroth grouped, yapping out cries, bearing teeth. 'This city sings for senseless minds!'

Carcarin closed his eyes and focused his rage to a fine point, burying it deep within him. It burned him. 'This city is all you have!'

'We don't need it. It serves us nothing but bitter compromise, and without it our people survive this cold. Our hands …' It raised them up, clutching at its long whittled staff. 'Our hands can give us our own city.'

The Wroth masses gave up a great cry, 'We shall build our own city! Our own city!'

The First City groaned. A deep hollow rattle. A creaking that crept along the bows of each wall. It coursed sleek and rhythmic, and carried with it a desolation felt within them all. A slick empathy crept into synapses, and all at once, like some shared fever dream, they felt the will of the city.

Its heart was breaking.

Carcarin recoiled, his words were so coarse they had flayed hope like so much flesh. He suddenly felt regret, fear, lust and desire, and a terrible sickening guilt. It was acrid and filled his senses. He saw the lights of the Umbra recoil from him. The Wroth seemed to forget their zeal and began to drift away from the herds.

Carcarin felt a grey haze engulf him, and ran from it, galumphing after the Wroth, corralling them, herding them, making feeble attempts to placate.

'The city is falling!' he snarled, but they were terrified and didn't understand him. Pushing back his slathering muzzle, their hands on his fur made saliva seep like oceans in his mouth, and soon he lost the words to ask them to stop and consider, to find peace; and his words became precise bites as he tore at throats, and his desperation became anger as he fed upon the arrogant fools who had dared defy him.

Eschea cried out for him to stop, but the warm iron slick in his mouth gave him rapture, consuming any wrongdoing. At length he felt the hunger of his feasting ebb, the tar-like comfort of his lust sated.

Eschea drove his horns against Carcarin's hide, and in sublime pain his thick and heavy euphoria cracked like sheets of breaking ice, thudding dully on him, his body crashing against the sodden floor of the great hall, bringing a sense of clarity, crisp and harsh and painful. He looked up at Eschea, his voice angular and incoherent, and in a fleeting moment of clarity, as the low hoots of the stag resonated obscurely within his shaken thoughts, realised what had happened.

They could no longer know the Umbra.

They could no longer understand each other.

Rune saw the city collapse; shedding skin, decaying from the outside, suddenly drained of its once potent beauty. The walls fell about the thousands; he saw them flee with terror as the earth reclaimed their sanctuary. He felt the bite of sadness, but read its reason. The arrogance of the Wroth had enraged the city, its hackles set against those who dared question all that it had done for them.

The veils of chronology flickered; Rune witnessed the many herds and packs of animals lose all sense of trust, hurry in any direction to escape one another's presence.

Bewildered, they found their way back to their kin, impotent without speech, they struggled to comprehend one another. Roars and hollers were empty of meaning, they were fearful signs; scaremongers, harbingers. Each a warning to stay away. In the furrows of snow and ice the parties dispersed without the warmth of one another.

The Wroth returned to their own, and kept their word. In the wake of the terrible loss, they began to build their own cities and erect walls around them. The other species floundered, their numbers always falling in the bloody rasp of survival.

Yet something began to grow amongst those whose lives were entwined by their nature. Amidst the dense forests, where many sought food on fruit-bearing branches, avoiding one another was impossible. Eventually fear was quenched with knowing gestures and telling eyes. Body language held meaning. Exchanges and signals became common, and here, amongst the furtive tells, the beginnings of a fragile language began to form.

Generations fell away, spawning complexities, symbolism, and a frantic desire to understand. They mourned inherited memories of the First City, could still discern its song in the eloquence of Naa, the comfort it once offered. They shared an old prayer, the knowledge they once owned, the mythology engrained in the bones of that hallowed place. They held titbits, shadows and half-truths, fragments of what had been. They pieced the remains together, constructed mythologies from the debris of their collective memory.

All they had was the desire to know. They tried with all their might to rouse the First City from the earth, to prove that they were capable of knowing its intention, and that they were sorry for the error of their ancestors. The silence left a deep and certain void, and they cradled effigies of vacant messiahs and made fetishes of false prophets in hope of kindling truth.

Eventually, within the fibre of their imagined past, filaments were coaxed that held a glimmer of that lost megalopolis and its purpose. In this they dwelt together, and built their world of it, hid themselves from the Wroth and sought a delicate language and creed.

Rune sensed familiarity in their vocalisations, the roots of his own shared tongue, Ocquia. In all of this he felt the sorrow of the First City, an organism, a living metropolis, an extension of the vital pith of all life. Rune could taste the source of the Umbra within its meandrous tendrils, it was a physical tether.

He felt its pull, and saw the keen eye of it on him. Beyond oceans, beyond the cusp of all he knew lay the First City, the place his father had sought, the seed of the Umbra. In his mind's eye it was three blistering lights held in a pattern he had known all his life, in the marking upon his armour, churning endless appendages extended, sewn to the magnetic pull of Naa

It was Naa.

It was the vocal chords, the throat from which all life sung.

His heart swooned, and he saw the fragrant emanations of the Umbra about him, saw that each glowing point of light signified lives that toiled. Those lives never ceased their apology; they held the note of the city and bound it to the ache of generations, it became imbued with the litanies of every culture. Their regret became gospel; the burgeoning language braided words within the melody and in the face of extinctions and murder and loss, and the gospel became the only mechanism by which to preserve their hard-fought language. The more they learned of one another the more they secured an urgency, as though they were honed to burst, and finally, in the warm caves and secret places, amongst the clans of Rauka and Grim, they saw the light of the Umbra once again.

The city lived.

They breathed in the fire, sought its place and purpose. Ocquia was their legacy, it had reconnected the clans and cultures of Naa; even in the shadow of the murderous Wroth, they had seen, against all odds, that a language might be shared once again. This was the key. To sing out to the Umbra, to tempt it to listen, to allow the city to know they hadn't failed. This was the Meridian, the musculature that connected them to the city.

Great joy was felt in this rekindling, eager paws hastily etched their epiphany into the stone and they sang and danced amidst the roots of the earth. They forged the Singing Stones to bind that connection.

But their voices were heard by the Wroth, who feared these great beasts in the wild dark. They too held slivers of memory, almost entirely empty of meaning; all they knew was to kill that which might kill them, to extinguish those who might defy them. And so they dug into the earth, seeking such animals.

Below the earth the Grim felt the tells of impending death. With no time to complete their plea to the Umbra, with precise fang and claw they took their scripture, all they had learned of the city, of the Meridian fouled by the Wroth, and carved it across the walls of their home. The Wroth blocked their escape, and they died, choked of food and water. Their bodies rotted away, leaving nothing but bones and Revenants, and the hope that one day someone else might know the Umbra, and others learn from them.

Despite the ever-present Wroth, the caves did not remain empty for long. Stone might be worn down over hundreds of millennia, yet it was mere centuries before the Cini found the hollow dry spaces beneath the hill and made it their home, found the sigils of a lost culture and learned, of its name *Orata*, the spoken history of Naa. Within its address, the ritual of the Fouled Meridian, the failed attempt to bring their achievements to the Umbra.

But the meaning was misconstrued, its interpretation bound to the present; the Cini looked upon their territory, where the Wroth had built settlements, beginning the gradual dominion of the land, and the Foul Meridian became synonymous with ending the occupation of the Wroth, with returning the land to those who dwelt there first. Clan leaders would invoke its name with ever growing import. The Foul Meridian lost its origins and gained new meaning; it was the end of the Wroth, the reclaiming of the Stinking City.

The Vulpus would inherit this creed, they would cherish its urgency. The Corva Anx embellished it with their stratagems of magic, felt the poignant pull of the Umbra in their wishes. They saw the Singing Stones, they knew the Revenants waiting in the Oscelan, heralds of the city waiting to be set free.

The Corva Anx knew the truth. They had tricked the Vulpus to do their bidding. Rune saw his own light, dancing between each party, lacing connective tissue.

He was a pawn.

But the Foul Meridian was not emancipation. Its true purpose lay dormant, a conduit, an invocation of something far older, primordial. The final apology, willing the First City to return, to reclaim its seat, to dwell above the earth in all its visceral, infuriated, wrathful glory.

The Foul Meridian was the end of the Stinking City, the end of the Wroth.

The end of all they knew.

He must warn the Vulpus. Warn them all.

*

Aggi watched Rune sink into a stupor, listless, as though asleep standing. Tor's strikes lessened as he turned to see the outcome of their venture. Suddenly Rune collapsed, head lulling awkwardly under his wing. Onnar rushed to pull his head free so that he could breathe, and tried to stir him. She placed her paw on his tiny frame and felt a rapid heartbeat.

'He lives!' she exclaimed.

Tor dropped the flint in dismay and lumbered over to examine the little feathered. He scooped Rune up and cradled him in his open arms, carrying him towards Erithacus.

'Let me see him.'

Tor saw a glimmer of concern in the old Grey Ghost, who swung his cage door wide so that he could see the frail Startle. Tenderly he lifted Rune's head, checking to make sure his tongue had not been swallowed. He sighed heavily and patted Rune upon the head with his wingtips.

'It is perhaps a great shock to him, whatever he may have witnessed, we can only assume our plan worked. He will need to rest and we will have to wait for this fugue to pass. Please take him somewhere so that he may recover.'

Tor held Rune high against his chest and loped three-legged to a quiet corner, where he covered him with torn newspaper. He returned to Erithacus, whilst Aggi went and sat beside Rune.

'What do you make of this?' Tor asked.

Erithacus sighed. 'I believe that, given time, he might have earned the title Umbra gradually, much like his father. What we performed was perhaps something of a short cut.'

'Will he survive?'

'I have no idea. His mind is in trauma. It might take some time for him to make sense of everything.'

*

The streets clamoured with the presence of the Morwih. Flock song was silenced; all but a few stragglers had made for the skies. Above, the tired brickwork impressed a thin configuration upon the deep blue of evening. The fluorescent eyes of felines crept the conduits that connected the districts, taking residence where they had once feared to tread.

Dwindling fires consumed the mirthless edifice of empty blocks of flats. A few Wroth still clung to their dwellings, watching the Vulpus with resentment and envy, their flicker of life untouched by disease. Vorsa and Oromon were alert to the enemy, yet it was not blood that they sought. They skipped puddles and avoided the chasmal stench of forgotten waste bins, their contents spread wide by hungry creatures seeking sustenance. The city felt old, it stank of the unclean, a giant corpse on its back staring up at the stars.

They reached an underpass, allowing safe passage to a woodland trail. It took them north, though it was not long before they had to leave its relative shelter and traverse the roads and gardens of suburbia once again.

Oromon paused, head low, feeling for the quaver of company. They could see a few Morwih pacing the fences of an adjacent building. Vorsa rushed behind a stationary car. Five, then six Morwih were present. Oromon motioned to her to run on without him, yet she waited for him to join her. The Morwih saw the sheen on his armour and were upon them instantly; a large white feline, a patch of black over one eye, hissed her intention to the Vulpus.

'Thought we wouldn't see you?'

Oromon pulled his haunches in, the fur about his shoulder blades protruding like horns, the glint of glass upon his armour glib with peril. 'We want no trouble. We are passing through. The truce still stands.'

The Morwih laughed. 'There is no truce and you know it. It's all for the taking!'

The other Morwih were circling. They drooled with frenzied whines that made Vorsa feel nauseous. She knew this behaviour, had seen this disquieting act before, alerting their prey with their hungry yowl, she felt its blood-curdling captivation.

The Morwih struck in a moment, tearing at Vorsa. Oromon leapt, knocking her free of their venomous bites, yet soon his own weight was overwhelmed, pinned back against the wheel arch of the car. Vorsa yelped as teeth enclosed upon her, zealous wounds burning under the intent of filthy mouths. Claws ran in incisor sweeps; back and forth she dodged the cruel nexus, blood ran from her, each wound upon wound weakening her further.

Oromon saw Vorsa struggling and pulled himself free of his attackers. He ran at the lead Morwih, turning into her knifeclaws and tearing her asunder with his glass armour. The other Morwih suddenly lost their hunger, the sight of so much blood a stark reminder of their own mortality. They cursed the fleeing Vulpus. Oromon snarled in response, slowing to nurse the cuts across his limbs. Vorsa limped beside him.

'They fight well.'

'They have had no greater cause; this is as much their world as it is ours.'

She looked at him with admiration he enjoyed.

'There is always a loser,' he said.

*

The path to Erithacus was not one Vorsa knew. However, Oromon had on some nights heard the call of the Speaker flocks concentrated in the slender parkland besides a canal which retreated into empty expanses of concrete. Sometimes these vacuous grey slabs were filled by masses of objects placed there by unthinkable metal mouths with vast necks, or vomited up by moving caverns. He could not make sense of them, knew they were harmless unless you were unlucky enough to stumble upon their trails, the movement of behemoths to and from places he might never know, running over any who stood in their path. He had lost many friends to these monsters.

It was beyond this place that the Grey Ghost and his fortress resided. Glaspitter sat atop the fence that hemmed his home. He eyed them cautiously, these bloodied Vulpus in their war armour.

'I am Vorsa Corpse Speaker, and this is Oromon, guardian of Orn Megol.'

'We are here to speak with Erithacus.'

'Follow me.'

Within the cloister of the laboratories they perceived an eerie unease. Unable to place the discomfort, they were glad to be away from it as they entered the broad seminar room. Below sat a strange entanglement, its curious gnarled symmetry of furniture, collapsed metal and books, and at its centre, the Singing Stone. The primitive oval possessed its own archaic presence amongst the Wroth debris. This was very much a thing made by other minds.

Drawn to it, the Vulpus were greeted warmly by Onnar and Aggi, who sat at the foot of the stone, conversing with a shadowy figure behind the bars of a cage. At first, Vorsa was confused by this odd setting and the curious feathered who sat within, yet she too had heard the stories of Erithacus, and chose to not question. She approached cautiously, the intimidating curve of his black beak and eyes held her in reverence.

'I am Vorsa, Corpse Speaker, this is Oromon of Orn Megol. We are friends of Onnar and Aggi and know the Speaker Anguin, who can vouch for us.'

Anguin greeted them both, 'They helped free us from the Crool.'

Erithacus nodded, 'Yes, I know of you Vorsa, daughter of Satresan. Thank you for your assistance in the liberation of our brother Anguin. We feared him dead. It was a great joy to reunite him with his flock. What brings you to my House?'

'The Morwih mass in the city to sabotage the Foul Meridian. I know this is not your war, yet I believe it will affect your sovereignty.'

Erithacus laughed, 'I am no king, Vorsa. But I am sympathetic to your cause. Yet we are feathered. Your war over the Stinking City is of little consequence to us.'

'They have made a treaty with the Gull clans to the east. There are many thousands. I fear this war will spread beyond the city, become the business of Esperer, and bring enemy flocks from the coastal regions once again, much as his father Malca once did.'

Erithacus nodded with knowing discomfort. 'The young Gull Roak, guardskin of Esperer came to me, seeking fealty. He spoke of a coup, that he wished to take the kingdom from Esperer. The old Elowin should be long dead. It seems it is only time before either Esperer or Roak bring the coastal flocks to the city. What do you seek?'

'We seek the Speakers. We hope you agree that the current state of things has been beneficial for all. The Vulpus do not ask for more, we simply wish to claim that left by the Wroth. Nothing will change, and as you said, the affairs of ground dwellers rarely affect your kin.'

Erithacus turned to Glaspitter and Anguin. 'What say you?'

Anguin nodded. 'I owe a debt to this Vulpus, I would be no better than the Morwih If I were to turn her away.'

Glaspitter puffed his chest. 'We haven't seen war in an age. It will be good to air out these old wings!'

'There you have it,' Erithacus agreed. 'The Speakers will ally with the Vulpus clans. But you must understand that come what may, even if you manage to invoke your Foul Meridian, the ambitions of the Gulls will continue. We will have to drive them out of the city. They will no doubt flee to the Pinnacle, we will follow them if we must and vanquish them. Let it not be forgotten that the Startle have lived under that tyrant for countless turns of Seyla.'

Vorsa agreed, 'Perhaps that will be a fine recompense for what Rune will do for us. How do his teachings go?'

Erithacus breathed heavily, 'The little Startle has seen the heart of the Umbra, I am quite sure.'

'That is wonderful news! Where is he? We have much to discuss.'

Erithacus smiled sympathetically. 'Whatever glorious things he saw, it has taken its toll on him. He is in a deep sleep, and may take many turns to wake. He must rest and allow his mind to fathom his abilities.'

Vorsa looked to Oromon with desperation. 'But what of the Foul Meridian? As we speak the Morwih mass upon the Moterion. We have so little time!'

Erithacus reeled, 'Corpse Speaker calm yourself! Nothing can be done to rouse him. It is an unknown world, how one perceives such esoteric things. There is no means of saying how long it will take him to learn these truths. It was foolish to imagine we could rouse these abilities in him.'

Vorsa shook with desperation, 'Then I must perform the Foul Meridian!'

Erithacus frowned, 'You wish to invoke the Umbra yourself?'

Oromon interjected, 'Vorsa, no, you are not ready!'

'I have trained my whole life for this. I know the rituals and I know the danger. I was taught under Dominus Audagard. My Revenant is strong!'

With a gruff cough Tor made himself known, fastening his armour once again to his body as he strode within the circle. Erithacus greeted him and picked up the remaining farnikan root. He gave it to Tor, who thanked him, and threaded its withered stem upon his shoulder plate. He sidled up beside Vorsa and placed a paw upon her.

'You are Gasp Listener? Your brother or sister?'

'Brother, Petulan.'

Tor smiled, held his gaze on her for a moment, grunted and then approached the Singing Stone. They watched him in silence as he picked up his flint, paused once again to catch Vorsa's gaze, nodded, and then struck the stone hard.

Vorsa swooned. She could not understand the static tingle within her bones.

'You feel that, yes?'

'Yes! I felt it, what was that?'

'That was the Umbra. If you imagine the Umbra as the hard stone at the centre of a fruit, the Gasp is the flesh that surrounds it. It is in itself a facet of the Umbra, yet far more tangible. You felt the chords that exist within the Gasp, within your brother. You are tethered to it. Strike the strings and you evoke a sound. We call this the Song.'

Erithacus pushed his cage open and stepped onto the threshold.

'Choir lauds the melodies, written in matrices, primordial symphony in stones yet to sing. So we pray for the mantle to offer its sanctuary, bequeath to us the love of the city and its song.'

Vorsa smiled, 'You know the Orata?'

'I do, and I know of the Meridian, and of the Corva Anx and what they charged you with. I cannot say that their interpretation is entirely accurate, but I believe at its centre is something just.'

He considered his next words carefully. 'Vorsa, I believe you have conviction in your abilities. If you truly think that you can do the work of an Umbra, and I believe you can, then trust in it. We are much more than these bodies of Naa, be that spirits of the Gasp, or indeed something beyond that; we can use our minds to create, to feel, to see, to love and cry and shout. We are only what we at least try to be.'

Vorsa felt a swell of confidence, and she saw Oromon resign himself to her decision. He offered his support with a subtle genuflection. 'Your father will take some convincing.'

'I know. But we must leave soon. We have no other option if Rune is unable. I will not force this upon him. I never agreed to that. I would be a hypocrite to do so. Thank you Tor, and thank you Erithacus. You are both very wise.'

She turned to Aggi who sat attentively beside Onnar.

'Aggi, the Starless Vulpus request your assistance in freeing the gods within the Moterion.'

'The god prison?' Aggi spluttered, 'what could they possibly need from me?'

'Part of our ritual is to free the gods caged by the Wroth. They have employed a number of Collectors, none of whom can open the cages. They asked for you by name.'

Aggi frowned. 'Other Collectors? I cannot. This is not possible! Not possible at all!'

Onnar leaned in and pulled Aggi close by her strong forelimb and spoke softly. 'You are greater than this Aggi old girl, greater than this. I will come with you. You will be with family.'

Aggi looked up at the mighty Drove, her huge ears twitching, and saw a dear friend.

She nodded her agreement.

Glaspitter hopped upon the pile of books and cocked his head back, issuing raucous commands to his soldiers. The paper racket of wing beats filled the auditorium and a green typhoon orbited the ensemble before disappearing through the opening in the roof. Glaspitter gestured to Anguin, 'After you, Lieutenant.'

Anguin straightened himself. 'We will meet you at the Moterion, Vorsa.'

Onnar loped to Tor and greeted him, 'Good to see you well Tor. We thought we had lost you.'

'Ah, perhaps you would have done if it wasn't for that old feathered.' He looked to Erithacus and saluted him.

'Do you have the means to make the cure for your family, Tor? It is not without irony that we find the cure to the disease growing underneath their discarded waste.'

Tor nodded. 'I have a few Wroth trinkets to make a flame, I can find some receptacle to hold the water. Wish me luck. I hope to bring my family to your fight, Vorsa. No war can be won without the Throa.'

Vorsa's eyes brightened. 'It would be an honour, daynight. I wish you well with whatever task you have to complete.'

Tor made his goodbyes and disappeared beyond the entrance. Vorsa turned once more to Erithacus.

'May I see him?'

He was so very small, curled up in the litter of literature, the heavy breath of whatever nightmare toiled within him. Vorsa lifted back the shreds of paper, felt a palpable sadness at such a sight.

Oromon leaned in. 'Perhaps we did ask too much of such a tiny thing.'

She sighed. 'I believe we did, and now he is like this, for us. We owe it to him to complete this task.'

They rejoined Aggi and Onnar.

'Wait!' Aggi cried. She disappeared beyond the piles of books, only to reappear dragging a collection of silver contrivances. 'Help please, Onnar,' she exclaimed, and Onnar recognised the armature. She helped Aggi dress herself in a fine armour, hewn of the scrap discarded throughout the laboratories. She pulled it taught, placing a crest upon her head.

They all nodded in agreement that it was fine work. Aggi looked to Erithacus, 'Thank you for showing me what I am capable of.'

The Grey Ghost sighed. 'You are very capable, Aggi of the Tempered Guild.'

She shook with pride. Together they said their goodbyes to Erithacus, and they made their way to the exit, leaving him very much alone.

In all the commotion, Erithacus had not even thought to question where his great claws lay, which were now beyond the threshold of his cage. He considered how he felt, wings pressed against the door frame. He offered his claws a little further beyond his refuge, felt no chill or resilience. He pulled himself back and felt a sense of achievement.

*

The legions of Vulpus collected upon the slopes of Orn Megol. A portentous dusk swept the evening warmth, prickled with distant stars, bowed in subservience to the luminal moon. Below, their red fur appeared deep blue, splintered by the prisms of glass upon each and every slope of spine. These were the Cubs of Seyla that danced in the livid nightfall, exclaiming the Orata with deft recollection. They listened and replied to each line, passing in domino screech, the vixens with their perforated howls, each intonation the venerated soliloquy, the ancient charge.

They filed into procession, and despite the solemnity, there was visible excitement. The Orata was their childhood, the ritual of Meridian the most cherished of verses. Not one ever thought they would live to see this, to go to a holy place and ask of Naa to bless its children, to know the city free of the Wroth.

They began their funeral march; to put the city to rest. They sung the homilies that bound the city in funeral shrouds, exorcising the last of the Wroth from its hollow places, platitudes to sate the lust of envious eyes. With baritone thrum, the packs of Acrathax headed the charge, the Esk Vorn and the guards of Orn Megol. Behind them the Infantry of Scaevi, Vamish ferals and forest born Fraurora, each a hundred strong, fetched up the brave souls who lived in dens hidden away amongst the thorn mass and broken step, the collapsèd sheds and overgrown allotments, quiet spaces that were the refuge of the city cubs. Now they were military reserves, gathered up in fabled rite.

Towards the city proper, the towers and scaffolding that marred and maimed, the procession moved on to a bruise of tarmac within a gentle loam of parkland. Grazing the ground with eerie portent, the rhythmic kiss of glass shard against glass shard proceeded the train; the patter of a thousand paws upon stone, the low intonement with each break, the Esk Vorn cackling the Orata.

The gloss sheen of moonlight upon the damp asphalt lit their tread. Many enemy intelligences watched with great trepidation, this swell of brilliant vigorous beasts on black roads, beginning to split into separate ranks, flooding each path that wended its way towards the gates of the Moterion. Onwards they coursed, a river of dark presences, each clarion call held aloft with sombre presage.

The Morwih watched from every roof terrace and balcony, sending tailswipe signals across the countenance of the city to the cathedral and its Feline eminence.

Yoa'a beseeching prayer

The Blithe Priestess

Did you see the lily white of her eyes?
As the grey heather seethes and slides
In the cool elated breath I see
For the life that she has blessed for me
I am the cut in bones and fevered night
In the wrinkled fur set by my rest
For she had seen my ragged breath
And she has seen our recompense

Sister bleed no more for us

Chapter 11

Atop the Pinnacle, Ara read the winds. The raw spray breeze brought autumn's introduction, offering him the residual tells of distant uprisings, wars and certainties. He found the note of the city amongst the bouquet of resonances. He felt for inconsistencies, changing tides and stubborn currents. He felt a warmth in the sharp chill, recognised it, saw the lineage of his dear friend passed to a bright child. He looked back towards the land, the ramparts that bordered the theme park. He was conscious of a gust of activity in the Gull ranks. Once again armour was present, hauled from the barrack nests, wiped clean of white excrement and worn with steely resolve.

Amidst the stationary feathered and the flitting restless Gull guards he saw an approaching blemish. In time it became recognisable, its shabby scrap armour in stark contrast to the black crag of slate worn by its seaside cousins. City Gull. Ara stepped closer to the edge and studied its flight path. Its aim was true.

He departed the roof, into the abdomen of the Pinnacle. The flight chiefs greeted him tersely. All were alert.

Elistis stood atop a supporting beam, overlooking the aerial manoeuvres of his flock. He too wore his High Wrought plates. Warmly, he said, 'Chief Ara, how is the wind?'

Ara smiled with wistful spirit. 'I hear the cause of Esperer's recent movements. I feel perhaps our Rune made good. Grom smiles on us. How go the preparations?'

'We have made every effort to protect the young. Everyone wishes to fight. The Muroi offer us their hardiest cache of armour, with which we have equipped all able bodied Startle. We are as ready as we can be.'

Ara looked to Elistis, 'Come with me.'

They flew once again to the roof, to the side facing the sea, hopping down to the trembling balcony. Much of this edge was damaged by weather and rot, yet it was also a perfect place to listen to the scheming incumbent.

They peered through a hole into the sanctum of the Great lord Esperer. The visitor was escorted by boisterous guards yet he held a certain girth that even they found threatening.

Esperer recognised the Gull's provenance, the slurred breeding of city flock. Such Gulls did not hold the grandeur of his own kin, and he found himself scowling at the gall of the impudent peasant entering his kingdom.

The newcomer bowed, 'I am Tawk, lieutenant to Roak. I have been sent with news.'

'Roak no longer has the time for me, I see?'

Esperer circled Tawk, his clever eyes searching out weakness in any who stood before him, the flinch of a wing, the unsteady footing. He read this proud Elowin and sniggered at each imperfection.

'I come to bring you glad tidings.'

Esperer returned to his throne. 'Go on then, impress me with my protege's advances.'

Tawk read the condescension. He cleared his throat and continued, 'Roak has made a treaty with the Fractured Sects, he ...'

Esperer bolted forward. 'The Morwih? He made a deal with Morwih piss?'

'Yes.'

'How? Why! Sisters of the Flock forgive us, what is he hoping to achieve?'

'The Vulpus wish for sovereign rule of the Stinking City. The Morwih defy their word, and so Roak employed my people to ensure that the Morwih win this war. Roak hopes that by securing a place amongst the infantry of the Morwih our occupation of the skies will increase the size of your kingdom and your rule. Perhaps even control of the fabled Speaker flocks.'

'The Fractured Sects accepted fealty from feathered! I must say I am impressed.'

'Roak is a fine captain of the guard. He requests that you join him with your own army. We face a strong opposition. Word on the wing is that the Speakers are a formidable enemy.'

Esperer scoffed. 'That they are. We will see to it that we make good my father's failings. Come.'

The Gull Lord guided Tawk to the balcony facing the land. Esperer shrieked, and immediately his highest ranking officers appeared upon the rail. 'Ready your legions. We fly to the Stinking City.'

The officers saluted and fell into flight, the shrill call rousing languorous troops.

Hidden amongst the saturated timber, Elistis looked to Ara with a knowing realisation. 'If Esperer leaves with his entire army?'

'They will leave the Pinnacle unguarded. Perhaps there will be a squadron that remains, but nothing we cannot defeat.'

*

Vorsa and her party reached the rusted edifice of the Moterion that evening. Aggi was noticeably agitated; Onnar kept close watch of her as she settled upon the exterior wall, whilst Vorsa slipped between the bars, letting out a cackle-call to alert the Starless. Their Delphic forms moved in the shadows, presenting themselves in their curious cabal.

'Ora bring peace, Vorsa Corpse Speaker.' Nox uttered.

Vorsa returned the courtesy, then gestured towards the hesitant Collector perched upon the perimeter wall. 'We bring you Aggi to aid in your task.'

Aggi flew down and stood sheepishly beside Onnar. Onnar nudged her forward, and she presented herself. 'What is it you wish me to do?'

The Collectors had done their best to help in feeding the starving, imprisoned gods, every moment, grasses and seeds being gathered or dropped within the cages. Lacking the sheer size to bring a great amount at once, they were now exhausted, and had been overcome with relief when they had seen the lope of a large Yoa'a, trailed by the dry thwack of familiar wing beats.

As Aggi stood before her estranged kin she felt such a weight of chagrin upon her, yet she focused on what she had now been asked to do. She buried her resistance and approached, passing her audience of Collectors, surprised in herself that she had heeded their call.

She said nothing, flitting to stand upon the large lock which fastened the first cage. Within, a collection of tiny eyes watched from the dark. She hesitated as they reached out toward her in kind. Nox urged her to proceed, and she began to examine the lock, noticing the screws which held it in place. They were tight and immovable. She peered closely into the lock itself, tapping it and listening for weaknesses. She then pulled a length of wire from her armour and held it out before her. She shied away from watching eyes but began to explain what they must do.

'Think of this Wroth thing rather like that of a Crechlin or Torplic. It has a hard shell, yet beneath the shell there are many parts. Some, which are like teeth, move. Others do not. The shell must be removed to get to the meat. How can one get to the meat if you cannot remove the shell?'

She tapped the hard metal covering of the lock, 'You take a piece of thin metal, like this, shape it, and thread it within the shell. You listen hard, feel the tool graze the teeth. The shell will open once the teeth are pushed free. You may need two pieces of metal to push the teeth apart. I will show you how.'

She twisted the metal between her beak and claws, with each nibble, knuckle and kneed, shaping a key. This was inserted into the keyhole, and she went to work. The lock eventually clicked open, and she pulled the bolt free. Once she had succeeded, the Starless beckoned to the creatures within. As the occupants were cared for, she looked beyond to the adjacent cage, which had a different sort of lock. She flew towards it, her captivated flock following eagerly, examining the fruits of her labour.

This next lock could not be picked, and so she fashioned a flint to unscrew each fastening. The lock fell away. She performed the act a number of times, so that the Collectors could gain a sense of the skill. Soon she had them reconstructing the discarded parts of the locks, or fashioning keys from scrap.

Onnar followed her lesson with an immense feeling of pride.

Atri, the largest Collector placed her wing upon Aggi's. She flinched, yet gradually accepted the affection. 'Aggi, you have become a fine teacher.'

Aggi nodded, 'thank you.'

The Collectors looked to one another and all offered their thanks to Aggi. They took to wing, seeking the various flock who might assist them in their task.

'Well done, Aggi.' Onnar said, walking beside her. 'It's never as bad as you think it will be.'

Within, Aggi smiled.

The friends followed the paths that wove about the strange collection of barred enclosures and glass windows. A quiet had fallen over the Moterion, its usual cacophony of cries subdued to a murmur, as though the occupants knew of the coming end of their imprisonment. Within, the companions could make out the shadows of gargantuan beasts, horns and thick hair, wide heads and bright eyes. These were the gods of myth. It was invigorating to be in their presence.

The miniature mountain offered various levels and apogees upon which the Corva sat, clothed in black ceremonial bonnets, wreathed in elaborate, symbolic trinkets, twists of wire and spillikins of bone.

The foot of the stone fascia served as a meeting point for the pious. Vulpus shared in their interpretations of the Orata. They deconstructed each syllable in hope of gleaning a greater comprehension. Armours hewn of wood and glass and smelted metal were brought forward, placed upon ornamental boulders, the glyphic renderings of the Meridian etched upon every surface.

Satresan emerged before the red fang of dawn, heading the troupe of the Vulpus clans, the jubilant yelp of a hundred cubs serenading their arrival. Scores of infantry filled the roads that converged upon the Moterion, securing it against the coming Morwih siege.

The Speaker of the Clans was greeted by his daughter, whose demeanour spoke a thousand words.

'The Umbra?'

'I am sorry father, his journey has ended. We asked too much of him.'

'Yet he lives?'

'Yes. He lives.'

Dominus Audagard recited his dissonant prayers at the flat peak of the false mountain. The Meridian altar neared completion. Though he was weak and frail in life, had been the runt of his clutch, in the Gasp he might become the enviable poltergeist; able to dwell in both worlds. But that was only one inkling, for beyond this, was infinity.

He was giddy, and danced beneath the venerations of the Gasp, the conjunctions of many circles that honed themselves of perpetual dark. They mirrored his own perception of the hallowed realm; with precision he had made these physical representations of the phantom spheres. The constraints of life waned in the Gasp's lightless halls, and he felt an awakening of his senses; with each hurdle vanquished he felt his knowledge broaden.

He would be a Revenant, whose weight within the Gasp could bridge the vast expanse between the mantle of Naa and the imperceptible Umbra, no longer picking and teasing answers from falling leaves and blood. All his sorcery, the many turns of scrawl and guarded decisions had finally culminated in this. He hoped his deceit would be forgiven in the fount of the Lacking Sea. The Umbra was a worthy cause, despite his desire.

Vorsa stood at the foot of the terraces and looked up at the Dominus. He shook his head in disapproval, flying down to greet her.

'If I did not know you better I would assume you deliberately foiled the chance for the Umbra to perform the Meridian so that you might prove some selfish need.'

Vorsa dismissed him, 'Dominus, we have done everything in our power. Rune has fallen ill as a result of his struggle to become that which you seek. We are left with one option.'

The Dominus peered closely at her through his chasmic black pupils, abruptly pecking her upon her headplate. 'Can he hear me in there? Petulan? Do you hear this? Your sister wishes to join you in the Lacking Sea! What say you ghostpup?'

She shooed him away, 'Do not mock me, Audagard. I have trained under you for so long. Do you have no faith?'

He looked at her again, this time with an inkling of remorse. 'I have all the faith in Naa and the Gasp for you, Vorsa Corpse Speaker. Perhaps I am becoming sentimental in my old age.'

She forgave him his objections. 'We have no other option. If we call upon the help of as many Revenant twins as possible it will surely be sufficient to achieve our goal. Petulan will act as emissary. It will work.'

The Dominus acquiesced. 'As you said, we have no other option.'

*

Roak flew high above the Moterion, passed the vast array of cages, saw the focal point of the crowds below, the unbroken parade of Vulpus soldiers staged along the borders. He saw the counterfeit terraces and the Corva, black across its countenance. He made note of the placement of the Vulpus guards, the scores of feathered amongst the trees. There was no sign of the Speaker flocks, yet an army readied themselves beneath his wings. It was no longer a possibility, both sides had committed to war.

He cut a path back towards the tenebrous glare of the cathedral. Rooftops swelled with coveting claws and determined beaks. Roak swooped low, cawing vitriol to his winged brethren. The Morwih had begun their slow descent to low lying buildings, treacle black, their elegant motions masked serrated intent.

He reached the mesa of the cathedral, upon which Hevridis paced nervously. Fraubela had just finished commanding the final attendants to her campaign, and now she dismissed them.

'Roak, tell me what have you seen?' she said.

'The Vulpus occupy the Moterion, as you predicted. There are many clans, it is entirely encircled. They busy themselves at the centre of the god prison. There is a series of stones upon which the Corva congregate, I assume this is the place where they will perform their ritual. I have determined the whereabouts of each troop, and I have identified possible paths for your ground soldiers to take. My soldiers can centre their efforts on killing their guardskin.'

Hevridis's hackles rose. He could barely contain his apprehension. 'My love ... I.'

'Speak Hevridis.'

Earnestly he said, 'It is not too late to reconsider this venture. How many lives will be sacrificed? Our force alone will surely prove to the city that we are formidable. A show of our prowess, to take these troops and fill every path, every corridor, every avenue with our presence. Surely this alone will sway opinions far enough that any meaningless ritual will no longer hold the influence it might once have done.'

Roak glared. 'Fruitless. We have not come this far to shirk our responsibility. I have trained a legion in your name to fight the Vulpus scourge. My people will die for your cause, and I do not falter.'

Fraubela refused to acknowledge Hevridis' arguments, ordering Roak, 'Begin the raids.'

Roak waddled to the edge of the cathedral and signalled his makeshift flight chiefs. A host of Gulls corkscrewed up from lower inclines. 'Arm yourselves, arm your squadrons. We will head for the Moterion. Focus your attention on the Vulpus that protect the borders.'

Hevridis made one final plea.

'Fraubela, I do not want to lose you in the pursuit of this city. There is something greater than this.'

'Do you mean love Hevridis? Love cannot exist in such a world as this, where our oppressors seek to silence us.'

Hevridis thought to question her, but saw her unshakeable faith in her plan. He shook his head and slinked off. He leapt between buildings, ignoring the knowing glances of his kin, who saw his lack of conviction in their war. At length he found himself overlooking the gates of the fabled prison, silent and strong. Did he feel as though he was betraying Fraubela? He only wanted the best for her. But sat close to this building, he found himself anxiously awaiting the presence of the gods.

The Moterion now harboured the marrow of Vulpus society. Long suffering, families left gaps amongst the crowd for missing brothers and sisters, lost to the cruelty of the Wroth. They both mourned and rejoiced; for so many the Meridian held a penalty for the aeons in which the Wroth had sacrificed empathy by their own despicable practices. Every clan bowed, reciting the Arantheen Trist; the passages upon which the Foul Meridian was interpreted.

The Starless Vulpus drifted to the base of the escarpment. Above the Dominus and his bishops narrated their blessings, conducted a pandemonium of jarring consecrations. They threw clawfuls of skull spurs and wooden tiles decorated with blood black symbols. They swore oaths to infernal conspiracies. Rapturous, they directed the black athelings of the Oscelan, the Starless, towards a particular quarter of the Moterion.

The Bellows of great beasts rose to greet them. They felt the guttural shudder of impatient breath. Above, the ballet of Corva-il; the white of their wings penetrating against the dim light. They each darted to a cage and its obstinate lock, each whetting their picking skills, becoming nimbler in their new art. The largest locks were easily vanquished, careful beaks threading needle wire into reticent keyholes. The rewarding whine as mechanisms relinquished their grip and doors swung wide reverberated out, and soon almost every lock was open.

The Corva-il reached an imposing enclosure. Amongst the pantheon of stolen deities, the Wroth had appeared most proud of ensnaring these particular celestial beings, embellished their cage with large sandstone steps that led to a wide viewing platform adorned with pillars and motifs. The Starless mounted each step deliberately. Three aside, they cautiously directed other Vulpus towards the large metal doors. The lock dismantled, they began, gripping with their jaws, to drag the doors wide with their mouths.

A second set of gates confronted them and the Collectors descended upon the peculiar lock. They looked to one another with bemusement. The bolt was buried behind a curious paraphernalia of metal squares set within a larger rectangular box.

Atri called out to Aggi, who perched in an adjacent tree. She descended, eying the device. She picked at it, yet found no mouth, no obvious point of entry. With her flint, she removed the tiny screws upon its side, pulling the plate back to reveal coloured vines and complexities of metal. She frowned, and pulled at the wires. She peered into the viscera of it, and with precision beak, removed every last facet. The gate glibly yielded with an agreeable click.

Silence enveloped. Beyond the doors, a tunnel, broad featureless slabs of concrete, unfamiliar scents wafted out. Those gathered could detect fear, trepidation, notes that carried the sensations of impending liberty. And another note, the scent of a predator long caged.

The heavy vibrato growl rolled ahead of its host; a hot and damp breath spilled forth.

The first emerged. Massive and pale golden, her agile musculature clear under a short coat. Curiously reminiscent of the Morwih, the Vulpus retreated ever so slightly. To see a god was both awe inspiring and terrifying.

The god looked down upon the congregation. She was weak with starvation. Nox yelped the psalm of intention, bowing low.

She dipped her broad head in return, throwing it back to let out a rumbling roar. Within moments, three more gods joined her upon the steps.

Low percussive barks heralded a number of Vulpus, atop their backs, four large ornamental crowns, dark berry stained pleats of wood and metal, fringed by gold and silver. Artefacts of the finest Muroi craft.

The mother god stood taut, summoning her family to stand beside her. They loped with unease, timid before the mass of eyes, despite their size. She spoke with melodious weighty tongue, words so infrequently spoken that she struggled to articulate, for the Wroth had stolen such intimate possessions, rendering it impossible to cry out with any meaning. Any ideas of Naa beyond their cages had been merely daydreams. Empty mouths and minds desperate for nourishment had bred illness, and some of the gods had even coveted death. Yet despite the pain of realisation, despite the unknown time of their release, the Starless had given them their words, taught through the bars, whispered determination, the romance of freedom, the untamed curse and blessing of the world beyond the Moterion. This all sat upon each awkward syllable and consonant, every curl of lip and bleating throttle held the pang of liberty.

'I am Carcaris, I hereby claim the lineage of the Rauka, and the name of Carcar. Our paws held stead in this land before the Wroth drove us away and made us slaves.'

Her voice quaked, battening the furore of her release, determined to speak these words.

'I am a mother. I am the clan chief of our tiny pride. Esit and Prauva, and my adopted son Maro. We have known a life of captivity, and known only of your world through your loyal and attentive kin. You bless us with our freedom. We accept our crowns and place amongst this world of Naa.'

The bearers moved before the gods and stooped low, allowing a pair of Starless to lift each headplate from their haunches with delicate mouths. Carcaris leaned in so that her muzzle was level with the crown, allowing it to be slid over her brow, arching across her forehead, great jags of tempered metal rising to a crest behind each ear.

Her children also received their diadem, and felt the acceptance of the Vulpus. There was a great howl of jubilance, carried forth on impassioned breath, the Starless commanding the Collectors to pull back every lock; every obstacle, until every cage was empty.

At first hesitant, the gods offered out digits and limbs. Naa wasn't real until they could exist within it.

The trumpet of Oraclas, the raw announcement of Grim, swept the zoological gardens, ridding any sense of entitlement the Wroth once held. They were no longer present to know their throne dismantled, no longer alive to claim such dominance. Now the strident weight of massive bodies broke the chains that bound the main gates, and the herds of rare and enigmatic species claimed the expanse of night. There were those who would stay; who would accept their roles in the greater treatise of Ocquia. Yet for many they could not slow their limbs, and galloped, ran as fast as their legs could carry them out into Naa. Their journey's might end in death, unable to survive outside of the Moterion, but it no longer mattered.

The crowd parted before the Rauka, allowing them a path to the gates. The Starless guided them beyond the black enclosures, out into the streets. Carcaris turned to Nox and bowed. 'You have fulfilled your promise, we are free.'

Nox nodded. 'Heed our word Carcaris, this world gives and takes. Know the lives you must consume to survive, know their families, know their own suffering.'

'And the Morwih? They are in some way our kin?'

Nox shook his head, 'This is not your fight, not your burden.'

Nervously the Rauka paced out into the world, claimed the sable appeal of shadows, and with the teachings of the Starless held as sacred, hastened their escape.

Above, Hevridis watched his very distant relatives attentively. He recognised himself in them. With glottal purr, they spoke softly with the Starless; he thought he heard thanks. Until this moment he had not known of their existence, that his own gods, the heritage the Morwih sought above everything, had been imprisoned here by the Wroth, had been cared for by the Vulpus. It was almost laughable how wrong he had been.

The Starless guided the congregation back towards the terraces.

Vorsa climbed the many levels of stone, entering the circle of Corva Anx. The Priests of Bone Char kneaded coal dust and saliva to form a black paste. They marked Vorsa's fur with it, drawing the final matrices upon her face; the cicatrix of the Gasp, each line an offering to the Lacking Sea.

Audagard composed himself, closed his eyes and perceived the great circle of shrines, riven the city in a perfect scalpel cut, saw himself at the centre. He was the pupil in the great eye, allowing sight to those ancients who had not wished to see. With his final mark upon Vorsa he felt the fragile thread, he felt those oldest eyelids part and perceive the Stinking City, see the nations of Naa and the mark of the Wroth.

Vorsa held herself firm, glancing down at Oromon, beside her father, each face thick with worry. She gave a faint smile. They each accepted, understood the profundity of her sacrifice. Vorsa returned her attention to the Dominus, whose eyes were now covered by his cowl.

Willing Revenant twins were brought forward by the Anx. Marr and Tetek, Muroi and Creta, they would offer their ghostly siblings to Vorsa, to assist her in the Gasp. They stood beside Vorsa, looking to her with fear and admiration. They each carried a piece of mirrored glass. Vorsa recited the *Nash Aka* over and over again; she wished to live through this, yet it occurred to her, despite the many times she had debated the outcome, that there was a distinct possibility that she would lose her life.

Corva flew in a shabby halo above her and she watched their dizzying strokes. She tried to focus on this alone, their stigmata bodies perturbing the grey shroud. It calmed her thoughts of fleeing.

With his beak the Dominus pushed forward a collection of pebbles. She chose three, full of quartz crystalline formations. She stared at each, capturing their imprint. The Dominus spread his wings wide, and with one final prayer, he stooped low, his gaze unknowable, and whispered to her.

'Come back my child.'

The Gasp
Blackness.
The quagmire was reticent. It did not like her there, it did not enjoy the vitality of life.

She waded through the transcendental muck, molasses thick, tentacle arms embraced her, lusting to snuff out her light. She pushed on, holding on to the truth of this insubstantial state, this was ghostflesh, immaterial, merely the barrier between life and something else, the cold longing of the Lacking Sea.

She felt the unsure winds of the Gasp, and pulled herself free. Chilling folds of vapour buffeted her, she could make out the pinpricks of light that signalled her fellow Revenant twins; they seemed so distant from her, held in the draw of dead nebula.

Far away, she could discern a vast white light. At first she was sure it was Petulan, yet its attention remained upon the face of the Gasp, the very edge of which made her sick to focus upon, existing in so many planes of reality all at once. She tried to rouse its attention, and for a moment it looked to her with sad eyes, all melancholy and want. She knew this want, knew it in the trillions of souls which formed the opaque constellations that vied for her mortality.

'Hello sister.'

Petulan hung in phantasmal bloom behind her. He was huge; an expanse of sallow light.

'You have grown brother.'

'I am fat with joy. Joy to know the Umbra sister.'

She placed her paw upon his gigantic face, felt the silky flux. 'I am glad you are happy to assist with our cause.' She looked to the vast disquieting entity who stared back at her. 'Who is that?'

'Why, that is a certainty.'

'A certainty?'

'A Revenant with purpose. He is fat on rage. He will do terrible things.'

'To whom?'

'Someone deserving of them, dear sister.'

The Revenant twins began to orbit Petulan, much smaller yet carrying their own wraithlight, they offered up themselves to him. He drank in their ectoplasm, lapped at the soapy liquid, smiling wide at Vorsa's revulsion.

'Come sister, let me open up the world for you.'

She felt the tug of invisible musculature, the part of Petulan that burrowed itself in her, and at once he dragged her with him, pulling her violently up and out, deeper into the chasm of the Gasp. She perceived the wretched mouths that reached for her, craved her. Petulan wrenched her from their grasp, and down into the glacial white that revolved amidst the blistering, starveling sorrow.

Further they fell, into its desolation, the frigid ache as her life left her.

A deep cold
colder
colder

'Petulan I am dying. Petulan.'
'Petulan?'
'I know, sister.'

She saw Rune, disembodied, only recognisable from the vivid elation she felt as she fell into the well of his gravity. She perceived a warmth emanating from him, and was drawn into its embrace. Pulling her limbs close, she wished to stay there forever.

Suddenly it dawned on her.
'Wake up Rune!'
'You must wake up!'
And so he did.

*

Rune flung his eyes wide. He kicked hard against his frailty and dragged himself up, crawling, pushing his useless body. Gradually he gained clarity, stretched his wings wide, and awkwardly staggered out towards the Singing Stone.

The auditorium was empty, the Speaker flocks absent. The great stone loomed. It sang to him; all the wondrous voices. He sat in the aura of it, traced his wings on its ligatures, striking the fibres. The pulsating light of Erithacus remained, and he hurriedly stumbled towards the cage.

Erithacus smiled heartily when he saw the little feathered standing at his door. He stepped forwards from his slumber and peered down at him. 'What do you see, son of Grom.'

'I see everything!' Rune shook his head. 'We have to stop them! We have to stop the Foul Meridian!'

Erithacus frowned, 'Why my child?'

'The city, the city is the Umbra, the First City, it is a place, something old and strong, it is this city that sang to us! The Corva know!'

'Calm yourself Rune. Explain to me what you saw.'

'I saw the past, I saw beasts great and glorious who shared a language, it was part of the Umbra; they could all see it, all of them shared in its aura. But the Umbra came from somewhere, there was a place. They called it the First City. They came together to share ideas. But the Wroth; they came, they wanted more. They refused to follow the song of the city, threatened to build their own. Then the city disappeared and took the Umbra from them all to teach them that they must work together. The Wroth no longer saw the other beasts as equals, saw the world as theirs to control. The other beasts spent an eternity trying to prove their worth to the Umbra, trying to seek forgiveness, to coax it to return. They forged Ocquia, regained their voice, and made the Singing Stones. But the Wroth heard them, hunted them and silenced them forever. The Orata is the memory of this.'

'So if the Vulpus perform the Meridian, the First City will know of their achievement, and will return? And we should fear this?'

'The Vulpus want control; they want the city, and the Morwih will go to war for this. There is no peace, there is no communion, there is only war! The Corva crave the knowledge that lies beyond life, they want the First City to return!'

'It will think we … it will know we learned nothing!'

This was not so hard to fathom. Erithacus had always questioned the Corva's interpretation of the Orata; from his own learning of deep time, the Stinking City was young. He recalled the Wroth literature that spoke of the first wooden foundations found buried within the clay embankments of the river, the source of both water and the outlet of waste for the Wroth. This literature was recent, documents. He imagined the tread of the Rauka, so long absent from this land, before the Wroth made meaningful testament of their empire. The Orata was far older, a vivid, permanent conversation with the past.

He imagined the Umbra, imperceptible yet entirely real, it dwelt within the spectrum of gravity; pulling the life into a measurable, knowable field. In the case of gravity, Naa itself was the attractor, drawing everything towards its centre. It remained to be seen what dwelt at the centre of the Umbra. A city? It seemed far too complex for the species that eked an existence in the primordial earth. Yet the pained expression upon Rune's face indicated that whatever it was, good or bad, it was far removed from the fate divined by the Corva Anx. They saw only prophecy, saw only a chance to commune with the realm beyond realms, though, perhaps, ultimately there was good intention in their infernal chanting.

Rune flapped his wings, he was weak, and he could barely raise himself from the ground.

'I can't fly!' He cried. 'I must!'
'You are too weak Rune.'
'But I must!'

Erithacus looked once again at his feet. He closed his eyes, took a deep breath, and stepped outside his cage.

*

Petulan strained to reach the zenith of the Gasp, punctured the epidermis, opened his mouth wide and bit hard into the rind of the Umbra.

His thick blue tongue licked nerve endings, sent raw sparks of perception along febrile arteries. The Umbra noticed him; cast out germinating proboscis that raced and traced the trailing fibrils of his being. They teased and tickled the interior of his mouth, plunging deep into his throat; threading needle-like within his whisper guts, and deep within his innards, they sensed Vorsa, her tangible presence, stark against her ghostly brother.

She was lost in him, the clumps of ether suffocating her memory of living; pulled into the well of unending gloom. Despairing talons found her, mauling her with desire, to taste the verve of her, the sheer wealth of life.

She sensed the colour drain, her potency seeping into the lustreless barrens of her brother's body. She could no longer sense herself in Naa. She was here, in the Gasp, and a gaping, immeasurable void opened, swallowing the sensations of sunlight on her fur, the impact of rain upon leaves, the delightful brush of long grass upon her face. She felt the fatigue, the apoplexy encroach as she became one with the dead, accepting the languor, losing to its despondent tones.

The Umbra saw her, wrapped resplendent petioles around her ruddy coat, reminding her that she was once living. It looked inside her, writhed under her skull, in the meat of her brain, and saw the abstractions of the Corva, their ambitions; saw the lusts and carnality for death, saw the Vulpus and their imperfect sensibilities, their petition for the City. Saw the good in their vanity, but also saw the Morwih, the chaos, the nihilistic urges of a people stripped of their past by the Wroth.
The Wroth!
Their filthy mark upon everything!
The probing fingers recoiled.
Sensations coursed impatiently along veins; rampant flares, thrilled in their cargo. Somewhere, the physical apogee of the Umbra received these observations.
Beneath the earth of an old land the First City stirred, lifted its tuberous arms beneath oceans of sand and rock, drained subterranean reservoirs for life blood, sprouted woodlands and commanded garrison roots; onwards to the sea, where water sought its conference, and asked of kelp forests to extend their arms in exaltation. Each undulation, every movement gave it girth, and it towered above the land, absorbing the ruins of the Wroth, reducing their foundations to dust. The First City sank beneath the waves with determination.
The Bishops of Bone Char stared with worry at Vorsa, her body still and lifeless. Violently, she awoke; drawing Naa into her lungs. She lifted herself before the Dominus, opened her eyes wide.
The Dominus pulled back his cowl, and for a moment he saw hollow voids where eyes should be.
'Petulan?' He whispered.
'We are here.'
He beckoned for a piece of mirror, guided it before her face. The reflection held two qualities, that of Vorsa, and the harrowing visage of Petulan.

'You bring news?'

'I come to tell you that the city sees you. It is coming. Summon the heralds.'

Suddenly those gathered felt a seismic shift; the earth seemed to slide, a creaking sonorous whine issuing beneath their feet. At first it was difficult to discern, but soon it gained volume, rising up.

The world groaned.

Petulan relinquished his grip on Vorsa and retreated into the Gasp. Vorsa blinked, her eyes regaining their clarity.

Suddenly the Dominus was ecstatic. He spilt forth his spellwork; cracked the glass and bled upon it. He looked to his bishops, who stared knowingly back. The volume of the tremors increased. Below, convulsing ripples scattered the Vulpus. They considered this as success, and a cheer rose to greet the Song.

'The city sings!' They cried. 'The city is ours!'

Confused, Vorsa shook the fog of death from her head, steadied herself. Her memories were soupy and made her gag to recall. Yet it was clear. 'Something is wrong Dominus.'

'What my child? Nothing is wrong. This is Naa telling us the spell worked.'

The city Gulls heard the quake too. They took to wing, dropping their first wave of stones, catching the Vulpus in the throes of elation, their missiles falling hard; puncturing skin and cracking bone.

In terror, the ceremony dispersed, a trail of feathers and fur left in its wake. The Vulpus withdrew from the terraces, found shelter, as wave after wave of sharp rock and glass plummeted down upon the Moterion.

*

For Erithacus the world was a piercing terrible place. He was flying. Each wingbeat ushered the deepest anxiety, he battled against the incessant whine of panic, tidal in its indecision; his mind both desperately cloyed and abandoned completely. His wings were atrophied, long had it been since he used them for any meaningful flight. He saw the extent of the landscape as jarring facets of an ugly jewel, and the wind repelled him, it seemed actively against him. Holding Rune carefully between his sickle toes, he tried to focus on the task at claw.

The little feathered directed him back across the city, yet did not know the location of the Moterion itself. He had no point of reference, and whilst alternately cajoling Erithacus and assuring him that tearing himself free of his sanctuary was done for the greatest importance, his eyes studied the features of brick below. It was no longer a question of whether they might ever see the world again, they were in it.

Erithacus had studied the aspect of the city on maps, followed the designated roads, the motorways that sprung forth and connected this to other lesser Wroth settlements elsewhere in Naa. It was upon these maps that he had formulated his precision commands to the Speaker flocks. For all his contemplation, to see the articles of his research now in life bred in him a new hunger for knowledge, and he chastised himself for allowing his past to so completely absorb him.

Before him the formulaic rows of houses and office blocks receded around an open parkland. An odour very familiar, the pungent smell of caged animals, suddenly rose to greet him. He spied a great signpost, upon it Wroth scrawl.

Zoological Gardens.

Erithacus began to descend, and from below the ebullient squawk of the Speakers rose to greet him.

'Do my eyes deceive me!' Glaspitter shouted above the zealous gale, and was at once flying beside the Grey Ghost with much joy. Erithacus kept his focus straight.

'Rune must reach the Moterion, and he is unable to fly.'

Glaspitter cawed to his eager companions and the entire squadron of Speakers fell into a ragged formation about their father. Daring not to topple from the sky, Erithacus managed a single glance at his remarkable family. He never thought he'd fly with them, and despite the throttling fear, so far from his shelter, he felt safe amongst his children.

They scanned the ground for movement, eventually spying reams of Morwih soldiers whose positions faced the huge walled enclosure. The bawl of a tremendous wind hit them hard as they set course. It held with it a peculiar wresting howl, as though stone raked against stone. Rune perceived its origin, a distant horizontal light within the Umbra which gained clarity as he focused.

It was massive, and moving.

Moving towards them. It was the First City.

He was too late.

*

Ground soldiers sought any overhang or place that might offer shelter, while Roak commanded the city Gulls with deadly charge; they battered the asphalt with their terrible cannonade, tearing brilliant white against an ardent sky.

The Morwih moved from the rooftops, slipping silently on to the streets. With careful brutality they sprinted at the Vulpus guard; daggerclaws raised they aimed their pillage. The Vulpus found their courage and, steadfast, turned into the avalanche, all red fur and proud rage.

The marauding Morwih saw the fury in their enemy; focused their lucent eyes, thought nothing more of the Vulpus than a festering blight, running directly for them, yowling a hunger waiting to be slaked. The Vulpus rolled against the surge. Their denticulation of glass a deadly wall. The Morwih collided; cleaving limbs and torsos in fits of hot blood.

Further ranks of Morwih spilled over the bodies of their comrades using their mangled corpses as leverage, pouncing with ever more bitterness. They overwhelmed the bastion; scaling the walls with deft paws; swinging up and over into the Moterion. With sweeping bedlam, the Vulpus charged deeper into the fracas, tearing, gnawing; the slit and crack of armour clash, the sputum eruptions of winded chests, the wheezing insistent grope of death.

The rain of stone came again, angular concrete rubble, the Gulls' aim careful, deadly. The Vulpus retreated ever further, finding themselves seeking refuge within the cages they had liberated. The Morwih were ruthless, hunting down any straggling foe hemmed by inescapable corners and dead ends.

Erithacus made for the terraces, 'Attack the Gulls!'

The Speakers engaged with relish. Glaspitter recognised the pompous manner of their commander.

Roak was oblivious, and thought nothing of the determined green feathered now careening towards him.

The Speakers threw themselves bullet-like into the fight. They swiped at the Gulls, knocking them from their paths, cajoling, deviating, splintering their enemy. They confused their trajectory before finally, as the white streaks of the Elowin became senseless in their erratic wake, they struck hard and fast. They became death dealers, dropping from the sky, cudgel strong and silent, bottle green spines projecting like pine cones. They hit their targets, rending wings from bodies, necks cracked, spines severed. They left their foe bloody, yet many Gulls remained, and soon they had regrouped, cutting a path back across the Moterion in search of the Speakers, who awaited amongst the trees with grinning certainty.

Below, Oromon let Vorsa lean into him. He led her to a safe place to rest, where Satresan waited. She felt the warmth of her father's muzzle against hers, reminding her of her youth, of days in the sun with her brother, and it carved back her exhaustion. She managed a smile and Satresan beamed back.

'I am so proud of you my daughter, you gave us back the city.'

With perfect irony, another hail of stones rattled the roof above.

'They are not taking the news very well,' Satresan said.

Outside the battle raged, the Morwih pushing further on. More projectiles fell and Vorsa looked up into the lugubrious heavens, witnessed the collision of warring flocks, the flail of bodies dropping like inverted stars. One such star reared towards her, clutching something in its talons. It made a cumbersome landing upon the plateau.

Erithacus could just about make out the dark visage of the Starless below. They looked at him with resolute eyes.

The Dominus scratched in a congealed muck of coal slurry and blood, splaying his clawed toes to lay provocative lines. As the lines met he saw some great quandary manifest. Its impetus moved in the lights' reflection, taking form – a face, full of puzzling brilliance.

The image spoke.

'Dominus Audagard?' Erithacus leered at him, his reflection within the glamour. The Dominus reared up, puffing his chest and spreading querulous wings.

'Stay back, ghost!' He screeched.

Erithacus frowned.

The Dominus looked cautiously at the grand feathered, and a spark of recognition materialised. 'How can this be?'

He moved towards Erithacus, placing his flight feathers each side of Erithacus's face. 'It is you, old Grey Ghost. It has been an age!'

'What have you done, Dominus?' Erithacus boomed.

Rune stumbled forward before the Corva Anx.

'The Umbra!' The Bishops of Bone Char whispered.

'So you come after the fact little Startle. I am afraid we have achieved that which you could not.'

'No!' Rune exclaimed, 'You did not. I have seen the Umbra. I know everything!'

'He has seen the Umbra!' Around him the Corva swooned in adoration. 'What did you see? What did you see?'

'I saw the truth. The Foul Meridian. It is not a spell for this city, it is a message to something old, something powerful!'

'It is nothing of the sort!' The Dominus exclaimed, the mask of his own deception fading away.

Erithacus leered at the Dominus, 'What will it bring?'

The Dominus could not hide his zest, 'Everything! You were right Grey Ghost! All the wonderful perplexing vitality! It is beyond this, beyond life, and we wish to know it! All of it! How could we ignore its call? We cannot live not knowing!'

'We must know! We must know!' The Bishops of Bone Char shrieked.

Erithacus sneered, 'What have you done?'

'We have freed us all!'

The Dominus coughed up quavering orders, and he and the entire havoc of black priests took to wing; screaming their incantations to the wind.

Below the Starless hung on the echo of Audagard's words. They felt a sickening numbness. They were immediately on foot, running beneath the wingspan of the Corva.

'What did you do?' They barked incessantly.

'Come!' The Corva screamed back.

The Starless did not falter in their pursuit. The Dominus looked down at them, the violent stygian river of teeth and fur that chased him, and though they were intimidating, he fostered a spectral smile.

Above the Moterion the battle went unabated, the vaults berated, dazed in fissures by mordacious wings, claws with scheming minds at the helm.

Satresan gave the order to retreat to Orn Megol.

*

Fraubela watched from the cathedral. She could discern the feather war, the endless advance of the Morwih, the retreat of the Vulpus. She sighed with contentment, glancing back as Hevridis rejoined her on the roof. He dared not look. 'Hevridis,' she said, 'what ails you? Do you still question me?'

Hevridis heaved himself up and shook his head. 'I do not know what to think anymore my love. It is best I say nothing. We shall see the results of this war soon enough, and then we can debate who was right or wrong.'

'There is no right or wrong, there is only who wins, and who loses.'

She gestured towards the edge of the roof. He declined, turning away. She realised the folly of tempting him and made for the Moterion.

Hevridis chided himself. He saw the bloody exasperation of Vorsa, her appeal.

He was upon the railway once more, a momentary glance east, to a lost life, before bounding down the cambering tracks that took him west of the Moterion. Soon he came to the parklands upon which the Moterion dwelt, and he winced at the sight of so much carnage. Vulpus and Morwih alike, their strewn entrails, the arterial red in vibrant smears.

Stones fell, meteoric grenades ricocheted upon corrugated metal, the threatening gall of Speakers picking off the Morwih with blades of glass held in their talons. He suddenly realised, despite his objection to this war, that he was a target. He entered the shadows, whittling his way into the safety of each dim crevice.

The west wing of the Moterion was quiet, the Vulpus clans driven back east. The Morwih were within the enclosure, and from his vantage Hevridis could see the terraces. He saw a large feathered, its beak short and curved, much like that of the Speakers who wheeled above him. At its feet something moved.

It was Rune.

Rune was still alive.

*

Erithacus picked up Rune gently in his claws and joined the Vulpus retreating towards the shadow of Orn Megol.

*

Onnar ran with the Vulpus, Aggi flying above as lookout for the legion. The appearance of Erithacus brought Aggi down to ground level excitedly as the Speaker landed beside the Yoa'a, who eagerly took Rune upon her back.

Aggi jostled him, 'The Sisters of the Flock bless you Rune!' She nuzzled him lovingly.

'We were all very worried, where did you go little Startle?' Onnar asked.

'I went into the past!' he said.

Onnar laughed, 'Well that must be quite a tale to tell!'

Anguin circled down to keep Erithacus abreast of their strategies. 'We will stay with the Gull flocks, fight them at this position whilst you pull back. We will join you at Orn Megol and plan our final offensive.'

Once they reached the hill of the Vulpus enclave the Vulpus divided into parties. The exposed parkland was no place for the Morwih, they would be far from comfort, which boded well.

Satresan and Vorsa were escorted by courtiers back to the caverns, while Oromon stayed to oversee the clans.

The grass around Orn Megol, unmanaged, had grown tall. It was perfect. The Vulpus spread wide, in eager columns they lay spry and ready in the lush green. Above, the ragtag Speakers reformed and flew back towards the Moterion in search of the Gulls.

Oromon paced the stone path at the hilt of the hill. He strained his eyes to make out the greyish guise of the city. There was peace at this distance, the subtleties lost in wispy haze, removing all sense of the tragedy that had befallen them. Still, he knew the Morwih, knew how thick in number they were. He gritted his teeth.

*

Esperer and his army passed over the rivers that marked the boundaries of his land and that of the Vulpus. Apart from a row of old oak trees that once flanked a now dried river, there was no physical barrier, no obvious landmark. He felt a sense of pride, not fully realised, not in any way deserved. This land was not yet his, might never be. His chest was tight, nerve endings reminding his brain that long flights were not good for him, that for whatever time he had left any strenuous feat might shorten it even more.

The white graze that haunted him washed the detail from everything. He seemed to have locked eyes entirely with it, as though he now stared through death to perceive Naa. At times he saw dark and foreign skies where there were none.

The day broke as they made landfall on the gravelled roof of a multi-story car park. Hundreds of coastal Gulls preened and readied themselves for battle, Esperer straining beyond his cataracts to make out their final destination.

The city was vacant. There were Wroth bodies upon the streets, in the open stomachs of Wroth machines. He peered through windows where many lay within their nests, long surrendered to death. He felt the desire to enter these dwellings, places he had never been allowed. Always a Wroth to push him away. He bathed in the exquisite thought that all of this would be his to know, to ransack.

They made for the Moterion en masse, each brandishing cruel slate armour, missiles held fast. As they approached Tawk joined the coastal flock. He studied the stiff and obedient manner of Esperer's army. He felt them judging him, mocking him and he knew that his kin would have no place with them once the war was over. He was quick to remember this as they neared their destination. The silent battlegrounds held a potency all of their own, a far cry from the green plots and curvaceous paths that adjoined the once equally well kept contours of the Moterion.

That was now a hellish collection of sodden bodies, those that still lived heaving in an agony of smashed glass and blood. The corpses of many Gulls were suspended by their necks and wings from trees, fallen from the sky. Morwih crawled up in foetal balls, amongst them the sanguine fur of Vulpus guardskin.

The terraces offered a perch, and so they descended, flinching at the sight of Corvan architecture atop the rock. Esperer knocked the artefacts from the peak with little effort, all stick and Wroth debris. It was light and flimsy. He hissed at it, at these superstitions. In his city the Corva would be driven out with the Vulpus. He made a mental note of this, as ambition once again brought vitality to his almost senile brain. As if in direct retaliation, his eyesight dimmed.

Roak was bruised and battered. His fight had been short; knocked to the ground by a single Speaker. He had landed on his weak wing, still suffering from his ordeal in the mud, and cursed its continued deterioration. Soon he would be grounded if he did not take better care. He righted himself and cawed to the remaining city Gulls. The wounded gathered together, tending one another. Above, the thwack of wings enclosed, the coastal flock set down in imposing ranks, gawking at their city allies with disparaging glances.

Tawk was glad to see his friend, and flew down beside Roak. Esperer landed in ungainly fashion upon an empty cage, and peered at Roak.

'Your army is a little worse for wear!'

Roak could not mask his limp and bowed self mockingly, 'It was quite a fight, yet we still stand. The Vulpus have been driven back towards their hole in the ground and the Speakers fly in retreat.'

'You fought with the Speakers? Remember Roak, we must not kill them, they are a prize, my spoils of war!'

Roak choked back his infuriation. 'You have not met this force. They are ruthless. I have not known such an adversary. They fight like they are weapons themselves.'

Esperer smirked. 'For that you need brawn, not intellect.' He flung his wings wide and his squadrons took flight, the titan escadrille of the Naarna Elowin.

Roak had quite forgotten the sheer scale of Esperer's army, including his small yet imposing flock of Larn Elowin, a breed of massive Gulls stolen and enslaved from birth to carry the ballast of war. Huge stones bound in dried seaweed hung below their powerful wings.

Esperer hopped down towards Roak, 'Despite your many losses, you have done well here, made the city Gulls useful. You will not be forgotten for this. I can see myself in you Roak. For many, this would be a boon - a strong, fearless, intelligent Gull who I would gladly see as a successor to the throne.'

He smiled churlishly.

'But you couldn't even hide your lust if you tried Roak! You wish me dead. I understand that, and if you had just waited, then perhaps my death would usher in your rule. But you were too impatient. I am far from ready to give up my throne. Your father was much the same. Arrogant, foolhardy. Like that ne'er-do-well, you render yourself useless to me.'

Roak spluttered, saw Esperer shudder, the delicious exhilaration of his mistaken admission.

'My father? What of him?'

Esperer frowned. He feared perhaps he had betrayed himself, letting that morsel slip. He dismissed it, it was all immaterial.

'Your father? A vainglorious Gull. A ruler cannot abide vanity. It leads to delusions of grandeur. Why should it bother you what fate befell him? Look how far you've come. Such a shame this final hurdle bettered you.'

'My father died at the mouth of a Vulpus, the same beasts we fight this day.'

Esperer raised his brow, 'Perhaps. Or perhaps he was just another pretender to the throne, willing me to fail where my own father once did the same.'

'What did you do to him! Tell me! Did you kill my father?'

Esperer composed himself, and waddled towards Roak. 'It matters not how he met his fate. I am a far more forgiving ruler than I once was. In those days you would have been killed. Today I hereby strip you of your rank, you will serve as infantry, nothing more.'

Roak wrenched back the urge to attack his king, felt the sobering gaze of Tawk upon him. He pulled the venom within, where it ate like the bile in his stomach.

'Save it,' Tawk whispered.

Roak swooned in the pang of rage, he thought of his family, how his mother had been shunned from the nests upon the cliffs, how his brothers and sisters were mocked and spat upon. His father might have become nothing more than scraps of memory, might not have been a good father, but his death had rendered his family little but pariahs.

The welt of reasons why Esperer would die pained Roak. He longed for home, for the time he could have spent nursing his mother's grief, and instead wasted it in pursuit of acceptance by that wretched Gull king; had risen in his corpulent presence, each success, each victory, to regain what had been lost in the shame of his broken family. He scolded himself, he had even seen Esperer as a father figure.

To know he was complicit in his father's death? This was a bitter truth.

*

Fraubela walked the paths of the Moterion as Ora began to rise, behind her a cortège of Morwih, each a loose affiliation with her sect, their dandy mannerisms brazen in the face of so much death. She stepped astride the body of a fallen comrade without a moment's thought.

The zoo was desolate. She leered into the interiors of the cages. Things had lived there, things she might have called family. She shook the thought of such an existence from her and proceeded on to an enclosure unlike the others. Here was no cage, just a wide mote and beyond, a thick wall. Upon it sat many of her soldiers, enjoying the scant sunlight, blinking in its aura.

Esperer's flock whorled down and surrounded her. The well-fed troops of the Gull Lord were formidable, stinking of Ungdijin entrails. She chided them, drew her claws at them, though they cared little for her outburst, the strange furry creature. Morwih were not a common sight for these coastal kin.

Esperer stepped close to her, sized her up and down. She looked back at the ageing king, his body pitted with scars, his down unclean, his white eyes furious orbs, armour scabrous, crude. She was impressed.

'I am Esperer, the Gull Lord of the Pinnacle. My Lieutenant Roak has been my right wing, so I extend my left in greeting. I hope that his efforts have been to your liking?'

She was flattered by his manners. Like Roak, his size and strength were almost Wroth-like. It was akin to being spoken to by her Familiars, the few words she could understand of their gargling, insensible drawl. She liked it.

'Your soldiers have done well. Our forces combined have driven the Vulpus back towards Orn Megol, their hole in the ground. The Moterion, their most sacred land is vanquished. However, it may be that they were successful in completing their ritual. Many will follow them blindly as a result, regardless of whether it garnered any real change. Whatever they accomplished, we must undo. Kill them all if need be. One cannot rule if one is dead.'

Esperer smiled. 'I know nothing of this Vulpus ritual, nor do I care. My intentions are plain. We shall organise our squadrons, adding what remains of the city flocks to our own. If it is agreeable with you, we shall fly towards this Orn Megol. Take the fight to them.'

Fraubela nodded, 'Our ground soldiers are numerous. What you see before you is but a fraction of our force. Once we gather we shall follow in your stead, and clear those left alive. I hope to take Orn Megol within the next turn of Seyla.'

'So be it.' Esperer barked orders and his flock took to wing, leaving the Morwih unperturbed.

They lounged back and embraced the warmth of morning.

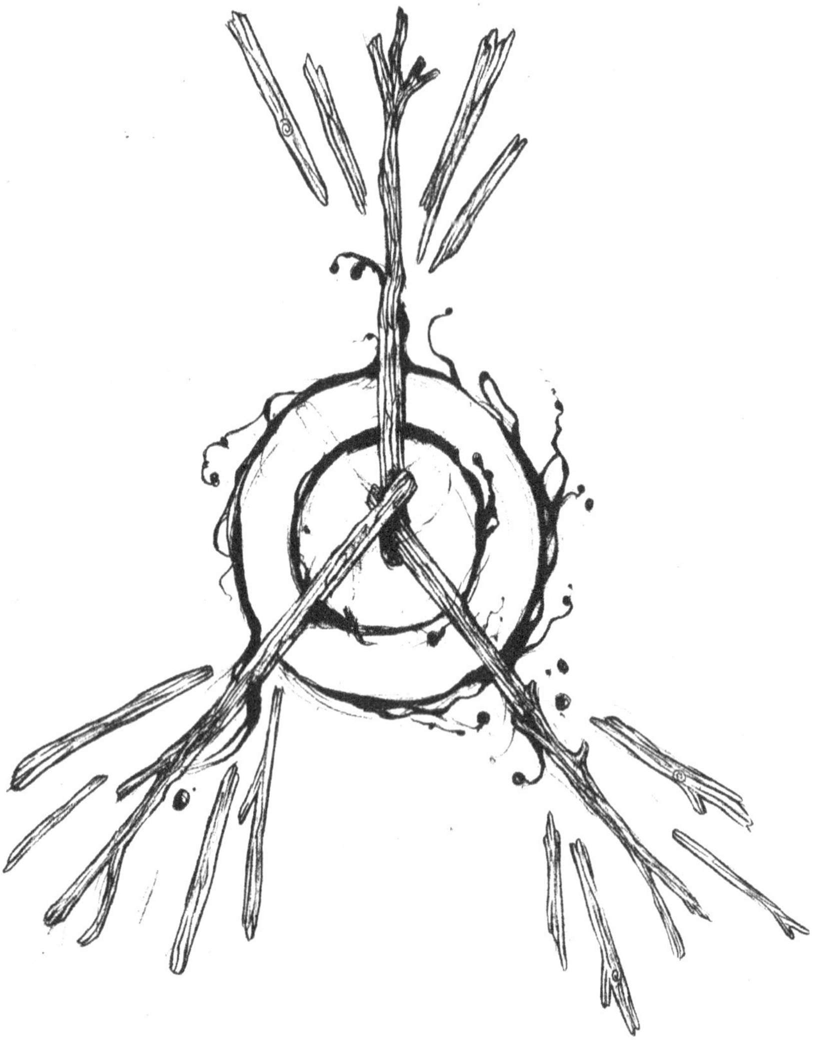

Chapter 12

Tor returned to his sett to find many dead. Of his family, his youngest had perished. His son Tordrin was barely conscious when Tor coaxed him to drink the farnikan root elixir. Alberi, his mate had taken their child's death very badly, and despite her sickness, it was grief that consumed her entirely. He cried out in the agony of it all.

Tor nursed them back towards health. Of his extended family, only nine remained. He lay their bodies amongst the leaf litter of the woods, blessed each with tiny petals plucked from esphani flowers.

Tor sat with Tordrin until he was able to speak.

'You saved us father.'

'You are my son.'

With time the Throa regained their strength. Food was foraged, they rested as much as possible. Tor had found a second strength, though he knew it was temporary. He felt the nag of something rotten inside him, yet he could not identify it. He hoped it was the final fleeting charge of the sickness.

One evening the earth stirred and he perceived the Song. He could not know if Rune had achieved that which the Vulpus wished of him. But he felt a draw back to the city.

Each morning he sat at the entrance to the sett and listened to the dawn chorus. His knowledge of the war was sparse, but amongst the prayers to the Sisters of the Flock, news came. A Yowri took notice of him, and once she had completed her verses, she approached him.

'You listen?'

'Yes' he said, 'I listen for news of the war.'

'Ah, the Stinking City. There is much to tell. Many go there to fight, from lands far from here. The Vulpus are now rulers, yet the Morwih have driven them back to Orn Megol.'

'Naa accepts Vulpus as rulers?'

'You felt it? The Song? They call it the Song. The Stinking City sang for the Vulpus, and so it is theirs.'

'And of the Morwih?'

'No one ever wished for them to rule. But perhaps they will if they defeat the Vulpus. They have made an alliance with the Gull clans, the Lord Esperer himself is in the city, he fights alongside the Fractured Sects.'

'Esperer? The Gulls fight with the Morwih?'

'Yes, they have torn up the ground with their stone weapons. The Vulpus hold many injured. The allegiance might end the Vulpus rule. The Speakers have fought back, yet there is no other winged force as large as the Naarna Elowin.'

Tor shook his head. 'Yes, there is.' When he had finished speaking with the Yowri he went to his son. 'I have to leave, return to the city. I have a task to complete. Will you stay and watch over our family. Be strong for them?'

Tordrin agreed, and Tor dressed himself in his armour, attaching a myriad of tools to each plate. He gave the last piece of the farnikan root to Alberi, and hoped that she would not need to use it.

He left the following morning, out towards the Stinking City. His progress was slow, yet unhindered.

Among the weathered structures of the Wroth, he sought a statue.

*

Rune and Vorsa could see something in each other that had not been there before. He saw a facet of her that was not fully realised, a strange aura that appeared to swell in the afterthought of any movement she might make. She saw this in him too. Some quality of the Gasp remained in them both.

Orn Megol was empty, its children above ground, awaiting the Morwih. Erithacus asked to speak with Satresan, and they discussed dark tidings within his sanctum. When they emerged Vorsa saw that her father looked drained.

'The Corva Anx are no longer to be trusted. They have used us in their diabolical plans!'

"I do not understand.'

Erithacus sighed. 'The Corva are not as eccentric and foolhardy as I once imagined. I have known Dominus Audagard and his fanaticism for many turns. I have known of his desire for the Gasp.

'They used you and your knowledge of the Orata to further their ambitions. To what end I do not know, but they knew the true intention of the Foul Meridian was not to free this city from the Wroth. They may have indeed seen good in their plight, that the end result would assist the Vulpus, but that was not their true goal.'

Satresan shook his head. 'We should have known this would come to pass. They betrayed the Starless Vulpus, forever cursed them. We should have abandoned our treaty with the Corva long ago.'

Vorsa was perplexed, 'If the Foul Meridian had a different intention, what was it?'

Rune explained his experience, leaving Vorsa breathless.

'What will it do?' Vorsa shook.

'We cannot know.'

*

Great statues of animals guarded the approach to the column at the centre of the Stinking City. Tor pondered their significance, he knew that the Wroth were not all bad, knew some that had even helped his own family in the past. Such occurrences were not quickly forgotten. He had never known what the Wroth made of the other species they shared Naa with, and perhaps now they were gone he never would.

The wide courtyard of granite sat amidst a convolution of major roads. Tor wound about the dead vehicles. He imagined this might be a place the Wroth had come to meet, to enjoy the company of one another. The only Wroth here now were decomposing bodies, lain in black bags. Faces covered with cloth, hiding the wretched smile of withdrawn flesh.

At the centre, a vast pillar. Somewhere stretching to the clouds an effigy of a Wroth stood at its peak. Tor marvelled at the hands that must have built this. It was quite something. He cleared his throat. He looked up at the massive buildings which stared inquisitively back with their yawning grills of columns. Upon the roof of each were thousands of feathered.

He gurned his lips, finding the right shape with his tongue and muzzle. He cocked his head back and warbled. It wasn't his best attempt, but it got the attention he required.

Suddenly the trilling hoot and tumble of wings filled the circumference of the square. The grey purple hew and nodding gait of the Baldaboa beset him, landing in a circle around him. They leaned their heads to one side to perceive the old daynight, and with each step, and each jolting neck movement they knew him intimately. A holler began to grow in their craws.

'I know you speak Ocquia, please do not think me stupid. I am here as a friend!'

The crowd parted to allow a rumbustious old Baldaboa to stand before him.

She spoke, 'I have only ever known one Throa, he came to me as a cub and showed me kind. I taught him a little Baldaboa, he was never any good at it.'

Tor replied. 'I once knew a fat Baldaboa whose greatest joy was finding sugary treats in the waste of the Wroth, and hiding them from her children.'

They both laughed and Tor embraced her. 'Troon'aubada, it is good to see you friend.'

'Tor, a face I thought to never see again! I believed you to be far from here, lost in your travels!'

'For a long time, yes. I travelled great distances. But I returned to my home and had a family. Naa gets pulled away from you when other mouths need feeding!'

'Too true! I have many mouths to feed old Throa!' They laughed together. 'But why do you come to me now? Does it have anything to do with the troubles that plague the city?'

Tor nodded, 'Naa is at war with itself. I know you are aware of the Vulpus Orata and their quest to take ownership after the Wroth.'

'We felt the earth quake like everyone, and more this morning. I assumed the power had been handed to them. We may understand its tongue, but you know all too well that we do not trouble ourselves with the notions of Ocquia. They have made it very clear we are not to be considered part of that world.'

Tor told of Rune; of the death of Artioch, of the little feathered's expulsion from the Pinnacle, and his many triumphs and tribulations that culminated with the war for the city. He explained the intricacies of the friendships formed in the shadow of these events.

He knew it would take a great deal to convince the Baldaboa to fight for anyone. Long ago, their ancestors had been domesticated by the Wroth, but some had escaped their clutches and started new lives within the ever changing landscapes of the city. They saw similarities in the fascia of these endless buildings that triggered memories of the rock faces and clifftops they once knew as home.

Much like the Morwih and Caanus, they had been stripped of their history by the Wroth, yet made the best of their freedom, constructing their homes amid the heights inaccessible by the hands that built them. Despite having been bred by the Wroth, it was the Wroth who set about making it impossible for them to even find places to roost. Surfaces were covered in sharp objects, smothered in substances that would ensnare their feet. The Baldaboa lost limbs to the cruelty of the Wroth.

They bred quickly, which was perhaps their downfall. There was not enough food in the city, and though this was shunned by many flocks, some turned to Wroth waste for sustenance and became insensible. They lost their footing in the world. They succumbed to the ways of the Wroth, cutting themselves off from Ocquia. Even the forest-dwelling Baldaboa distanced themselves from their city cousins, and a once vibrant people was forever looked down upon.

Tor had seen their brightness, and had gone to them in kind. He wished to know of their culture, and had found a deep and caring flock.

'We have no reason to help the Vulpus. Would they ever deign to help us if the roles were reversed? I think no.'

Tor agreed. 'That is quite true. Yet that is not to say that by helping, you would not be helping yourselves. The Wroth are dead. Your people, like all, will have to survive in a world without them. We are all thrown together, like it or not. The war is but the beginning of this.

'The Vulpus have been great wards of the city. They have kept the

Morwih at bay. But now The Morwih wish to own the city. They have even employed the Naarna Elowin as their aerial stooges. Such a force is almost impossible to defeat, unless ...'

'Unless the Baldaboa fly against them.'

'Yes.'

'It is true that if the Morwih were to win this war, our lives would be in peril. Such a predator cannot govern. Without the Wroth or the Vulpus within the city we would be quickly hunted to extinction. But Tor, we have spent endless turns living outside of Ocquia. We have been cast out for a reason.'

'Consider this a chance to shift the balance. Your people are strong, this is as much your city as it is theirs. If not for the Vulpus, then for the Baldaboa.'

Troon pondered, and spread her wings. 'Let my people discuss this.' She took to wing, her family following in a dizzying hail. Tor thought on his words as he sat under the great column. He felt an exhaustion deep in his bones.

As night drew close, the Baldaboa returned. 'We will fly for you Tor, we will fight the Naarna Elowin with all our might. But I must ask. The war is not in the sky alone. We can, perhaps, destroy the Gulls, but we cannot begin to stop the Morwih. The Vulpus are brave fighters, but I do not imagine there are enough of them to defeat their enemy in numbers. You will need more ground infantry.'

Tor agreed. 'I have an idea for that too.'

He promised to meet the Baldaboa on the fringes of Orn Megol, and then retraced his steps, his nose to the air, sniffing for a particular scent. His hackles raised, he was soon out amongst the wide roads and he strained his short neck to look between the barriers to see the city in all its festering glory.

He continued on, galumphing along the road until he reached an overpass. The smell became potent, an odour he had learned to fear above all others. It made him wince to even court the idea of what he was about to do. He looked down upon the road below.

The Caanus packs were anarchic. Without the Wroth to feed and guide them they had no sense of purpose. They had found one another in the search for food and shelter, seeking comfort in ramshackle hordes, lumbering innocents frightened without the voices of their Wroth companions. Together they found a substitute for the warmth of the families they had lost. Tor felt sorrow as they sniffed aimlessly at strewn remnants, searching for fleeting echoes of their masters, scampering in the litter of memories.

The bridge upon which he stood was inaccessible from the road below. This was as good a spot as any.

'Caanus brothers and sisters!' he bellowed.

The whole troop looked up at him, all saliva-strewn jowls and lolling tongues. They gave him the ubiquitous look of the Caanus; utter confusion. A huge boxy-faced Caanus teetered his head with curiosity.

'What are you?'

'Why, I am a Caanus, come to bring news!'

'You're a very strange looking Caanus.'

'Short legs!' yapped a tiny wrinkle-faced creature who looked even less like a Caanus than Tor.

'What do you want? We are busy looking for food. We haven't eaten in many turns and we are hungry!'

'Will you eat Morwih?'

They looked at one another with something resembling contemplation.

Tor frowned. 'You chase them. That's what Caanus do isn't it, chase things?'

'Yes, we chase them, but I don't know anyone who has ever caught a Morwih. Have you?'

Tor nodded, 'Oh yes. I have caught a Morwih. They are a little stringy, but food is food.'

They all agreed, food was definitely food. They were beginning to come round to the idea when Tor noticed a very specific scent. It made his teeth hurt. A group of similarly patterned Caanus appeared from beneath the bridge. They looked up at Tor with suspicion.

'We have hunted you, have we not?' They spoke with dry wry voices. Tor felt his heart sink.

'You hunted Caanus?' The boxy-headed canine looked to his kin.

'This is not Caanus, this is Throa. Our Wroth wished us to kill them. I have tasted their flesh, far tastier than any Morwih.'

Tor felt the need to run. He held the fear in himself and centred it, felt its grip. He buried it down deep. The hunting Caanus bolted.

Tor ran as quickly as he could, which was not very fast. He felt the strain in each muscle, every single fibrous tendon telling him that his heart might explode in his chest if he continued on, but he did, away from the bridge. He felt them behind him, felt the drive in their blood put there by their masters, who had taught them to murder and kill. The thought was so raw that it made him want to cry, and yet he took it, and forced it within his bones, and ran ever faster.

He reached another overpass, looking down on a wide stretch of road. The tarmac was utterly throttled by bodies, hundreds of Wroth, dead, piled, left to fester in the sun and coagulate in the rain. The smell was appalling, and every escape route was barred by the deceased.

He closed his eyes tight, felt the spittle fall upon his fur as their mouths enclosed.

No pain came.

He opened his eyes. The hunting Caanus stood in silent shock.

'They are all dead?'

Suddenly the bloodlust vanished. They resembled puppies, all floppy tan ears and drooping eyes. They looked to him for guidance.

'You must have seen the dead, how long have you been in the city?' Tor asked.

'We arrived this turn, we came from the north, looking for food. We found these Caanus and ran with them for a while. We had seen many dead masters. But not like this!'

Tor pulled himself up with a stuffy wheeze and brushed the saliva from his fur. They looked to him with such sadness. The other Caanus reached them, huffing and puffing through malformed faces, struggling on legs that could not carry such frames. He saw the hand of the Wroth in these poor souls.

It suddenly came to him that his hatred for the Caanus was misplaced. He thought of all that Erithacus had told him of the Wroth, how they owed a debt to these beasts.

'You are Caanus. You are the same blood as the Cini, yes?'

They stared back in confusion.

Tor took a deep breath. 'Long ago, your people were called the

Cini. You lived in the woods, away from the cities. The Wroth came to you, because you were strong. They asked you to hunt with them, asked you to protect them in the dark, made you family. But in this they took part of you away. Your true families were driven from the land. They were hated and hunted until they were all gone. They were murdered by the Wroth, by your own kind. The Wroth Cini became the Caanus. When there were no more true Cini, The Wroth made you hunt the Vulpus, who still live in the woods that were once your home. They too are your distant family, by blood. Your Wroth companions lied to you, and now they are all dead. You can no longer rely on them for your supper, for your comfort. You have to be each other's family now.'

The hunting Caanus looked worried. 'We do not know how to live in this world! How do we live without our Wroth masters?'

'The world is changing for us all. With the Wroth gone, the Morwih wish to own this city. They will drive you away, they will make you suffer at their paws. I ask of you to join me, and your Vulpus kin, and push the Morwih back. Together we shall find a place for us all.'

The boxy headed Caanus barked. 'I am very good at chasing Morwih! I like this idea!'

His companions howled a chorus of agreement.

'Then you must let go of your Wroth. You must remove your bridle, and you must shed your Wroth name.'

'But without my name, I am not Rex. I am nameless.'

'Choose a name, a name you like.'

'I like Rex.'

'Then Rex you shall remain.'

Tor chuckled to himself. The hunting Caanus looked to one another for guidance. They seemed completely lost in the delusions of the Wroth.

Finally, they asked, 'Are all the Wroth dead?'

'Yes.'

'All of them?'

'Yes.'

'Then we will fight for you.'

*

The chimney stacks pierced the evening grey like spears in empyrean's stomach. The Corva Anx and their lesser disciples found their roosts within the factory, cold and unkempt. The Dominus looked down upon the courtyard of the soot-encrusted ruin and became one with the dark.

Azrazion shifted in his tattered nest beside his son, beneath a velarium of suspended skulls and glass beads, his body distorted with old and new wounds from every desperate incantation. 'I felt it! I felt its coarse voice!'

The Dominus leaned close and calmed the frail Corva. 'The City sings. It is almost done, my father.'

Audagard clambered to the window ledge, from where he saw the Starless Vulpus below.

'What did you do!' The growled words hung in the black. 'What did you do? Dominus!'

'We held back our real intention, that is true, but with good cause! That cause is marked upon the sinew of each vow in your Orata, we speak only from its need!' We wanted the best for you all!'

'What does that mean? No more of your nonsense Dominus, tell us the truth!'

The Dominus consented.

'This is far greater than any Vulpus war for some wretched Wroth settlement. There is no magic in the Wroth, they were all brawn and material. Your desire for the city was all your doing, it was Vulpus creed!

'We did not make you go to war, you would have fought regardless! You wanted the city, so you took it!'

Nox seethed, 'We believed in your words, you told us that the Foul Meridian was for one purpose only! To assure the city for the Vulpus! We didn't want to take it, we wanted to save it from the Morwih!'

'You would never have done it for our cause. We never lied, we simply found the truth within your belief in the Orata. They serve the same ends!'

The Dominus dismounted his perch, gliding down to the Starless.

'The outcome of the Meridian remains the same. All of Naa accepts its significance. The Meridian was performed and was successful, the land and all its direful rotting planes are yours. If our spellcraft and witchery is fulfilled as well, then all the better, yes? Would you deny this old feathered his just desserts? The Morwih would still go to war with you, the Vulpus would still have to fight. The war was inevitable.'

'But you guided us, you guided my great grandfather, our families, to seek the Revenants in the Oscelan. You cursed us with these visions, for what? For this end? Did you not get what you wanted from that act? And what of Vorsa, you almost lost her to the Gasp? You lied and you continue to lie!'

He pounced on the Dominus, 'And for what!' Nox pinned his wings flat against the earth, pushing them into the coal slurry. 'We will die and the Morwih will take the city, we cannot win this war! Their forces are too strong. You wish to know death so much, then have it. Have death!'

The Dominus wriggled against Nox, squealing in terror. His Corva took to wing, diving at the Starless, pecking, tearing, yet the Dominus remained underfoot.

'Wait! There was always a reason!'

Nox reeled. 'A reason?'

'Your curse! It is far from a curse! You are Sentinel! You are the Proclamation!'

'What do you speak of?'

'The Revenants! In The Oscelan! You are their hosts, bound in blood! There is reason! the highest reason!'

Nox removed his paws. 'Tell me.'

*

The Starless Vulpus stood at the threshold to a cave shaft. Long ago a seam of coal had been found by the Wroth, had brought with it the promise of industry. Yet its yield was overestimated, and any hope of profit lost. Now it was nothing but a scar in the earth, its silent maw spilling fear.

The Starless felt a potent, undeniable dread that was etched into their bones as much as their fur. It was transcendental. The foreboding gloom shocked the fabric of them, their very cells were in mourning for what their forbears had seen. What dwelt below was inconceivable.

The Dominus hopped before the orifice, 'We came here seeking the Oscelan, beneath the earth it screamed for us. We were naive, our necromancy infantile and incomplete. We sent your ancestors into the earth to find the Revenants, to understand their forbidding purpose. In the dark we found them, the dead with unfinished work, held in the earth until their role was fulfilled.'

Nox glowered. 'What was there role?'

The Dominus grinned, 'Spirits bound to Naa always have business! For these old haunts, they awaited you!'

He skittered off, searching for something.

'Come,' he called and they followed his voice to a spot in the earth where white ash collected. A fire had once burned, Wroth vagrants seeking shelter in the factory. He picked up a lump of dried moss, wiped it in the wet ash, and with their permission cautiously applied the pulp to form a crude skeletal mask upon each of their faces.

'Why?' Nox asked.

'A face for you, and a face for them.'

Nox took a deep breath, and with his kin beside him, entered the mine.

The roof bowed, rotten beams that no longer offered support bedecked the tunnel walls. They trod carefully where the roof had collapsed. The walls were wet, and a slither of a stream ran ahead of them, sending back broad uncanny echoes through the ponderous gloom.

The path veered downward, into the coal seam itself. It opened on to a vast void where the floor gave way into a subterranean cavern. Above, the light of Seyla shone down through fissures in the rock. A steady flow of water joined the stream, falling away into the pit below.

The coal seam was a wide black band in the rock wall, a strata weave that bloated and thinned.

'I can feel them.' Nox said nervously.

Sheepishly, the Dominus took to wing, flying before the Oscelan. He could sense the presence of the Revenants, the writhing stream of torment and woe. He was utterly terrified, amid the earth, no place for his flock, no place for any living creature. Suddenly exposed to the thing he longed for so much, had craved, sought in blood, maimed for, killed for, lied for, and suddenly all at once, lost his taste for.

Regardless, he flew towards the rock, eyes shut. Something unnatural reached out from the coal and pulled him in.

He felt the cold hard Oscelan against his face. It whispered the unspeakable, and words like the spines of insects crawled into his mind, injecting venom deep. He saw their faces, horrifying, malnourished, not meant to be. He saw their desire, oh! the endless, ceaseless, incorrigible desire to live, pressed down under the weight of millennia. He saw it all, the infinite turns of Seyla, her glow like a white line across time, unable to turn away from her constant cold stare. *You are dead* she said, *and you will live in death forever.*

It was glorious.

He screamed out, saw the black lick of the coal absorb him, pull him down into the seam; and he strained, as hard as he could, tearing feathers from flesh, until he was free, falling, gaining flight, flapping with exhausted wings, until he lay upon the rock.

The Oscelan rippled. Ventricles of white aether seeped from the rock; tortuous lurid arms of mist, followed by trunks, torsos, awful misshapen guises of animals none of the Starless could recognise. These were the oldest kin, buried within the petrified forests millennia ago, those who had died beneath prehistoric canopies, crushed to black carbon. As a projection; the vaporous dead gloated from the coal, floated about the Starless, sniffing their vivacity. A face formed above the Vulpus, an emaciated skull, long and wide, primordial teeth designed for tearing at unimaginable prey. It looked into Nox, saw the stubbornness, the determination. It spoke with the sound of muscle being torn from bone.

'EROUA OAZA VAS! THE CITY SINGS FOR YOU!'

Nox cowered beneath it. 'What do you want from us?'

'TO BE FREE OF THIS GRAVE'

Six presences emerged, squirming masses that wheeled towards the Starless. The Vulpus looked to one another in despair, set to run, yet were too late. They closed their eyes, and felt the excruciating defilement.

*

The Dominus spat himself free of the mine. He felt the storm of death behind him, the pull of war in the east. He dismissed it all, all mere wisps of consequence, all carrion of prophecy made good.

His bishops flew to him, haranguing him with questions.

'Is it done?'

'It is!'

*

Rune and Aggi sat upon the music hall. From here they could see great swathes of the Stinking City, and they watched anxiously for signs of the Morwih.

'What is the Umbra like, Rune?' Aggi moved closer beside him for warmth.

'When leaves become old and rot away, they leave a skeleton, lots of little threads, all interconnected. It is there, and it is not there. It has form, but most of it has withered and disappeared, yet it is a leaf all the same. That is the Umbra, like lots of strange lines, all connected, across everything, and all of us. All life moves across it, I can see every life.'

Rune closed his eyes tight until patterns emerged, the tighter his eyes, the more vivid the lines. He opened his eyes and the lines remained, dancing off into the far distance. There were many bright lights, yet the brightest still hung far off, to the south, and it grew ever brighter with every passing moment. The lines that conjoined with his own were now fuller, as though some aspect of the First City already had a presence here. He imagined it like many insect legs stretching out.

'I think I can see the First City.'

'What does it look like?'

'A great light in the distance.'

'Do you think your Father is there?'

'I hope so.'

Aggi sensed anxiety in the little feathered. Below, Oromon was greeting mercenaries who had come to join the fight. She saw Throa from distant sets, Tril and Nighspyn. Amongst those waiting she saw the tall and elegant presence of the Drove.

'There are Yoa'a, like Onnar!' she exclaimed, and they both flew down to greet them.

Some carried whittled sticks with glass and metal bound to each end. Their armour was beautiful yet robust. Aggi could see wood and metal, root and twine lashing each resilient plate, adorned with Drove glyph work, to one another.

'Tarmisil!' Onnar exclaimed as she bounded to joined her sisters upon the terrace. They graced one another's faces.

She turned to Rune and Aggi. 'My dear friends, you are requested below.'

They left her in the safe paws of her fellow Drove and descended into the subterranean stronghold. Entering the great hall of Orn Megol, they found Erithacus and Satresan deep in discussion.

Satresan sighed, 'Now that we know our lot, we must plan for the future of the peoples of Ocquia. Rune, what can you tell us of the First City, what does it want?'

Rune recalled his visions, 'I fear the city saw our greed. It is not like the Stinking City, it is not just stone and rock, it is made of trees, and bone and living things. It moves with a will of its own. In many ways it is the Umbra itself. All I felt was sadness. Loss. We cannot stop it, whatever it will do.'

'Then we must try to withstand the Morwih, and whatever fate exists beyond that, we can only hope that it does not end us all. The earth shakes beneath our feet, which does not bode well. I have not known such a thing in my whole life.'

Rune shook his head. 'I do not think it will kill us, but it will bring change. The First City wanted peace, its greatest move was to disappear, not to attack. It left our ancestors alone so that we might learn to work together. The city is not a Wroth thing. It is made of us. It exists for us. My father saw good in it. I trust his judgement. We must not fear the worst.'

Glaspitter entered the hall in a hurry, 'Erithacus. The Gull army approaches.'

They all made their way to the surface. They saw the formations of the Gulls, who marked the sky with their pallid bodies, each tinged with the black of their armour.

'We cannot possibly win against such a flock,' Erithacus whispered.

*

Amidst the city, Tor looked to the sky and saw the Gulls. The Caanus in his tread saw them too. 'What are they?'

'They are the enemy we cannot reach.'

*

In the quiet streets the Baldaboa sought their extended families, jostled them from beneath arches and alcoves. They persuaded those resentful of Ocquia with the prize of a new world. All saw the empty squares and parks, the retreat of the Wroth. All feared what would become of them, and with little effort they left their nests and roosts, bustled and hooted and cooed to one another in the draw of new fortune.

Troon greeted the increasing flock with pride; covert messages were carried wide, a point on the land to converge. A few Gulls who flew overhead looked down with vague curiosity, the flick flack warble, the telltale accent of the Baldaboa, garnering little beyond a frown. None contemplated such an uprising. The grey-green flutter was inconsequential.

Troon caught the gaze of the enemy, decided their disinterest was to her advantage. No one would see them coming. She followed Tor's instruction to the word – fly north west, towards Orn Megol. They flew in staggered succession beneath the oblivious wing of the enemy.

*

The Caanus romped through the streets, noses to the ground, yelping gleefully at the few Morwih unlucky to stumble into their path, fleeing the rough bark and scamper. Strange earthquakes continued below. Tor's companions looked to him for understanding, of which he could offer none. He could see hairline cracks in the ground; occasional breaks and faults yawned. Muroi and Creta hurried away from their underground homes, fearful of what was to come. Their fear was shared by all who sought shelter away from the tremors.

The Wroth had built tunnels. They seemed to bury streams beneath their cities; some reeked of faeces, other carried fresh water. Tor wished to make sense of the disturbances, and he asked the fleeing Creta where he might find an entrance. They directed him to an old access tunnel, where a gate had long rusted from its hinges.

Tor and Rex walked along the passageway, stooping under pipes, avoiding the various detritus that had collected in the dark sewers. The concrete and brick was split here too, meandering cracks that Tor followed until he reached the source.

The floor and walls of the channel had been torn open. Here, amidst the foundations of the Stinking City giant roots had emerged; vast as tree trunks, they were ploughing the defiant stone with serpentine determination, reducing it to rubble. Tor placed his paw upon one of the roots and felt its strength. The roots had wrapped themselves around beams and pipes that held the city firm and they were undoing the very foundations, tearing away the underpinning.

'What is it?' Rex barked.

'I do not know, but it means to pull the city down.'

They climbed out of the drain, faced by many packs of Caanus, all eager and excitable.

They strode north, below the flight path of the Gull army.

*

Fraubela and her cortege had left the Moterion. She kept her distance yet assured her troops of her presence amongst them. She had no intention of fighting.

The Vulpus were all but driven from her city. Her city. She had won. Their archaic rites so much dust. She smirked, there was a skip in her stride. She had one more task to complete.

Hevridis trailed her. He saw nothing but the dead. Every few feet another Morwih, another Vulpus. The slain allies of both sides beside them – Harend, Aven, Maar. All pathetic carcasses amongst the debris of a fallen civilisation. Suddenly any sense of pride, something his kin were so very good at feeling, seeped out of him like the dark pools of haemoglobin where something bright and thinking once dwelt. He kindled a new feeling, something that was not so easy to discern, for it held great discomfort. He felt shame.

The day's terminus beckoned, lustral folds of violet and orange sinking beyond the hill. In shadow, the black bulk of the music hall gave their goal an imposing end point. Hevridis kept his distance from his love, listening to her boastful serenade. It was nauseating.

It began to rain.

He found a tree to climb, a large oak that blended with the thicket which lined the lowlands. He could see the flicking black of Vulpus ears in the long grass. They listened intently. Once he had seen one pair, others became apparent. The Morwih would not expect an attack here, and his entire body yearned to go to Fraubela, to alert her to the foolhardiness of her commands. She would send her soldiers into these enemy lands and they would be slaughtered.

This was his conundrum. He was Morwih. He owed the Vulpus nothing, their lives were nothing more than obstacles to the Fractured Sects. The Morwih feasted on the mere thought of dominion, and they wished for it. They wanted it.

Above all, there was no stratagem, no design, and no hope for tomorrow. Fraubela's thought was simply to vanquish.

And what of the Vulpus? What did they want? To be left to live. To protect Ocquia. Protect even those who might be food.

He pressed himself close to the tree, felt the dull ache of the raw bark against his fur, pinning it in places, pinching flesh, felt the grain. He heard the rumble of some unknowable thing working in the earth. It was almost inaudible, yet once he had noticed it, he could not ignore it. It became as obvious as the Vulpus in the grass. He watched Fraubela, her expression so glib.

He chose a side.

*

Roak flew beside Tawk, far behind the lead squadron and their commander. During his sojourn Roak had considered the Gull Lord a weak and fragile fool, but Esperer was far from it. It vexed Roak no end that, surrounded by the trappings of war, the old king had regained a youthful clarity.

Roak spied the music hall, the territory of the Vulpus. He could see the tide of Morwih close to the green of the grass slopes and the buckled tarmac path. These lines perhaps had served no importance for the Wroth, but the Morwih knew their significance. They began to collect in rough lines along the edges, their incisive gaze upon the silent acres they craved.

Roak, though, no longer cared about the war. He returned his caustic glare to the tail feathers of his glorious leader. Tawk followed his line of sight, knew his intention. He flew close, careful not to speak too loud.

'Roak. You mean to kill him.'

'Yes.' Roak said, without hesitation.

*

Amidst the rain and wind Esperer signalled the first battalion; they dropped low, silent wings motionless in the updraft, so many sharp extremities. They made for the grass, enacting their first sweep. At their speed, amidst heaven's spittle, it was hard to discern the shapes moving in the grass. They made a second pass, grazing the tips of the meadow.

Oromon slinked low, he saw the first run, the white down in Seyla's glare. He positioned himself just beyond the wake of motion left by the flock. He attempted to glean the second trajectory, the return pass, pulled himself down, feeling his hind limbs coil.

He leapt.

Webbed foot in mouth, he dragged the great Gull into the grass, rolling over it, down into the taller growth. He broke its wings with violent jerks, pulling its face close to his so that it could see its murderer.

He bit into its neck.

Above, Esperer could only make out the slightest disturbance. The battalion regrouped, only then realising they had lost a soldier.

'Down there!' one gestured, and they perceived the spiral formation of a struggle within the grass, and the still corpse of one of their own.

'There are Vulpus in the grass!'

The squadrons dropped, seeking targets barely perceptible, and they made the same mistake; each run losing a second and third comrade. Yet the next run knew better, and the hail of rocks fell with deadly aim, cutting and killing without remorse.

*

Fraubela shrieked her command, and at once her platoons bounded from their stations into the fray, all brindled fur and ruthless armour amongst the wet cascade.

Hevridis watched with trepidation as the Morwih met their enemy. Cirrus blades distorted their feline paths; with no idea of the whereabouts of the Vulpus, they could not predict their movements.

The Vulpus began to move on them, using the incline and throwing themselves at the besieging soldiers. Hevridis pulled himself up to a stronger branch, high above the battle. For a moment the Vulpus held back the advance, yet with each new volley of stones from above their defence was further breached.

Onwards leapt the Morwih, grim fervour, exacting mortal wounds.

With her command given Fraubela veered right along the curving path, avoiding the Vulpus soldiers, heading towards the brink of light, beyond the music hall. Hevridis knew she sought the entrance to Orn Megol, and so he followed.

Oromon ran towards the path that encircled the music hall, where the hundreds of reserve allies stood ready, prepared their chitin armour, bound pieces of bark to their tiny hides and broad snouts. He commanded each according to their skills, and in moments they took to action; the Bloodsons and Aven carried ammunition, tossing it to the Collector flocks midair, who concentrated their aim entirely on the Gulls. The Collectors were much faster than the cumbersome Elowin, and although made little physical damage, they threw the Gulls off their aim as they severed the sky.

Oromon made for the Drove, whose number had grown significantly. Through wet fur and bloodied teeth he panted, 'I implore you, we must hold the line.'

The Drove nodded assuredly, looking to one another. Tarmisil took the lead.

Onnar rushed to her side. Tarmisil glanced at the brave warrior beside her, and then to her own weapon. 'Your mother would want you to have this.' She lifted the Halberd, which slid within the cuff of her gauntlet.

Onnar noticed the worn wood, could make out the cut marks made by her mother's own teeth.

'This was Laudinor's blade?'

Tarmisil nodded. 'I killed the Morwih who took her life with it myself.'

Onnar smiled, 'I will cherish it.' She strapped it to her own gauntlet, so that the blade now ran along the back of her forelimb. It would do much damage.

Their ruddy grey tirade plunged over the top; down into the yolk of battle. They ran against the grain of muddy eruptions, the cleft of disembodied limbs, the black alluvium filth torn up, cast across incensed mouths, wide dextrous tongues throwing profanities and teeth. Chests splaying; the raking cry of hungry scorn, the swollen glee of a hundred crushed skulls, pierced arms, exploded eyes. They desired their ire, thick and deep in disemboweled guts. Onnar brought down her vehemence in clever curves, spattered the warm and stinking death upon her armour, wiped the slather from her vision and pummelled on, cutting, smashing.

Each movement slowed to a point; with perfect brevity she timed each clout, each battery. The Morwih twisted under her, distorted in the wet of their compatriots' gore, slick, unrecognisable; bone white crack and splinter, so sure, so perfect and crisp against the clotted septic turf beneath their feet.

Onnar stopped for a moment, amongst the throng, breathed in deep, felt the guilt of death on her fur, in her fur. She sobbed for the loss of her enemies, sank down, listening, watching the waves of Morwih, the Vulpus clans, the Drove, the Maar, the uniform vermilion that covered them all. The grass reduced to filthy crowns, grass follicles pulled, wrenched by desperate mouths hauling themselves free of their enemies. The rain was blinding, yet it diluted the blood. Onnar was thankful.

She was engulfed, the pale enmity of a blank lustre fogged with haze; marshalled ranks of Gulls stooped and flung their deadly blessings, augural formations, inverted hope. The roar of bodies pinned and sliced against one another. She was knocked and shoved as Vulpus guards ran to pull soldiers from the botch.

The sloping field presented the sight to her in clear mutilation.

The Morwih were making progress. She could see the continuous sweep of new soldiers feeding from the city. There were so many! A ceaseless onslaught, the defenders could not stem the flow. The Vulpus were pushed back, further and further towards the top of the hill.

She heard the muffled cry of her name, so tiny, so weak. It pierced her tarry perception, and she pulled herself down, just in time. A massive stone crushed against the skull of an aggressor. Eyes up, she saw the humongous Larn Elowin, still clutching its second ballast. She searched frantically for the source of the warning, and there, hovering low, ducking the meteoric stormfront, were Rune and Aggi.

'Get back!' she cried, 'Get back!'

They looked confused – they only wished to help. She knew this, saw the desperation, 'Please, for the love of you!'

She saw their realisation, saw Aggi beckon Rune back. This war had never been mercenary work. She was no longer mercenary. A life of no real purpose, of adopting the ambition of others, being the courage for others. That had evaporated. For a moment, she saw herself above it all, above the flayed skin and hair and death, saw her friend dead on the road, pulverised, unthought of, a moment's regret by whatever killed her. She was not forgotten, not empty.

'Don't just stand there, proudfoot!'

Tarmisil stood on hind legs, a Morwih attached at her shoulder, its eager eyes so determined. Onnar broke her trance and loped to her friend, raising her halberd arm, bringing it down hard on the Morwih's head.

*

Vorsa had regained her strength, and despite some peculiar aspect she could not place, she was well enough to fight. Her father objected, asking her to stay with him, protect Orn Megol from within. His plea was fruitless.

She was soon upon the esplanade, saw the myriad wounded dragged free of the fight. The Morwih were halfway up the hill. Upon the roof she saw Erithacus, conducting his flock from beneath a slight recess in the stonework. Statuesque, his divinations were perfect, each command rewarded with a fallen Gull. The Speaker flocks were few against the Elowin, yet they were resolute.

'Oromon!' She shouted.

'Vorsa, you are well?' He was tired, his armour loose, falling free of his back.

With her mouth she deftly pulled it taught. 'They are pushing forward.'

'We cannot hold them,' he said with despair. 'We are trying, but it is the numbers, we simply do not have the numbers. For every dead Morwih, two will rise up. They are fine fighters. They are fearless.'

'I will fight with you,' she said.

They leapt forth, teeth bared, into the fight.

*

Hevridis ran along the embankment which curved with the path leading towards Orn Megol. He could hear the patter of Fraubela's guard, and he was soon stalking through a line of withered trees as they approached the loading bay behind the music hall, down into the shrubbery. He bound forward, his presence unnoticed, blending with her entourage.

The entrance was unguarded. The worn earth thick with scent, as much a warning as the Vulpus themselves that this place was not meant for the Morwih. As they descended into the hole he pulled back. Fraubela centred herself amongst the group. Multiple paths lay before them. She placed her face close to the floor, then commanded four of her troop to disperse through the passageways. They waited in the wet earth.

Only one returned. She beckoned them on, and for a moment

Hevridis felt the urge to know what fate had befallen those who had not come back.

Orn Megol. He had never thought to know its belly. The Fractured Sects knew almost nothing of the earthen kin. Dragged back from the primitive cults of Ocquia, Morwih recognised their civility amongst the Wroth. Yet that eve he had seen no sign of that refinement. In Fraubela he saw a thirst that no quiet home could quench.

The jewelled walls of the tunnels beguiled them all. Even Hevridis felt the need to exclaim his awe at that which the Vulpus had built. Each shard of mirrorglass reflected the infinitesimal light, carefully tempted into the earth by cleverly angled pieces through shafts above. Seyla was with them, in the dark, and it adorned every raw surface as exquisitely as lace.

The passage guided them downwards, until they reached a broad entrance. This, he thought, the meeting place for the Vulpus, a gallery of bone fragments, skulls of loved ones, a multitude of glyphic reliefs. He wished to know what it all meant, and yet he lacked any grasp of the Vulpus' runic alphabet. He held himself in shadow.

'Come forth, ruler of Orn Megol!' Fraubela cried.

Satresan emerged from his cloister. Despite his fear the ghost white Vulpus held himself firm. Hevridis saw that fear, but he also saw courage. Beside the old leader were his stewards. They encircled him.

'I do not know you.' He spoke with a whisper.

'I am Fraubela. I am the Consul of the Fractured Sects. Leader of the Morwih.'

'Why are you in our home, Fraubela?'

She smiled, lowering her face. 'It's quite obvious, I am sure.'

'You are here to kill me, Morwih?'

Her soldiers fanned out, yet Satresan stood fast.

'I will not fight you.'

'I do not wish to fight. We can make this as painless as you allow it to be.'

She moved close to the old Vulpus, her eyes provocative. She traced the contour of his crown, the subtle grey and white of his coat.

Hevridis saw it all before him. He saw Vorsa. How she had held him in her maw, how she had choked him, bled him, all to make a point.

She had broken it all for him, all the games, all the subterfuge.

He saw the countless turns that he had served his love. How he had loved her! It was a painful, vital thing in him. But it was love pulled taught, spread to breaking point, and the weight of his realisation was all too much for it to survive. Despite her best efforts to dismiss him, he knew she loved him, but it wasn't enough.

Her soldiers pinned down Satresan's guards. Outnumbered, they were unable to free themselves. They did not struggle; Satresan would not have it so.

'Do not fight them!' He cried as Fraubela pushed him back against the wall. He was far larger than her, yet he knew he was too frail to fight back.

Her aim was cruel. She held his throat in her mephitic jaws, yanking him down. His front limbs buckled.

Hevridis did not falter. He dodged the lone guard still accompanying her, he pounced, feeling his claws flex from cuticle sheathes and bury themselves in her flesh.

The shock jolted her free of Satresan. The confusion had dizzied the Morwih guards, whose momentary lack of concentration allowed one of the Vulpus to struggle clear, who now bore down on the Morwih.

Hevridis dragged Fraubela back, back against the wall. She kicked out, she tried to free herself.

'No!' He cried. 'I will not let you kill him!'

'You coward! You cur!' She hissed. She tried to pull herself from him, yet he would not let go.

'Please Fraubela, You cannot. You are better than this! You can love, you have a heart. I have felt it in you, you are capable of more than this!'

'I am nothing without this! Nothing! What are we, strays, orphans? We deserve this! Deserve it all! Let me go! I will prove it all to you, prove to you just how strong, how brilliant we can be!'

'Will you kill him?'

'Of course!'

There was clarity. He saw the Fractured Sects win. He saw the city in their stead. He saw nations of Ocquia migrate, avoid this place completely. He saw the Vulpus clans that survived withdraw from the land. He saw the city decline, deteriorate. The Morwih would suffer the most. Without food, without the knowledge of the many species whose treatise and understanding allowed for hunters and grazers to live amidst the same land, they would decimate what was left and starve in the aftermath.

He placed his weight upon her, holding her close, and bit down hard at the base of her skull. With a violent jerk, he snapped her neck.

Fraubela fell limp.

He carefully lay her down. He turned to her guardskin. He said nothing, yet his face told everything. They withdrew, and made for the surface.

Hevridis stared at the lifeless form before him. He shook his head.

'I cannot stop the Morwih.'

Satresan paced beside him. 'No one can.'

Hevridis nodded. 'It will end, and when it does, we will have much to talk about. You can thank your daughter for this.'

Satresan exhaled. 'She is a clever soul.'

'That she is.'

Hevridis moved to leave Orn Megol.

Satresan turned his neck, feeling the bite wound. His guards rushed to his aid, yet he assured them he was able to stand and walk unaided.

'We must alert my daughter to what has transpired here. We must alert our people that the Morwih leader is dead!'

The guards rushed to the surface, greeted by a number of Vulpus kin.

'The Consul of the Fractured Sects is dead!'

The word was carried forth, cried to all who would listen. Yet the Morwih fought on with scythe fangs, impervious to the news; they shirked any ruse, clever though it may be. They pushed the Vulpus back against the low wall that hemmed the music hall, pinning the final line that held Orn Megol, their yearning eyes hungry, insensible.

With snarling contempt, Oromon was beaten back beside the Drove. Pitted with weeping cuts, they fought with depleted breath. Vorsa leapt from the terrace into the foe, all feral in their striking claws and snapping mouths. The fatigue had sunk long into the defenders, yet they held themselves in the fount of life and struck back with every ounce of strength. They pushed down together, Vorsa sharing a glance of dwindling hope with Oromon. Despite their best efforts, they were crushed against the perimeter, lost below bodies.

She strained to reach him, lashing at the Morwih's legs. Vorsa bit and bit, tearing flesh. They howled at her, threw themselves upon her, and their weight had her down in the crimson, the gagging glut beneath the bodies. She heard the call of Oromon, she heard the hollow hoot of the Drove.

Low, crushed flat against the earth, she saw Petulan.

*

Hevridis emerged from Orn Mogol only for the Vulpus scouts to be upon him. He vaulted up onto a supporting wall, daring not to look back. Soon he had scaled the red brick and found safety upon the long collapsed glass-domed roof of the music hall. He climbed precariously up until he was far from any who could touch him. Here he sat and mourned Fraubela.

He saw the battle, closed his eyes and imagined it over. He straddled the iron lattice and found himself upon the rafters' edge. Croaking voices reached his ears, and periodically, the green flick of a feathered, darting to and from the sky. They were Speakers, he had heard their cry often above him, and yet they were here, and they were fighting.

Chapter 13

Seeping through membranous layers, permeating nerves with glorious carnality, the Oscelan Revenants stitched themselves to the Starless Vulpus. The pain was profound; they convulsed, eyes confronted with visions of maddening descent into fathomless eons spent bound in the coal, the strobe of eras spasming, forcing themselves with great pressure, binding the tallow of forests with every molecule, making themselves indistinguishable from one another, mutating their presence into neutron stars, enfolded cataclysms, focused, unending, psychotic.

Nox considered his form amongst his kin. He felt the beat of another within his chest, a strong, imperfect drum. His limbs were no longer his to control, there was something incomprehensible in him.

They turned to one another, saw that the crude skulls drawn upon their fur had adopted a new quality – carrion protrusions, the deathly expressions of that which now invaded their bones.

The Revenants overcame them, took the reins, and they left the mine with unnatural speed.

The Starless Vulpus inscribed a peculiar line across the land; the dismal cavalry enveloped in strange mist. They were part living; black fur and virulent eyes and part dead, for their bodies were two-fold, that which deigned to walk in Naa, that which walked the vaults of the Gasp. One overlapped the other, veils of perplexity visible only to them – the host and the parasite ghost.

Within their sight, the Stinking City, which drew them in with its splendid life, its pain and ecstasy, and they pulled it close, as though the cloth of Naa were in their mouths, the grotesque undead.

They set foot upon the westerly edge of the fields, tearing clods of earth as they careered up towards the battle. Morwih funnelled in from the south, following the worn track of their kin. The Starless felt the yearning of the Oscelan, all the bountiful verve, all the zest the Revenants had desired for so long, now before them. Together they surveyed the landscape, strewn with the dying. Nox could feel the spirit, feel its anger. They despaired in it, licked at the bloody wounds of fallen bodies and gained knowledge of lives lost. The roar of onslaught before the music hall caught their attention, their brimstone eyes blistering as they ran towards the fight atop the hill.

They fell together, becoming one Starless Creature, binding their extremities in the slick of black corruption, an orgy of gnashing teeth lost in liquid dark. This monstrous mass lashed forth. No longer six, but one senseless debauchery.

Above, the Collectors were snatching ammunition from the Bloodsons when the black void opened in the heart of the battle.

The warring parties scattered, something hideous had pulled itself out of that dark, it scurried and gnawed through the mud, yet no one could be sure what it was. The sea of soldiers ran from the festering thing as it flailed scythe limbs toward them. Some brave souls turned to confront it, yet their aim was lost with terror as it whipped them up and tore them apart. Garlands of fur and blood erupted.

As if to meet this unseen force, Esperer's troops assembled midair, concentrating their efforts upon the clans who now sustained the weakening barricade atop the hill. Aggi conducted Rune away from the bombardment, directing him east, to find the source of the Gull army.

The pair kept pace with the squadrons above, until they dropped to collect new ammunition. Rune and Aggi continued onwards, until they reached a series of low lying Wroth structures, vast grey platforms, where a few weary troops of Esperer rested. The pair found a place from which to watch.

*

Tor stopped for a moment to catch his breath. The pain in him was growing. The Caanus had formed one large pack, running through the streets, picking up the vagrant canines that could only dream of such a sight, a tide of eager barks, clumsy feet and boundless enthusiasm. Tor struggled to keep up, did all he could to ignore the worrisome ache within. Yet the Caanus were patient with his little legs, and eventually the end of their journey neared.

The Baldaboa were nowhere to be seen. Their path took them to a quiet track, a rough road strewn with pine needles, copses of evergreens, dark and ruddy wood, and fine-toothed spurs that swayed under the weight of their cone fruit. They progressed with caution, the dense branches consuming any light, until it was difficult to discern where they trod. Again, Tor found use for his lights, and with a little fuss, managed to trigger them. Their path was at once a flare of yellow, which as they continued widened until it was swallowed by a large clearing. As Tor considered their next move the Caanus were unusually silent.

The trees swayed, held amongst their bows a forbidding manner, the light that filtered through the gaps between the branches making faces at them, eyes and mouths of gruesome pareidolia.

Rex's great head darted this way and that. 'There are eyes here, in the trees! Watching us!'

Tor dismissed him, 'It is but a trick of the light boy, don't worry. I will have our destination shortly. Would you like to see a much cleverer trick?'

Rex broke from his fear, 'Oh! A trick, yes!'

The giant bodies of many Caanus surrounded the Throa, who pulled a length of strong wire from his armour. A puddle was close by, and he made for it. He located a large leaf, and placed it in the water. It sank. He tutted to himself, and found another, he hoped more buoyant leaf. Once it floated he took the metal spur and began to rub it on his belly. They all stared with curiosity, until finally he lifted the wire and placed it daintily on the leaf.

The leaf moved.

'This points north, and our destination is just a little off north. Now we know our direction, we can follow this path onwards.'

'This is some strange magic, Throa,' one of the hunting Caanus offered.

He picked up the wire and slipped it back under his armour. 'This is no magic my friend.'

'The eyes are still watching us!' Rex added.

Tor shook his head, and turned off his lights. Thousands of eyes glowered down from the treeline.

Tor was startled, and then smiled with realisation. He pursed his lips and let out a warble. The trees warbled back. Their foliage became a shadowgraphy of silhouettes and wing beats.

The Baldaboa.

Troon flapped down and landed in front of Tor. 'Ora bring peace my friend.'

'We have seen the Gulls, they are very close. We shall begin our assault.'

She took to wing, and Tor began to lope towards the music hall, his giant pack of Caanus in tow.

*

The yap and growl of the Caanus was unmistakable, few would stay long in the presence of such a threat. Rune skirted the edge of the warehouse and tried to seek the source, and suddenly the mob of hounds emerged from a copse of pines to the south.

Aggi was on the wing before he could alert her. They swooped low, pitching over spry ears and excited tails. At the centre of the pack the bodies divided, and there waddling as fast as he could, was Tor. Rune recognised his lumber and landed upon his armour. 'Hello Tor!' he exclaimed.

'Rune son of Grom! I am so glad to see you well!'

'The war?' Tor asked.

Aggi said, 'The Vulpus are losing, pushed back against Orn Megol. You could not come at a more urgent time.'

The pack continued onwards towards the eastern edge, until finally they broke onto the field of battle. 'Remember my Caanus! Morwih are the enemy!'

*

'Morwih! Morwih! Morwih!' They roared, picking up pace. The pack fragmented into groups running riot amongst the confused and frighten enemy. For many Morwih the lust of war was quashed in an instant, and they retreated in haste the way they had come. The Caanus pursued, whilst others launched at the belligerent huddle before them. They lined the lowland path, cutting back the flow of Morwih from the city with angry barks.

Above, dank piles of leaf litter mired with rain water into a lake of decomposing muck such that further up the hill no paws could gain traction, and so the battle slid away from the hilltop.

The conflict splintered; an obstacle slowed the fight at the core.

Tor guided a small group of Caanus carefully up the muddy bank. Infantry of both sides ran toward them. He braced for their slathering jaws, but none came. They were fleeing. The fighting ground to a halt, the cries of victims trailed the great wound that opened at the centre of the battle. Troops held a wide berth, but could not escape it. Amongst the incoherence, something great breathed through alien lungs.

Tor saw the nightmarish entity that had burrowed to the heart of the battle. It stalked the vacated ground, all spindle legs and eyes. It held a Morwih in one scissor claw, a Vulpus in another. They convulsed, held from the neck, clinging to what little life remained. The entity was black and sodden with rain, and none could look upon it without feeling nauseous.

Soldiers of both armies pleaded for its victim's release. It held them like trophies. The jaundiced notes of dawn shed little light on this terrible thing. Tor could not believe his eyes.

Above, Erithacus flew up on to the roof. Cumbersome and stone grey, he leered out at the disturbance below. Hevridis slinked in the shadows, intent on not being noticed.

'What do you want, Morwih?' Erithacus boomed.

'I came up here to flee the Vulpus. I am something of an outcast.'

'And what pray tell makes you an outcast?'

Hevridis smirked. 'Ah, well I killed my lover, the Consul of the Morwih, to save the life of the Vulpus king.'

Erithacus swivelled his neck to eye the feline. 'You have my ear.'

Hevridis put on a brave face.

Erithacus leaned towards him, 'What is this? Sadness?' Erithacus could sense guilt.

'I saw the future ruled by the Morwih. It was desolate.'

Erithacus dipped his head, 'I have seen that future too. A similar fate was wielded by the Wroth, and yet that did not come to pass. It seems Naa does not will such things. I believe your sacrifice was not in vain.'

Erithacus returned his attention to the sky, conducting the Speakers as they wheeled above. To the west the sky was besmeared. Like a lone cloud on a clear day, an aberration loomed. The shapeless form gained clarity, wings, eyes, and the grey green sheen of plumage.

It was the Baldaboa.

They blinkered the sky. The Gulls turned with fright as Seyla regressed. They saw the dark upon them, the weight of shadows. And as suddenly as the light waned, so too did it blister and crack, as wings were pulled tight against bodies, falling from the sky.

The Baldaboa poured down upon the Gulls, tearing at them with voracious claws, jabbing, pecking, confounding. Esperer was forced down by their weight, barely pulling himself free. He cursed the wretched flock, calling out their leader, 'Come forth damnation, come forth and face me!'

Troon surfaced like the figurehead of a dark galleon, her flock a turmoil, a constant helicoid of threshing feathers, they whorled towards him with alarming vivacity. Troon was silent, holding herself steady at the head of the flock, the swaying legion.

'This is not your city Esperer.'

Esperer guffawed, 'It is no more yours than mine Baldaboa, transient, scum feeder, damnation!'

The mass of Baldaboa lurched forward, frightening Esperer, his eyes fixed on the conical vortex extending up into the sky. He fled down, the enemy flock in tow, some breaking off and spreading wide, curdling the sky in search of his remaining troops. Their presence overcast the war below, the Baldaboa a sullen shroud that choked back the Gulls. All at once the sky was silent but for the rain.

*

Vorsa fought herself free of the Morwih. Drawing breath through gritted teeth, she hauled with sluggish forelimbs until she reached the iron railing that encircled the music hall. The enemy glanced and hissed, yet their attention was quickly drawn back to the filthy battalions, rain soaked and mud sullied. The battle raged, yet at the centre, the fight withdrew.

She saw the black thing; the mass of limbs amid the turbid dirt. The pervasion lashed at any who approached. She could not make sense of it, revulsion and curiosity struggled until she could no longer stand and watch, and she leapt down, pushing through the enthralled enemy, who did not even notice her, all focused upon the abomination as it gnashed and drooled.

With caution she entered the clearing, her soldiers warning her back. She lowered her face to perceive its own visage, and saw that there was not one, but six faces, fused and protruding from one mass, twelve eyes watched white and baneful, each orb incensed with some unimaginable vileness. She recognised them, despite the spoiled flesh.

'Nox? What have you become?'

The face darted to meet her, phosphorus eyes shone, globules of saliva leaked from its grinning jaw.

'A REFLECTION. WE ARE THE MOCKERY OF LIFE, THE CONSEQUENCE OF ILL DEEDS.'

She recoiled as it stalked beetle like towards her, the wretched pop of cartilage seizing and releasing. It looked into her, beyond the fur and bone. She felt its many eyes burrow.

'WE DWELT LOW SO LONG, WE DREAMT OF THE PRIVILEGE OF THE LIVING, THE RESPLENDENT VITALITY. ONLY TO FIND LIFE SODDEN WITH BLOOD. YOU SQUANDER THIS GIFT.'

Vorsa flinched from its rancid breath. She peered through the perversion, in hope of finding her kin.

'We never wanted for war, we wished only to protect our home! We followed the words of the Orata, nothing more!'

'Let them go!' A voice rose from the field of combat.

'AND YET HERE YOU STAND, MURDERING, MAIMING? HOW IS PEACE FOUND IN SUCH THINGS?'

Vorsa shook her head. 'No! This is not what I want! We are defending ourselves! We cannot allow the Morwih to simply murder us!'

A Morwih guard stepped forward. 'We never asked for your rule Vulpus. You simply took that choice from us, we will fight for it because it is all we have! Creature, let our soldier go!'

The Starless Creature tightened its grip, its victims squealing in pain.

'YOU HAVE TRUSSED YOURSELVES IN THE TRAPPINGS AND ORDER OF WAR. IS IT THAT ORDER THAT FORGIVES YOU, THAT SEPARATES MY ACT OF VIOLENCE FROM YOURS? THESE SOLDIERS WOULD DIE AT YOUR HANDS, WHY APPEAL FOR THEIR RELEASE WHEN THEY WILL DIE ON THIS LAND FOR YOUR CAUSE?'

Vorsa closed her eyes. She thought of Hevridis and her request for peace. 'We wanted the city because we thought our rule would be more just.'

'THIS IS A FALSE CITY. THE TRUE CITY SINGS A SONG OF SORROW.'

'What does it say?'

'YOU ARE SINCERE, BUT IT IS DEAFENED BY WANT, THAT WHICH THE WROTH CRAVED ABOVE ALL. IT SEES YOUR DESIRE, SEES THE UGLY NEED. YOU HUNGER FOR IT, YOU MURDER FOR IT.'

'We want only for the peoples of Ocquia to find peace in this land, free of the Morwih!'

'THERE CAN BE NO PEACE WHEN THERE IS WANT. WANT AND DEATH, GREED AND HUNGER. THE WROTH WANTED FOR MORE, THEY WERE NEVER SATISFIED, AND NEITHER WILL YOU BE IN THE PURSUIT OF THIS FALSE CITY.'

The Starless Creature let go of its prey, who both slumped to the earth, gasping for breath. Quickly they were proffered assistance by their respective kin and lead away.

Vorsa felt Petulan rise in her oesophagus, saw his wide smile, saw his vapourous form turn in on her and grin.

'Listen!' he said.

The Starless Creature lifted itself on a collection of hind limbs, and with multiple mouths exhaled a clarion cry; dissonant groans of many tongues, languages old and forgotten. The wind grasped each sharp tone and carried it afar.

As though the sky itself inhaled, every living soul upon the battlefield felt their lungs starved of air.

A grinding, incomprehensible roar swelled. It choked the sky of sound, stole away its voice. Every pair of eyes looked towards the Stinking City.

The sound came again. It emanated from the heart of the largest buildings, those entwined in the Corva binding spell, now bound beneath by giant roots, the brazen glint of steel that shirked the green folds beyond.

Metal creaked. Concrete moaned. From the hilltop, the dawn gave a perfect sky upon which to see the Wroth acropolis. They heard it transmit its call of distress, the bleating, stumbling tremors that whisked up the air between each structure and reverberated out with lamenting tenor.

Belligerent roots expanded, pushing their girth up and out; skewering the cars of underground trains, their fleshy rind bursting each shell. Water mains ruptured and spilled their gallons. Encouraged by the myriad fuels and furnaces throughout the toppled streets, fires eagerly tore.

Windows exploded in confetti fervour, doors bowed against flame's inhalation, contorted fissures chittered in plastic distortion, becoming liquid, charring black. Iron and steel protested against shaking office block summits, whining under its own heft, crashing down at the feet of proud monuments, whose brief pity went unheard as they too felt the grip of strange plant limbs.

The Wroth themselves no longer held conference in the city's emptied bowels; their remains glaring through sunken eyes as the facades of brick and slate teetered and slid from listing structures, plumes of dust belching forethoughts, until the gagging cornucopia buckled under its own weight.

Peeling acres of stone hurtled down upon low lying buildings, crushing their ribs and spines. False giants of the Wroth held themselves in twisted repose, collapsing down in an asbestos bellow.

Vorsa felt the rumble of appendages beneath them, seeking the music hall. The First City found the warmth of Orn Megol under its shallow foundations. It hesitated, feeding cautious roots into supporting beams, it then recoiled and deviated the path of its burrowing.

As Ora rose to greet the empty horizon Tor sat beside Rex in disbelief. Rune was resting quietly on his back.

'What do you see Rune? What does the Umbra show you?'

'I see the First City, its arms reaching.'

The great roots entangled beneath the metropolis. The First City wriggled fat arms, tore out girders, constricted each supporting beam until it weakened and failed under its own weight. Thriving trunks expanded, cracking every obstacle, weakening the substance upon which the Stinking City stood. Without this vital skeleton a sea of brick and concrete sunk in on itself, swallowed by its own subterranean stomach.

*

'What is this?' Esperer screamed. Stupefied, he flew out towards the rubble sea. His guardskin freed themselves from the throng of Baldaboa, who quite forgot their victorious fight, the unfathomable destruction stripping all impetus.

Esperer landed on a listing traffic light, looking out upon the grey expanse. This had been a remarkable citadel. He flew further, seeking some kind of explanation, yet there was none. Nothing to rule.

Nothing.

The Pinnacle.

He straightened himself. 'Back!' he harooed. 'We must go back!'

He thought, *I have a kingdom, I have a city, I have a people to rule.*

He did not need new territories, he did not fear his death any longer, he could not see the flicker of it in his vision. It was fear that had plagued him, fear for a death that was not to come. His children were dead because they were weak, and he was not. So often told he was too old to rule, and yet he was here, alive, despite all.

He stirred up his kin. 'Back! Back to the Pinnacle!'

Back to his stronghold.

Roak hung static as Esperer fled, then he turned on the updraft and followed in pursuit, the remains of his City Gull army in tow.

*

The sea bloomed with excitement. Beneath the waves the First City moved on the seabed; neither dragging or rending where it stepped; becoming one with each aspect, absorbing, renewing, replenishing every coral frond or life-teaming steppe. Its song was present in the currents, in the flagella of plankton, within the membranes of jelly creatures. It sunk to the lowest depths and sang to unknown minds far deeper than light, and raised up far higher than any breath. It saw the land with its trillion eyes, and it flourished.

*

Vorsa saw the same destruction and rebirth. A hapless, knowing smile formed. She shook her head and acknowledged the monstrosity made of the Starless.

'DO YOU UNDERSTAND?' It snarled.

Vorsa did. The Stinking City, the object of war, was no more. She stared with disbelief, an incomprehension shared by the weary soldiers of both armies, whose vitriol was now snuffed out. They shed their gluttony with their armour, and stupefied, drifted with vague curiosity towards the remains of the city.

The beast turned its attention south.

'THE TRUE CITY SINGS.'

Vorsa followed its gaze beyond the destruction and felt the whine of something bewildering upon the horizon. Petulan felt it too. The Creature beckoned her to go towards it.

'THE CITY SINGS.'

*

Glaspitter guided the Speaker flocks to the roof of the music hall. Erithacus greeted his chief with wide eyes. 'Do we know what has become of our home?'

Glaspitter shook his head. 'I fear it is lost, and the Gulls have fled for the Pinnacle. Do we follow?'

Erithacus glanced down at Tor and the little companion upon his back. 'We drive them from the city only to let them return to punish the Startle? No. We drive them from there too.'

'So be it.' Glaspitter puffed his chest and commanded his squadrons.

Below, the bruised and battered, yet determined Baldaboa rested upon the terrace. Troon hobbled beside Tor. Tor lay a gentle paw on the feathered and looked towards the ruined city.

'I am so sorry old friend. We shall find a better life in this new land. I promise you that.'

Troon sighed. 'It seems there is more to this war than the desires of the Vulpus.'

Tor agreed. 'There are greater things at work, things that need your presence.'

She smiled again, 'I have a memory of a place. It may not be my memory, maybe one my parents cherished, perhaps a distant ancestor. I know that we once knew a different life, one without Wroth things. We will find such a place again. But for now, I believe I will make time to listen to your allies. Perhaps with the Wroth and their city gone we can find a place in your Ocquia.'

'I truly hope so.' Tor said.

Tor looked to Rune. 'Your journey might be turning full circle, little feathered. Are you ready to go home?'

Rune felt the ominous light brush his down. It was a light no one else could see, and he feared it. Its longitude and latitude flexed and fizzed upon his retina. Its path clear. It too set a course for the Pinnacle.

Rune shivered.

'I am ready.'

*

Onnar limped from the peak of the hill. Her fellow Yoa'a departed with goodbyes, and promises of future battles, heading for grass unfettered by carnage. She wiped the dried blood from her face, removed the halberd from her forearm and strapped it to her armour.

'Is this your doing Rune?' She said with a wry smile, gesturing to the remains of the city. Rune looked unsure.

Tor greeted her, 'Rune's First City rises in the south, in the land of his former home. We take this as omen.'

'Or Fortune!' Onnar replied.

'I will travel there by foot. It will take me a fair while, yet I feel Rune's father has a hand in all of this, and I must see this to the end.' Tor said.

'I agree,' Erithacus landed beside him, 'I have broken a vow I made with my old self to never set foot in the world of the Wroth again, yet I feel that world has ended, so I will not chastise myself for such a sin any longer.'

Erithacus turned to the little feathered. 'Rune, will you lead the charge back to the Pinnacle?'

Rune nodded, 'I will. Onnar, Aggi, will you come?'

'Of course, my dear,' they said together.

They descended the slope to find Vorsa and Satresan amongst the tall grass, before the blackened visage of the Starless Creature.

Its delirious eyes looked upon Rune, and Rune could see beyond the revolting entity. He discerned the mantle of the Gasp in this emissary, saw the light of Umbra brim around it. It bowed to him, on multiple stalked legs. He nodded nervously in return.

Vorsa said, 'Father, I will go to The Pinnacle, will you join us?'

'I am too old for such a journey, my daughter. With the city gone we must assist where we can. There is much work to be done here.'

Oromon stepped forward from the crowd of tattered soldiers, gracing her face with his. 'Be safe Vorsa Corpse Speaker, come home to us.'

They rested for a while, gathering strength before Rune took to wing with Aggi in tow, and Onnar, Tor and Vorsa began their journey by foot. The Speaker flock launched from their roost upon the music hall, their distinctive call rousing Erithacus to make his goodbyes and join them in flight.

Their path took them through the outskirts of the city. Loud claps echoed from gas explosions in the distance.

Many of the smaller Wroth dwellings remained intact, yet pulverised mounds of concrete were all that was left of the heart of the city itself. Aggi spied new shoots amidst the earth. She looked to the vacancies where once towering buildings stood. New life would grow here, consume all of this stone and metal, forests would reclaim their footing, the many voices of Ocquia would drown the failed eulogy of the Wroth.

She recognised the low bridge that sloped over the muddy stream where Onnar had almost lost her life. Its flow was much more substantial now, vast quantities of water from fractured mains gushing uncontrollably out of the earth.

They made slow progress, the Speaker flocks above, all exhausted in the wash of war. Tor grew tired and they took time to rest. He spoke of his journeys as a young Throa, of the wars he had fought against the Maar, stories of his father, of the songs of his kin.

Whilst they paused in their travels Vorsa sang the Orata, adding her own interpretations to the Foul Meridian, knowing that much of what they had cried out every night would need to be rewritten. Despite her disillusionment she thought of her prophets, the old gods of the soil, Vorn, Vors and Alcali, of their struggles that had led them to forge the Orata. It was a story worth preserving.

Rune thought of his father. What he would say to him if he were to find him at journey's end? The Umbra was now fused with his own sight, and in the light of the First City he perceived presences, some of which he felt he recognised.

The Creature hewn of the Starless Vulpus danced under Seyla, a numinous entity caught in her motes of light; it pivoted and glided with inorganic gait, haunts uncoupled with the earth, leading the party with restless zeal. Its arachnid-like collection of eyes ever watching, studying every living, moving thing. Vorsa observed it with morbid fascination. Her companions distanced themselves. She saw the Gasp in it, as she had her brother before his death. It lived in both Naa and the Lacking Sea. The light around it shivered.

'Petulan, what is it?'

'It is a Herald, a steward of the First City. A golem made of the living and dead.'

'It looked inside me,' Vorsa said with chagrin.

'That is its purpose. The city must protect itself. It must know your true intention.'

*

That night the party rested in fields where pylons rose. The power lines no longer crooned their monotonous serenade, now nothing more than relics. The group huddled in their presence.

Dawn broke with unusual radiance, a bright enamour encouraging them all from sleep, and they felt invigorated. They found food where they could, and began the day's progress towards the sea. Erithacus took Aggi under his wing again and described a myriad of shapes and objects upon the landscape. He gave her the Wroth names, which she was able to mimic with a little effort. The Speakers parroted back and forth stunted sentences until she could speak them with some degree of fluency.

'Why must we learn their words, if they are gone?'

'The Wroth were not all bad. They were clever, they could create beautiful things, things that lived without life, things that clicked and whirred and allowed them to see and do things beyond our comprehension. Yet for this they suffered. They damaged Naa, they burned it up.

'There are places upon this world that will take countless turns to heal. The world they have left us might suffer further, we may see changes in the sky and seas that we struggle to overcome.

'Perhaps the answers to our woes lie in the words of the Wroth. They held the highest perch, and many of them looked upon us with scorn, or pity – or worse, as nothing more than things to be used. We must at least try to not follow in their flight.'

'Their mistakes might be in their words too,' Aggi said.

'Yes, that is very true. We can learn from their mistakes. So we must keep their words alive, much like the Orata.'

The river spread its broad body on the land, its babble accompanying them south. Rune dallied above Tor and Onnar, recognising places he had hidden and slept.

Herds of curious Effer flocked to the eccentric caravan, offering their best wishes. The smell of salt upon the air was soon apparent to them all, but most of all to Rune.

Chapter 14

Ara was conscious of scents on strange winds, sounds that spoke of peculiar tongues. There was a voice in the breeze that he somehow knew, though it was as vague as his dwindling eyesight, and that frustrated him. For a moment he considered the Gulls might attack from the sea, that the Startle would be caught unaware. Yet this was no Gull army. He knew their smell, he was thick with it, sick of it.

The Startle had quickly retaken the Pinnacle from the small squadron of reserve Gull guards. They had offered the remaining Elowin an ultimatum. Leave under the terms of wrongful occupation, or be driven out under pain of death.

Few remained. Stubborn, they stalked the outlying lands, throwing empty threats. The Thousand Headed King would have none of it.

Elistis circled above with his kin, banking hard until he settled beside his chief.

'The Startle are ready. We can do nothing more but wait.'

Ara thanked him, and they both flung themselves from the ledge and up into the murmuration. Radial recitals spun and spasmed over the shabby fort, altering, throwing themselves in elastic arcs, exhilarated.

*

The Gulls regrouped beyond the scrublands. Esperer glowered at his kingly seat, soon to be home once again. He liked his brackish bogs, his acres of tufted sea grass, his wiry, water-logged kingdom.

He would grow strong again, he would make his subjects know his might. He would usher in a new era, for with the Stinking City gone many would come looking for a new home. His kingdom would flourish. He would gain longevity from his sovereign acts, he would live forever in his briny stronghold.

He crossed the sentry gates, saw the undulations of the Startle, like any given day, folding folly, their pointless dance. He spat at them. No Gulls came to greet his flock. He sent his guards in search of answers, they scoured the stooping outbuildings, the collapsed ghost train, the idle teacup ride. They found the remains of their home front, despondent and embarrassed. They had lost the Pinnacle.

'Where are my soldiers?' He vomited the words towards the Startle flock.

The Startle ignored him, turning, turning, folding, the asymmetrical loops and figure eights.

'Where are my …'

The Startle dropped. Arrow like, the violent configuration blindsided the Gulls, forced the very air to submit, all but terror and incapable torpor remaining. The Gull Lord's soldiers crashed into wooden towers. Esperer screamed, he would not give up, he would not give up. Higher and higher he flew, seeking their lives, all of their lives. He would crush them all to bloody pulp.

His soldiers darted with fatigued rage up into formation, only to be repelled. The Startle boiled, flumes of High Wrought moiled before the Pinnacle. Esperer pulled his weary troops back beyond the faux castle walls.

'We cannot fight them! They are too strong!' His tired troops looked to him frantically.

Esperer felt the dull realisation of failure creep in. It held a form, liquid white, eyes level with his own, looking right into him.

'No!'

He barrelled up, towards the murmuration, kicking his legs to gain traction in the air, his beak javelin-like. But the Startle were cerebral, a syntax of colloidal prophecy, all feather and brain and perfect union.

He lashed at them, and they reeled. He dived at them, and they parted. He could not inflict a single wound, for they had learned his ways, his blunt attacks, his weight over intellect. They had seen their loved ones murdered by this foe so many times, and for the Gulls, their strategy was not broken, so never changed, never knew to fix the glaring weakness in their attacks.

Esperer fell back, exasperated, swivelling once more to vie for the throne room. The Startle blocked his ascent, the silent front a thousand spurs, all for him.

He coughed and cursed in a bevy of white down, torn from him with each vicious pass. He pulled back.

His guardskin pleaded with him. 'We cannot fight. We must plan a new strategy!'

'You are weak! This is my kingdom, you will fight for my kingdom!'

He looked to the ranks of Gull, who stared despondently back.

'Full force!' He screamed through saliva strewn beak. 'Soldiers up!'

They dragged themselves to fly, and with every able Gull he sloughed forward towards the Startle.

'My king!'

He ignored the call.

'My king! Look!'

Esperer shirked any distraction, he found his focus, despite the rancour of his muscles, his lungs, all raw and spiteful of their host, all embittered, all ready to pack up and give in. He saw his bane, the fog of infidels, curs, peasants, all of them parading for him, all for him, all their hatred was for him.

He had taken it all from them. He was proud of his wars, of his land grabs, he hadn't failed like his father. He was strong, brave, a king, *the* king.

'My king!'

The Startle abruptly jarred left, vanishing. He saw the Pinnacle, an open path to his beloved haunt, its adamant facade beckoning his return, his Gull kin beside him. He turned to give a self-satisfied nod to his soldiers, to let them drink in the zeal of their king.

But there were no Gulls beside him, and with dumfounded fear he lost his focus, looking up to see his entire flock in a frenzy, flying away from the Pinnacle as fast as their wings could carry them.

He then heard it. A searing shout. It shook the air. Dust vaunted from the crumbling structures; a bold shockwave. The Pinnacle quaked.

He scrambled up, higher, above the peak so that he could witness the capacious blue of the sea.

He could not comprehend what he saw.

*

Roak heard the strange drone on the wind. It held in it a tone that struck something primordial. The trees beneath him shook with it too. He swooped up towards the Pinnacle, his city Gulls in tow, ready to vanquish the coastal Gulls. Yet the ragtag flock that greeted them flew with a mindless fear. Tawk flew up beside him.

'Do you see Esperer?'

Roak shook his head.

Flying free of the Pinnacle, they too faltered in sight of the sea. Beyond the glare of the horizon, where there had once been the flat ocean and endless sky, a mountain now heaved. It was formed of that ocean, a gargantuan mound that drew the water up into itself, grasping the diurnal tide.

Roak reeled in disbelief, 'Is it a storm? A great wave?'

Tawk could offer no insight. 'I have seen harsh storms, have flown amongst the crowning seas, but I have never witnessed anything like this before!'

They flew out to greet it, the cyclonic winds eclipsed the titan wave, debris revolving in rabid tumble. They ducked and dodged as they pushed on into the maelstrom. Tawk joined his city Gulls and flew above the excited waves.

Roak looked back to the Pinnacle, to the harsh edge of the cliffs that flanked his home.

Hovering before the decrepit tower was Esperer.

*

The closer they came to the Pinnacle, the quieter Rune became. Onnar checked to assure herself that he was well. They could all hear the baritone call of whatever lurked beyond the shore. Rune was plagued by the source of it, blinding him with feverish lights. He found himself batting at an invisible foe, every bout seeming to stoke its determination.

The party moved up to a path which gradually turned towards the theme park. Tor remarked that he had not seen such a place before, its sun-bleached sidings, amongst the run of rust and filth. The remains of fairground rides sagged above them.

Erithacus and the Speakers flew ahead, impatiently seeking the source of the deep sound. They soon made out a distant disturbance upon the sea, a swelling aberration on the horizon.

Although frightening, sight of the mountain in the sea seemed to lessen Rune's attacks, and he flew high with Aggi so that he could obtain a better view. The wind blasted the distant flocks of Gulls, indistinguishable from one another, the Pinnacle an exclamation mark black against a boisterous sky.

The wave was suspended beyond the bay. Now a fierce mass, half a mile high, water vapour tremoring in frothy banks of mist atop its peak, caught and thrown wide.

'What do you see? Vorsa cried.

Aggi dropped low, 'It is a great thing, the sea has risen!'

Esperer reached the Pinnacle, landing haphazardly upon the balcony, lost in his own maddening desire. He peered out to sea in confusion at the monumental anomaly, its sonic invitation. It tugged at him yet he cared nothing for its threat, for what it might be. Only that he was king, and that this was his throne.

He scrambled upon the wooden step and sat heavily upon the skins of his children, where he felt relief and curled into himself. The dim light and distant roar caressed him. All of that effort, and for what? He had all he desired before him.

Outside the daylight thrilled stormy white and the Pinnacle shook against alien winds staggering in the path of the vortex.

Esperer's eyes narrowed with fatigue. The wooden walls shook, yielding a shrill, chilling whistle.

The gaze of his ghostly companion appeared before him once again. Esperer threw his wing dismissively towards the entity.

'Be gone forever!'

'You do not recognise me?'

Esperer sobered immediately. He choked on his spittle, 'You speak?'

'I have watched you from oblivion your whole life, Esperer.'

'Who are you, demon?'

'I was the chick you crushed in the nest, who you throttled, who you consumed to make yourself strong. You punished me for living, like so many of your own kin. I have watched you inflict endless suffering, watched you skin the bodies of your own children. I have seen your intentions and your actions. I condemn them all.'

Esperer's mind was slow to recognise the significance of these words, encouraging him to ask again who this wretch might be; and then the revelation finally transpired, like a dumb weight upon his thick skull.

'Elion? My brother?'

'Yes.'

'Oh Elion, you were weak, you would have lived a few turns at best! You made way for your brother. Let me thrive, carry on our name, our lineage. Have I not ruled with all the might our father lacked? You should be proud, ghoul. But you are jealous, jealous of life, perhaps? Has jealousy driven you to haunt me? Then you are pathetic.'

Elion accepted this. 'It is true, I have wanted for life. Yet my hatred of you did, eventually, dissolve. I no longer wished you dead, I felt sympathy. I even felt love. Yet it has been a long time in the Gasp, where time is immaterial. I cannot see the turns of Seyla, or the Opalescent glow of Ora. I am of the dark. I am Gasp. I am made of stranger things than you. But I could never let you go.'

'You are a sick thing brother, and a dead thing. Be gone!'

'Oh I wish I could.' Elion sighed, still a formless veil with eyes that mimicked Esperer's own.

'But I cannot, even if I try.'

'Why?'

'I am your twin, Esperer, Naarna Elowin. I am your Revenant. You are a Corpse Speaker.'

'I am no such thing!'

'Oh but you are. I have toiled in the dark seeking this conduit. I have shirked every law of Revenant speech, I have betrayed many cordial acts to make this journey. I have supped on the nectar of the Umbra. I have grown stronger than most. Stronger for you.'

'For what purpose?'

'A certainty.'

*

The shoreline soon heaved with onlookers. Hundreds of feathered, amongst them the many Speakers who had found no enemy to fight, now rested along the harbour. The boulder groins held impatient mammals, all straining to find a better view. Vulpus clans that lived in the thickets of the coastline sat patiently, their armour hewn of driftwood.

The Caanus pack that had followed Tor like faithful subjects ran ahead and now frolicked in the sand. The sky was eminent, an exalted golden white, the terrific head winds invigorating, the warmth of Ora offering a caress between each crisp gust.

The tired caravan made its way through the tangled wreckage of the rollercoaster and emerged upon the beach. Ahead, the Starless Creature, feverishly seeking the sea.

The coast stooped to the water, cliffs rising either side in the distance, yet before them, endless ocean and the mountain made of water.

Rune saw the Startle turning this way and that above. He gleefully flew up to greet them, vivid radial lines of light shuddering out from their cluster, joining with the lustre in the sea.

Silence. The great crowd listened intently. The breeze carrying with it a saline kiss, eyes stung in the light of Ora.

They held their breath with unknowing.

The mountain fell.

Receding, tugged into benthic depths, from the shore the water parted across its vast brow, gently, as though a titan might raise itself. A dark shape beneath the waves began to surface, an outline perceived through the shallow water.

The ocean clawed back the colossal shroud, and before the eyes of the many cultures of Naa appeared the First City.

It towered above the Pinnacle.

Its shape was like that of a vast flower bud, unfolding in the presence of all who gathered before it, incongruous abstraction of bone and bark, florid acres and dense primeval forests formed each petal. It was unimaginable, groaning with size as its elevations settled; its waterfalls sought new paths. New shoots grew upon cliff faces. It threw out more giant roots, burrowing down beneath the earth, setting itself into the land.

It made landfall; dragging itself free of the water, its arms lashed around gigantic stones which it held like anchors.

*

Roak gaped, he drank in the glorious, impossible sight. Losing wing beats he fell and recovered, yet his path remained. He reached the Pinnacle, landing upon the balcony. Within the throne room he could hear two voices.

'The Umbra has risen in Naa. Will you not take a moment to look?'

'I will not leave my throne again!' Esperer barked at his brother. 'I will not cave to your whims you … dead thing!'

The First City sent its tendril arms down into the earth, beneath the Pinnacle.

The Startle had by now evacuated their families, leaving Esperer alone above their former home, clinging to his seat of power. And cling he did.

The tower began to creek. 'The Umbra sees you Esperer, I have whispered your deeds to it, and it knows what you have done. It sees the same venom in you that it saw in the Wroth.'

'This is all bunkum, chick stories, make believe! There is no Umbra, no Gasp, You are old age, and you are guilt!'

'You admit you are guilty?

Esperer sobbed. 'I know I have squandered my office. I know I have been cruel. But I have learned from my father's mistakes, I have made up for my past improprieties!'

'You will die here, Esperer.'

'I might! But I will die a king!'

Roak stepped hesitantly within the throne room.

Before him, Esperer cowered low against the floorboards. The smell of urine and fear was about him. In the mute daylight Roak could just make out the slightest disturbance hovering over the Gull Lord. As his eyes adjusted to its presence it became more apparent; an entity, a pale wraith creature hungered above Esperer.

At once it noticed Roak. It looked at him with eyes that spoke of fathomless betrayal, of a long and withering sadness.

In a single glance Roak read its reason. Recognised that desire all too well. Another soul had longed for Esperer's life. And deserved it over him.

The presence returned its gaze to the king, and Roak fled the

Pinnacle, into the living day.

The splintering snap of the foundations turned Esperer's stomach, and the Pinnacle lunged wildly in the forceful wind. Outside the crowds parted as the stems of the First City rifled the base of the tower. They began to pull the Pinnacle towards the sea, tearing out its backbone. The iron frame distorted, warped and snapped. It expelled a final seizing cry.

The Pinnacle began to fall.

'I am king!'

Elion smiled a forbidding smile, and tore open the reluctant gulf that stood before him and his living twin.

Esperer's heart stopped.

He saw the terminal dark of the Gasp, the wavering morass of its insipid depths.

The remaining weight-bearing beams relinquished the Pinnacle, and it fell.

'You are dethroned.'

His brother wrenched Esperer through the veils of life into the unliving dread beyond. As Esperer had once done to him, amongst the leaves and twigs of their childhood nest, Elion swallowed up Esperer's apoplectic body, gnawed the ether bones until there was little left. But the dead could not die, and Esperer's remnants, the shaking, powerless ribbons of ghostflesh, drifted into the perplexing gravity of dead nebulae.

Forever voiceless, forever alone, forever aware.

*

The Pinnacle disintegrated upon the concrete at its base; spilled its guts; the empty nests of a hundred generations of the Startle. Rune looked down upon what had been their home, a place for which so many had died.

The rotten edifice suddenly lost its importance, became no more than the tired remains of another Wroth-made thing. Amongst the broken wood and myriad nests he saw the mural, their desperate wish for freedom now exposed to the elements and quickly blurred into obscurity.

The Startle joined the crowds below who stood in the shadow of the First City. Rune sought Ara amongst the excited, terrified ranks.

'My dear boy!' Ara exclaimed when Rune found him on the sand. Rune could see the glimmer of joy in the old Startle's eyes.

'I can see it!' Ara said, 'I can see the city!'

'This is what my father sought!' Rune exclaimed, 'He went into the world seeking this, and it has come to us! He has returned to us!'

Chapter 15: Grom

Grom was born Umbra. Very few feathered were even aware of their own limited experience of it. The spectral apparition was responsible for the feathered's awareness of magnetic striations, and yet it was so weak within most of them that it was impossible for them to consciously perceive. In Grom it was overwhelming. Others shared a measure of his clarity; it was lauded and honed among some, given arcane significance with ritual and dogma, yet even those with philosophical inclination, who had built belief systems upon their vague experience, did not understand the Umbra's true purpose.

Grom had found it frightening. Each and every night of his life had been awash with oscillating gyres of black, lit by make-believe light. An endless inverse of crude organic lines, knitting and mending upon the surface of his subconscious. Each and every sleep was exhausting, a cycle that only broke after many years. Eventually he taught himself to make sense of what he saw and heard, that it was not entirely a figment of delusion or a sign of illness. He only came to know this for certain when the Umbra warned him of his father's death; fraying threads of light, lines that withered away, meant impending mortality.

He came to recognise movements within the Umbra; one or two were loved ones. He knew Rune, and Lauis, amongst many. In the coming years, the lines and their cargo – countless amorphous shapes, would offer up their significance with little encouragement. The abundance of the Startle was dizzying and induced pain, yet soon he understood that the ballet of the Startle was a product of the Umbra, and within their murmuration he found solace.

Grom came to understand the Umbra as his own perception of the interconnections of all life and death. It was a visceral tether to time, to Naa, and to other life.

When he was very young, when he himself had just flown the nest, he had seen Lauis amongst the other fledglings. He had felt some preordained notion, a draw to her. Turns later when he accepted rank in the Startle, he would rise before dawn to assure he would be beside her in flight. They would meet upon a tile on the roof that he had marked with a curious symbol, three lines, pointing towards one another.

Once they paired Lauis gave birth to a single clutch of eggs, and all but one perished. Grom feared that Lauis would suffer this loss, but each day she tended that egg with such affection, he soon realised she was strong, more than a mother, more than a mate.

When the child was born they named him Rune.

The infant was very strong, and learned fast. Grom saw so much of himself in the little feathered, but was taken by how much his son reminded him of Lauis. They did not force the Startle on him. But very few born to the Pinnacle chose to leave. It was not indoctrination, quite the opposite. It was in their nature to desire to fly with the flock, the murmuration was an unavoidable urge.

Grom knew the hand of the Umbra dealt in their orchestration, grazing an unseeable veil that spilt over everything, and with eyes closed, each discernible movement was realised before it occurred. Taking flight with the Startle was as much a choice as breathing.

Rune had climbed out of their nest, perched his little body upon the edge and looked straight up, at the opening above, the frequent flyby of the Startle encouraging excitement, his fragile wings shaking with enthusiasm. Even once he had taken those awkward first attempts and tumbled back into the nest below, it did not take long for him to get back up and try again. When he did fly, he flew straight out, out into the opulent sky, and Grom and Lauis had followed, giving him room to find his tack, and they were filled with an overwhelming joy as their son embraced each effusive wind with untrained grace. Current heaves might try to throw him off kilter but he was steadfast, and it made Grom swoon with pride.

As Rune grew, he became increasingly inquisitive. Grom assumed the role of teacher, and would take Rune on adventures along the coast, away from the scrutiny of the Gull sentries. They would visit the slate cliffs and examine the ossified remains embedded there, splash in rock pools and marvel at the fluorescent anemones whose tentacular limbs swayed and groped below the water. They would tumble through woods and observe the practices of the creatures that made those places their home; the courtship dances and nest building, the silent ceremonies of the forest. Rune would bear witness to his father's second sight, whose observations had two perceptions, what was seen, and what was felt.

Grom understood the Umbra with increased deftness. He saw obstacles manifest days before they appeared in reality, and made adjustments and calculations against the shadows cast by Ora, and the increments of Seyla. The Startle became stronger for it. He was a modest and retiring feathered, but soon his word became inviolate.

He frequently travelled to converse with other thinkers, and although he met no one who could see or interpret the presence of the Umbra, he found an earthen knowledge far richer and far more rewarding than anything he'd known before.

Few Startle had forged relationships with ground dwelling mammals, and so he sought them out. The Muroi taught him their grasp of heating ore, how they learned of the softest metals and where the Wroth made them. He was taken through an entanglement of tunnels that ended in the oven of a restaurant. In the hidden crawlspace behind the stone mantle the Muroi had carved simple moulds in sand for High Wrought armour. It was here that he had asked them to carve the family sigil into his own plates, the armour that Rune would one day inherit.

Grom asked the Muroi for further sources of inspiration and they spoke of their mythology of Erithacus and his student the great Tor, a seer, a mammal able to harness the power of the Wroth. This would be his next destination. He would entertain Rune with fanciful stories of these thinkers and their esoteric abilities, and he felt something stir within himself that was exciting and prescient.

When the Gulls invaded, the light went out.

The blood had stuck, it cloyed, it sunk deep and wrapped him in itself, told him of its nature, of how it had once lived and gave life, and once it was lost, once it no longer knew its course, it gave in. It could not find its way back into its veins, it could not give back life.

Grom stood listless and dizzy that evening. Her body was torn, a great gash ran across her head. Her flesh was punctured.

He pleaded for the wounds to heal, yet the skin was shattered, it could not mend itself. He was feeble. The grey blurs of anxious bodies rushed about him, the bedlam, the screams and cries, the thick vomitus stench of Gull.

The Gulls had forced themselves into the Pinnacle, blocked every exit, stolen every scrap of food and had begun to kill anyone in authority. Ara had hidden as many away as he could deep below the nests, in secret places. The Startle fought back, slaughtering many Gulls, but finally exhaustion and fear got the better of them and after turns without food or water, they had surrendered.

The Gull lord Esperer took power.

Lauis lay before Grom, her body broken in so many ways that it no longer made sense. The Umbra had failed him, had not warned him of this fate. The void that opened up in him swallowed his sensibilities, drained him dry of hope.

The blood had pooled and smeared and dried, her frame remarkably small where once had been such a large and vivid soul. He studied the arc of each spasm, each death throe, the red echo that encrusted on the ground before him. Circular motions and half-moons, dark celestial orbs of crimson that trailed each sense of life. The formations were entirely random, yet the viscera spoke of something far more meaningful. He saw form and function.

His vision blurred as he trembled. He felt fevered, numb with cold. Crouching low, he stared hard at the pattern, trying to discern some point to this loss. Her life bled from her so black against the matted straw beneath her. He dared not blink, searing the image into his mind.

He closed his eyes. In the dark the image inverted, light spheres and flanking lines. The Umbra came with little effort. His imprint shuddered, vanished and manifested with each jolt of his vision, swallowing it, embellishing it within itself.

The pattern moved. At first he perceived it as a figment of his imagination, absorbed within the shadowlines, needling out from infinity, tethering itself to his offering. At once the coagulating blood splintered into arching lines and markers, assumed new positions within the concentric mass. He considered each formation, how each mark across a line signified something. The Umbra collapsed, leaving the desolate, lightless hollow behind his eyelids.

He opened his eyes again. Her body remained.

When the Startle came and carried her corpse away he stayed. He did not break the fasting of his senses, his ears mute, voice a dry rattle. He felt the warmth of Ara, of his many loved ones desperate to illicit some emotion. Soon his gaze fell and he collapsed within the nest.

Days drained away and with each mournful moment the loss hung heavier on him and asked for all of him. It was in the Umbra that he now dwelt, his sleep the only remedy. Sometimes the loss cloyed, sometimes his guilt seethed as the thought of Rune danced across his mind, and soon that single thought would break the Umbra and leave him cold and alone.

It was very early when he woke to the blunt tug. Sluggish and angry he stumbled out of his hovel into the world. Dawn had not risen and he wandered about the damp earth. He had not fed for a long time and found scratching and picking at the ground somewhat indulgent, yet necessary. He pulled himself close and sat down, his focus on Seyla above, pearlescent. About her hung infinite lights, grains of stone that blinked and swooned. Of all the mythologies and rhymes spoken of these infinitesimal specks, none caught their majesty. There was a depth in the sky, he had once flown so high the horizon revealed itself as a faint barrier, the sky beyond a gulf, a grand drapery of unknowing where those phosphor grains held dominion, far beyond Naa.

He studied each constellation, recognising the various patterns that held deities in their grasp. He followed the motes of stellar gas and rivets of luminescent matter that strayed and flurried amongst the heavens, and he recognised their significance. He had seen these arrangements before, amongst the shadows of the Umbra.

Patterns. They stirred something of consequence. What he saw in the death of his love was not inconsequential. There was meaning within her death.

He began to see these same forms within the folds of seedling plants, the concentric wakes of rain on water; what had once been an abstract nightmare gained a new clarity. He readily savoured each pattern, staring long enough to capture its inverse, further offerings to the Umbra. With time a language and semblance of logic exalted itself upon him.

It was a map.

Grom remained in the Umbra. It staggered reality, engulfed every sense and dulled the nag of grief. It was here that he could sort through the tatters. The maelstrom of memories invoked and eroded, unable to take root. All he was left with was one perfect violent image. The body of his love. His futile attempts at fatherhood only ended with further agony; Rune reminded him so much of Lauis.

Amidst the carnage Ara bargained with Esperer for an armistice. They needed time to collect themselves, to find a new home. Esperer had granted them banishment, and all but a few were keen to leave the Pinnacle.

Ara made sure Rune and Grom were safe. Rune was not old enough to care for himself entirely, and the loss of his mother was confusing and deeply upsetting. Grom remained unreachable within the deepest recesses of the nest. Ara took Rune to be cared for by others, whilst his father healed.

On the eve of their departure Ara had gone to Grom to explain that if he chose to stay he would be at the mercy of the Gull Lord, and that Ara would take Rune with him to assure his safety. In this final attempt to rouse Grom he had succeeded; Grom was shaken with grief and pleaded for forgiveness for not predicting the massacre.

Ara explained that no fault hung on him, but entirely on the cruelty of the Gulls. Grom found a little comfort in this.

As he lifted himself from his stupor he absorbed the news of Ara's intended departure. The Umbra hung in his field of vision like a fever and he perceived things with curious resolution. He saw a time when the Gulls would leave. It was so clear in him that the Startle should stay that he shouted it out, demanding that the flock remain.

Ara saw such conviction in this, reminding him of all the times that Grom had shown them the clearest path, that the flock stayed.

Grom however did not. He asked Ara to care for Rune, tried to find the words to convey what he now sought. He embraced his son and promised him he would return.

He flew north, towards the House of Tor, the abandoned scrapyard that stood like a Neolithic stone circle above the subterranean maze of the Throa. He had come to seek guidance, from one who studied under Erithacus.

This almost mythological name was as intangible as the Umbra itself, so much so that it was impossible to get close to Erithacus without first establishing a connection with his disciples. There were very few who had learned firsthand from him. Tor was one.

The Throa and Grom became close friends, and it was here that the grip of the Umbra took root in the mind of one desperate to acknowledge its presence. Grom agreed to try to show Tor the effect of the Umbra, although he did not know how this could be possible.

Beneath that automobile graveyard Grom and Tor plotted and pondered over the complexities of nature. Tor wished to see Grom invoke the Umbra, and so they wandered to a nearby hill and Grom flew up amongst the leaves of a tree. His vision obscured by the vibrant green foliage, Tor sat below, watching the little feathered lull into a state of torpor.

Grom saw stars; the undulating map of busy ordinations, each star a single life. From his tree he conducted the sky, predicted the path of each flock, the ambulations of the groundswell. The bioluminescent throngs of every microorganism, although almost indiscernible, made themselves known. At first the overwhelming abundance sent him spinning, but with time and concentration he found subtle shades, a dimness or novel glow to each marker. Then, each star offered deeper meaning, he deciphered form and function and cause within their scintillations. Soon their size upon the map was not a hindrance.

Each life became clear. He could know things of those not ready to offer up their secrets. As he stood upon the branch of the tree, he saw all that Tor was. Every facet of him spoke clearly. He saw the sadness at the hands of the Wroth, he saw the beauty in all that Tor had created. He saw the death of his parents, and he saw the desperate need to understand it all. Grom saw himself in the Throa.

When the Umbra subsided he joined Tor on the ground. He placed a wing upon Tor and wept. He explained all that he had seen and apologised for the intrusion. Tor was noticeably moved by the feathered's honesty.

Grom picked at the earth, scratching away until the roots of the grass were revealed. 'The Umbra is here, it is in everything, it connects us to one another. These roots sing, they beckon to us, but we simply cannot hear.'

It was in the ground that Grom found the Settling Stone. It called to him as they approached the sett, still under the influence of the Umbra. He saw the threads weaving below the earth. They fed to an unknowable distance but were clearly a vital limb, a milestone, evidence of Grom's intentions. Beneath the House of Tor, Grom found a physical facet of the Umbra.

The Settling Stone lay grave in a cavern filled with earth. Set free by the Throa, the crudely marked object was suffused with purpose. To seek reason. The friends knew not what they sought, it was not clear to Grom, yet every time he closed his eyes his mind was filled with the penetralia of life. He saw it in the fibrous tendrils of saplings and the sediment in rock, as he had seen it in the blood spirals of his lover. The nagging wrenching, unceasing pain that felt like barbs in his flesh was real, and there was an answer within it. There was consciousness that exceeded him, it was not a figment, or a flight of fancy. It was raw and tangible. To explain this to Tor, to show him the effect of the Umbra, was as much for himself as it was for the Throa.

Tor explained his family's history of the Stone, and as the words were spoken Grom coaxed an apparition of truth from it. Yet this artefact knew a deeper time, it was geological, cleaved of history. It sung to him, asked him to let it speak.

He told Tor to strike the Stone, and he did. The sound reverberated with siren clarity. Grom instructed Tor to find smaller stones, and together they marked the sound's direction.

There was something drawing the tone towards it. As it sung, the earth began to vibrate, and the dry soil shook. Grains of dirt separated to form vein-like patterns upon the ground, snaking out from beneath the weight.

Grom squeezed his eyes shut and felt his mind swim. Before him the horizon line of shivering light, stretching beyond his periphery. He saw the Stone as a pulsating disturbance in his vision, and the magnetic pull upon it as shimmering lines, like that of heat plumes on a hot day. He could sense that same pull on himself. Beyond the great Wroth settlements, beyond the ocean, a land mass of immense size, and within it, something stirring. At first he could not see it, a conglomeration of writhing orbs of light, folding and enveloping one another, a seamless, endless menagerie of life, and yet it held a quality like no other. It scared him, moving organically, with certainty and aim, and most disturbing of all, it noticed him.

He felt its countless eyes look within him. It was not malevolent but it spoke to something deep in his marrow, a cutting sensation, as though to pull the sorrow from him like a diseased organ. He knew it could see that which he sought to rid himself of, and it hurt. It hurt so very much that he fell from the Umbra, crying out for his lost love.

Tor sat with the little feathered and spoke gently. Grom pondered what he had seen and eventually saw some semblance of meaning. This was what he wanted. He had not known what waited for him, just that it did, and in his sadness something primitive and true had reached out for him. He had now seen his goal.

The Umbra took him to the Stinking City. He tuned to a single intelligence whose causal fronds splayed out and touched many minds beyond itself. He felt as though it sensed his prying, as though one might speak through the Umbra.

Erithacus could not see the Umbra. It was as invisible to him as the wind and yet he felt it. He imagined that this might be where their mouthless words resided, their decisions and consequences manifest. He alone amongst all he knew felt the resonant pull tease at him. Like Ara he read the Umbra as a code; the sensations dismissed by many alluding to some enigma that Erithacus found to be a puzzle waiting to be cracked. Through contemplation he took each subtle nuance that his senses identified as the Umbra, and built his own map.

As Grom navigated his way across the choking skies of the city he became aware of many lives that blushed and swelled with importance. He was amidst an event, a seismic change that he had not felt before.

Erithacus, the Grey Ghost shared with Grom the wonders and miseries of the Wroth; a soul who had seen so much pain it was no surprise he was cynical and damaged.

The vagaries of the Umbra began to take on further facets, and make ever more sense to Grom. Erithacus showed him the complexities of language, how the Umbra could break down the barriers of sounds and allow meaning to be found in the most alien tongues. The same tools had been used to allow the Speakers to grasp Wroth speech.

Erithacus took time to tell Grom of Naa, that it was a sphere of rock amongst an endless universe, that it revolved around a star, Ora - a ball of fire that lit the heavens, and that every star in the sky was the same.

He explained that Naa held the sky in place with the same magnetism that pinned the Umbra to Naa. The Umbra was a nascent conduit through which all of Naa might communicate.

But Grom saw more, he felt the Umbra had a physical tether, something he could touch.

Erithacus had felt it like dust in his eye. It shouted at him to be noticed. Too old and too afraid to leave his cage, he encouraged Grom to seek it. So Grom left the Stinking City the next morning, finding a stray current that lifted him up and out towards a coast he had not known before. The air was cool and fresh and full of familiar scents that wrapped around him and inspired hope.

The beach he came to was endless white sands drawn up into pleasant curvatures and crescents. Ora shone still against the white surf. For a few turns he dug around for insects in the tufts of grass, finding as much nourishment he could muster for his final meal. He stood resolute on the beach, feeling the sand grains lock and loosen as he lifted each foot, felt the salt breath against him. He tightened each plate of armour, recited endless rhymes that gave him comfort. He saw lone Gulls leaping and gliding on ocean currents. He closed his eyes and listened to the Umbra.

Fly it said.

So he did.

He had never flown so far from shore. The many strands that tethered him to the land tore with unease, and he felt the nauseous fear of letting go of any chance of rest. He strained behind him to see the distant beach, but the current took him up and out across the lambent waves, their dark marines and blues and greys, the cresting white that frosted each spur, a lattice of endless evolving shapes.

As he flew higher cloud cover stole the sea away from him. The awe of sunlight upon the ceaseless canopy of massing cloud, mountain ranges of nimbus, valleys of ashen wisp that moved with grandeur. He hollered loud at these massive balusters, falling within them, to emerge wet with nascent rain. He dived low below them, their shadows merging over the ocean, blotting the light that accented the briny din.

The rain came. He immersed himself in the clouds, attempting to fly above their bombardment, to find the light. Thick and vehement, the path was impassable, no longer offering haven above, so he flew low, following the profile of the waves, throwing himself over them, tumbling and cavorting. He knew he would have to save his energy, and he could not call on the Umbra for guidance, far too dangerous to let go of reality, here, far from shore.

The sea spray kept him alert, he laughed as the waves riled and sent him careering upon their vibrant eddies. He fought the sea squall; it became an opponent, desperate to push him back. He pulled himself close and dived against the invisible adversary, sometimes gaining ground, often falling back into the maelstrom. He was cold and began to wane, fighting his impossible foe.

A cataclysm of charcoal black opened up above, held within it an enmity, screaming out at him with bellow lungs, its cold spittle unrelenting against his face; clouds erupting with harrowing veins of light, seeking him out, tethering themselves to his path. He flew as fast and hard as he could, darting right and left, angles that confused the battery. He was so very tired, the grey fascia low against the sea, feathers soaked, and each cold raindrop a barb in his flesh. Exhaustion joined the ranks of his enemy; he saw it as a red tedium in his vision, the tickling, nagging strain in each limb. His wing strokes became slower, and from deep down, below the tiredness, something laughed as if to say, 'You thought you could traverse the ocean!'

For days the storm remained unabated. He assumed that his flight path mirrored its own, Ora no longer willing to manifest. His only relief was a current that allowed him to glide for great distances with few wing beats. It gave him time to rest and seek nourishment. He drank the rain as it ran down his face towards the corners of his beak.

Food was scarce; the odd insect would pass him by, and sometimes he was lucky to catch it. Tiny Ungdijin revealed themselves like mirages below, tempting him to hunt. It was ungainly and incredibly dangerous, but he managed one in the days and nights he had flown. The fat he had built up before he began this dangerous flight would not last.

He tried to focus on anything that brought him hope, to find a sense of rhythm within all that he had learned of his life, of the world, and of the Umbra. He pieced together the fragments of his burgeoning belief. The foundations lay on his evidence, that somehow the ideologies of the flocks had roots in the vortices of the Umbra; and that the Umbra was somehow connected beyond the stories of religion; it was intrinsic to the muscle and sinew and organs and bone of all of them, and it was more than the whim of superstition.

He thought of the first time he had seen Lauis fly with the Startle. She wore her great grandfather's armour, it was red and silver, folded and torn, not cast like his own. It was beautiful against her dark plumage, iridescent greens about her flanks. She had strong wings and under her control her feather barbs seemed effortless, whereas his had always been somewhat stubborn.

He watched her flick the blades with an assured pivot of her shoulder, each leaping from their sheath and locking into their stirrup. He was far too young to understand love, or the desire for a mate. This was simply awe. He was impressed by her confidence. Later he would learn that she was just as nervous, that day when they noticed one another on the slate roof of the Pinnacle.

The terrain of sea and sky merged before him, a chasmal sepulchre, walls of sable black borne by the waves, lifting up and out to form a cathedral corridor; a choir of thunder rolling about him, spurring him ever onwards and deeper into the abyss. His exhaustion hung from him, his endless battle to maintain a glide on uncooperative currents, soon his wings would seize. Below, again the shoals of Ungdijin, teasing him with precious sustenance, yet he was too weak to take such a plunge, and so he watched them move as one, multitudinous slivers of silver, caracoling about one another, countless lives arranged in a fluvial ballet, a marine Startle.

He saw the Umbra take of these forms and add them within its complexity. The Ungdijin knew its presence, they too used its sight.

He started to falter.

The pain in his limbs was unrelenting. The fact that he no longer cared stirred him, as though remembering an old nemesis, indecipherable, dread was no longer comprehensible. These thoughts would surely kill him. He shook himself free of the torpor, sought the nerves in his limbs for sensation. He sang aloud the songs he had learned as a child, the songs he had sung to Rune when he was a fledgling. He felt the warmth of those memories and he embraced them.

> Winding roots of the tree embark
> And reach aloft thine branches
> Sing for the sky oh leaf and twig
> Sing for the bark and bramble
>
> Oh how we wheel about your fruit
> And taste of your fine sweet bounty
> We long for the sky just as you did
> And we bow to your task so humble
>
> For we are of the heavens borne old tree
> We do not take the sky for granted
> We venerate your gradual plight
> From tiny seed once planted.

The black below seemed familiar. He coveted it as it sank, ink-like, within his grasp. He breathed in the salt and felt it encrust his eyes and blind him further from sense. With each flash of lightening the surf illuminated, webbed across its surface, geometry in the fervour of the sea, and for a moment the Umbra enveloped, sublime and intoxicating.

He fell.

In that half-moment formations made sense. He saw the parameters of the Gasp, he saw the bone matrix of the Corva Anx, saw their meanderings and prayers and gods split and spit out fricative invocations. Their dark paths and avenues of direful mathematics.

He saw the crudity of it all.

It was beautiful.

His body hit the water, awkwardly splaying him out, saturating his feathers. The Umbra spread wide. Its many protuberances, the spirits of the Gasp suddenly ceased their consultations and turned, coalesced upon his own sentinel; they recognised him, their alien sentience threatened with iridescent limbs, reaching for him, coaxing him, asking too much of him, telling him that he was dying, that he must get out of the water, out of the Gasp.

His head lulled back, the water pouring through his nostrils and down his throat. The Umbra collapsed in on him, the revolving mass that held so much fell away, leaving him alone in the black.

He considered his life, what he had lost in this pointless journey. He hadn't even known what he sought; all was effigies of ideas, all seeking purpose where there was none. He had been hunting the ghost of his love. And within all that, all the flights of fancy and fate, he had forgotten the one real thing, the sharing of his blood with the person he had loved the most, the culmination of all they had been, and he had abandoned him.

Rune danced endless across the vacant space that had once held the Umbra. Grom cried out for him, for everything he had lost.

Deep down, Grom was dead. It felt like death, bleak and breathless. Death was not what he had expected. He was ashamed, and he felt surprise that he could feel at all. He felt a horrific burning in his lungs, a rising stomach acid that seemed imprisoned behind some dumbfounded wall, a dull empty aching throb.

It was black, completely black. He supposed the abysm beyond the sky was of a similar magnitude of nothingness. Yet as his eyes stung he saw particles dance before him, like stars, though lacking their significant light.

Beyond the dark a cold shaft shone within the nothing and played against a length of rope. There were crustaceans attached to it, writhing arms of seaweed and the knotted remnants of a net. Decidedly earthbound things. Things that held weight and mundanity.

Grom wasn't dead. He was drowning.

He strained against the drag of each feeble limb until he found his footing on the rough fibres of the rope, wrapped his wings around it, with beak and claw hauled himself from the depths, each grievous yank one less ounce of energy, each fiery belch, each whining wince of muscle.

And

Breathe

Breathe deep with all your might

The navigational buoy had escaped its anchor and floated listless in the flat sea. Grom had dragged himself atop a small raised shelf that held a malfunctioning light and rusted antenna array.

He slept.

He slept for a long time and only woke to pick at the barnacles upon the carapace of his host. He failed where better equipped feathered would have succeeded, so making the most of what he could find, he ate the seaweed and devoured every last winkle he could prize free.

The pain in his limbs did not cease. In his right wing the pain was excruciating; he had hit the water hard. He sat for a while and attempted to flex it, but to no avail. He had lost all of his armour save his headplate, which he now removed. It was heavy and awkward, and he let it sink into the water. He realised now why migratory Startle flew with wooden armour. High Wrought was very much for show.

For a while the buoy would serve as a place to get his bearings, to ready himself for the flight ahead. The realisation that his wing was broken had not fully entered within his plan, though it was unlikely he would fly again. In the meantime he tried not to think about it, regaining his strength with plenty of rest. He hoped that his injury would turn out to be a far less damning wound.

He remained on the buoy, drinking the water that collected in the small concave dish above the light. He had copious barely edible seaweed, molluscs could not escape his beak, and the various Ungdijin that appeared within spearing distance allowed him one or two lucky strikes. But for this to be the rest of his life was not an option to be considered.

The lapping of waves lulled him and he cast aside his feelings of failure and embraced his fate. It was cold out on the water and without the continuous effort of flight he no longer generated the body heat that kept him warm. He would surely die of the cold, battered by the sea. He felt the sleight hand that had dragged him beneath the waves creep back under skin and muscle, tugging at his bones with a deliberate veracity. He welcomed it.

The Umbra coagulated before his eyes and showed him his own

light. It shook like a dying flame teased by a wind. He knew this aspect of the Umbra, the tells and nuances, the same patterns that once fated his own father's end.

Amidst his defeat he felt a sure and gravelled roar; it groaned beneath, enormous currents dragging with them mountains of water. He knew their sound as orchestra, knew a gentle sea before the rain fell, knew the storm in the breathless warmth, a yellow yawn that dried his eyes. He dreamed deep in the ocean, feeling the crushing, enveloping weight of all that lay above.

His buoy swung wide. He slid across the platform with speed, hitting the rising antenna. He steadied himself on his good wing, as again the buoy rocketed up and down. Mounds of water began to erupt, the wash of foam swelled and broke across the marine surface, his tiny metal island listing deep on its axis.

Something was rising.

He coughed up his delirium to see the world cold and fierce. The violence that belched below him gained height as countless tons of water shed off the arc of whatever leviathan bayed to breach – and breach it did – a dizzying grey mass, valleys and hillocks, black wet, Crepic and star-shaped Lanfol clung for dear life with pincers and adhesive arms; the island rising gradually, water gorged across cliff faces.

Grom squeezed his face against the cold steel, his wing seized with unforgiving pain; he held his breath as the water below him was drawn away, leaving a gulf between himself and the surface of Naa.

He felt the nauseous pull as once again the earth invited him back. He smashed against the expanse, setting him free of the buoy and out on to the raw island. He sank in the water that pooled in crevices, took fitful breaths as the island swung wide and pulled the water with it.

He cried out, 'no more!' helpless in the grip of an unsympathetic thrall. The stone mass finally came to a halt and he lay, crumpled amongst strewn seaweed.

He dragged himself up and out into the sun, felt the graze of warmth upon him as the light rose and quieted the stormfront. Here he would lie and collect himself, tend his wounds and discard his plans once and for all. It was perhaps an impossible task, and he wished he did not know regret, but it was all he felt.

He placed his ear to the stone that warmed as the sun reached its apex, and he felt a swell of contentment; a rhythm lay below him, perhaps water rushing through subterranean caves, the roar of weathering rock. It pulsed with a remarkable vigour which lulled him into a deep sleep. Here the Umbra enveloped again, whispering snags of secrets and guarded truths through plays of light in the dark.

He saw the billions of lives that sank within the sea. He saw the livid avatars of aquatic families; cunning predators, the cruel and kind in ceaseless theatre. He saw what he had always seen at home, amongst his own family, here, out where sky and water seemed lifeless, grey and black and unfathomable. A fragment of intrigue ignited and burned away within his cerebrum.

He saw the island had its own light.

Its scale dwarfed all other lights; and it too was flanked by similarly gigantic forms – graceful teardrops that swayed with knowing temper, whose inner mechanisms coiled around the spring of the Umbra; they too sung with it, a song that resonated with chords low and ancient, they sung these notes with quiet brilliance. The Umbra guided their movements, they were harnessed by it, followed the cartography embellished within it. The Umbra was alive with their hexes, their marine magic. These swimming landmasses were the true heralds of his goal; the source of every tangential spell. They sang loud below the water, raising their massive heads to breathe deep, expelling vast quantities of water through their nasal caverns. Fractals of coral sat in grandiose slabs, affixed and flanking sheets of granite, sandstone and flint.

These living islands wore armour made of stone.

He did not know the species, but he knew that they had been sent to find his little life and bring it home, that they knew that he would soon die.

From beneath him a voice reverberated. It whirred and clicked and sang in peculiar tones, and yet he understood it.

'Grom, I can feel your exhaustion, and your desire for death.'

Grom smiled and rolled towards the source. He could no longer speak, yet his words were heard. 'I am very tired. I was not made for such a task.'

The voice was harmonious, it softened the bites of his pain and battened down his fears. 'You defied all the odds, we are very proud of you.'

'I failed! I abandoned my son for flights of fancy. You should not be proud.'

'Oh but we are, for you may not see every facet of the Umbra, but you had the foresight and curiosity to look beyond. Your son carries in him that singular sight and it will bring him to find you, and in him is much more than this. Hundreds of generations have carried that particular sight to deliver it to you and your love, and in that sharing of blood it found resolution. Your journey in life may end here, but that is far from the end, little Startle.'

Grom could no longer open his eyes, yet the warm prickle of sunlight embraced him. The fractured bone in his wing now gave way to an infection that coursed in his veins. He knew this, yet he felt no pain.

The swim of black before his eyes enthralled him, and he was at once covered with a singular warmth far greater than the sun. The black took shape; he saw the glorious streams of light that ribboned up into conical ebullitions of green and white and yellow against the pitch of nothingness. Faces boiled up in the froth of etheric plasma; faces he knew.

His father, his mother.

They were here, in the salient landscape beyond all landscapes, and amongst the dark, a single perfect light, the light of his love.

Lauis.

*

A legion of bright red Crepic jostled out of the crevices in the Norn armour, those huge slices of rock that lay across the great beast's flanks. They circled Grom's tiny body, gently lifting him on precise claws and skittering across the stone to a sheltered indentation. Here they lay him amidst a nest of seaweed, drawing close over one another, interlocking pincers to form a living mausoleum, steadfast against their host. They would protect Grom's bones until the Norn reached their goal, the land to the east, which Grom had sought.

Days passed and the pod reached the coast of the great land mass. Through fear of beaching themselves they dared not get too close, yet the mammals that heard the beckoning call of the Umbra collected on the shoreline, great Oraclas, their tusks held high, blasting the call to aid. Horn-nosed Tasq swayed their heads in jubilance, Rauka and Eprica forgot their endless chase and held rank together, and each species lined the surf as the armour of the Norn surfaced.

The Oraclas filed out into the breaking waves, amongst the ruddy sands and flecks of light in the shallows, their young giggling as they did so. Soon they were swimming, their grey muscular limbs no longer asked to support these great walking giants. They spread wide of their ocean kin, terpsichorean displays, as water jettisoned from trunks, this gesture returned by the Norn; watery eruptions and jittery calls of play. They shared their stories and excitement, and then returned to the task; to escort the tiny prize to its resting place.

The Crepic unlocked their vice grip and in solemn geometric patterns they processioned along the spine of the Norn, down to the tip of its rostrum. Here they were greeted by the great head of an Oraclas, who's gentle trunk formed a loop in which the body of Grom was placed. She turned and swam to the shore; her trunk raised above the water. Her entourage sounded out their love and joy to the Norn family, who chattered and clicked, their great tails rising and falling amidst the breakers.

Once at the shore the many animals came to witness the little corpse that lay in the cradle of the Oraclas' trunk. They studied its desiccated contours, its sadness pungent and empathetic. They moved as one, from the beach and into the dense forest that flanked it.

Necros Anx sat in low branches. The congregation headed for a clearing amid the trees. Once there, the emaciated flock descended from their sentry posts and formed a circle. The Oraclas who held Grom stepped forward and lay his body amongst them.

The Necros Anx wore armour made entirely of bone; splinters of it splayed and sewn into sawtoothed angles. Their faces, painted white with chalk, held a spectral quality. On this land they held the same position as the Corva; death priests, whose stratagems coveted the Gasp.

The Necros Anx closed in on their quarry and murmured to one another. They urinated upon themselves; the ammonia cleansing their claws. They bowed to one another, and from the clatter of their headdresses a dry and rasping tone emerged.

Their voices rose as they cocked their heads back, their audience adding to the throng. Through these throats this sound was impossible, and yet regardless they sang. It shook the earth with a fervid resolution, a focused cacophony that burrowed deep.

Here lay the old roots of the First City; yet they fed no tree or plant. These roots exotic and anomalous had burrowed within the world for millennia. They bonded with the life-giving tubers of the forests above and whispered with them. Prehensile and wanting, they felt the tone that descended into the dark below; they listened, and then they moved. They broke the soil, cavorting about the ground, feeling the presence of the host of animals who had come to deliver the body.

Each gentle limb teased the skin and sinew of Grom, they fed the slightest threads within and unwound each connective bond. The bones began to tease away, wound within the grasp of these knowing roots. Then, with each particle, every cell left of Grom, they pulled back down into the warm earth –

He began his next journey.

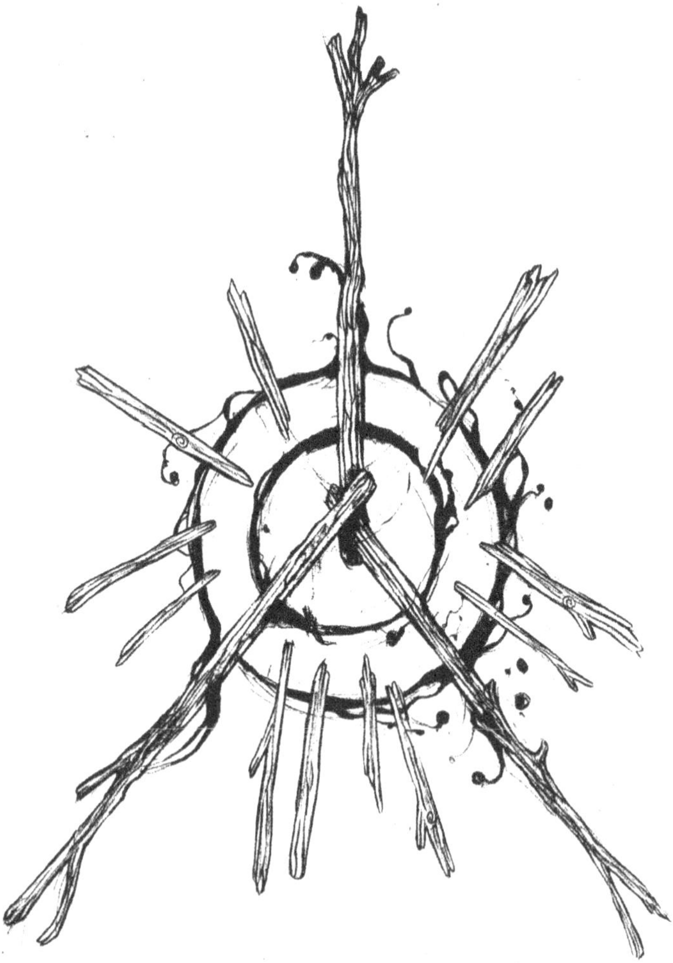

Chapter 16

Rune flew before the city, landing upon the twisting carpet of roots that now extended upon the sand. Beneath his feet mosses and grass appeared, seeking the light. Rune found no entrance to the city, yet knew one existed. He began to search its woody exterior in search of a way in. The Starless Creature crept along the perimeter, amongst the pools that collected at the foot of the city, inky execrations floating about its bestial body.

'Let us in!' Rune cried.

The Starless Creature skittered towards him.

'IT WILL NOT LISTEN TO MERE WORDS.'

Rune looked to his friends.

Erithacus bobbed with apprehension.

'What do I do?' Rune asked.

'The Umbra,' the Grey Ghost said.

The little Startle closed his eyes tight, let himself drift into it, the gentle patter of a low, restful heartbeat, his own, the city. He breathed, and it breathed, and he fell down into the auroral sopor.

He saw everyone, every light, those he knew, and those he loved. Lights that shimmered with anticipation, fear, excitement. He saw them all, and he saw the city.

The city saw him.

An aperture retracted before him, a ruckus of clattering, chattering osseous fragments, pulled and pushed by eager vines, sliding each parched, gnarled twig and splinter away to form a circular opening. There was a deep exhalation; the calming scent of new blooms and forest dew cast forth from inside.

It was dark within, against the bright day. Rune was scared. He looked back to Tor, Ara, Onnar, Aggi and Vorsa, who drew close to the entrance. Erithacus was quick to follow, and, with courage, Rune entered.

The floor was thick with soft moss, the walls steeped in ancestral fog. He could see dim, sylphlike presences in the walls. There were many minds here, untameable, brilliant, older than Orn Megol, older than the Singing Stones. Erithacus and Aggi flew above, marvelling at the immensity of the interior, trees that might have dwarfed the Wroth city reached with gigantic digits up into the athenaeum.

The Starless Creature ran forth with intent; beyond the apprehension of Rune's party, deep into the vague brume ahead. Rune continued on, listening to the gentle rattle of unseen things; illegible sounds that echoed around them.

'What do you seek?'

The voice boomed. Hollow grating words, contrived of the emptiness.

They looked to one another. Tor spoke in a hushed voice, 'We seek so much.'

Erithacus set down beside Rune. 'I think Rune knows that which we seek.'

Rune nodded. 'I do.'

He shouted, 'We seek the throat, from which we sing!'

The voice appeared to inhale; a short affecting tremor. The walls clicked and fussed and creaked.

Rune watched in awe as streams of parched bone moved across each wall, drawn to a source in the dim beyond. In the distance, a faint light shone down, breaking, rippling, as though filtering through foliage.

The friends moved forward, carefully traversing the knit of rhizomes and radicles beneath their feet. Eventually the mist dissipated and they came privy to a beautiful sight, the vertebral walls contracting, enfolding in the red and amber hues that reached from the shaft above.

The Starless Creature was here, captivated by its light.

'Come forth,' they whispered.

The foundation trunks amalgamated here, the fine circuitous veins drawing down to the centre of the floor. Erithacus traced the source of every limb, each coiling off into the dizzying height above, as though the whole structure balanced upon this place, a raised shelf of sandstone, coddled in supple branches.

They stepped forth. The floor was worn by many ancient feet. Rune looked to Onnar with hesitation, and she encouraged him forward. As Rune got closer, he noticed patterns on the surface of the rock. Dark shapes, curvatures pitted and embossed. He knew these marks, his father had shown him such, hidden in the layers of slate within the cliff faces.

They were fossils.

Tor stood wearily beside him and looked down at the shadows in the stone. He placed a shaking paw upon the relief, felt the smooth indentations. 'This once lived, many turns ago.'

Erithacus took to wing and flew over them. 'Aha!' he exclaimed. 'Wonderful, truly wonderful!'

They all looked to him for explanation, making way for him as he landed clumsily. He peered excitedly, pushing past his comrades, tutting, laughing and chortling to himself.

'Three! Three of them!'

Rune looked to him for explanation, 'What do you see?'

'Look Rune, look!'

Rune flew up so that he could get a better view. There were skeletons, petrifactions, curiously familiar and tiny, each one reaching to the other two, their dainty snouts touching, frail claws stretching forwards to form a three pointed star.

It was a moment, a fragment in time forever imprinted. He landed beside it, hopping along each limb. He saw tiny filaments against the rakish formations, he saw the rough impression of feathers.

'They were feathered?'

Erithacus smiled, 'Almost, my boy!' He guided Runes eyes, 'Look at their little heads, do you see their beaks?'

Rune stared intently. 'I see teeth! These little feathered had teeth?'

'And claws too, you see.' Erithacus spread his wing, a mirror of the fossil forearm. 'These are very old, they are your ancestors Rune, mine too.

They are your kin.'

Vorsa studied the bones. 'They are children, are they not?'

Aggi cocked her head to one side. 'Three, three who lost their lives, lost each other.'

She hopped beside the one closest to her, placed her little clawed foot upon it.

"Emini.' She skipped to the other two, 'Abriac and Alauda.'

Vorsa narrowed her eyes and gestured to each in turn, replied with quiet realization. 'Vorn, Vors and Alcali.'

'The Sisters of the Flock!' Rune declared.

'Could it be?' Tor looked to Erithacus.

The old feathered sighed, 'I believe so.'

'Their death made us.'

A voice drew up from the fibre of the city. It owned a sadness that they all sensed. Like an organ, acutely they perceived the intention of the First City. The ligament wall began to unravel, skeletal bits and bark nubs skittered; tenaciously seeking positions amongst the burgeoning jigsaw. A huge skull emerged from the wall.

'I am Lendel, caretaker of this city.' The ancient warden gaped down upon the caravan. He lowered his voice to a delicate clatter. 'Amidst a storm their mother tried desperately to save them. Lost in a deluge of mud and water, they were dragged down into the silt, reaching for one another in the dark. She could not rouse them, and in the earth she lay them to rest. This was the first grave. But her sadness did not go unnoticed. As she wrapped herself around their burial, the quake of her heart stirred the smallest life in the earth, infertile seeds germinated so they could keen to it.

'Pebbles were jostled by the tendril reach of flora, the grave became a pilgrimage. Life blossomed in the wake of it, and the mourning encouraged, did not hinder, it inspired cooperation. The first flowers bloomed upon archaic storks, tempted insects to wreath the tomb. They lived and died such short lives, and their bodies fell amongst the new growth. The groundwater convened beneath, channels sought routes that crisscrossed this tiny tomb, its precious occupants forever hugged close.

Their death taught the living to know one another, to covet one another. And in this sharing, the Umbra was born.

'Trees sought its sensation, they tied themselves around one another to form an impassable barrier. Those whose feathered arms later became wings built their homes within their branches, conjoining to forge the first stays of the city.

'The untiring dance of countless millennia fused a thousand fold. Forests begat forests, aware, elaborate, intrinsic to one another, they fed from the same light, the same soil. All for the three sisters who lost their lives in the silt.'

Erithacus looked up at Lendel's great skull which jutted from the wall. 'The city could think?'

'In a way, yes, all life is aware to some degree. It became greater than its parts, became more than a grave. It became the repository of tired souls, what you call the Gasp. With its vitality the city opened conduits to tangible places. The Umbra grew to encompass all life, a connective tissue that did not need a physical form, it simply lay in the fabric of us all. But the city was its birthplace and it would forever be tethered to the real.'

'What of the Wroth?' Tor asked.

Lendel seemed agitated, his form shifting, rippling.

'It is not our place to know or dictate the whims of Naa; we are of Naa, we are not gods. All we can do is offer that which we learned, and the Wroth chose to ignore our plea.'

Erithacus peered through questioning eyes. 'Did you kill the Wroth?'

'We cannot kill. But there are some far older than the Wroth, minuscule, infinitesimal, whose behaviour is not so different to theirs. They looked upon the Wroth with envy, perhaps felt that their role had been usurped. Perhaps they realised the grave potential of their own actions, that life truly hangs on such a fine thread. Perhaps they asserted themselves, through fear of losing all, and the Wroth died.'

Onnar stood tall. 'We come seeking a loved one.'

Lendel nodded gravely. 'There are many loved ones here.'
As the words drifted, the skull mass began to recoil and morph, erecting fresh growths of leaf litter and chitin, a new face constructed of the paraphernalia of the city walls. Angular horns jutted wide; beneath

was the skull of an Oreya stag. The skull changed once more, becoming Bronordean, the Grim, who once sheltered in Orn Megol. 'We find our peace in this place, all of us together.'

'All of us.'

Rune stepped forward, shaking. He looked up at Bronordean.

'Is my father here?'

The scrolling debris disassembled, ribs and jaw bones parting into dextrous patterns, nut husks clinkered under the guiding streak of new shoots, diligently each splinter of wood trickled into place, to manifest as a body, wings of chaff and seedcase, a neck of bramble sinew and a head, a face, the gleam of bone, feather jags of dark wood. It remained part of the wall, layers of tail feathers undulating twigs and vines. The face looked down at Rune with love.

Despite it being hewn of the city Rune knew this face. He flew up to it and with utter relief, with joy and sadness, he embraced the collection of forgotten things, felt the raucous thrum of every loss, every terror and trifle, every sympathy and every malice inflicted. Not in flesh, but in form.

Tor felt the deepest relief, watching the little Startle embrace Grom.

'Hello my dear friend,' Tor grinned, unable to hide his elation.

'Hello old Throa,' the hushed voice uttered back.

Then Grom looked to Erithacus, 'Erithacus, you came!'

Ara flew up before him.

'I heard you, I heard you in the wind!'

'You did! I hoped you would listen, you are always listening Ara. Thank you for caring for my son.'

'Did you find what you sought?' Erithacus asked.

'I did, at some cost. But it is quite astounding. I am part of all of this, part of all of us. I can see the breadth of time, I have found my peace here, amongst the memories of all our kin. It is loss that coaxed this city into being, it is loss that helped me find it.'

He turned to Rune, 'My son, I am so very proud of you. I have seen you through the eyes of Petulan, through voices and songs and air currents. I have seen you in the darkest days and brightest nights. I have wrestled and wept for you, but I knew you would succeed, would become strong.

'We knew from the very first moment you opened your eyes, that you would do great things. You are Umbra, one of the first in a very long time who can see the Umbra, and you will help your friends in finding a union in this world, without the Wroth. The most important thing I can teach you is what you already know, why this city exists.'

'We are better together than apart,' Rune said.

Grom beamed.

'Someone else would like to speak with you Rune.'

Grom dispersed for a moment, reforming with another face Rune did not, at first, recognise. She peered down at him, and he looked up, into her wide and empty eyes.

'My beautiful, beautiful boy,' she said.

Rune recognised his mother's voice.

Erithacus sat beside the rock in which the sisters dwelt, amongst his friends, watching the little Startle flit between his mother and father, Lauis and Grom, exchanging stories and discarding the sadness and dangers that had affected them all so gravely. Events that had brought them here, within this house of shared stories. The Speaker placed these strange and wonderful truths amongst all that he had learned of the Wroth, the knowledge gained in the face of hardship.

Rune embraced the avatars of his parents and went to the old Grey Ghost, 'Something troubles you Erithacus?'

'No my boy, not at all. I have lived much of my life in a cage, learning of the world through its bars. Were it not for you, not for all of you, I would have dismissed the idea of such a place as this. We stand on the edge of great things, and we must rise up to greet them. The sisters ask us to learn one more lesson.'

Aggi hopped close. 'I am here to learn Erithacus!'

'We are now wardens of Naa and we have a responsibility. You told me a tale of this city and its purpose Rune, that the Nations of Naa came here to settle their differences, to learn from one another. I once attempted this myself and failed. But we must try once again. My Speakers will go out into the world and seek out the leaders and guardians of the flocks and herds, clans and packs, they will bring them within these walls and we shall find resolution.'

Tor lumbered towards him. 'This is an honourable task. I say this to you Grey Ghost; in this new land, there will be many lost souls. The Caanus and the Baldaboa have stood beyond the sight of Ocquia for too long. Both deserve a place here.'

Erithacus agreed, 'There will be a place for all. You will not join us in this restoration?'

Tor smiled faintly. 'I believe I am not long for this world, I can feel death's tug under my fur.'

'Something ails you?'

Tor nodded, 'There was something inside of me long before the sickness of the Wroth, something that has taken advantage of that weakness. Someone must go to my family, make sure they are well.

'My son Tordrin and his loved one, Alberi, they have seen much pain and loss, but they are very strong, very brave. They will tend to my House.

Please make sure they know how much I love them all, and perhaps they might come and find me some day.'

'Where will you go old friend?'

Tor looked up to Lauis and Grom. There was endless kindness in their faces.

'I saw so much ingenuity in the Wroth. I could never forgive their violence, for what they did to my family and to many of my friends, but I saw their creations and wished to know how such intricate things could exist. I see the genius of this citadel, of the life within it. So many of my answers lie in its roots and walls. I believe I shall lay here amongst the leaf litter, if you will take me?'

Grom skittered across the walls. 'There is a place for us all here, old friend.'

The First City sang once again.

Tor's companions encircled him. He looked to each of them, and finally to Rune.

'Well done my little feathered, well done.'

Tor was raised up by the arms of the city, feeling the perfect verity of the Umbra. It numbed his limbs, entwining every consequence of his life. The city unravelled him, every vital part of him, until he was the city, and the city was of him. He knitted within it, and absorbed the indescribable wealth of knowledge held in its bosom.

His face emerged within the tapestry and he looked down upon his friends, who looked back with sadness and admiration.

*

Upon the shoreline, in the presence of the First City, they said their goodbyes.

Vorsa offered a farewell. 'I will return to Orn Megol to help my father. I will bring the Morwih and the Vulpus here, we shall find peace.'

She looked to Rune with wide eyes. 'Rune, I cannot ever thank you enough for what you did for us. Even if it was a fool's errand, I hope you have found something far greater than our vain desires.'

'I found my family Vorsa, I found everything I hoped for!'

'Onnar, will you return to the city? There is a place for you amongst the clans.'

Onnar stood tall, pondering the offer.

'As much as that is tempting Vorsa, I shall fulfil Tor's wishes and seek out his family, and then I shall make my home here. The sea air does me good, and I have grown fond of this Startle and this Collector. I can find much work to do in this new land. But I thank you, and hope to run with your clan again someday.'

'So be it Yoa'a, we shall travel together.'

*

Erithacus stood deep in thought, his eyes closed, he felt the sea winds upon his tired body. He felt invigorated in this, in the tangible sand beneath his feet, and in the friendships he had made. Rune hopped before him. 'Thank you Grey Ghost, for helping me find my father.'

'Thank you for freeing me from my cage, little feathered.'

He commanded the Speaker flocks out into the wide lands to search for the ambassadors of each and every people. To draw the marrow of Naa together once again.

*

Vorsa and Onnar began their journey, turning back one last time to see the majesty of the First City, and to smile farewell again to their many new friends. They struggled up the sandbank, amidst the tussocks of grass, only to be confronted by a vast swathe of white; the remnants of the Gull armies. Battle weary and aimless, the coastal and city flocks had abandoned their armour and offered no protest against the Vixen and her Drove companion.

Amongst the flock stood Roak and Tawk, unsure of their place in the land. Onnar recognised the proud Gull. Roak did not shy from her.

'When I crawled from that mud, I wanted to kill you Yoa'a. I wanted to kill you because you stirred something in me I had not felt since I was a fledgling.'

'And that was?'

'Compassion … isn't something I have known much of in my life. When you saved me, you made me question how I saw the world. That made me feel weak, unsure. I only knew how to control things with force, to punish. This day I learned a lesson, that my King murdered my father, and set me on a path of blind ambition. I have served myself long enough. Now I must serve my people.'

Vorsa stepped forward, noticed Roak give the slightest flinch.

'This is the First City, a place of communion. If you speak for your people, then go to the city, find Erithacus. Request a voice amongst the nations of Naa.'

Vorsa and Onnar, Vulpus and Yoa'a, continued on, beyond the sand dunes and wreckage of the Pinnacle.

*

Roak looked to Tawk. 'You have been a faithful lieutenant and a better friend than I have ever known. I believe you will make a far greater leader than I. Will you lead the Naarna Elowin to the First City?'

'I will,' Tawk said. 'Where will you go?'

'I will join you, fly beside you, but first …'

Roak launched himself up into the wail of wind, breathed deep the reward of home.

*

Rex emerged from the surf with his Caanus pack, shambolic and full of joy, he sniffed for the scent of Tor. It was lost amongst the endless fragrances of the many animals now present, for all of which he felt a great and incomprehensible affinity.

Eventually Rex found the scent he sought and followed it into the great cavern of the First City. It ended at a vast wall. He scratched at it, hoping to find some hole or crevice within which Tor resided.

'Hello Rex.'

The voice came from above. Rex looked up and he saw a face in the wood, much like the faces in the trees. He was frightened, and so he barked.

'Rex, it is I, Tor. I have passed on, to the Umbra. I am now part of this place.'

Rex did not understand, yet he recognised the scent of Tor and the lilt of his words.

'Will you come play with us in the sea?' Rex asked eagerly.

'I cannot Rex, I am here now, forever. But perhaps we can talk awhile. You have a whole world to explore, and your pack will look to you for guidance. I will teach you all I know of the world, and with time you will understand the rhyme and reason of Naa.'

*

Dominus Audagard and his congregation of Bishops made their final blessing upon the beach before the First City. They watched Vorsa and Onnar leap beyond the dunes, the Speaker flocks arching out above the land.

They sought sticks in the wiry scrub and with ingenious beaks drew hexing marks in the sand. The spheres were finally whole, the Gasp and Umbra sat square within their line of confounded sight. Each tore a feather from their bodies and placed it at the centre of their scrawl, a personal endowment to the world beyond. They squawked and bounced upon the sand until the rings were no more, dizzy to behold the First City's vast escarpments and forests before them.

They sought entrance above; through the shafts that let light within the City's womb. They flittered down with rapturous cackle; encouraging the teetering vacillations of the dead to rise and greet them, their black knights. They danced and conjured in the presence of spirited skulls, who chattered many glorious, obscure things to them like excited children, until they lay their eyes upon the stone that held the sisters. The Starless Creature, the amalgam of life and death stood as sentinel.

'They are here!' The Corva Anx rejoiced. The Dominus lowered his head, felt the bristle of energies, potent and bewildering.

The Starless Creature regarded the fossils in the stone.

'The sisters call for you,' it whispered.

The Dominus tiptoed to the fossils. He nervously placed his head flat against the stone's surface, fearing it like he had the Oscelan. At first he felt just the grain, the particles of dust rough against his down. He searched for something less tactile, more than the reality of the rock.

'I did all you bid me to do! Let me know it all! Let me know what lies beyond this trivial existence!'

And then he keeled in the presence, a storm sheered into him, and he felt a pandemonium of emotion. The hideous loss and gulf of guilt, dread and longing, he felt the stupor of feeling knotted tight amidst the stone. He knew all of these emotions, all that lay within the Gasp, but he wanted more. He could sense the tiniest burs of something beyond, the crack of salience that hemmed the lip of all consequence. He strained towards it, pulling himself through the gulf of screaming sensation.

At the brink, he felt warmth. A deep and impenetrable gravity, which was baffling to him. He became aware of shards of consciousness, fleeting notes of experience, he welcomed them into him, allowing his body to be riven. The prickly barbs of their aether snagged on his soul, causing bursts of memory to shimmer caustic in his eyes; the lives they had lead before death, the bright tangle of pain, of happiness and excitement, the anxious, seemingly endless, yet essentially brief encounter with life. He felt the sisters' love for one another, for their mother. So much life, taken so quickly.

He felt his own magic inhale the splendid ravishing of such a simple idea, elucidations far beyond the spectral realm. Their light eclipsed the Gasp. He could not see it, but he felt it. He felt the Umbra.

The Starless Creature keened skeletal faces to him, seeking his revelation.

'WHAT DO YOU SEE?'

The Dominus stuttered. 'I see ... I see life.'

'AND?'

The Dominus felt deep within for understanding. 'There is so much.'

'There is so much in life. So much more than death.'

The Starless Creature laughed a guttural croak.

'LIFE IS FAR MORE FRIGHTENING A PROSPECT, SO MANY UNKNOWNS. DEATH IS ENTIRELY PREDICTABLE.'

At last, the Revenants began to unfold from one another, six presences, six celestials. Their fur undulated as the plasmatic dregs of their ghoulmatter heaved from the living bodies of the Vulpus. Nox felt the cold leak from his bones, and for a moment the ireful beings, primal things, hung above them like afterthoughts.

Through terrifying mouths the Revenants offered their thanks, and then in a blink they were gone.

The Starless Vulpus collapsed, crawling to one another for comfort, and to share their thoughts.

The Dominus looked at them with worry deep within him, suddenly feeling the guilt of his choices. Nox peered back at the old Corva with curious eyes.

'Something has changed in you Dominus. What did the spirits show you? What did you see?'

The Dominus suddenly looked very frail. 'I saw the brevity of life,' he grumbled as he sat down. 'Just how beautiful it is, perhaps far more perplexing than the dead.' He lifted his head and sighed. 'I am sorry Nox. In my devotion to this cause I cheated you and your forbears of a happy life.'

Nox considered this. He looked to his siblings, who imparted their feelings in the slightest inflection.

'We forgive you. You wronged us and yet we see the delicate lines you followed to bring the First City back into the world. We see those who stood as emissaries, those who suffered for this act. We recognise our place in this. Perhaps you sought a selfish reward for these deeds, yet your deeds have changed the world. We ask one favour for our part. I have seen the world through the eyes of the dead. It has left a quality in us. We feel the Umbra, and we wish to share it with all of Naa. All must learn to know it. You must serve us in this pursuit, as we once served you.'

*

Vorsa and Onnar journeyed through a land in flux. Feathered song offered excited declarations of strange and beautiful things, of fallen lords, of destroyed cities. They stole glances with great Rauka moving between rusting cars and trucks, stalking the desolate motorways in search of an understanding beyond their cages.

A herd of Oraclas bathed in a lake beside their path. They watched them for a while, until the giants emerged with joy to see the agents of their freedom, told Vorsa of the tattoo of distant trumpet blasts, of other kin, other god prisons held in other fallen Wroth cities. The Oraclas would traverse great distances in search of their splintered herd, hoping to reunite with relatives parted by the Wroth. Into the countryside they strode, an armada, whose triumphal call attracted a bevy of lone beasts seeking a family. In those leathery giants they found just that.

The friends travelled through the tall grasses of wheat fields, bounding the tracks of land where fences and hedgerows no longer determined paths. In the evening they sat amongst the golden crops and watched Seyla rise. Onnar could see the billowing afterthought of dust that hung above the Stinking City, and the conglomeration of flocks that now sought the sea. She cast her gaze to the river, and for a moment discerned some movement along the bank. There were large shadows beside the water, bathing. She thought nothing of it and lay down.

As Vorsa's eyelids closed Petulan opened his, and basked in the radiant cold of the moon.

The morning brought them to the empty House of Ror, where they made their final goodbyes. Vorsa travelled on until she reached the border of her land. She could smell the trails of burrowing animals who had left quickly in fear. At last she stepped upon the spoiled slopes of Orn Megol.

Vulpus and Morwih alike were still working to clear the corpses of the dead away from the hill, dragging them down into the sparse woods. They lay them beside one another, covering their bodies with leaves and shallow earth. Vulpus priests said final words for all of the dead. A battle-worn Morwih stood beside them in quiet reflection.

Vorsa made her way to the terrace, upon which stood Oromon and her father. Hevridis sat deep in thought beside them.

'My daughter!' Satresan exclaimed, and they graced one another's faces.

Oromon beamed. 'What did you see?'

She shook her head. 'Such sights, I wouldn't even know where to begin. But it is a tale worthy of the Orata.'

'Hevridis.' Vorsa turned with a stern expression to the furrow-browed Morwih.

Satresan interrupted her. 'My child. Before you chastise him, know that he sacrificed his true love to save my life.'

Hevridis gave a weary sigh. 'There were things I could see that made it my only course of action. I hate to admit it but you were ...'

Vorsa stopped him. 'We were all wrong, both the Vulpus and the Morwih. We have seen greater things. We were all the sum of influences beyond us, the Stinking City, the Wroth. They made of us something unnatural. We wove a life within the limits of their world, but it is our Naa now, so we have to find a new Song. We have to find it together.'

Hevridis smiled, 'The Morwih don't like working together.'

'They came together for Fraubela,' Vorsa said.

'She promised them the city. But we will be a scourge, and we will ruin this land, and decimate families, if we do not find a way to lessen our impact. We are hunters. I saw the city dead and I could not let it be ... but perhaps we can offer more.'

'Then be their leader, Hevridis.'

He shrugged. He looked out over the fields, saw the Vulpus and his people working to gently move the lost souls to their resting place. He saw no argument, no anger.

He looked to her, his decision made. 'Yes. I believe I will try,' he said.

She smiled.

'We will go to the First City, together, and there we will find resolution.'

*

The Speaker flocks divided across the land, listening for the dawn chorus. They passed on the news, the call to all who spoke for their people, a summoning. The great pilgrimage began, beneath the wing of the Speakers, herds of Athlon, Aurma, anxious Oreya from the forests, and the chatter of all manner of tiny mammals.

Their flight took them back along the river, witnessing the same creatures that Onnar had seen bathing in the water. Curious, the flock landed en masse on the river bank.

Filthy clothes had been removed and the remains of a campfire crackled. Conversation drifted from the water, words the Speakers recognised. When the makers of the fire came out of the water they were met with a host of bright green feathered, all adorned in armour made of metal and shattered glass.

Anguin hopped along a branch that brought him very close to the largest of the creatures. The beast peered down with delight, which was quickly replaced by confusion. The creature could quite clearly see the fine clasps and detail upon Anguin's chest plates and beneath his wings, and somehow knew, despite his common sense, that this feathered had made these himself.

Anguin looked to the Wroth, and cleared his throat.

'Who's a pretty boy then?'

The Wroth laughed nervously. 'It speaks!' He turned to the two smaller Wroth behind him, who looked frightened. 'It's okay children, they're just birds!'

Ominiously, Anguin said, 'I do speak, and you will listen. We have much to discuss.'

*

Erithacus returned to the fluctuating shapes that constituted the walls of the First city. Grom, Lauis and Tor elegantly danced about the mural, arranging in reticulate patterns, histories and motifs, ideas and loved moments. The living tapestry taught the Speaker much of the past, unrecorded in any Wroth tome. He learned through these semblances, incarnations of his beloved friends, of endless voices within the Umbra. He would one day add his own voice to the Song.

*

Rune flew above the tremendous contours of the First City, considered its place amidst the land. He had seen kings fall, nations war, a city crumble into ruin.

He summoned the last of his energy and flew higher, wide of the shore, above the dark cliffs either side of the glorious structure that now towered above the land and out over the ocean. The magnificent sphere of Naa lay salubrious, despite the sins of the Wroth.

The Startle began their evening flight, unhindered by that which lay below. Despite war, despite the horrors that had plagued them for generations, they had flown every night. Perhaps they had finally found peace.

He closed his eyes and felt the Umbra turn and turn with Naa. He invoked its filigrees, saw the lineal weave. He saw it concentrate above the First City, the converging, bewildering source of it all. He saw it in the land, in the herds and packs and clans and flocks.

He saw it in the harmonious paradigm of the Thousand Headed King.

Acknowledgements

With great thanks to Gary Dalkin for his considerate yet firm advice during the editing and proofreading process, Mark McClure for his assistance in typesetting and laying out the book before you. My friends and family who encouraged me to keep writing - Melanie, for her tireless support, Tabby for her literary advice and lifelong friendship, Suzanne for her kindness, patience and friendship. Steve for our friendship and the conversation we once had that inspired the idea of this book. To Dave for taking the time to read rough drafts, Laura for steering me in the right direction, my mum, for always being the most enthusiastic and reassuring person, whose support of my nonsense is unwavering. To all those people who offered ideas, inspired and motivated me, thank you. Last but not least, the Squirrel, Magpie and Jay, and two rather greedy Wood Pigeons who frequented the roof outside the kitchen window where I wrote the majority of this book.